P9-DDA-103

SONS
of
ZEUS

ALSO BY NOBLE SMITH

Sparks in the Park
Stolen from Gypsies
The Wisdom of the Shire

SONS

of

ZEUS

NOBLE SMITH

THOMAS DUNNE BOOKS ᐱᐱ ST. MARTIN'S PRESS
NEW YORK

This is a work of fiction. All of the characters, organizations, and events portrayed in this novel are either products of the author's imagination or are used fictitiously.

THOMAS DUNNE BOOKS.
An imprint of St. Martin's Press.

SONS OF ZEUS. Copyright © 2013 by Noble Smith. All rights reserved. Printed in the United States of America. For information, address St. Martin's Press, 175 Fifth Avenue, New York, N.Y. 10010.

www.thomasdunnebooks.com
www.stmartins.com

Design by Steven Seighman

ISBN 978-1-250-02557-9 (hardcover)
ISBN 978-1-250-02642-2 (e-book)

St. Martin's Press books may be purchased for educational, business, or promotional use. For information on bulk purchases, please contact Macmillan Corporate and Premium Sales Department at 1-800-221-7945 extension 5442 or write specialmarkets@macmillan.com.

First Edition: June 2013

10 9 8 7 6 5 4 3 2 1

For Yohanyn

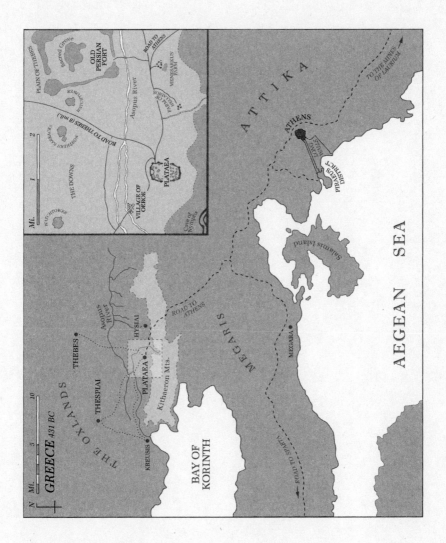

GREECE 431 BC

N

Mi. 5 10

THE OXLANDS

THEBES

THESPIAI

KREUSIS

HYSIAI

PLATAEA

Kithaeron Mts.

Asopus River

ROAD TO ATHENS

BAY OF KORINTH

MEGARIS

MEGARA

ROAD TO ATHENS

ATTIKA

ATHENS

LONG WALLS

PIRAEUS DISTRICT

TO THE MINES OF LAURIUM

Salamis Island

AEGEAN SEA

Mi. 1 2

THE DOWNS

WATCHTOWER

VILLAGE OF OEROE

Cave of Nymphs

PLATAEA

Asopus River

ROAD TO THEBES (8 mi.)

NORTHERN BARRACKS

PARK OF HERA

WATCHTOWER

Sacred Grove

PLAIN OF THEBES

OLD PERSIAN FORT

MENDESARCUS'S FARM

ROAD TO ATHENS

SONS
of
ZEUS

PROLOGUE

———◆———

The God of Death was in the stadium that blistering summer day. He was among the forty thousand impatient men stomping their feet, calling for the pankration championship to begin. That is what warriors would say years later—during the endless war between Athens and Sparta—when they talked about seeing the ill-omened match between the two fighters known as the Bull and the Centaur.

A scourge of black flies had plagued the athletes and the crowds all week—flies that nipped a tiny piece of flesh and then lapped at the blood. No one had seen these vile pests before in Olympia. Rational men thought the flies had been blown on a powerful wind from Africa. The superstitious believed they'd sprung from noxious vents that led directly to the underworld—a dire forewarning of death.

**—Papyrus fragment from the "Lost History"
of the Peloponnesian War by the "Exiled Scribe"**

440 BC. THE EIGHTY-FIFTH OLYMPIC GAMES

Nikias could ride like the north wind, take down a red-breasted goose on the wing with a shot from his sling, break a man's shin with the flat of his foot, and snap a horsefly off a wall with his ox hide whip from ten feet away.

He was eight years old.

That's how boys were raised in the wide plains north of the legendary Kithaeron Mountains. The women of the Oxlands produced survivors. Nikias's ancestors had lived through the invasions of the Sea Raiders, overthrew the Last Tyrant to create the democratic city-state of Plataea, and helped push back the might of the great Persian Empire itself from the very gates of their citadel.

When Nikias was born, his father had held him up to the sky and called out to Zeus that another hero had been delivered to Plataea. Three years later the boy had cradled his father's funeral urn in his arms. Another Plataean hero had died in battle.

Nikias was tall for his age, and strapping. He had the scabbed knuckles of a fledgling boxer; long, curly hair bleached blond by the hot Greek sun; bright blue eyes; and a gap-toothed rogue's grin. He lived for the pankration, the combination of boxing and wrestling famous to Greece.

And he hadn't come all the way from Plataea to the sacred city of Olympia with Grandfather—ridden two hundred dusty miles!—just to stay in the stifling tent with the slaves guarding the baggage, killing flies with his whip to pass the time. Not while the greatest fight in the history of the Olympics was about to take place! Two undefeated pankrators. Mortal enemies whose city-states had been at war for a century. Blood and revenge. It was enough to make him tear out his hair in frustration.

"Why should boys be banned from watching the pankration championship, anyhow?" he fumed. It wasn't as though he were a woman or a slave. He knew that Grandfather would flay his hide for disobeying him, but he didn't care. He bolted from the tent and into the marketplace outside, darting through the throngs of men like a fox in a field of wheat, clutching his coiled whip in his hand.

By the time he got to the Hippodrome entrance he was breathing hard and his throat was parched from the dry heat. He saw spectators swarming in through the gates—men from all over Greece and even as far away as Egypt and the Persian colonies.

Citizens from the democracy of Athens—those masters of the sea with their vast, unstoppable fleet of triple-decked warships—were easy to spot. They were lordly men, big and muscular, with the bodies and faces of heroes, well dressed in fashionable linen clothes, their curling hair and beards clipped short. Athens was Plataea's friend, as Grandfather always said. But the Athenians never seemed very friendly.

He caught sight of a pack of Spartans, subjects of dual kings. Grim and lean, with incongruously long manes of dark womanly hair. Naked except for their soiled and threadbare bloodred capes. Terrifying warriors—raised in packs like wolves—whom no Greek army dared meet on the field of battle. "Never break an oath and never turn your back on a Spartan," as Grandfather liked to say. "And fear slavery more than death."

Fifty years earlier the Spartans and Athenians had joined together with Plataea to defeat the Persian king Xerxes. But now they fought over Greece like two dogs who wanted the same bone. It didn't make any sense to Nikias. Why not break the bone in half?

He tried to sneak in to the Hippodrome with a group of Makedonian jockeys who weren't much taller than he, but an attendant spotted him, yanked him aside, and painted a red *X* on his tunic to show he was banned.

Nikias cursed and ran around to the opposite side of the enormous Hippodrome, where the poorer visitors had set up camp in the shade of the northern wall. There were pimps and whores, seers and wizards, seedy wine bars and brothel tents. The place reeked of hemp and wood smoke and greasy meat burning on fires. He pulled off his tunic and tossed it aside so that he was wearing nothing more than a loincloth. An obese Thracian pimp with tattoos up and down his arms grabbed Nikias by the neck and squeezed hard.

"What's this pretty thing doing here all alone?" asked the pimp, pushing Nikias toward a tent filled with writhing bodies and the blare of orgiastic flute music.

Nikias stomped on the pimp's foot and the Thracian bellowed and let go. Nikias leapt back, uncoiled his whip, and cracked it at the man's face. The pimp touched his ear, saw the blood on his fingers, and shrieked as the pain surged through his brain. He called for his henchmen, who grabbed their clubs. Nikias dashed toward the Hippodrome and its walls rising forty feet high. He pulled himself onto the top of a shed built at the base of the stadium, kicked off his sandals, wrapped his whip around his arm, then started climbing up the chinks in the stone with the agility of a lizard.

Nobody had the guts to follow him. They waited for him to drop. But Nikias had scaled more difficult and precarious cliffs in the Kithaeron Mountains when he was no more than six, urged on by Grandfather, who loved it when his scion did anything bold and brave. In a matter of minutes he was at the top, gazing at the forty thousand spectators and the still-empty fighting arena below him. A combination of smells punched him in the face: the spicy odor of unwashed men and the pungent reek of fishcakes sold by vendors as snacks.

He rolled over the edge and tumbled onto the wooden benches, startling some Athenians who were singing a patriotic song in praise of their city. "The flies are getting bigger and bigger," said a wit as he shoved Nikias out of the way. The boy snaked his way to one of the aisles and sprinted down fifty rows to the wooden rail at the edge of the arena.

A weird noise erupted from the spectators—the ancient ululating battle cry of forty thousand men shouting the word for "freedom"—"*Eleu-eleu-eleu-eleu-eleu!*" It was an unnerving chaos of sound that penetrated down to Nikias's bones.

"The Centaur of Thebes!" cried a herald through a speaking trumpet.

Damos the Theban entered the arena to the thunderous shouts and applause of his supporters. With his almond-shaped eyes, beard ringlets, and shoulder-length hair, he made Nikias think of a carved temple guardian from the olden days, when the men of Greece were vassals of the Persian Empire and imitated their overlords in appearance. His upper body rippled with muscles and his legs were as solid as a warhorse's. It was easy to see how he'd gotten his name. He really did resemble a centaur. And like those ancient creatures he was deadly. His last pankration opponent had been dragged from the arena with a broken neck.

Nikias felt a surge of hatred for this man. He might have been the same Theban who had killed his father at the Battle of Koronea. "I'll drown myself if Damos wins today," he thought.

"The Bull of Plataea!" called out a herald from the opposite side, and Nikias's stomach lurched in anticipation.

Half of the assemblage cheered wildly as Menesarkus—hero of the Persian wars, general of Plataea!—entered and strode around the small sand-filled square with a lumbering grace, waving to the crowd. Like Damos he was naked and, at the age of fifty-three, a remarkable specimen of longevity. His broad body was muscled and tanned from a lifetime of plowing the earth on his farm and training with weapons of war at the gymnasium. His hair and beard—refusing to gray—were still blacker than the glaze of a funeral jar. In the five days of events he had devastated his opponents, snapping two jaws and one elbow, shattering a collarbone, and collecting a handful of teeth on his path to this championship bout.

Nikias loved the Bull more than anybody in the world. He was a god walking the earth. Surely he would crush the Theban upstart. He watched intently as the fighters circled each other like two snarling dogs.

"Remember me?" Nikias heard Damos yell across the fighting space. The Theban's face held a twisted smile. "We met after the Battle of Koronea—during the sorting of the dead."

"I remember it well, Theban," barked Menesarkus. "As well as you'll remember my fists after today."

"Perhaps I'll see you weep again like a woman," said Damos. "Like you did after the battle. Who did you lose that day? Was he your beloved shield man? Tell me his name?"

They charged each other like wild boars in a wood, slamming together chest to chest. The crowd went crazy, pumping their fists, shouting encouragement. The two pankration judges, bearing long sticks made of cane, darted into the arena and quickly separated the fighters before they could throw any punches. The judges were responsible for keeping the opponents inside the boundary of the small ten-by-fourteen-foot marked area. They checked Menesarkus's and Damos's fists to make sure they weren't concealing iron rods or spikes, and warned them against biting and eye gouging. Then, with a ceremonial slap to the contestants' backs, the judges shouted in unison, "Now! Now!"

Menesarkus and Damos circled each other, bobbing their fists up and down.

They each threw a couple of trial punches, and then exchanged a few powerful blows that would have felled an ordinary mortal. The assembly of forty thousand started shouting all at once. The prolonged roar of their voices, to Nikias's ears, was like a massive wave crashing endlessly against a rocky shore. His skin erupted in gooseflesh.

Damos kicked out with one of his long legs at Menesarkus's left knee—the knee that Nikias knew was wounded from an earlier bout. Menesarkus moved his leg to the side just in time but winced with the effort. Damos grabbed him around the neck and Menesarkus grappled back, rabbit-punching him on the back of the head. Damos kicked at Menesarkus's knee again with the flat of his foot, over and over, with Menesarkus dancing backward to avoid the blows, digging his fingers into Damos's back for purchase.

"Boundary," snapped one of the judges, and stung Menesarkus on the buttocks with his stick.

"Break!" commanded the other judge, prodding them both with his stick.

They came apart throwing long punches. Menesarkus missed, but Damos's longer reach helped him land a crushing uppercut that smashed into Menesarkus's lower jaw. The fighters backed up to the sides opposite where they'd started. Damos was right below the rails near Nikias. He was so close Nikias could see the beads of sweat on the Theban's back and the crescent-shaped marks where Menesarkus's nails had dug into his flesh.

A Plataean standing next to Nikias leaned over the wooden barrier and yelled at Damos, "Hey, Theban. You look like you're doing the harvest dance out there. Why don't you try fighting?"

Damos turned and spat a gob of yellow mucus into the heckler's face; some of the spittle hit Nikias on the cheek and he wiped it off angrily. Then Damos went straight for Menesarkus, head down, tackling him around the waist and slamming him to the ground. Menesarkus squirmed and twisted. He pounded Damos on the back while Damos's hands reached up and sought out his throat. Menesarkus rolled over, kicked, and jumped to his feet. The Centaur sprang to a fighting stance.

One of the judges struck a stinging blow to Menesarkus's leg—he had gone outside the boundary marker again—and the old pankrator growled at the judge and swiped at his stick. The judge poked him, spurring him forward just as Damos jumped up and kicked out. Damos's heel smashed into Menesarkus's left shin, completely dislocating his knee.

Menesarkus howled in pain, hopping away on one foot. Nikias's stomach churned. It was all he could do to keep himself from jumping into the ring and attacking Damos. Menesarkus was in grave danger now. Nikias said a quick prayer to Hermes, god of luck.

Damos wasted no time. He charged in for the knockout blow. But Menesarkus flopped on his back in the defensive position called the crab and kicked up with his good leg, striking the surprised Damos in the groin. The crowd groaned as one man.

"That's it!" shouted Nikias.

As Damos leaned over in anguish, Menesarkus kicked up again, hitting the Theban a glancing blow on the nose with his heel. Blood spurted from Damos's face. Menesarkus made to wrap up his opponent's legs with his brawny arms, but Damos slipped away, viciously elbowing him on the side of the head. Nikias let out a cry.

"Boy!" yelled a voice in the crowd.

Nikias turned and saw a red-faced Hippodrome attendant running toward him along the walkway. Nikias sprinted in the opposite direction, zigzagging between a gang of snack sellers pouring from one of the access tunnels. He made his way to the other side of the stadium and took up a place in a section almost directly across from where he'd stood before, near the wooden rail close to the arena. He glanced around him and saw red cloaks everywhere. He was surrounded by Spartans! They sat as still as statues and none even glanced his way.

Except for one man. A hideous noseless Spartan who was as big as Menesarkus. He sat on the bench right behind Nikias and cocked his head with a quick jerk, which made Nikias think of a praying mantis. Grandfather had pointed him out earlier in the week. "That's Drako the Skull," he'd said. "A famous Spartan warrior and a ruthless killer."

"Get out of here, beardless boy," said the Spartan in a gravelly, constricted voice, as though he'd been strangled nearly to death and never fully recovered the use of his larynx. He transfixed Nikias with his wolf's eyes.

"Leave him," said a deep voice full of authority.

Next to Drako was a regal youth in his late teens who was regarding Nikias with a benevolent smile. This other Spartan looked different than his kinsmen. For one thing, he wore sumptuous red silk robes and had jeweled rings on his fingers. And he could have passed for a Plataean with his curly sandy-colored hair, blue eyes, and square jaw.

"Of course, Prince Arkilokus," replied Drako in a tone that was neither submissive nor respectful.

Nikias nodded at the Spartan prince by way of thanks, then looked back at the arena. The Bull was resting on hands and knees, breathing in ragged gasps, and shaking his big head in confusion. The Centaur was crouched down low, also panting for air. His nose gushed blood from Menesarkus's last blow, covering his upper lip, mouth, and chin with red gore as thick as potter's slip. Damos spat out the blood, plugging his nose with his fingers. He tilted his head to one side as if it now weighed too much for his neck to support.

Then the flies came. They descended upon the pankrators and lapped up the blood from their wounds, even settling on the saliva that dripped from their mouths.

"Plataea!" yelled thousands of voices.

Menesarkus was mumbling to himself. Nikias couldn't hear what he was saying. The judges prodded him, but he could not move.

Damos tilted back his head, fingers held to his nose to stop the vital fluid from gushing out. His hair had come loose from its thong and hung down like a horse's mane.

"Thebes! Thebes!" screamed thousands of men. "The Centaur for Thebes!"

Damos reached into his mouth and pulled out the mastik, the gummy resin that fighters used to protect their teeth. He wadded it up in his fist and then bit it into two pieces. He shoved one lump of the resin in each nostril to staunch the bleeding. He got to his feet and pointed his outstretched hand at Menesarkus.

"Show your finger and it's over," he roared. Nikias knew that raising one's little finger meant you were done. That you'd had enough.

"Never!" Nikias said to himself. "Don't do it, Bull. Don't listen to him."

"You! Plataean!" Damos snarled. "Show your finger. Submit to me."

A cacophony of counsel, encouragement, and slurs erupted from the forty thousand. Menesarkus began to lift his arm as if to offer the sign of defeat.

"Grandfather, no!" screamed Nikias.

Menesarkus froze, then turned to where Nikias stood by the rail. The boy's face was contorted in dismay. The old fighter looked startled at first, but then a faint smile broke across his bloody mouth. Nikias made the pankration sign: a fist slapping into a palm. Menesarkus squeezed shut his eyes. When he opened them, the Bull raised himself up on one foot and stood there swaying.

"Won't give up," croaked Menesarkus. "Can't submit to a Theban goat lover."

"Then I'll rip the eyes from your skull!" shouted Damos.

The Theban charged across the arena and sprang on Menesarkus, clawing at his eyes. Menesarkus was caught off guard by Damos's sudden burst of speed. The two were face-to-face, locked in a grim dance, with Menesarkus hopping frantically backwards to stay upright and Damos pushing him hard. Damos finally kicked Menesarkus's good leg out from under him and landed on top.

"He's down! The Bull is down!" declared Menesarkus's stunned supporters.

"The Centaur! Damos the Centaur!" the fans of the Theban shouted with joy.

"No! No!" wailed Nikias.

The pankrators rolled and thrashed in the sand, writhing like snakes. The sand stuck to their slick bodies—greasy with oil, sweat, and blood—until they appeared to be men made of living stone. Suddenly they stopped moving. Menesarkus had managed to cover Damos's mouth with the huge palm of his hand. The Centaur couldn't breathe. The resin he'd stuffed in his nostrils to staunch the bleeding had turned out to be a fateful blunder. Panicking, he released his grip to claw at Menesarkus's face. This was just what the wily old Bull had anticipated he'd do. With a skillful twist of his body, Menesarkus swiftly slipped behind the Centaur and put him into the Morpheus hold. His forearms locked around Damos's neck, creating a vise that cut off the blood to his brain. It was a move Menesarkus knew well. He'd been practicing it since childhood.

The shocked Theban reached back and scratched helplessly at Menesarkus. The crowd stood up as one man, yelling, shaking their fists.

"You asked my beloved's name!" shouted Menesarkus above the pandemonium of the Hippodrome. Damos's eyes opened wide in terror as he started to black out. "The one I cried for after the battle?" continued the Bull.

Damos reached up and clawed the mastik plugs from his nostrils, but it did no good: Menesarkus's arm had shut off his throat.

"He was called Aristo," sobbed Menesarkus. "He was my *son*!"

Nikias thought back to that horrible day, after the Battle of Koronea, when his grandfather had pulled Aristo's white corpse back to the farm in an old handcart. Menesarkus had wept over the broken body of his only son for hours while the women had stood by stern faced and silent. Nikias remembered the feel of his father's black funeral jar as he hugged the clammy clay urn against his chest. How that cold had penetrated into his guts. It was still there now—a cold river stone lodged in his stomach—as he clutched the wooden rail of the Olympic stadium, staring at the pankrators. The vision of the fighters seemed to be dissolving before his eyes. He was nearly blinded by his tears. And there was a strange taste on his tongue. The coppery tang of blood. Revenge, his grandfather always told him, had a distinct flavor. Like seared meat plucked from a sacrificial fire. He was right.

Damos the Theban raised his little finger—raised it high for all to see. A moment later his arm went flaccid. The judges ran to the fighters. "Break! Break!" they commanded. But Menesarkus would not yield. He shoved Damos's face into the sand and held it there, shifted his arms to a choke hold to crush his windpipe. The judges beat him with their sticks. Menesarkus flattened himself onto Damos's back and thrust his mouth to the Theban's ear, ignoring the flurry of increasingly desperate and violent clouts that rained down on his unfeeling hide, as though he were some insensate creature.

"He's standing on the other side of the river Styx," wailed Menesarkus. "Can you see him now? Can you see my dead boy's shade?"

Dozens of men stormed the arena. "Damos yielded!" yelled the judges, stabbing Menesarkus in the ribs with the sharp points of their canes. A young man from Damos's entourage grabbed the dead fighter's legs and pulled with all his might, shrieking insanely at Menesarkus, "You murdered him! You murdered him!" But Menesarkus would not let go of his enemy. He held fast to the Theban.

Nikias turned away, wiping the hot tears from his face, holding his stomach with both hands, afraid he might be sick. He glanced up and saw the Spartan prince Arkilokus watching the struggle in the arena. The young man was smiling with satisfaction. Drako, however, was looking straight at Nikias, studying him with his cold murderer's eyes. Nikias stared back without flinching, instinctively curling his fighter's hands into hard fists.

PART I

"Love death and hate your foe!"
—**Tyrtaeus of Sparta**

ONE

———— • ————

The fighters' torsos were locked in place like two beams hewed and fitted by a master joiner. They leaned forward, heaving in unison, chest on chest and cheek to cheek. Both men's fingers dug into the flesh of his opponent's back as anchors and they struggled with bare feet to gain purchase in the deep sand of the farm-yard arena.

Despite the cold evening the fighters trained naked and dog tied—the uncir-cumcised foreskin of their penises wrapped with a leather thong, pulled down, and knotted to the scrotum to prevent an opponent from taking hold and seizing their manhood. Their skin was coated with olive oil and sand to keep their hands from slipping on each other's bodies. They wore thin leather boxing gloves that did little to deaden their brutal blows. They were the two best pankrators in the Oxlands. Maybe even the finest in all of Greece.

"You're like the pig who rubs the stone for water," growled Menesarkus. "And you'll get no satisfaction from me," he added, punctuating the age-old platitude with a strained grunt that escaped from his lips in a burst of vapor.

Nearly ten years had passed since he'd fought and killed Damos the Theban, and the Bull of Plataea had aged little in that time. His beard was streaked with gray, his hair was thinner, and he had gone almost completely deaf in one ear. But he was still as muscle-bound as a warrior half his age. The only outward sign of that terrible championship fight was a thick leather brace that supported his crippled knee, and the mournful cast to his dark eyes.

Nikias twisted his neck so his mouth pressed directly against one of Mene-sarkus's cauliflower ears and replied playfully, "Stone-rubbing pig? Know thyself, old man," and pushed back with all his might.

Nikias, in stark contrast to his grandfather, had altered much over the last decade. He was now taller than Menesarkus by six inches. Even though the Bull outweighed him by fifty pounds, Nikias was as hard muscled as a professional oarsman on an Athenian war galley. His hair, worn long to signify he was not yet of age, remained a golden blond. Despite his slightly crooked nose—broken three times in bouts since he was a child—his striking looks made girls and old women and everything in between swoon.

"The Old Bull and the Young Bull," thought Menesarkus, straining to force Nikias in the opposite direction. That's how he saw them in his mind's eye. But right now the Old Bull was losing ground. His legs were starting to tremble. It felt as if he'd run around Plataea's walls a dozen times. . . .

"Break," hissed Saeed in his thick Eastern accent. The wiry Persian slave danced around the two pankrators, prodding them in the calves with a pointed training stick until they released their grips. Saeed's intervention was just in time for Menesarkus, whose legs were about to buckle. He glanced at his old, faithful servant and the slender Persian smiled back.

"Fight!" barked Saeed, smacking them on the backs of their legs with his quick stick.

The men squared off, rotating their forearms so their fists bobbed and weaved. Menesarkus's lower lip was puffed up and trickled blood. Nikias had already suffered two hard blows to the face, and one eye had nearly swelled shut.

Menesarkus had been taught by his own grandfather that Pythagoras of Samos was the first pankrator to box scientifically with set moves and feints. But Menesarkus believed that a psychological war against one's opponent was just as important as technique. The old fighter liked to dig at his combatants until they lashed out in anger.

"You can't beat me, Nik," said Menesarkus. "I'll get you in the Morpheus hold and then it's good-bye, sun, just like always."

Nikias had never once broken free of the hold in all their years of training and had suffered numerous blackouts for his efforts. But he'd never given up. Menesarkus admired Nikias for his persistence. And at the same time resented him for being so strong willed, a constant test to his authority. He knew the youthful fighter had the talent and physique to surpass him in skills someday. The thought was both reassuring and unsettling.

In three days Nikias would cut off his hair and burn it on the altar of Zeus with all of the other young men in Plataea turning eighteen this season. With the completion of that highly anticipated ceremony—the lad talked about it incessantly!—his grandson would officially be a man with the duty to serve as a warrior until the age of sixty-five, and the right to vote in the Assembly Hall until death.

"Maybe once you've burned your hair and stood in a phalanx," suggested Menesarkus, "you'll grow balls big enough to beat me."

But Nikias wasn't going to let himself be goaded. He curled back his lips. The smile of a hunting dog as it approaches a wounded boar. "You missed your calling, old man. You've got more lines than Euripides the playwright."

Menesarkus felt a strange fear he'd rarely experienced in the arena. Or was it a thrill? "Could this be the day he beats me?" he thought.

Nikias threw a sweeping punch at Menesarkus's head, a knockout blow. But the young fighter had put too much force behind it and stumbled when Menesarkus ducked aside. Menesarkus seized the moment. He jumped onto Nikias's back, clamped his arm around his grandson's neck, and dropped his head down low so Nikias couldn't whip back his head and smash him in the face.

"Say good-bye to the sun, Nikias," called out Saeed, stabbing his stick into the sand and crossing his arms on his chest. His job was done for the day.

For a moment Nikias did nothing.

"Come on, boy!" Menesarkus growled through clenched teeth. Two seconds had already passed. "Do something. This is too easy. . . ."

Nikias leaned forward, dug his feet into the sand of the arena, and started moving toward a storage shed a few paces away, the veins bulging at his temples, face turning bright red. Menesarkus hopped along on his one good leg, squeezing as hard as he could to stop the flow of blood to Nikias's brain, trying to drag him down. But the young man's legs were too strong. He made it to the shed, grabbed one of the poles supporting the overhang, twisted his body with a violent effort—sending the startled Saeed scurrying out of the way—and flung Menesarkus against the wall with the force of a bucking horse. Menesarkus winced from the blow. Nikias dragged him along the wall, using the rough stucco wall to scrape the skin off his grandfather's back.

Menesarkus yelled in pain and relaxed his grip. Nikias broke free, pounded him in the face with his fist, and danced away, raising his arms in the air with jubilation, whooping at the top of his lungs.

"Surprised you, didn't I?" Nikias shouted. "I've been planning *that* for a month! Now you know what the hide of the stone-rubbing pig feels like."

Menesarkus shifted his jaw back and forth. It made a crunching sound in his ears. He felt foolish. Nikias had used his strength, his powerful legs, against Menesarkus's weakness. He had turned the wall of the shed into a weapon. He glanced over at Saeed, who wore a stunned expression on his usually placid face. The Persian raised his eyebrows as if to say, "Clever boy."

"The sun seems brighter," Nikias said to Saeed, shading his brow and squinting at the sky. He cavorted like a Thrakian minstrel. "No dirt naps for me today."

"Take him down, Master," urged Saeed in a harsh whisper.

"Think you're tough, Nikias?" Menesarkus limped back into the practice arena. "You beardless piece of dung." He raised his gloves and bobbed them up and down menacingly. "Pythagoras of Samos was the first fighter to box scientifically, but—"

"Quit giving lessons!" ordered Nikias with a force that stopped Menesarkus's words in his throat. Nikias appeared to have grown in stature. He moved slowly forward with such confidence, it seemed as if he carried an invisible shield—a shield that pushed Menesarkus backward.

"Come on, old man." Nikias was puffed up with the thrill of having escaped the older fighter's famous hold. "No more Pythagoras or pigs. Let's just throw some punches." He descended upon Menesarkus with a torrent of blows and then backed away.

Menesarkus realized, with a sinking in his gut, that he was afraid of his grandson. He did not want to fight him anymore today. He did not want to be beaten.

"What is Helladios's daughter doing here?" asked Menesarkus angrily, pointing a stiff finger and peering across the arena toward the women's quarters.

Nikias asked, "Where?" and whipped his head around, looking for their neighbor's daughter. But he saw no one there. He snapped back his head to face Menesarkus, and a spray of sand from Menesarkus's hand blinded him. It was followed by the Bull's perfectly timed leather-clad fist, which caught him squarely on the jaw. Nikias's knees buckled and he toppled like a dead man.

Saeed dashed across the arena and adjusted Nikias's head to free his airway, so he would not suffocate while he was unconscious.

"Old tricks still work," said Saeed, shaking his head at Nikias's folly.

"He got too excited," said Menesarkus softly. "He should have gone right for the kill when he caught me off guard."

He stood over the prostrate body, rubbing his tingling knuckles with a lopsided smile on his face. He was suddenly aware of singing coming from the women's quarters where his wife, widowed daughter-in-law, and granddaughter were hard at work, weaving cloth that would be sold in town. The movement of the wooden machinery sounded like percussion instruments, tapping and drumming in rhythm to the song.

Menesarkus recalled his earliest memory: lying on the floor next to his mother as she worked those same looms, watching the oil from the new-spun wool collect at the bottom of the tapestry and drip onto the dirt floor like dark dew. He was overcome by a disconcerting feeling. His heart was filled with incalculable joy mingled with profound sadness.

He could not hide from the world any longer. The pipes of war were on the wind. The Athenians and Spartans were on the verge of open conflict. And Plataea would get caught in the middle like an olive pit between two massive grinding stones. Would Nikias prove himself in battle and live to be a hero? Or die in ignominy like his father?

"Your grandson almost defeated you," observed Saeed.

"Almost is the same as dead." Menesarkus glanced up at the ancient olive grove on the slopes above the farm where his ancestor, the founder of the Nemean tribe, had planted them over three hundred years ago.

Hiding behind the largest tree was a stranger who had been spying on the farm for most of the day. But Menesarkus's myopic gaze saw only gnarled limbs—twisted trunks and branches that reminded him of tired old men.

TWO

———————◆———————

The stranger wore a hooded cloak of earth-colored yarn that had been cleverly woven together with bits of twigs and leaves. His face and curling beard were daubed with watered-down clay. He blended into the landscape as though he'd sprouted there. He watched Menesarkus with a catlike intensity, his eyes peering from the shadow of his hood, wondering what the famous Olympian was thinking right now as he stared forlornly at the hills.

The stranger briefly worried that Menesarkus had seen him, and the flesh on his neck and cheeks tingled with alarm. But then Menesarkus passed a hand over his face—an expression of resignation—and turned back toward the barn, where two big male slaves were working on a broken plow.

"Bring the young master to the women," ordered Menesarkus.

The slaves dragged the unconscious Nikias across the sand and into the house. Menesarkus entered, followed closely by his man, the one called Saeed. The Persian paused in the doorway and looked back over his shoulder toward the foothills and the olive orchard, his dark mouth shaped in a disconcerted frown, as though he could sense being watched. Then he, too, disappeared through the portal, leaving the yard empty except for a few scrabbling chickens.

The stranger relaxed a little. He was safe. Yet he did not leave his post. Over the years, in perfecting his craft, he had developed the patience of a spider. He remained behind the screen of trees, as still as a statue, until the sun's chariot sank below the horizon.

He'd been spying on the farm for the last season and could recite with numbing detail the routines of every living thing on the farm, from slave to cow to master. Today he'd watched the pankration match with particular interest. Especially when it looked as though young Nikias was about to defeat his grandfather.

It struck the stranger that Menesarkus's name—in the language of the Greeks—meant flesh that endures. The Plataean seemed to be cheating death in the same way he'd just tricked his opponent.

A crow landed on the roof of the house and let forth a throaty caw, bobbing its head up and down. The black bird, the stranger noticed, had one white tail feather. The crow lifted its rear end and deposited a drop of purplish feces onto the path in front of the doorway, then flew away. The stranger let forth a gasp. This was a wonderful sign! An ominous portent!

From the stranger's vantage point Menesarkus's abode resembled a miniature fortress. It was a two-story tower with a flat roof and had only one entrance, the front portal. On the first floor the small windows—too small for a man to crawl through—were high up on the wall and shuttered from the inside. A low breastwork along the rooftop afforded protection for archers.

There were several other buildings in the farmyard, including a large storage room, a barn, a pottery shed, an olive oil mill, and a dormitory for Menesarkus's fifteen slaves. Menesarkus's prosperity was a direct result of the defeat of the Persian king Xerxes. The Plataean's wealth—like that of so many of his fellow citizens—had been gleaned from the nearby battlefield, where nearly a million Persians had been crushed by the allied Greek forces. The victors had gained Persian armor, weapons, horses, and human chattel—the spoils of war.

And gold.

For Persian princes always went to war with their purses stuffed with darics and their bodies festooned with the trappings of their family wealth: rings, crowns, gauntlets, swords, and helms made of the yellow metal.

The watcher had bribed a Plataean public official for a copy of the most recent Plataean census, and so he knew there were exactly 179 farmhouses scattered throughout this part of the Oxlands, though few were more prosperous looking than this one. The city of Plataea alone contained twenty thousand men, women, children, and slaves living behind its high walls. The Plataeans could field a phalanx of almost two thousand fully armored and experienced fighters, along with cavalry support of one hundred riders and another thousand lightly armored archers and sling-wielding peltasts made up of foreign residents and slaves.

Three thousand men. A formidable army. More than a match for smaller Thebes in a battle of phalanx against phalanx.

The stranger scoured the farmstead with his eyes one last time to make certain no one was walking about, then wrapped himself in his beggar's cloak and hood and strode vigorously up the hillside. He found his exquisite horse—the mount of a wealthy man, not a vagabond—where he'd left it grazing in a secluded meadow on the edge of a pine woods, patiently waiting his return. He worked his way along the base of the mountain eastward, in the direction of the town of Hysiai. Then he headed north at a swift canter cross-country, avoiding the main road and the easternmost Plataean watchtower. He crossed the Asopus River where a small footbridge spanned the shortest distance between the banks. In less than an hour, from Menesarkus's farm to the end of his journey, the spy had ridden the eight miles back to his home—to the walls of Thebes and safety.

The sentinels at the heavily guarded city gates recognized the rider immediately and shouted, "Open the sally port!" A door set into the gate swung open from the inside, and a groom ran out and took the reins from his master. The rider dismounted and darted through the door and into the city. He walked swiftly through the winding streets to his regal home. He had composed a letter in his head on the ride back and he was anxious to put the words on papyrus.

"I don't want food or a change of clothes," he said brusquely, waving away his many slaves. "I'll be in my library. No one is to disturb me."

An hour later he had written a coded message with Persian glyphs. The jagged black strokes and wedge shapes made it look as though a crow had tracked ink across the papyrus with its sharp claws. The message read:

Greetings my most beloved and honored King Artaxerxes, son of Xerxes, lord of Persia and blessed of the true God Ahura Mazda. I, Eurymakus, magistrate of Thebes and your loyal vassal, offer news that will gladden your heart. By the time you receive this letter your father's bane—the Greek city-state of Plataea, where he suffered his greatest defeat—will be under my control. With your gold I have bought a traitor who will bring about his city's doom. Once we have seized the citadel, the men will all be put to death in tribute to your father. And the women and children I will send to your capital as a token of Theban allegiance, to spend the rest of their days as chattel. . . .

He thought of the handsome young fighter Nikias and smiled as he envisioned the special torture he had in store for him. The young Plataean's screams of torment would be as sweet as the music of the aulos pipes.

After he finished the letter, he rolled up the papyrus scroll tightly, poured wax from a candle onto the edge, and sealed it with his gold signet ring, the bloodred carnelian gemstone carved with an image of Artaxerxes. He hummed a Persian tune as he worked, smiling contentedly. But then he thought of the surprising way in which the clever young pankrator had broken free of Menesarkus's terrible death grip. He shivered, and the smile faded from his lips.

He closed his eyes and said a silent prayer to his *fravashi*—his guardian angel: "Daena, my beloved goddess, guide me and protect me." He kissed the stone of his signet ring. It was still warm from touching the hot wax, and it felt as though it were a living thing.

THREE

It was early morning and Nikias sat at the cluttered table in his bedchamber, trying to construct a love poem, listening with half an ear to women's laughter from the courtyard below his second-story window. Kallisto was down there, he knew, practicing archery with the women of his family. Her voice was so distinctive—husky and melodic at the same time.

She was the daughter of their nearest neighbor, General Helladios. He and Menesarkus had been bitter enemies for decades, fighting in the courts over disputed boundary markers between their two properties. Helladios had produced five ugly and worthless sons over the years, and Kallisto, the youngest child, was his only daughter. And in her it seemed Helladios had saved his best seed for last. She was wildly ravishing yet exhibited none of the traits that men desired in a wife—modesty, frugality, steadfastness, a civil tongue, and a shy demeanor. In fact, she was as spirited as a Persian colt with a trident's barb for a tongue.

And Nikias felt he would die without her.

The poem was for her. And he wanted it to have the sentiment of Sappho but the strength of Homer. He had already rubbed out numerous lines on the sheepskin writing pad using a pumice stone. Those barely visible but still legible words he'd effaced seemed to mock him and his failure as a poet.

He glanced at the bowl on his desk that his mother, Agathe, had brought to the room before dawn. It was filled with water, wine, and honey, with little chunks of bread floating on top. He could barely open his jaw from the fool's punch he'd taken from his grandfather the day before, and this spongy bread was all he could manage. The fact that he'd gotten knocked out didn't matter. What counted was that he had beaten the Morpheus hold. Something none of his grandfather's opponents had ever done! He'd trained for a month, strengthening his legs in the gym by squatting with iron bars on his shoulders to gain enough extra power to surprise his grandfather.

He popped a soggy piece of bread into his mouth and thought, "A morsel of victory is much better than none at all."

A high-pitched chirping erupted from the bucket of scrolls next to his desk. "Good morning, Ajax."

A green wall lizard, four inches long, popped its head over the edge and tasted the air with a quick dart of its tongue, scanning the room for insects with its black-bead eyes. Ajax was a fierce creature that kept his room free of mosquitoes, flies, and even the occasional scorpion. It crawled out of the bucket, up the table leg, and onto his desk to perch in its preferred spot: draped over the back of a small bronze sculpture of a pankrator, looking as though it had the statue in its own reptile version of the Morpheus hold.

Nikias set down his stylus and flexed his aching hands. They were the ugly, nearly deformed hands of a lifelong pankrator. He wore his late father's signet ring on his littlest finger. The band was set with a stone of carved jasper, bearing the image of a boxing Minotaur—the sigil of their family—and the circle would never again pass over his swollen knuckle, which had been fractured last year in a pankration match. It was now as much a part of his body as his broken nose.

He thought of Kallisto and her perfect hands—the hands of a goddess carved from the finest marble. He imagined engulfing one of her pretty palms and fingers between both of his own, like the rough shells of an oyster protecting a smooth pearl.

"Now, that's poetry," he said to the lizard, and wrote down the simile. But the words came out all wrong. He wrote Kallisto's name over and over again, surrounding the appellations with little key patterns and other designs.

"Phile looks nervous," he heard his grandmother, Eudoxia, say from outside.

"I think her hands are trembling," added Agathe with a mellifluous laugh.

"Pity," chimed in Kallisto. "So close to beating us."

Nikias went to the window, opened the shutter a crack, and peered down. The women were all unveiled and barefoot, and wearing nothing more than short tunics. Here in the countryside, among their own sex, women could be free in their dress. If they were to go out like that in the citadel, however, any male citizen would have had the right to thrash them for being promiscuous.

All the women of Plataea had been trained as archers for as long as anyone could remember. Once a year they were allowed to leave their men at home and wander the fields and mountains together, drinking wine and singing bawdy songs. The event ended in a feast and sacrifice to the Goddess. A happy Artemis ensured healthy offspring—preferably boys.

Kallisto, Eudoxia, and Agathe stood off to the side while his sister, Phile, took up a battlefield archery stance—a sitting position with her left leg curled under her buttock and the other knee bent with the foot flat on the ground.

Kallisto seemed to sense she was being watched. She glanced up at the window and squinted, then turned her gaze back to Phile, saying, "Come, girl! You're taking as long as your brother Nikias does to shoot."

Nikias smiled wryly at Kallisto's barb, though he wished he could be down there proving himself to her. Showing her his prowess.

Phile gripped the handle of her goat-horn bow with her sinewy arm and stared straight ahead at the target, a stuffed goose at the end of a pole held by Saeed the Persian.

"I've got wax in my ears," she said with a laugh. "I can't hear you."

From the opposite end of the yard, Saeed called out, "Three—hundred—and—one—paces. Exactly."

"You can do it, Phile," urged Mula, Saeed's gangly ten-year-old son. He was in charge of collecting the shot arrows and bringing them back to the archers, and went about his task with the seriousness of an Olympic Games attendant. Nikias knew Mula was in love with his sister and worshipped her.

Nikias watched Phile rub the horsehair string meditatively, take in a deep breath, and focus on the target. She brought the bowstring back and held it to her chin for an instant, then released her fingers. The arrow flew across the yard, grazed the goose's neck and hit the wooden wall behind the target with a dull *thudunk*.

"I knew you'd miss!" called out Nikias.

Phile glared up at the window with an expression of hostile surprise in her slightly bulging eyes.

"You're not allowed to gape at our sacred practice," said Phile, outraged. "Close your shutters this instant!"

Nikias's silver-haired grandmother raised a wagging finger. "The Goddess will not look kindly on your spying, child," she scolded, and made an attempt at an angry scowl, but the expression looked ridiculous on her sweet face.

"Saeed," called Agathe with an imperious tone. "Where is your master, Menesarkus? Nik should not be spying on us." Nikias's mother was nearly forty years old, but she looked more like her children's older sister than their mother with her smooth, flawless skin and plait of black hair that reached nearly to her buttocks.

"Master is to bed," replied Saeed. "His spine is sore from fighting Nik."

"Why don't you fall out the window onto your fat head," Phile suggested to her brother. "Do us all a favor and die."

Nikias opened the shutter all the way, swung his legs out over the windowsill, and dropped the twenty feet to the sandy arena.

"You will break your leg one of these days, my child," warned Agathe, shaking her head.

"Let's hope," muttered Phile.

Agathe went to Nikias and looked him over with the air of a gymnasium physician inspecting an injured athlete. "How's your jaw?" she asked, poking him on the side of his face a little roughly, causing him to wince.

"Hurts," he said. "Especially when you do that, Mother."

"Does it hurt when you speak?" asked Agathe.

"Yes," he replied.

"Then keep your mouth shut," said Agathe dryly.

Nikias glanced at Kallisto, who was laughing at his mother's joke. Her brown curls fell in thick spirals across her green flashing eyes, and he felt a lurch in his gut. Phile was tittering and repeating their mother's words.

Nikias strode over to Phile and grabbed his sister's bow. "You need to work on your form, Sister. In battle—"

"But what do *you* know of battle?" Kallisto strode up to Phile's side, wrapping an arm around her friend's waist. "You haven't even burned your hair yet!" She was smiling, but there was an edge to her voice, and she spoke with the confidence of a woman who had grown up with five older brothers. She squinted at Nikias expectantly to see how he would react.

"More than any of you." Nikias instantly felt stupid for the defensive tone in his voice. "And I cut my hair in two days," he added proudly, swiping the long hair from his eyes with an irritated gesture.

"But you've never fought in the phalanx," observed Kallisto, putting a hand on a hip, reminding Nikias of the curve of a water amphora.

"I've fought men face-to-face with my fists," said Nikias.

"I challenge you to a contest," said Kallisto.

"What?"

"You're not afraid of me, are you?"

"Of course not. But I don't spend all day shooting at targets—"

"Oh, the young warrior makes fine excuses," said Kallisto, turning to the other women.

"Nikias wouldn't lower himself to play with you," said Phile.

Nikias shot a withering look at his sister but she smirked back, emboldened by Kallisto's swagger.

"All right," he said, turning to Kallisto. "I take the challenge, Helladios's daughter. One shot at the target. First miss loses."

"Excellent," said Kallisto. "But let's make it a little more interesting. Let's have your man Saeed throw the target into the air and we'll shoot on the wing."

All the women clapped their hands with delight at this suggestion.

"Oh, Nikias," said Eudoxia. "You've stepped into bilge water, Grandchild."

"You first." Nikias handed the bow to Kallisto with a smile. She took it and squatted next to him, taking up the archer's stance. He studied her face. In profile her looks resembled the exaggerated features of a goddess's face stamped on a coin. She had a long, straight nose, perfectly outlined lips, and a prominent chin with a deep cleft in it—a feature he found particularly appealing. He imagined kissing that chin, her cheeks, her lips . . . dear Gods, even her feet were sublime! He glanced at her plump high breasts and the dark nipples pushing against her thin hemp tunic. Zeus would have ripped apart the thunderclouds merely for a glimpse of her!

"You look worried," said Kallisto, glancing at him out of the corner of her eye.

"Just shoot," replied Nikias, and swallowed the lump in his throat.

Phile laughed. "I heard you gulp from over here!" She mocked her brother with a ludicrous gulping sound. Nikias's grandmother and mother took up the taunt. Mula couldn't help himself and imitated the sound, then covered his mouth with a palm the moment Nikias shot him a dark look.

"Is this a frog pond or a training ground?" asked Nikias.

The women giggled and became silent.

Saeed took the goose in hand and swung his arm around in a big circle, waiting for Kallisto to call out. At her side was a bucket full of arrows, shafts down. She plucked one out, strung it to the bow, and brushed the arrow's fletched feathers against her cheek.

"Now!" she cried. The goose flew into the air, and the moment it reached its apogee the arrow sang. The target tumbled to the earth with a shaft straight through a wing. She got to her feet and held out the bow for Nikias to take. She leaned forward so her face was hidden from the other women.

"Where will we meet this time?" she asked in a hurried whisper.

"The Cave of Nymphs," he answered quickly, hiding his mouth by wiping his face with his forearm. "In two hours."

She nodded and said in a loud, chiding voice, "Don't miss, now."

Nikias took up the squatting stance, clutched the bow in his left hand, fingered the strings. He glanced at Kallisto and saw a smile pulling at the corner of her mouth.

"Concentrate," he thought. He loved Kallisto, but he didn't want her to beat him. He focused on the target. *Knowing* the distance and *feeling* the distance, he'd been taught, were two completely different concepts. Saeed had given him that lesson before he could even draw a bowstring. *Feeling* the target brought into play the force of the wind and humidity, and the mysterious magnetism the earth goddess Gaia exerted on an arrow that pulled it downward along its trajectory even over a short distance. He took a deep breath, focused on the target until his peripheral vision blurred and dimmed. The mock goose going round and round in Saeed's hand seemed to grow brighter—it actually appeared to be flapping its wings. The thought of the stuffed goose taking flight made him laugh.

"He's nervous," said Eudoxia.

"Look at him sweating," said Phile.

"My poor child," said Agathe.

"Now!" yelled Nikias.

The goose went straight up in the air. His arrow flashed. The target plummeted to the earth, the arrow through the body. A perfect kill. Kallisto bit her lower lip. Nikias tossed her the bow.

"Your turn," he said with a smile.

Kallisto was rattled. She took longer to shoot this time. The women shouted encouragement and Kallisto mumbled to herself under her breath. When she finally plucked the bowstring, she cursed the moment the arrow was released, thinking she'd missed. But the arrowhead clipped the goose's neck and they fell to the ground as one.

She passed Nikias the bow and he could see that little beads of sweat had formed on her upper lip and brow. He was sure that *that* dew would taste better than wine.

"Lucky shot," he said.

Kallisto shrugged and said, "Artemis loves a huntress."

Nikias got back in his stance. He was enjoying the game. He loved how Kallisto would not back down. That she wanted to beat him more than anything in the world. But he wouldn't let her win. He respected her too much for that. Saeed grasped the target and starting spinning it round. Nikias felt a surge of confidence, as though the bow and arrow were an extension of his arms, hands, eyes, and brain. He knew he couldn't miss.

"Now!" shouted Nikias.

The target flew up into the blue sky.

"Boy!" bellowed Menesarkus the instant before Nikias let go of the string.

Nikias hesitated a fraction of a second and tried to catch the goose as it plummeted, and his arrow went sailing straight into the chimney of the slaves' dormitory, bouncing off with a metallic clank.

Menesarkus was leaning out of the window of his bedroom, clenching his teeth in pain. "Get up to the mountains and check on the shepherds and their flocks, or I'll have Saeed flay the skin from your rump with his Sargatian whip!"

The women howled with laughter and Phile danced around Kallisto, shouting, "She won! She beat you!"

Nikias handed Kallisto the bow, gave her an admiring look. "Congratulations."

"You were distracted," she said with an apologetic smile, and made the slightest wink—a gesture that sent a thrill through his core.

"That's no excuse," he replied happily, thinking of how close he was to taking her in his arms. "There are many distractions in battle." He held out his hand and shook hers, slipping a folded poem into her palm.

FOUR

———————◆———————

Nikias put a bridle on his tempestuous white mare, Photine. She was shying and snorting peevishly. She wanted to stay in the fenced pasture, nibbling grass and rolling in the dirt all day.

"Can I ride with you?" asked Mula as he mucked the stalls. "I promise not to fall behind," he added meekly.

"Not today," said Nikias vehemently. The boy's shoulders sagged and Nikias tousled his head of woolly hair. "But tomorrow you can ride with me to the pine forest and we'll hunt together."

"I can't wait!" shouted the merry boy.

Nikias grabbed a short sword and his Sargatian whip from its peg on the wall. Saeed had made the weapon from an entire flayed ox hide, weaving the pieces together to make a supple cord that could take off the flesh down to the bone when properly wielded. A white scar emblazoned on the young fighter's chin had come from his youthful attempts to master this weapon and not from another pankrator's fist.

Nikias rode across the farmyard and toward the gate where Saeed stood holding a short thrusting spear. The Persian tossed it up to Nikias, who caught it as he trotted by.

"Watch out for Dogs," said Saeed.

The Dog Raiders were an enemy tribe from the other side of the mountains who covered their helms with the skins of black canines. Two had been spotted last week sneaking over the mountains and into Plataean territory, stealing sheep. Nikias wrapped the whip around the spear so he could carry them both in one hand.

He and Photine climbed into the hills above the farm, taking a steep goat path, until he came to the Lookout, a massive ledge of rock that stood halfway up the mountainside. This place afforded a sweeping view of the plains of the Oxlands. From here he could see the farm below and the empty courtyard. The women had put down their bows and gone back to their labors.

He smiled at the thought of Kallisto's triumphant expression when she'd beaten him, and turned his gaze northward to the earthen mounds of the Persian fort. Nikias and his friends used to go there as children, digging in the ground for rusty swords and the bones of unburied Persian warriors. In the distance beyond the fort stood the sturdy northern watchtowers, gray pillars guarding the border with Thebes. If an enemy army invaded from that direction, it would have to pass right under the sleepless eyes of Plataea's vigilant border guards.

Across the verdant plains over the downs the sun was burning off the morning's wintry mist, and the vapors receded like a backwards-rolling wave in the direction of Thebes, eight miles north along the Kadmean Road. Nikias was reminded of a funeral shroud pulled back to reveal a corpse's face and he shuddered, thinking of one of his earliest memories: his father Aristo's bloodless corpse in the back of the cart after it had been brought home from battle. The dead face had been streaked with dirty tears where he'd cried out his life into the dust.

Nikias turned and looked to the west along the Cypress Way. This was Plataea's main thoroughfare, connecting it to all of its outlying villages. The road was alive with horses and carts going to and from the citadel. The tops of the tall conical cypress trees that lined the avenue swaying gently in the wind, like the swishing tails of contented cats. Two miles away, at the end of the road, stood the familiar bastions of Plataea.

"A city's walls should impress one's friends and depress one's enemies," his friend Chusor, who lived in the citadel, had told him once. Plataea did just that. The sturdy, high-walled bastions surrounding the citadel were interspersed with two dozen square guard towers. The walls in the northern half of the city formed a rambling rectangle, to the south a warped triangle that abutted the steep foot of the mountain.

The stronghold enclosed several marble temples gleaming in the sun; a large open agora—the city's main public square—near the gates; an assembly hall; and a small amphitheater along the northernmost wall. All of these public buildings were made of the local black or gray marble, a somber contrast to the garishly painted buildings of Athens—a city Nikias had only visited once, when he was a boy, as it lay a hard four-day march to the southeast through dangerous territory. Even though Athens was twenty times the size of Plataea, this view of his citadel always filled Nikias with pride. It made his heart swell.

"I am a Plataean," he said softly, reverently. In two more days he would be named a citizen and given ceremonial black and white ballot stones. He could almost feel the cool, smooth rocks in his palm. Such power in those small pieces of the earth. They meant he was part of a democracy. A strong voice to be heard amongst many. He would also receive a complete set of armor that had been fitted especially for his body—helm, breastplate, and shin guards. Chusor had been working on it for the last year at his workshop. Nikias had caught a glimpse of it there. He couldn't wait to try it on and see his reflection in the burnished shield.

Chusor was a metic—a foreigner, born in Athens, who lived and worked in Plataea but didn't have the legal rights of a Plataean citizen. He couldn't vote in the Assembly and couldn't even sue a citizen unless a Plataean man acted as his sponsor. Still, he seemed content with his position. "There are enough intelligent men in Plataea without me casting a ballot stone," Chusor had said to Nikias once. "And any pair of fools can work out a disagreement rather than taking each other to court."

Nikias reckoned Chusor was right on both counts, but he couldn't imagine living his life as a lowly metic. Without the law on your side and the ability to vote, you might as well be a ghost. At least, that's what his grandfather would say.

He squeezed his knees against Photine and she headed upwards toward a grassy deforested area. The air smelled of the sea. The Bay of Korinth was an hour's ride to the west, and some days, especially when it was hot, Nikias would ride there and swim in the bay while Photine happily rolled in the sand.

The horse smelled the faint scent of brine, too, and she shook her head as if to say, "That way!"

"Not today, girl," said Nikias. "But—"

The horse laid back her ears and snorted. A rider was coming fast through the woods behind them. Photine whirled and Nikias had to grab her mane to keep from getting thrown. With a neat flick of the wrist he uncoiled the spear shaft from the leather whip, catching the spear with the opposite hand as it spun through the air. Spear in right hand, whip in the other—he was prepared for any foe.

The rider burst from the woods and rode straight at him.

"Are you going to kill me or kiss me?" asked Kallisto as she stormed past, her hair flying crazily on the wind, eyes wide with excitement.

Nikias laughed, tucked his spear under his arm with the point facing backwards, wrapped the whip around his neck, and took off after her. Kallisto veered off the goat path and headed straight up the mountain, scattering a flock of crows in a field of sage. Nikias gained on her, hugging his chest to Photine's pumping neck, becoming one with her body like a centaur, guiding her seemingly with his thoughts.

Kallisto jumped recklessly over an ancient crumbling wall and her horse's hind hoof knocked loose a stone, stumbling and slowing almost to a stop. She cursed and kicked her mount.

Photine took the wall like a hare jumping a garden hedge, and Nikias shot past Kallisto. Photine was galloping hard now, shoulder muscles bulging. Her short, stout legs were suited to this kind of terrain. Soon Photine charged up a stony field. Nikias breathed in the scent of sun-warmed grass and olive leaves borne on the wind.

He looked to his left. She was beside him now. They were so close together, their legs were touching. The lovers leaned over at the same time and their lips met briefly. Kallisto flashed him a smile and shrieked with uninhibited joy as her steed nosed ahead of Photine. She reined in hard below a jutting shelf of rock, then leapt off her mount and started climbing ancient steps carved in the stone. Nikias pulled Photine up hard, slid off, and chased after Kallisto, grasping for the hem of her dress to slow her down; but she kicked his hand away, laughing, and grabbed the whip from around his neck.

She sprinted ahead of him into the dark mouth of the cave, yawning in the mountainside like the jaws of a toothless Titan. Nikias stabbed his spear into the earth and chased after her. She led him to an alcove near the back of the cave. She was holding the whip with one end in each hand to make a hoop shape, slipping it over his head and and waist, pulling him toward her until they were pressed together. She was still laughing, but softer now. He could see her eyes in the dim light, staring into his with a strange ferocity. They were like the painted eyes on the statue of Athena the Huntress in the citadel. The eyes of a goddess—a goddess who was trying to decide whether to grant joy or to destroy.

"I beat you," she said with mock imperiousness. "Bow to me."

Nikias scoffed and grasped her in his powerful arms. They kissed savagely, like boxers throwing devil-may-care punches. Soon they were breathing harder than they had on that entire frantic ride up the mountainside. And then their urgent hands fought against each other's clothes, ripping them off, seeking out the hot bare skin underneath, feeling hard muscles and soft flesh. They pressed their naked bodies tightly together, coiling their arms and legs—they were like two supple grapevines that had become wholly intertwined.

Nikias could hear his own blood pounding in his ears and feel Kallisto's heart throbbing against his chest. She started to speak but he said, "Shut up for once," and leaned down, covering her mouth with his own until they were breathing the same air in unison. After a while she let forth a shuddering groan—a groan he caught in his mouth—and her knees buckled. He lowered her gently to the floor of the cave, where she lay down on their discarded clothes. He eased himself on top of her, supporting himself with his forearms to keep from crushing her against the hard stones.

There was a moment of stillness and silence as their eyes locked. Nikias tried to speak but his voice stuck in his throat, and so he raised his eyebrows as if to say, "Now?" They had met before in secret, but it had never gone this far. They were on the edge of a cliff above a rushing river. There was no turning back if they made the leap into *this* torrent.

"Of course, you fool," she whispered back, gently teasing. "I will—" she broke off as she opened herself to him, guiding him with firm but trembling hand. "I will have you," she said, and gasped as they became joined for the first time. "Slow, now," she commanded. "Like you're dancing for Demeter."

His hips moved back and forth in an ancient rhythm, the cadence of the harvest dance that every Plataean boy and girl had performed as soon as they'd started to walk. Back and forth. Slowly. Praising the goddess Demeter with their undulating bodies. Calling forth life. The cave surrounded them, cradling them in its deep solitude as though they were cupped in the palms of the Gaia—in the hands of Mother Earth herself. Nikias let forth a moan deep in the back of his throat that seemed to be swallowed by the cave and pulled down, down to the heart of the mountain, all the way to the underworld.

"There's no poem compares to this," Kallisto said softly after they were done. And a little later: "If I conceive, Father will have to let us marry."

"Yes," said Nikias drowsily, breathing in the intoxicating smell of her hair, like sunshine on wild herbs mingled with the robust scent of her horse. "I'll make you a fine husband"—this muttered as a dreamy afterthought.

They fell into a deep sleep. They did not hear the horses ride up outside the cave. Or the many footsteps creeping up to the entrance. Only when they were surrounded did Nikias's eyelids fly open. But it was too late. Wooden clubs slammed into his stomach, chest, and head, and he gasped in agony and surprise, the wind and senses knocked out of him. Kallisto's terrified screams filled his ears.

FIVE

"You whore!" bellowed Kallisto's eldest brother, Lysander. The sound of his hand slapping her face was like a snapping whip. He grabbed her by the arm and dragged her out of the cave and into the light.

Helladios's four other sons followed after their leader, slapping at Kallisto's naked body and yanking on her hair. They yelled hateful words at her, surrounding her in a hostile ring.

Nikias crawled on the cave of the floor, his head spinning, his ears ringing. His hand found his whip. He clutched it in his fist and got unsteadily to his feet, staggering after them, ignoring the searing pain in his stomach and head. He'd been beaten far worse than this before by his grandfather in the practice arena, and knew how to force himself to move despite the pain.

"Get away from her!" he barked as he came into the light of the cave entrance.

Lysander, a big thirty-year-old with black hair and an extended lower jaw, pointed his sword at Nikias. "Stop or I will cut you down," he said, spittle flying from his mouth.

"Nikias, run away!" screamed Kallisto.

The other young men were all armed with short spears and clubs. They glared at Nikias with burning hatred.

"You'll pay for this," said Isokrates, the next eldest brother. He was a scrawny man with a neck too long for his body and a nose too big for his head. "You know this is our right, Nikias. You'd do the same if we defiled *your* sister."

Nikias drew in his breath sharply as though he'd been struck again. He knew what Isokrates said was true. It was in their rights to abuse their sister for what she'd done. And he would have murdered any one of them if they'd dared even touch his sister, Phile. He glanced at Kallisto, her disheveled hair covering her face, her body wracked with sobs.

Lysander lowered his sword and sneered at Nikias with his cruel, thin-lipped mouth. "Go home, son of Aristo. We'll see you in the courts." He sheathed his weapon and regarded his sister with a look of utter loathing, as though he were inspecting the most worthless slave ever to come up for auction. Suddenly he grabbed her by the hair and twisted it around his fist into a single plait. Then he punched one of her breasts with all his might. Kallisto sucked in a gasp of air like an inverted scream.

Nikias was blinded by a red rage. He snapped his Sargatian whip twice in a lightning-fast motion, drawing blood from Isokrates and one of the other brothers. The wounded siblings screamed in pain and dropped their guard, giving Nikias the chance to pounce on Lysander with the swiftness of a predatory animal. He locked him in the Morpheus hold, dragging him away from the others, using the other man's body as a shield. Lysander clawed feebly at Nikias's arms but it was useless to struggle.

"If any one of you touches your sister again," said Nikias, "I will send Lysander to Hades."

The youngest brothers—the sixteen-year-old twins Orion and Theron—let go of their spears at once. The addled sibling named Akake, his chin gushing blood, looked at the struggling Lysander with confusion on his idiot's face. Isokrates held up a submissive hand, threw his weapons aside, then swiped at the blood dripping down his face where Nikias's whip had sliced open his forehead.

"We'll leave her," he said quickly, eyes full of fear. "Don't hurt Lysander."

Nikias eased up his grip on Lysander's neck and the man took in a gasping breath.

"Let me go," he pleaded. "Let me go."

Nikias kept Lysander trapped in his arms and turned to Kallisto, who was a few paces behind him. "Go into the cave," he said, "and get your clothes. You're leaving with me."

Kallisto dashed into the cave and returned throwing on her dress and slipping on her sandals.

"Now get on your horse," ordered Nikias.

Lysander made a sudden movement but Nikias squeezed hard, thrust his mouth next to his ear, and hissed, "Do not move!"

Lysander didn't listen. He started breathing hard. Panicking in the death lock. His eyes bulged out and his face went purple. Isokrates had moved around close to where Nikias's spear was stuck in the ground. Isokrates lunged at the spear, pulled it out of the ground, and thrust the point at Nikias's exposed side. Nikias instinctively brought Lysander's body in front of the oncoming point to protect himself.

"Gods!" shrieked Lysander. "Gods! You've speared me."

Nikias let Lysander go immediately and the big man fell to the ground. Lysander lifted his shirt in terror, staring at the wound—a tiny slit above his belly button. It opened slightly like a winking pink eye with every one of his gasps.

Isokrates stared in shock at what he had done, then tossed aside the bloody spear, holding a hand over his mouth.

"Help me, curse you!" raged Lysander.

The brothers all rushed to his side.

"Help me home!" bellowed Lysander. "I'm dying! I'm dying!"

"You're barely bleeding," said Nikias with disdain.

The brothers lifted up their wounded leader, carried him gently down the crumbling stairs, and heaved him onto his horse. Then they all mounted up and rode away, cursing Nikias over their shoulders as they went.

"What a pack of cowards," said Nikias.

Nikias beheld the bedraggled Kallisto. Her face was white except for the red shape of a hand where Lysander had slapped her. He wanted to go to her and hold her in his arms, but it was as if his body had become rooted to the ground.

"Let's go," he said.

She shook her head miserably. "They've done their worst to me. I have to go home and tell father what happened. That you weren't to blame. Otherwise there will be no hope for . . . for us."

He reached out and grabbed her arm but she shook him off.

"Don't touch me, Nikias!" she wailed. "Leave me alone!"

She covered her eyes in shame. Nikias tried to speak but no words came. Kallisto left him there in front of the black mouth of the cave. She mounted her horse and rode away.

He stood in shock for some time, then picked up his bloodied spear and wrapped his whip around it. He put a hand gingerly to his head where one of Kallisto's brothers had struck him with a wooden club. There was a huge welt there, but the skin wasn't broken. He checked his ribs. One of them might have been cracked. But it didn't matter. Nothing mattered now.

Nikias took a long time riding home, carrying a heavy burden of humiliation and sorrow. He thought about what his grandfather would say when he told him what had happened. The old man would probably foam at the mouth like a rabid stink badger.

He put Photine in the fenced pasture and took off her bridle. He hung the bridle in the barn's tack room and leaned his whip-coiled spear against the wall. Then he walked around to the front of the farmyard. He paused at the front gate and looked toward the mountains. Night had fallen. The crescent moon was rising. Just the tip showed above the mountains, like the curved blade of a hand scythe. Hesperos, the evening star, glowed red in the sky above it. He remembered a poem his father had written comparing the star to an apple on a high branch that was just out of reach—something you could never have. He could not stop thinking of Kallisto's white face with the slap imprinted there, like a scar that would never heal.

A whimpering sound made him turn toward the house. He saw one of their guard dogs wobble drunkenly from the dark. Was it dragging a stick? The skin on the back of Nikias's neck prickled as his brain made sense of what he was seeing: the dog had been skewered! The flight feathers of an arrow were sticking through one side of its rib cage, the metal tip poking out the other.

Nikias froze. He scanned the darkness, trying to pick shapes from the shadows. There was a lamp burning in the farmhouse, but none in the upstairs windows. No light came from the slave quarters. He squinted at the dormitory building and saw that somebody had barred it shut from the outside. A baby cried from inside—a girl who'd been born a month ago. He heard her father making a fearful shushing sound.

The dog lay down in the farmyard and stopped moving.

A barn owl hooted. But the sound was wrong. A human had made it.

Suddenly he heard footsteps on the road behind him: bare feet slapping on the dirt like the soft, quick clapping of hands. There was no time to turn and look back at who was coming. Nowhere to run but into the farmyard. He clenched his fingers, squeezing his knuckles into fists like hammers. Every muscle in his body tensed. He ran toward the front door screaming, "Grandfather! Saeed!"

Men lunged from the shadows and ran straight at him. The years of brutal training in the pankration arena made Nikias react without thinking. He knocked one down with a punch to the throat, pulled his elbow back and smashed another in the temple. He jumped up, kicking out with all his strength, and a third went flying. A fourth leapt on his back and got him in a chokehold, and Nikias flipped the man over his shoulder, kicked him in the head.

Something covered him smelling of brine. A fishing net. He flailed his arms against the net but couldn't get at the attackers. He struggled wildly but there were too many of them. He tried to shout, but one grabbed him from behind and shoved a cloth in his mouth. They carried him into the house, into the dining room.

Nikias saw Menesarkus sitting at the table, surrounded on all sides by cloaked warriors. At the head of the table, in his grandfather's place, was the noseless Spartan—Drako the Skull—his red robe illuminated by the light of a flickering oil lamp.

SIX

———◆———

"The grandson," said Drako, looking Nikias up and down. He frowned when he saw the number of his men who were bleeding. "You were supposed to grab him, not let him practice his boxing skills on you," observed the Spartan commander, oozing with disdain. He made a barely perceptible motion and his men pushed Nikias into a seat. "Take that out of his mouth."

One of the Spartans yanked the cloth from Nikias's mouth. He started to say something to his grandfather but Menesarkus cut him off.

"Silence. Where have you been?" A second later Menesarkus waved his hand. "Don't answer that. Just shut your mouth." He shifted on his seat and grimaced with pain from his sore back.

Nikias's mind reeled. What was going on? Were the women safe? How had these men made it past the border sentries on the mountain posts? Where was Saeed? He looked at the grim-faced warriors who stood in the shadows with their backs against the walls. He counted a dozen of them inside—all naked except for their soiled red cloaks. None of them were armored but each wore a short thrusting sword at his waist, gnarled hands clutching the hilts. They stood so still, they resembled statues in an artist's studio, but the threat of violence was palpable. Would they all be murdered? Nikias wondered. He wiped his bleeding nose on his arm.

"The women are safe," said Menesarkus softly, reading the look in his eyes.

"We have no intention of harming your family," said Drako in a rasping voice that did little to calm Nikias's fear. The Spartan commander was as big as Nikias had remembered him from the Hippodrome ten years earlier, with broad shoulders and the musculature of a wrestler—unlike his attendant warriors, who were all whipcord lean.

Drako scratched near the edge of the gaping hole in the middle of his face with a long, curved fingernail that resembled an animal's claw. "We merely came to talk."

Menesarkus threw back his head and laughed. "Perhaps I should get out the wine bowl. We could have a symposium. I've a few interesting neighbors I could invite. Oh, but I forgot: you Spartans only drink barley and river water. The dirtier the better."

Drako gave a cheerless smile at Menesarkus's sarcastic tone and turned his killer's gaze on Nikias. "Your grandfather has not lost his Oxland wit after all these years. I met him when he was your age. Fatter, now, yes. And hairier"— this in a disgusted aside—"but still the same Menesarkus."

Nikias knew that his grandfather had journeyed to Sparta after the Persian Wars—an exchange of heroes between the allies. Menesarkus had competed in the Games of Lysander there and won the highest honors, beating the Spartan pankration champion in a no-holds-barred bout in which, Saeed had told him, the Spartan had been maimed for life.

"Were you and my grandfather shield friends?" asked Nikias, and cursed himself for how high his voice sounded. Could they hear his fear? He glanced at the faces of the mute warriors standing in the shadows, but they were as devoid of emotion as a row of bronze helms.

"I told you to hold your tongue," Menesarkus said angrily.

"Please, Menesarkus," said Drako with false politeness. "Let the boy and me converse. We have already met before, after all. At the Hippodrome in Olympia. When you strangled Damos the Theban to death."

Menesarkus stared at Drako and the two locked eyes for long seconds. Then Menesarkus sniffed and shrugged.

"You're a guest in my house," he said. "Do what you will."

"Menesarkus and I fought side by side during the Battle of Plataea," said Drako, turning his ruined face upon Nikias and twisting his wolf's mouth into what Nikias reckoned the Spartan thought was a pleasant smile.

"Glorious days, those were," he continued. "When a hundred thousand Greek allies met five times as many Persians and reaped them like grass." His grating Doric accent lingered on the word 'grass' like the hiss of a scythe. Drako stood up and walked over to Nikias, lingering behind his chair. Nikias wondered if the Spartan was going to reach around and slit his throat.

"Soon after the victory," Drako went on, "Menesarkus was an honored guest at the palace, where I served as a royal guard. We practiced the pankration together. We shared meals in the mess hall—"

"And we had many scintillating conversations," blurted Menesarkus sarcastically, rolling his eyes. "By Kronos's balls, what is the meaning of this rambling preface? Why are you here, Drako? Why have you invaded my home?"

"This is nothing more than a visit," said Drako flatly. "An invasion involves considerably less talking."

Menesarkus sniffed and waved his hand for Drako to proceed.

"Tomorrow morning I will march to the gates of Plataea," said the Spartan. "And I will ask Plataea to sign a treaty with my kings."

Menesarkus took a deep breath then exhaled. "You will be spurned. Our laws forbid us from opening our doors to enemies of Athens. Our Arkon cannot even speak to you without Athens' permission. You know this already, Drako!"

"Are you an independent city-state or slaves?" asked Drako with a sneer. "For I cannot tell."

"Do not speak to me of slavery and freedom," shot back Menesarkus. "I've seen your camps of pitiful Helots working under the lash."

"Helots are barely human," replied Drako. "You Plataeans are more pitiful for having once been valiant heroes." Drako leaned across the table, staring straight into Menesarkus's face. "Once you were equals of the Athenians. But they have grown in might. And now you grab your ankles while they take you from behind like the rest of their so-called league!"

Menesarkus's face was a mask of barely contained fury. He glanced at Nikias and his eyes softened, then he cursed under his breath and shook his head slightly.

"Our conversations have not changed much since we were young men," offered Drako with a cold smile.

"They have not," agreed Menesarkus.

Without thinking, Nikias said, "I don't understand why we need the Athenians' permission to do anything."

Menesarkus glanced at him under his bushy eyebrows and replied without rancor, "Plataea is a warrior. Athens is the general. It's as simple as that."

Drako made a quick motion to his men and they filed out of the room, leaving him alone with Menesarkus and Nikias. Oddly, without his warriors in the room, Drako seemed even bigger, more terrifying and commanding.

"My ancestors were loyal to Agamemnon," said Drako. "Followed the fool to Troy. Look what good it did them." He paused and leaned on the table. "I respect you, Menesarkus. Always did. And I'm certain your fellow citizens would follow you anywhere. We need your support in the Plataean Assembly. You know what will happen to Plataea if Sparta unleashes its might against you. Athens will not come to your aid. They will leave you out to twist like a hanged man. Give your grandson here the opportunity to perpetuate your tribe. Otherwise, all is ashes. We will make camp at the Persian Fort, for we still claim that as a war prize and thus our territory. We will approach the city at the sun's zenith tomorrow."

Drako passed a hand over his missing nose and squinted strangely at Menesarkus, then left, shutting the door behind him.

After they had watched the Spartans slip out of the farmyard and disappear into the night, Menesarkus and Nikias went to the women's quarters and un-barred the doors. Saeed was standing there at the ready, holding a loom spindle, looking menacing. The women pushed him aside, hugging and kissing Nikias and Menesarkus.

"We were desperate," said Eudoxia, wiping away tears.

"We thought they would murder you," said Phile, looking even more bug-eyed than usual. She surprised Nikias by planting a tender kiss on his cheek.

"Did they hurt you, Nikias?" asked Agathe, holding her son's face in her hands.

Nikias shrugged. "We talked," he said as nonchalantly as possible.

Nikias and Saeed walked around the house bolting all the doors and shutters. When they were done, Nikias went back to the dining room table and found his grandfather sitting alone, staring into space.

Nikias said, "You never told me the name of the warrior you beat in the Games of Lysander. When you were a guest of the Spartans."

"He literally had me by the balls," said Menesarkus, nodding his head. "Drako tried to rip my heirs from my body! There was nothing I could do. Biting *is* al-lowed in Sparta," he added in a defensive tone.

Nikias was impressed. "You bit off your friend's nose."

"Drako was *never* my friend, Nik. Spartans don't have friends. Not like us. Never forget that. The Spartans are different creatures. They bleed like men, but they think like insects. We cannot bow to them, else we will lose . . ." Mene-sarkus paused, searching for words, then said ". . . whatever it is that makes us human."

SEVEN

Nikias carried a lamp up to his room, placed it on his desk, and sat on his bed with his back against the wall, holding his father's tortoiseshell lyre. He stared into the shadows thinking over the events of the day. How did Kallisto's brothers find them at the cave? Had they been spying on them all this time? Had one of the slaves been bribed to give them away? Perhaps Kallisto's maid?

There was a movement above and he saw the lizard Ajax magically clinging to the ceiling and crawling with its shifting gait.

Nikias's father used to sing a bedtime song about a lizard. But he had no memory of his father's playing or singing. If doomed Aristo's face hadn't been painted on a funeral jar—a jar that stood on a table next to his bed—he would never even have recalled what the man looked like. He stared at the jar now, at the miserable expression on Aristo's handsome face. "I should be alive, not sitting here in Hades," he seemed to say.

"What a terrible fate to die so young," thought Nikias. To live as a shade in dark Hades, where a man was constantly hungry but could never eat. And always aroused but never able to make love. A bodiless wraith that craved its old human shape and all the sensations that went with it . . . excruciating desire with no relief.

He reached for the urn but it slipped from his hands and dropped to the floor, landing on its side. The heavy lid came off and some fine ash slipped out like smoke, floating toward the lamplight. Nikias cursed, picked up the urn, and put the lid back on. He examined the container and saw a crack had opened up from top to bottom. He put it back on the table.

This was a bad omen.

He knew there was no way he was going to go to sleep tonight. Every time he shut his eyes, he saw Kallisto's humiliated face.

Where could he go? Who could he talk to? Demetrios, his best friend, had been virtually exiled by his father, the magistrate Nauklydes, to the island of Sicily to become "educated" at the court of the tyrant of Syrakuse. Nikias had received only one letter from Demetrios in the last two years, an ill-written missive describing the tyrant's hellish prison pits and an even more horrid courtesan he'd bedded. "Which one had the worse pit I can't honestly tell you," the wry Demetrios had written.

Stasius, Nikias's other friend, had become debauched and empty-headed over the last year, drunk on the praise heaped upon him for his exceptional beauty, and even drunker on the wine and hemp in which he stewed and steeped his body. Nikias could no longer confide in him, especially not about something as important as this.

The shutter opened slightly and an enormous mantis stepped through the gap. The slender insect, walking upright on two legs like a human made Nikias think of the desiccated Spartan warriors. The mantis was drawn to the oil lamp and a moth fluttering around the flame. The mantis crept forward, stalking its prey, triangular head twitching from side to side. It cut the moth down in midflight with one of its serrated arms, then picked up the trembling body and bit off its head.

Ajax caught sight of the mantis and the lizard wagged its tail like a dog, letting forth a happy chirrup—a lizard battle cry. It crawled down the wall and onto the desk, pausing a few feet from where the mantis stood munching the moth. The mantis sensed the lizard's presence, for it shifted around and faced the lizard, tossing aside the moth and waving its arms menacingly, like a pankrator warming up for a bout.

Nikias watched intently. He'd seen many fights like this before. When he was a child, Stasius and Demetrios used to stage epic battles, pitting lizards and mantises against each other in a wooden box. Boys would crowd around, cheering like crazed spectators at a championship pankration bout, betting on the outcome. Nikias had never liked watching these forced battles. It didn't seem right to make dumb animals kill each other for sport. And the lizards hardly ever won against the armored mantises.

Nikias had instead preferred to experience the thrill of death in a more intimate way. He was the one who'd invented the dangerous game he'd called "piss on the tower," and his spirited friends, terrified of looking like cowards in front of Menesarkus's heir, had agreed to his reckless challenge of crossing the disputed unoccupied land separating Plataea from Thebes and sneaking into enemy territory.

It began one misty winter morning, before the break of dawn, when Nikias led half a dozen boys north on foot, crossing the wooden bridge over the River Oeroe, which flowed down from the Kithaeron Mountains and ran to the west. The boys stole past the Plataean borderland outposts positioned on the downs and eventually reached a larger stone bridge spanning the mighty river Asopus, which cut through the Oxlands from east to west. They could see the silhouette of a lone

Theban watchtower in the distance. The boys knew this tower was manned by deadly archers—warriors who would relish the chance of taking target practice at some Plataeans, however young they might be.

In the end Nikias was the only one of the boys with the courage (or lack of good judgment, as his friend Chusor would tell him after hearing an account of the story years later) to sneak up to the enemy tower. The heavy mist and dim light of morning hid his approach, but as soon as he'd urinated upon the ancient stones, the mist evaporated as if by magic, and he was left standing alone in the rosy sunrise, fully exposed at the base of the tower. He never ran so fast in his life. The arrows that zipped past his head sounded like hummingbirds in his ears. It was only when he fell into the arms of his friends—all of them laughing hysterically at his daring—did he realize his cheek was gushing blood.

"Missed you by a cunny hair!" Demetrios cried.

"Well," said Stasius, "he sure is bleeding like one!"

All the way back home they'd bellowed the "Song of Hate," the drinking song denouncing Plataea's blood enemy, the Thebans—that race of cunning men who'd tried in vain to destroy Plataea for a hundred years, and who'd bent over and grabbed their ankles for the Persian invaders.

In a cavern of the north
Skulked a dragon old
Zeus yanked it from its cave
And choked it, behold!
Ripped the teeth from its jaw
And sowed them in the ground
Up sprang the wily Thebans
With dragon's blood they're crowned!

Nikias came out of this reverie with a start. Ajax the lizard was about to lunge at the gigantic mantis on his desk. Nikias didn't want to see his little lizard gutted by this evil-looking thing. He jumped out of bed and swept his arm across the table, knocking the mantis out the window. Ajax chirped with fear and leapt to the wall, frightened by Nikias's violence.

Nikias opened the shutters all the way and dropped down into the sandy courtyard. There was only one person whom he could ask for help right now—his old friend Chusor the smith. He set out on foot toward the citadel, and with every step he took his shame and regret grew. He'd brought Kallisto low, and his heart was as heavy and dark as the black marble lid of a tomb.

EIGHT

———————•———————

Nikias entered the Gates of Pausanius a few minutes before they were to be shut and locked for the night. He passed through the tunnel that cut through the fifteen-foot-thick walls leading to the open space of the agora on the other side. It was only a few hours after sundown and the city was still alive with activity. Torches burned in sconces on buildings; lamplight flickered in the windows of homes. It always struck Nikias how much later city people stayed up than folk in the countryside.

He turned left and headed down Sex Factory Lane. The brothels were alive with activity and the food stalls crammed with patrons. Music sounded loudly from open doorways and grunts and cries came from open windows on the second floors. When he got to the Golden Thighs, the last brothel before the Old Market, a young man's head popped out a window, laughing crazily. He let out a yell of delight when he noticed Nikias.

"The great Olympian in training!" cried Stasius above the roar of the party-goers inside the room behind him. "I was wondering why you ignored the invitation to my symposium."

"I was busy on the farm," called out Nikias. Stasius was one of the fastest runners in the city—and so striking in appearance that his image adorned collector's plates with the motto "Stasius is beautiful." His father was the owner of the Golden Thighs, one of the least reputable whorehouses in the city.

"You country folk are so busy," said Stasius merrily. He flashed a disarming smile. "We were just talking about you. You've got to come up. We've been smoking some hemp that will float you to the clouds. Leo is—"

Another boy poked out his head searching for Nikias. "Where is he? Aha! Nik!" cried Leo when he'd spotted him below. "Stasius isn't joking. We had to tie a rope to his leg to keep him from floating off to Thebes where those infamous boy lovers would surely pounce on his backside with abandon."

Leo was the homely opposite of Stasius with his broad face, squat body, and thick forehead. He was an up-and-coming wrestler and a ward of the city whose father had been killed fighting for Plataea, and whose mother had died while bringing him into the world. Both young men were approaching eighteen and would participate in the hair cutting ceremony with Nikias two days from now. This symposium—a glorified drinking party—was Stasius's way of celebrating the end of childhood . . . the beginning of manhood.

"I'm on my way to see Chusor," said Nikias. "I'll come back later."

A broad-shouldered lad with a musical voice stuck his head between Stasius and Leo. "We'll be here all night," sang Hector. "We're going to fight with giant leather phalluses! Tra-la!"

"And Pelias the harpist is going to play," said Stasius.

"Ask Chusor to show you his Skythian!" shouted Leo, and the two disappeared inside the noisy room, laughing and calling to the others.

"What would Chusor be doing with a Skythian?" Nikias wondered. The Skythians were the barbarian race who inhabited a region far to the northeast. They were famous for their poisoned arrows and served as the Athenian police force. Nikias had seen one of them once—a freakish-looking man with red hair, eyes as blue as the sky, and a body covered with tattoos. Chusor was always buying curious slaves; after a time he'd grow bored with them and set them free, much to the amazement of the Plataeans.

The Old Market was crowded with people—mostly country dwellers visiting the city for the ceremony of manhood. A traveling seer stood nearby surrounded by a small circle of fascinated onlookers, poor mountain shepherds dressed in sheepskins. The seer wore a filthy robe embossed with hieroglyphics, and on his head was perched a tall, bulbous hat. He held a burning brazier in one hand. Nikias didn't like the look of this stranger, a man he'd noticed hanging about town the last couple of months. The seer was skinny and had a dirty, scraggly beard that reminded Nikias of a repulsive satyr. The seer glanced over at him and gave him a slanted smile.

"Swindling foreigners," said Nikias under his breath. He'd been conned years before into giving up a precious coin to a traveling stomach speaker—a man who'd promised to communicate with Nikias's dead father Aristo in the underworld. The stomach speaker had dug a hole in the ground and filled it with pig's blood, then told Nikias that his father's face was staring back at him, squeaking pitifully. But no matter how hard Nikias had stared into the blood, he hadn't been able see his father's face in the puddle. He'd known the man was a charlatan when he'd demanded more money to interpret Aristo's words—words only he could hear.

Nikias noticed Pelias walking by carrying his harp in a leather pouch under one arm. Pelias was a young Athenian in the employ of Magistrate Nauklydes and was one of the most sought after young men in the city. He had a beautiful voice and quick fingers that could pluck any tune called out to him.

Pelias bumped into the seer, and Nikias was surprised to see something pass between their hands. He'd done the same thing with Kallisto a dozen times, so he knew there was no mistaking it—the harpist had slipped the seer a note. And then Pelias was on his way striding quickly out of the market place toward the Golden Thighs. The seer looked over his shoulder before pocketing the object.

Nikias laughed. He was thinking of how Stasius would react if he told him he'd seen "beautiful" Pelias passing love notes with a greasy old reprobate.

He pushed his way through the men in the market and walked over to Chusor's smithy, a large domicile and workshop built against the city's eastern wall. Everyone in Plataea called him "the Egyptian" because of his exotic features, but the mysterious inventor was actually half-Aethiopian, and spoke Greek with the accent of a highborn Athenian. There was a rumor he'd killed a man in Athens and been forced to flee to Plataea, where he'd set up shop five years ago. But Nikias didn't believe the scurrilous tale, even though Chusor sometimes had a sinister air about him and his work.

An old shield painted with a picture of Hephaestos, the god of the forge, hung from a metal pole above the workshop entrance. Nikias peered through the large open window to the interior of the workshop. Sitting at a table near the back of the main room was the giant smith, grinding something in a mortar. On the table was a pile of yellow rocks. Nikias knew Chusor didn't like to be disturbed while he worked, so he watched in silence.

Everything about the foreigner was in perfect proportion—sturdy legs, V-shaped torso with defined stomach and pectorals as broad as serving platters, arms rippling with muscles, and a powerful neck. He had the full lips and broad nose of a Phoenician trader, although his skin was darker. His thick, curly hair was the color of a raven's beak and hung to his shoulders. On his chin was a four-inch-long beard braided in the Egyptian style.

Diokles—Chusor's servant—brought in a bowl with some finely powdered stuff that looked like bread flour and set it on the table. He had the nut-brown skin, a flat face, and straight black hair of his enthralled race, the Spartan slaves known as Helots. The Helots, Nikias had been told by his grandfather, had been the original inhabitants of the Spartan homeland. But hundreds of years ago they had been conquered and enslaved like beasts. Diokles's squat body was preposterously muscled from years of backbreaking servitude in a Spartan mine. It looked as though melons had been shoved under the skin of his biceps and calves.

Diokles had managed to escape from the mine during an earthquake and had found his way into Athenian territory where Chusor had taken him on as his servant. Nikias had never heard the full tale of the Helot's flight from Sparta. But he knew that Diokles lived in constant terror that "the Masters," as he called the Spartans, were hunting for him.

Chusor took several scoops from the bowl and put them into a clay jar. On top of this he poured in some coarse granules of the yellow rock. Nikias recognized these as Vulcan stones. He'd seen them in fissures on the Kithaeron Mountains and knew that Chusor valued them. Nikias collected them for Chusor in exchange for mastik and lead shots for his sling.

"Get the pot," said Chusor.

Diokles went to the furnace, where a pot was heating on the coals. He brought it to Chusor, who poured a thick, molten liquid into the top of the clay jar, then blew on it to cool it. Then Chusor stuck a lamp wick into the hardening wax.

A weird cry called out from a room on the second floor of the smithy.

"He awake now," said Diokles in his thick Helot accent.

Chusor stroked his chin beard. "Let's see if we can get him to talk." He pushed the chair back from the table. Diokles followed him up the stairs and out of sight.

Nikias pulled on the front-door ring and found that it was open. He entered the room, breathed in the reek of sulfur and the rich smell of beeswax. He picked up the clay jar Chusor had just filled, put his finger in the hardening wax, touched some of the fine powder in the bowl, and tasted it. It was gypsum, the main ingredient in plaster. He had worked with the stuff back on the farm, recoating the walls of the storage sheds.

He heard Chusor's voice speaking in Persian. Nikias had grown up with Saeed muttering at him in that language and knew enough to make out that the smith was asking questions: "What is your name? Who is your tribe?" Whoever Chusor was interrogating up there, however, did not reply in the same tongue. Rather, he chattered like a feral animal and then pounded something metallic on the floor—chains. He must be the Skythian who Leo was talking about.

There was a piece of papyrus sticking out from a folder on the table. Nikias pulled it out and stared at a strange drawing. He could not understand what it was at first because he had never seen anything like it. There was a dark outline interspersed with squares and circles, and inside this were boxes of varying sizes. Words were written on the boxes: "Assembly Hall, Jail, Temple of Athena, Gates of Pausanius . . ." He realized, with astonishment, that he was looking at a detailed map of the city—a map drawn from a bird's-eye view.

A door slammed on the second floor and he heard footsteps coming back down the stairs. He tucked the plan of the city back into the folder and sat at the table, crossing his arms on his chest just as Chusor entered the room.

"Nikias," said Chusor in surprise. "I didn't hear you enter."

"I knocked but nobody answered," said Nikias, forcing a smile. "So I just came in."

"I'm glad you did," said Chusor, flashing his huge white teeth. He glanced at the table and his eyes twitched slightly. "You saw my map?"

Nikias tried to keep his face from showing guilt. He shrugged and said, "I saw the folder there and—" He broke off, embarrassed.

Chusor pulled the map from the folder and spread it out on the table. "Nobody has ever made a schematic of this city before—at least, not in such detail. I did the same thing for the tyrant of Syrakuse when I was the apprentice to the great Naxos."

"What is it for?" asked Nikias, relieved that Chusor wasn't angry with him for snooping through his things.

Chusor scratched a scar on his left pectoral—a scar that could only have been made by a spear point, though he'd told Nikias once that it was from an accident in a workshop. He seemed about to speak, but then he shrugged as if to say, "There is no reason for the map. It just is." Suddenly he brightened and plucked something from a bowl and tossed it to Nikias.

"This is what I wanted to show you," he said.

"A plane tree seedpod?" said Nikias, holding up the hard circular thing with its dozens of spiky prongs. They were everywhere around Plataea this time of year, especially on the main road to Thebes, where hundreds of massive plane trees lined either side of the thoroughfare for miles and miles. Nikias remembered stepping on one of the pods when he was a child: its spikes had gone into his bare foot like a dagger.

Chusor grabbed a wooden bucket and dumped the contents on the table. Twenty or so metal replicas of the plane tree seedpods—about twice the diameter of the real ones—tinkled with the music of coins as they tumbled, gleaming in the lamplight. Chusor saw Nikias's look of incomprehension and laughed.

"Why do you suppose I made those metal versions?" he asked, stroking his braided beard.

"Some sort of trick?" replied Nikias cautiously.

"They're weapons."

Nikias picked one up and studied it closely.

"Imagine," said Chusor, "a battlefield strewn with these things."

Nikias saw the potential for Chusor's invention, or rather his re-creation of nature. "If they were on hard ground, horses wouldn't be able to walk on them. Would go right through the soft part of the hoof."

Chusor snapped his fingers as loud as a dry stick cracking in two. "I knew you would see it! Nobody else I've shown them to has understood the potential. Place these in front of a charging cavalry and they're as good as a phalanx of spearmen."

"Ingenious," said Nikias. "Truly. No matter how you throw them, they always sit with one of the spikes sticking up."

A constricted scream came from upstairs, followed by the sound of pottery breaking and then Diokles cursing in his own tongue. Chusor looked up toward the ceiling.

"I bought a captured Skythian from the Makedonian slaver," said Chusor with the same bored tone he would have used to describe the purchase of a new anvil.

"What for?"

"I want the secret of the poison his tribe uses on their arrows. One nick from a Skythian arrowhead will stop a man's heart in seconds."

More angry screams cried out along with the sound of breaking furniture.

"He's not cooperating," said Chusor, frowning. Then he looked at Nikias and his face brightened. "The last time you were here," he went on jovially, "you had the notion of running away with your beloved Kallisto to Athens and joining your cousin's fighting ship."

Nikias gave a wan smile. "And you told me the Athenian navy was so tight-fisted, you had to bring your own arse cushion for the galley benches." His smile faded and he stared at the floor morosely.

"What's wrong, lad?" asked Chusor.

"I did something foolish," said Nikias. "I need your advice. There's no one else I can talk to."

A loud banging on the door made Nikias start. Chusor strode to the portal and glanced through the small grated window set near the top. He looked at Nikias over his shoulder with a questioning glower and asked, "Something *very* foolish, perhaps?"

He opened the door. Standing on the threshold were half a dozen city guardsmen brandishing battle-axes. Their leader saw Nikias and announced, "Nikias, son of Aristo of the Nemean tribe. You are wanted for the murder of Lysander, son of Helladios."

NINE

Nikias no longer knew what time it was. He reckoned three or four days had passed since he'd been taken to the prison, but it was hard to tell in this windowless cell. The guards brought him food and took away the bucket full of filth on a regular basis, but they refused to give him any news of what was going on in the citadel. Once he had awakened from a nightmare to the distant sound of aulos pipes and cheers, and he'd known that the initiation of manhood was taking place in the nearby Theater of Dionysus. Never in his wildest imaginings did he think he'd miss that sacred moment of transformation. It should have been the most important day of his life. Only death would have kept him from it. The misery that had enveloped him in that moment was overpowering. It had felt as if his body were tumbling in a void, over and over again, only to sink like a ship with a gaping hole in its hull, down into Poseidon's realm and the cold emptiness of the sea.

He forced himself to get off the cot. He started doing push-ups. First on his hands, then his knuckles, then on fingertips. He did five hundred before his arms finally gave out and he collapsed on the dank floor. The smell of must and earth penetrated his nostrils. He wondered how long it would take before he started to rot.

"This is why we burn the dead," he thought bitterly. "So their shades don't have to breathe this stench for eternity."

He curled up in the fetal position on the floor. How long would they keep him here before having a trial? For the hundredth time he reimagined the fight with Lysander and his brothers. Why had he turned Kallisto's brother into the oncoming spear? Was it instinct? Or had he wanted Helladios's son to die?

The spear tip must have nicked Lysander's stomach. That was all it took. No man ever recovered from that wound. His father, Aristo, had died from a spear to the groin—a tiny puncture below his intestines. It had been the only mark on his body, his grandfather had told him. But, like a hole in a full wineskin, it had been enough to drain his vital fluid. How could men with the strength to claw ore from the ground, then melt and hammer it into weapons, be so vulnerable to their inventions?

If he were to be convicted of taking away Kallisto's virginity, he could be banished from Plataea for life. That he knew for certain. If he were to be convicted of murdering Lysander . . . well, he could be hanged or exiled, depending on the jury's decision. The trouble was all of the witnesses were on Lysander's side. And, Nikias knew, they would all lie. Kallisto's eyewitness testimony was invalid because she was a woman.

He wished Demetrios were here now. "If I can escape from prison," he thought, "I could go to Syrakuse and find Demetrios." He could take Kallisto with him and save her from the ignominy that was now her future life. They could ride to the Gulf of Korinth—be there within half an hour if they rode fast and hard. Nikias could sell his late father's gold signet ring and buy them passage on a ship for Syrakuse. Nikias could earn their bread by fighting the pankration circuit. This fantasy of escape kept him from dashing his brains out against the wall in despair.

Hours went by. Perhaps another day. Nikias awoke from a fitful slumber to the sound of a familiar voice saying, "Get up, now." He wondered if he was back on the farm in his bedroom.

"Grandfather?" he asked groggily.

"Come with me, boy," said Menesarkus.

As though in a dream, Nikias followed his grandfather out of the cell, down the hall, and up the long stairs from the underground prison. His legs felt weak and he was breathing hard once they got to the top step. It was brighter up there and he squinted. By the time they got to the prison exit, he had to cover his eyes with his hand, for he was nearly blinded by the white light of afternoon winter sun. The guards nodded respectfully at General Menesarkus and let them pass.

Menesarkus wrapped one of his massive arms around Nikias's shoulders and led him away from the jail. They walked without speaking and his grandfather guided him a hundred paces or so to a wide doorway that opened onto a walled quadrangle. Here Menesarkus released his grandson from his ironlike grasp, found a marble bench, and sat down, stretching his crippled leg out in front of him.

Nikias squinted at his surroundings. He realized they were in the Courtyard of Laws. Across this quadrangle were the two entrance portals to the sacred Assembly Hall building. He glanced up at the tall building. The structure, made entirely of local black marble, was the most somber building in the city. "A temple to the will of the people," as his grandfather was fond of saying.

Here, all of Plataea's citizens met to discuss important matters and vote on new laws. Nikias had never been inside the hall before. If he hadn't been in jail during the initiation ceremony the other day, he would have been allowed to sit with his fellow citizens and listen to debates, and vote by dropping a white or black ballot stone into an amphora.

He and his grandfather were the only two in the courtyard, and it was very quiet except for the cawing of a crow. The bird was standing on the head of an ancient statue of Plataea's first lawgiver. The painted statue had lost nearly all its pigment over the years, and the eyes, once decorated with lifelike irises and pupils, were now so faded that they resembled the clouded eyes of a blind man.

The crow was staring at Nikias sideways with one intelligent eye. He noticed that the bird had a single white tail feather, and it made him think of the story about how Apollo, the god of light, cursed a white crow and turned his feathers dark, thus blackening his kind forever. Nikias felt cursed right now. He'd "gone to the crows," as they said in Athens. His friends in town, however, would use the Plataean version of this old saw: "You're in such deep shit, even the oxen are keeping their distance."

Hundreds of marble headstones inscribed with Plataea's laws had been placed throughout this courtyard—a public record for all citizens to see. The courtyard always reminded Nikias of the cemetery on the outskirts of the city's western walls. Every time a new law was created, up popped a somber headstone, like a memorial for a man who had flouted convention.

He looked at his grandfather. Menesarkus was staring at the ground, lost in thought, until a fly buzzed past his head and he waved it away with an irked gesture.

Nikias gazed at a nearby law stone. The weathered rock had been carved centuries ago, at the earliest founding of the city. It read: "And if any man breaks the horns of an ox, even by accident, he shall pay the owner of the ox five drachmas. . . ."

"I didn't kill him," said Nikias at last. He was sick of the waiting game his grandfather was apparently playing—waiting for Nikias to throw the first punch.

"I believe you," replied Menesarkus calmly. "I saw the body. If *you* had been at the other end of that spear, you would have gutted him from hip to hip."

"So the brothers actually claimed *I* speared him?" asked Nikias, outraged. "It was Isokrates who did it, trying to murder *me* with my own weapon."

"They said more. They said you meddled with their sister. Do you deny that too?"

Nikias shifted his jaw back and forth. "I love her," he said. The crow cawed loudly just then as if to mock Nikias.

"Bah!" spat Menesarkus, losing all composure. "Love is for girls, not warriors. A marriage is nothing more than a political alliance between houses. Everything else is sheep shit and poetry."

"My father would have understood."

"Well, I'm not your father, am I?"

The sneering tone in his grandfather's voice was so hateful, it felt like a slap in the face.

The crow started to screech even louder, and Nikias took a pounding step toward it, moving his arms about wildly. "Get out of here!" he shouted, and the crow flew off with a startled flapping of wings.

Menesarkus said, "That crow is an omen from Apollo. We must be cautious."

"When is the trial?" asked Nikias softly.

"Trial?" asked Menesarkus with a laugh. "The citizens of Plataea have much more important business than murder trials, at least for the time being."

"I don't understand."

"Well . . . first of all, Drako the Spartan knocked on the gates of Plataea and set the city in an uproar with his request to hold talks with our city. Arkon Apollodoros and Magistrate Nauklydes left for Athens the next day on a special mission to meet with Perikles. We waited anxiously but heard no word from them until this morning when Nauklydes returned with news that Arkon Apollodoros had died before the council with Perikles could be completed."

Nikias pictured the eighty-six-year-old Plataean leader—bald like a tortoise, with rheumy eyes and a long white beard. But he'd been a hale and sharp-witted man who everyone in the city thought would live to be a hundred.

"How did he die?" he asked.

"Heart attack," replied Menesarkus in a disgruntled tone, as though he were piqued with the Arkon for having chosen such an inopportune time to perish.

"What happens now?"

"Grave decisions must be made. And a new arkon voted into office. Nauklydes would have us make peace with the Spartans. I am of another mind. More will be made known soon. I am here in the citadel to attend a special war council for generals and magistrates."

"And me?" asked Nikias.

"You are free for the time being," said Menesarkus with a wave of his hand.

"How?"

"I have offered my entire holdings to the city as bond that you will not flee before your trial."

Nikias shook his head in disbelief. "Grandfather, you can't—"

"Are you *planning* on running away?" asked Menesarkus with a piercing look. "Because no true heir of mine would do such a scurrilous act. I would rather he hanged himself from a tree or gutted himself. We will hire the best advocates in the city and we will beat this ludicrous charge of murder. As for Kallisto . . . well . . . you have ruined her and must face up to what you have done. Ten years of exile is all we can hope for. Ten years rowing in an Athenian trireme might do you some good. Your cousin Phoenix is a side captain now. He'll find you a bench on his ship. I've already sent a messenger to him at the port of Piraeus in Athens."

Nikias was in shock. The idea of running away from home and joining a ship had appealed to him only because it had meant he could be with Kallisto. But the thought of being *forced* into exile without her—to be sent away from Plataea like some sort of criminal—made him sick to his stomach. He felt dizzy, as though he'd drunk too much wine and was about to be sick.

He barely noticed Menesarkus had stopped speaking. His grandfather was shaking his big head sadly. He opened his mouth to speak then clamped it shut. He grabbed a handful of Nikias's long hair and his eyes were full of grief. "You should be shorn like your friends. Now you must wear this hair as an emblem of your shame."

"You did the same thing with Grandmother," said Nikias distantly. "You got her pregnant and her father was forced to marry her to you."

Menesarkus sighed deeply, an exhalation full of frustration and sorrow. "You inherited too much of my blood," he growled under his breath. "Those were different times, Nik. Those were the days of the Persian invasions. Our way of life was turned on its head. Rules were tossed aside like broken pottery from a kiln. Times have changed. Law is everything now. I should have taught you better."

"Maybe those were better days," said Nikias softly.

"Go home," said Menesarkus. "There's work to do on the farm. I must stay here and discuss important matters. General Helladios will be coming soon. I don't want him to see you. He might do something foolish." He got up and limped toward the entrance to the Assembly Hall.

Nikias left the Courtyard of Laws and wandered aimlessly past the stoas, the open-air hallways where classes were in session. He saw a mathematics class with several dozen young boys in attendance, fervently writing on wax tablets with their metal styluses. "I sat there once," he thought to himself bitterly, "dreaming of glory." He wandered for some time before he realized he'd looped right back to the area of the Assembly Hall.

Out of the corner of his eye Nikias spotted the ugly seer moving at a fast pace on his bandy legs, heading toward the Temple of Zeus standing directly behind the Assembly Hall. Nikias wondered what the charlatan was up to: What business could he possibly have in this part of the city? Maybe he was a thief who meant to steal from the sanctuary of the Temple of Zeus. Criminals were known for chiseling the gold leaf from wooden statues. Maybe he could catch the man and redeem himself a little!

He ran toward the Temple of Zeus and was about to go up the steps, when he noticed that some scaffolding set up against the back wall of the Assembly Hall was shaking, as if someone had just climbed the planks and poles to the top. A year before, a minor earthquake had damaged part of the façade and roof of the hall, and workers had started to repair it. But Nikias didn't see any men at work today.

He peered up at the roof and saw a pair of scrawny legs just before they scrambled through a hole in the pediment. He ran to the scaffolding and started climbing.

TEN

Nikias had never been inside the roof of a building like this and had no idea where to go. He stepped through the hole in the pediment and saw a passageway running along the length of the wall nearest him. There was enough space in this attic catwalk for him to move at a crouch all the way around the perimeter of the hall. Pigeons cooed nervously as he passed the nests they had built under the safety of the tiled roof.

If the seer had come up here to spy, he wondered, how would he ever find him? It was dark, and there were too many nooks and crannies for a man to hide. As his eyes adjusted to the dim light, he saw huge marble blocks, spaced roughly every five feet. On top of these blocks rested the ceiling beams that spanned the width of the hall. Nikias got on all fours and crawled into a cubicle created between two of the support blocks. Here he could gaze over the edge and onto the speaker's floor, forty dizzying feet below.

The Assembly Hall could seat every full-fledged male citizen of Plataea—around twenty-five hundred men—on a semicircle of wooden scaffolding rising nearly to the top of the ceiling at the back row. The black marble walls made the chamber seem cave-like and somber. The only light came from openings near the ceiling at the front and back of the hall, and this light reflected off the gray marble floor, making it shimmer like a swath of dirty ice.

Facing these bleachers and set against the center of the front wall was a magnificent seat carved from a single piece of black marble: the arkon's empty chair. This was flanked on either side by seats fashioned from gray stone, four on either side, all but one occupied by stern-faced men.

Magistrate Nauklydes stood before this small audience of seven fellow citizens with his back to the bleachers. Nikias had grown up around these men and knew them well. White-haired Magistrate Iphikrates, tenacious and haughty; dour old Magistrate Periander, practical to a fault; General Agape, a stalwart fighter but notoriously long-winded; General Zoticus of the cavalry, a lethal warrior and author of a treatise on cavalry tactics; General Alexios, Menesarkus's younger brother, quick to laugh but dangerous at war; General Helladios, tall and lean, with a hawk's predatory eyes; and finally the old man himself, the Bull of the Oxlands, the most victorious military commander in the history of Plataea, albeit nearing the age of sixty-five and his retirement from active duty.

Nikias knew Nauklydes, the man who was speaking, very well. For he was the father of his friend Demetrios as well as his grandfather's former Olympic herald and battlefield protégé. Nauklydes was a tall, muscular man with a handsome face and a dignified demeanor. Some people said he resembled a young Perikles.

The acoustics of the building brought Nauklydes's voice directly to Nikias's ears. ". . . and the reason for this meeting," the magistrate was saying, "is to inform you that our arkon did not die of natural causes in Athens. I believe he was given a poison that stopped his heart."

Nikias was stunned. Could the Athenians—their sworn allies—have plotted to murder the Plataean arkon? The chamber echoed with expressions of surprise and outrage from the generals and magistrates.

"Absurd," said General Alexios with a laugh.

"Preposterous," scoffed Magistrate Iphikrates.

"Perhaps he was suffering from some illness," ventured Magistrate Periander.

"I would not put anything past the Athenians," pronounced General Zoticus.

Nikias thought of Chusor and the Skythian slave he'd purchased. The inventor had told him he'd bought the man to get the formula for a poison that stopped men's hearts in seconds. So it didn't seem impossible that the arkon had died from such a nefarious cause.

Nikias watched his grandfather; he was stroking his beard, looking back and forth from Nauklydes to Helladios. He wondered what the old man was thinking. What was he going to say?

"Please," said Nauklydes, holding up his hand, "let me tell you the whole story." He stretched his neck and rubbed hard at the base of his skull as though trying to fight off a headache with his fingers. "Upon arriving in Athens we discovered that Spartan emissaries had recently been rebuffed by the Athenians. And so, too, had missions from the Persian king Artaxerxes. We immediately noticed that the Long Walls are now in use and manned by hundreds of Skythian archers."

"Athens no longer has to fear a siege like the rest of us poor landlocked citadels," said General Helladios with contempt. "They can get all of their supplies by ship from their port and cart them along this raised road to Athens proper."

"We cannot condemn them for being clever," General Alexios said. "Can we?"

"You might call it Greek ingenuity, Alexios," said Magistrate Periander in his clipped voice. "But I call it belligerence. The Spartans were against the Long Walls when Perikles initiated the building of them twenty years ago."

"During our first audience with General Perikles," Nauklydes said, "the Athenian leader informed us that a fleet of triremes is blockading Melos for refusing to pay their full taxes. And the colony of Samos in Anatolia is under siege for 'rebellious intent.' Athens is at war, my friends, with her own allies. Perikles then went on to say that their agents had recently captured a Spartan informant and his skytale. They deciphered the coded message, which stated that"—he paused and rubbed a hand over his face, took a deep breath—"Sparta intends to invade our land next month and lay siege to Plataea."

A collective chorus of groans, oaths, and prayers filled the great room.

In his peripheral vision Nikias saw a movement in the hall's attic catwalk a hundred feet away. He peered into the shadows. It moved again. It was a man, slipping into another cubicle.

"And did they show you this coded message?" Menesarkus asked.

"Yes, old friend," Nauklydes replied. "And they gave us more proof. They let me see the captured spy—a Megarian agent working for his Spartan masters—who had maps of Plataea in his possession. He knew details of our fortifications in the mountains. Strengths and posting schedules."

"Was this confession verified by torture?" asked General Zoticus.

"Yes," said Nauklydes. "I witnessed it."

Nikias saw movement in the rafters again. There was no mistaking it now. He was looking at a man who was spying on the chamber below just like him. It had to be the phony seer.

"We must reinforce the watchtowers on the mountain!" proclaimed Magistrate Iphikrates.

"And send out messengers to the countryside to bring everyone into the city," added Periander.

"This is a bad idea," said Menesarkus. "We cannot plunge the countryside and the city into chaos based on a mere rumor of invasion. We'll know if the Spartans come to Plataea. They can't hide ten thousand red cloaks. But I do agree we should reinforce the mountain strongholds."

Nikias eased himself out of the cubicle until he was in the passageway, then started crawling across the support beam toward the place where he had entered the building.

"I must agree," said Agape. "The Spartans have never invaded the Oxlands. And they have never laid siege to a city. If we were to make a list of all the city-states the Spartans *have* invaded and—"

"The Spartans are masters of deception," cut in Alexios. "This could just be a chimera to weaken our friendship with Athens."

Once Nikias was back at the pediment, he could stand up to full height. He ran across the wide beam to the other side of the roof, then paused to stare down into the hall. Here there was a large crack in the corner stonework caused by the earthquake.

He saw a box of tools nearby and grabbed a wooden handle sticking out from the box. It was a chisel for working with stone. He tested the weight. It would make do as a weapon. He started to move again when his foot kicked a piece of loose stone. It sailed over the edge—fell for an excruciatingly long second—hit the floor and skidded across the slick marble to rest at Menesarkus's feet. Nikias cringed, waiting for his grandfather to look up and detect his hiding place. But the men of the council were used to their crumbling building. Menesarkus reached over and picked up the fallen chunk—no bigger than a lead shot for a sling—and clutched it in his hand.

"Would you have us keep this news from the citizens?" asked Zoticus, tugging at the leather thongs of a riding boot. "The men in the countryside whose farms are in danger?"

"Indeed," agreed Helladios. "The citizens of Plataea deserve to know the Athenians are going to stab us in the back."

"I would have us think things through," replied Menesarkus, giving the piece of stone in his hand a toss and catching it again, "before running around proclaiming that the rafters are going to tumble down on our heads and—"

"Idiocy!" yelled Helladios, springing from his seat. "Blind stupidity, Menesarkus!"

"Do not let your wrath at Menesarkus's heir taint your words, Helladios," shouted Alexios.

Nikias crept along the support beam, counting the cubicles as he went. The seer, he knew, was in the middle one—the sixth space created by the rafter blocks. He wondered what he would do if he caught the man. Throw him over the edge to his death? Call out to the men in the hall for help, thus exposing himself? He glanced back at the floor and saw Nauklydes holding up his hand for peace.

"Please, General Helladios," said Nauklydes. "Let us conduct this debate with civility. Alexios is correct. We must set aside all personal affairs for this debate. You and General Menesarkus must solve the tragedy of Lysander's death and Nikias's punishment in another arena."

Nikias flinched at the mention of his own name. He glanced down and saw Helladios sit back in his seat and cross his arms on his chest, his jaw set in fury.

Nauklydes turned to Menesarkus and said, "I must also disagree with you, my old friend. I think that we have to act immediately. We should accept the Spartan emissaries, even if it means upsetting the Athenians."

Periander, Zoticus, and Helladios voiced their support of this plan. But Iphikrates, Alexios, and Agape remained silent, looking to Menesarkus for his response. The old pankrator sat with arms crossed, chin on chest, brooding. Nikias wondered how his grandfather could possibly disagree with Nauklydes's rational argument, especially after the meeting with Drako. What harm could be done by merely meeting with the Spartans? They weren't the sworn enemy of Plataea, after all. Not like the Thebans.

"I believe the Athenian stance is reasonable—" said Menesarkus, breaking the silence. He stood up and limped onto the floor, favoring his good knee more than usual. "—when one takes into consideration the fallout of Plataea breaking this alliance. The treaty we signed with Athens is written in stone and stands in our court of law for all to see. If we were to break this treaty, it is very likely that other city-states—ones with less love for Athens—would start turning away from the Delian League in droves and Athens's power would crumble."

"Perhaps that is not such a bad thing," said Helladios.

"Would you have Sparta be the master of Greece, General Helladios?" asked Menesarkus with ire in his voice. "Would you have us under the yoke of a dual monarchy? The citizens of Plataea would not stand for it. I have been to Sparta, my friends. I have seen what their way of life is like firsthand. And I would not be one of their so-called allies. We would be nothing more than slaves. Glorified Helots!"

"What would you have us do, Menesarkus?" asked Helladios. "Go blithely about our business while the Spartans amass an invasion force on our border? Have us hide behind our walls while the Spartans destroy our economy? While they cut us off from the rest of the world? Make us prisoners in our own city? And for no other reason than a fifty-year-old treaty we signed with a nation that has grown from a stalwart friend to a rapacious beast?"

Chisel clutched in his hand, Nikias peered around a ceiling rafter support block and into the cubicle where he thought the seer was hiding. But there was nobody there. He moved around the next support block. That cubicle was empty too.

"Hera's jugs," Nikias cursed softly. Had his eyes played tricks on him? He heard a strange sound that made him flinch and look up. Built against the rafter above his head was a nest. A pigeon sat on its clutch of eggs, eyeing him with fright. Nikias grinned and held a finger to his lips.

"We stand or die by our treaties," said Menesarkus. "The Spartans might invade the Oxlands and burn our farms and cut our vines, but they cannot take this city if we are unified behind its walls. Never forget that."

"Now is the time for bold ideas!" called out Helladios, and looking directly at Menesarkus he sneered, "Not an old man's babbling." Then he snapped his head around to face Nauklydes. "What would *you* do, Magistrate?"

Nikias peered over the edge of the rafter and watched as Nauklydes strode to the center of the speaker's floor with his back to the seated men.

"Not only would I have us become an ally of the Spartans," replied Nauklydes calmly, turning and clasping his hands together, "I would rejoin the Oxland League and ask Thebes to help us in ending this foolish enmity between our two states. I would make Plataea a powerful force in a new alliance of nations unwilling to bend to General Perikles's power-mad schemes. I would save us from . . . from this folly that Helladios spoke of . . . and lead us to new prosperity."

"Nauklydes, *you* are not arkon," grumbled Alexios.

"He's not arkon *yet*," shot back Helladios.

Alexios stood up and he and Helladios took threatening steps toward each other.

Just then Nikias sensed something looming in the rafters above and behind him, like a huge dark spider, ready to attack. His heart started beating faster. He heard the unmistakable sound of metal rasping on metal—some sort of weapon drawn from a sheath. Nikias made a sudden movement, turning to look behind him, startling the pigeon. The bird called out in fright as it flew into the hall. Another two dozen pigeons, fleeing from their nests, flapped about near the ceiling and rained white guano onto the men below.

The rest of what happened was a blur. A man dropped from overhead. Nikias felt a hand on his throat. He swung out with the chisel, hit soft flesh, and heard a groan. A fist punched him near his ear and he lashed out again with his weapon. He heard a man moving back toward the pediment and he followed, crawling—crawling as fast as he could. But the man was quicker and made it to the scaffolding before him. Nikias leapt through the opening and onto the wooden structure into daylight. A rope used to haul stone from the ground to the top of the platform was swinging back and forth. His attacker had already slid down its length and disappeared into the streets of Plataea.

ELEVEN

———◆———

Nikias pounded on the back door to the Golden Thighs. He'd sprinted all the
way from the Assembly Hall and had to bend over to catch his breath. He noticed, with surprise, that he was bleeding from a knife wound—a thin slit running along his elbow joint to the palm of his left hand, just missing the veins of
his wrist. The spy in the rafters—the fake seer—had tried to cut him open.

"Hey, open up. It's Nikias," he said, and shook the door ring.

The portal opened a crack and an ancient slave poked out his enormous, pit-
ted nose. Nikias pushed his way through. He took the stairs three at a time and
found Stasius in his chamber with Leo. The runner and the wrestler were smoking hemp and staring into space with bored expressions. Their hair was clipped
nearly to the scalp, making them, at least to Nikias's eyes, look more like little
boys than men.

They noticed him at the same time and sprang to their feet.

"Gods!" cried Stasius, delighted. "You're free."

"We tried to see you," said Leo, clapping Nikias on the back.

"They wouldn't let us in to the jail," railed Stasius, throwing up his hands in
indignation.

"We even made a feeble attempt at bribery," said Leo.

"But the guards weren't about to exchange your freedom for sex with Leo!"
joked Stasius.

They grabbed him from either side and hugged the air out of him.

"We missed you at the ceremony," Leo said, stepping back and rubbing his
own short hair self-consciously.

Nikias shrugged his shoulders. He couldn't think of anything to say. "Have
you heard anything about Kallisto?" he asked.

"I heard they've got her locked up on their farm," said Leo. "You're not going
to try to go there, are you? Because they will kill you, Nik. Helladios gave all of
his slaves bows and arrows and ordered them to shoot you down on sight."

Stasius noticed the wound on Nikias's arm. "Where did you get this?"

Nikias briefly explained what had happened in the Assembly Hall. While he talked, Stasius tore up one of his shirts and made a bandage to wrap his wound.

"I've seen that seer around," said Stasius. "Ugly as a dog's arse."

"He must be working for the Spartans," said Leo.

"That's what I believe," said Nikias.

"What can we do?" asked Stasius.

"Maybe he's joined the other Spartans at the Persian Fort," said Nikias. "That's where I need to go."

"We're coming too," said Leo.

The three friends jogged down the dirt road that led east from the citadel. Dozens of Plataean horsemen were riding back and forth from the mountain garrisons and the border stations on the downs. Even though there were only twenty Spartans camped at the Persian Fort, the cavalry had been on high alert ever since they had arrived. Now, with the news of the arkon's death, the watchmen were even more vigilant.

"I wish I were riding out with them," said Nikias.

"Hey, look," said Stasius, pointing to the northeast.

A thin line of black smoke rose in the air from the direction of the Persian Fort. They left the road and made their paths through a field toward it.

"The Spartans are making dinner," said Leo. "Maybe they'll ask us to join them."

"Spartans only eat congealed blood," said Stasius, joining into the banter.

"Do you think little Spartan boys really live in herds like cows?" asked Leo.

"Let's ask the Egyptian's pet Helot," said Stasius.

"They let their women wrestle naked in public—" said Leo.

"—so they can't be all that bad," put in Nikias.

"Your grandfather lived there for a year after the war," said Leo. "Didn't he, Nikias?"

Nikias nodded. "He went to train their fighters in the pankration. That was when we were allies of the Spartans."

"Did he wrestle any women?" asked Leo.

"I'll bet they're as ugly as the men," said Stasius.

They had come to the edge of the field. Here was a thick wooded area of oak where hundreds of crows and magpies sat in the barren treetops, squawking loudly at each other. Nikias looked back toward Plataea and, in the distance, saw tiny figures of women walking down the road with tall amphorae balanced on their heads. Pure-white clouds floated across the bright blue sky. A pair of red-breasted geese flew overhead, honking forlornly with each stroke of their wings. It felt like any other winter day. He entered the woods and caught up with Stasius and Leo, who'd gone on ahead. They crossed a small stream. When they came out the other side and up the bank, they saw the grassy berms surrounding the Persian Fort.

The makeshift fortress had been built five decades earlier by hundreds of thousands of Xerxes's slaves—a temporary citadel to house his quarter-of-a-million-man invasion force. The Persians had dug deep ditches around a square four times the size of the city of Plataea, and piled up the dirt to make ten-foot-high bastions fortified with timber walls at the top. At each of the four corners a crude stone guard tower was erected. The Plataeans had never thought to destroy the place. They'd left it as a monument to their greatest victory. Over the decades since the end of the war, the timber walls had rotted. The earthen mounds had sprouted grass. The ditches had filled with thickets, and the guard towers had crumbled. Nikias saw no Spartans keeping guard, only the black smoke curling up from inside.

The sound of horses made Nikias flinch.

"Get down!" he said.

They ducked for cover and watched as half a dozen riders galloped past. They were Plataeans, citadel guards patrolling the perimeter of the fort to make certain the Spartans didn't try to sneak out and spy on the city. The instant they were out of sight, Nikias ran from the woods and scrambled down into the ditch and the cover of the thickets at the base of the berm. A few moments later the others came bounding into the thickets.

"Not so loud," said Nikias in a harsh whisper.

As children they had all climbed the earthen walls surrounding the fort hundreds of times, and so they reached for familiar handholds. As he clambered to the top of the grassy mound, Nikias wondered what they would see on the other side. Probably just some Red Cloaks combing their long, greasy hair and washing down their frugal meal with water from the stream.

Nikias moved on his belly, inching over the top of the berm, until he could peer down into the square of the encampment. Leo and Stasius followed. It was easy to see why Xerxes's engineers had picked this place to protect his army and its baggage train. A small tributary of the Asopus ran straight through the center of the nearly flat area encompassing two square miles of land. The Persian engineers had created a duct for this stream that passed through a metal sluice gate embedded in the earthen wall. Access to freshwater, his grandfather had taught him, was more important than food: a man could live for weeks without sustenance but could expire in days without water, especially under the hot Oxland summer sun.

His grandfather had stormed this camp at the Battle of Plataea during the Persian Wars. Inside he had captured several slaves, including old Saeed—then just an eight-year-old groom—and taken valuable armor, weapons, and ornaments from dead Persian nobles. Hundreds of olive trees had been planted in the center of the encampment as a memorial to the fallen heroes of the war. They were the only trees in the wide space between the four walls of the berms. Nikias searched the place for signs of life, but all he saw was the fire burning near the olive grove.

"Where are the Spartans?" asked Stasius in a whisper.

"Maybe they're hiding in the olives," suggested Leo.

"Spartans don't hide," said Nikias.

There were only two entrances to the interior of the place, at the north and south walls—openings just wide enough for four horsemen to ride abreast. Nikias could see no guards standing at either one.

A weird screech made the hairs on his neck and forearms stand on end. At first he thought it was another goose, but then he saw the tiny yet unmistakable figure of a man crawling from the olive trees.

"What's he doing?" asked Leo.

The man appeared to be supporting himself on his fists and the tips of his toes and resembled a deer lifting its feet as it gingerly crosses a meadow. The man stopped and rolled onto his back and disappeared in the tall dead grass. Then he let forth again with the hideous gargled cry. Nikias wondered why the Spartans were nowhere to be seen. Why they weren't running up to this odd sight. But no one else stirred in the encampment. The crawling man raised himself up and shuffled a few more feet, then flopped over again, screaming piteously.

"Come on," said Nikias.

He made his way down the other side of the berm, sliding on his buttocks, and came to a standing stop on his feet. Leo and Stasius were soon by his side. They walked the quarter mile to the olive grove, scanning the area furtively with every step. The man had not stirred for a while, and Nikias had lost him in the tall grass; but then he heard the gargling sound again and saw a bloody stump of a handless arm rise up.

Nikias recoiled, hissing, "Zeus!"

The man raised himself on his knees. He was facing the opposite direction but Nikias could see that both of his hands had been cut off. His head was raised toward the sky and he pawed at his face, choking. Nikias walked hesitantly around the man until he stood in front him. His stomach lurched. The man's eyes, ears, nose, lips, and tongue had all been cut off. His teeth were covered with blood and chattered in his mouth as he attempted to form another agonized cry. Around his neck was tied a piece of wood with the words "Athenian Spy" scrawled on it.

Nikias tried to lift him to his feet but he struggled wildly, thrashing about in fear. Nikias saw that his feet had also been removed. All of his stumps had been tied off with tourniquets to stop the bleeding—so he would live to suffer. The mutilated man broke from his grasp and flopped on the ground, writhing in agony.

Nikias heard the sound of retching. He looked up and saw Stasius throwing up and Leo staring at the ruined man with mute horror, his face ashen.

"We're Plataean," said Nikias. "We won't hurt you."

The man stopped moving his body and turned his destroyed face toward Nikias. He pointed a bloody stump at his mouth and groaned.

"I'll get him water," said Leo, and dashed off toward the olive grove. He ran back a moment later in a panic. "I don't have anything to carry the water with!"

Stasius tore off his shirt and handed it to Leo. "Soak it in the water."

Leo came back with the sodden shirt, held it over the man's mouth, and squeezed, letting the liquid fill his bloody maw. The man tried to swallow and choked again, shaking his head angrily and pushing Leo away with his stumps.

"What do we do?" asked Stasius. He was on his knees next to the man, touching him gently on the back. "What do we do?" he asked again, tears pouring from his eyes.

"It's no use," said a voice from behind. "He's a dead man."

Nikias whirled and saw the seer clutching a gleaming sword in one hand. The stranger no longer carried himself in the manner of a marketplace charlatan. He stood in a fighter's stance, the sword held across his chest—the attitude of a trained phalanx warrior ready to strike. Murder was in his eyes.

TWELVE

———◆———

Plataea's fifteen thousand free inhabitants were made up of two hundred or so separate families. Each of them had its own cluster of tombs at the city's sarkophogi, the cemetery that was built a stone's throw outside the western bastions. The tombs were miniature versions of the city's public buildings. Houses for the dead. Inside these repositories were kept funeral jars that held ashes and bones. On the jars were painted portraits depicting the deceased in Hades. Usually the men and women were shown sitting on a chair, staring wistfully into eternity.

The Magistrate Nauklydes was a pious man, or so everyone who knew him thought. At least once a week for the past two years he went to his tribe's section in the sarkophogi and spoke to his dead ancestors. He had just come from the public bathhouse, and his thick auburn hair was still wet and clung to his forehead in little pointy-ended ringlets. There was an ache in the back of his head that was threatening to turn into a migraine. The masseuse at the bathhouse had been unable to work his muscles enough to make it go away. The stress of the Assembly Hall meeting earlier that day had been overwhelming.

Nauklydes stretched his neck, rubbed the base of his skull, and thought he could see a creeping blackness at the corners of his peripheral vision—an ominous sign that another skull-splitter was fast approaching. He willed his eyes to focus, fought to forget about the pain. He did not have time for one of his "episodes" today.

He knelt before his family's replica of the Assembly Hall, where all of their urns were kept, and bowed his head.

"I ask my tribe to guide me in all actions," he intoned. "Especially now in a time of great need."

After speaking to the dead, he went back to his pottery factory. He loved to watch the busy workers—like a hive of intelligent insects—taking slabs of raw clay and metamorphosing them into valuable merchandise. As he walked down the long colonnade he could watch the entire vase-making process from beginning to end. It started out with men kneading clay. Then assistants toted the pliant lumps to the wheels where the potters shaped the clay into vessels of many varieties. Here "spinners" kept the wheels turning with quick taps from long sticks. Next was the painters' section, where both men and women sat hunched on the floor, inscribing the pictures and designs on the moist clay wine cups and bowls with metal styluses, chatting and making jokes as they worked. Finally the items were carted to the glazers, who painted the muddy slip that would burst forth with black, orange, and white once the pots were fired.

Nauklydes picked up a finished plate with a teenage boy's portrait in a coquettish pose and the motto "Stasius is beautiful" written over it. Stasius was getting old, he realized. He had just come of age. Soon the factory would have to discontinue the young man's plate. The notion made him a little sad. He thought of Pelias, the young harpist he had taken as a lover a few months ago, and wondered why he had not shown up at his house today for their assignation.

He went back to his windowless office, locked the door, and sat at his desk. He reached for his water cup with a trembling hand and took a sip. Whenever a migraine was coming, his peripheral vision would start to darken, as though ink had been injected into his eyes as a frightened squid in a bucket of water would turn the contents black. With the blindness came flashes of light—"dragons," one physician had called them—spinning and sparkling and snaking across his sight. After that he would usually vomit.

He had inherited his pottery workshop from his father. But the business had been in his family for ten generations. For the past fifty years the workshop had specialized in erotic scenes: drunken orgies showing two men taking one woman at the same time. Satyrs with ridiculously huge pricks raping young men and girls. Young boys admiring the erections of handsome bearded men.

With the dowry Nauklydes had received from his wife—who had died giving birth to their daughter, Penelope, sixteen years ago—he had taken a huge risk and expanded trade to the semi-barbarous region of Italia and Sicily, six hundred miles to the west. The men of that land had an insatiable craving for this kind of erotic work—the more graphic the better. The biggest seller in Italia was a wine cup fashioned in the shape of a crouching Etruscan with a phallus as big as a tree trunk. The drinker put his mouth on the end of the phallus and drank through the hole.

Nauklydes's gamble in Italia had paid off. The people of that land might be considered brutish, but they paid in silver just like any civilized men. The workshop had received so many orders in the last six months alone that Nauklydes had bought another twenty slaves just to dig for clay on the riverbanks. He was able to lure away skilled artists from the workshops of Athens with higher wages and a percentage of the profits. He had even saved enough funds to build his own small fleet of transport vessels. The three ships were under construction at the nearby port of Kreusis in the Bay of Korinth and would be completed before the summer; the plans for the ships were laid out on his desk.

Most importantly, he had used his connections in the west to send his son Demetrios—his beloved heir—to Sicily and the relative safety of the court of Syracuse, which was a Spartan ally. Nauklydes had felt for several years that war was coming to Plataea, and he was not going to waste his precious heir's blood on some fruitless Athenian campaign against mighty Sparta.

He took another sip of water and tried to relax his shoulders, breathing through his nose. The earthy scent of clay emanated from the workshop. It had a grounding effect on him and the pain started to recede. He was beating it back, willing the dragons away. But then Menesarkus's face appeared before his eyes as he had looked at the special council . . . his old friend and mentor, staring at him with his fatherly scorn . . . or was it suspicion? He felt a stabbing pain at the base of his skull. A knock on the door startled him.

"Who's there?"

"Phakas, and a visitor."

"Who is it?"

"General Menesarkus."

Nauklydes went to the door and undid the latch. He saw his assistant standing there.

"He's waiting in the shop," said Phakas. "Should I send him away?" In this city of incredibly fit men—where a citizen was expected to be able to wear armor and carry a shield into battle up to the age of sixty-five—Phakas was a flabby, utterly bald oddity. But he was a foreigner and did not have to fight for Plataea. His job was to make his employer money, not go to war for him.

"Of course not," said Nauklydes. He went back to his desk and sat. "Bring him to me and get us wine."

Phakas returned moments later with Menesarkus. The old pankrator limped into the room and stood behind a chair that faced Nauklydes's desk. There was an awkward silence during which the two refused to look in each other's faces.

"I will not be scolded, Menesarkus, like a child," said Nauklydes at last. "I will not back down from my position. We must break with Athens."

"I did not come to scold," replied Menesarkus. "I came to talk, man-to-man."

Nauklydes nodded his head and ran a finger over a dented scar on the bridge of his nose. "Very well."

"I remember when you got that scar," said Menesarkus, and eased into the chair. "It was at the Battle of Etropolis when we fought side by side with the Athenians." He gave a slight smile. "You would have made an outstanding general, Nauklydes."

Nauklydes smiled sadly. "I am sorry I disappointed you," he said. He looked over his shoulder as if peering into the past. "We were the allies of Athens back then. At Etropolis. And Sardis. And all the other cities we helped destroy in the name of the Delian League." He stared Menesarkus in the face. "Now we are one of the miserable oxen that drags their cart."

"We made an oath, Nauklydes."

"Our ancestors made that oath."

"There is no difference," said Menesarkus.

Nauklydes took out a silver coin and spun it on the desk. Menesarkus watched the quickly rotating blurred disk form an illusory, transparent globe. As the coin lost momentum it meandered across the marble surface toward Menesarkus, wobbling more and more as it slowed, then finally fell flat so that half of the coin hung off the edge of the table. The image stamped on the visible side was the profile of Androkles, the hero of Plataea, slayer of the Last Tyrant.

"Hide some in a jar," said Nauklydes with a shrug. "Someday the descendants of your Nikias and my Demetrios can dig them up and see what a Plataean coin once looked like."

"What are you talking about?"

"Perikles is going to do away with all coinage in the Delian League and replace them with Athenian coins—their ugly owls. To add insult to injury, he is going to demand a reminting fee to melt nonstandard drachmas into Athenian coins."

"I reckoned this would happen eventually," said Menesarkus with a sigh. "But a set currency will boost the economy in the long run."

"It will be a strain on Plataea's coffers for decades!" said Nauklydes with a sneer. "The reminting fee is nothing more than a war tax imposed by mighty Athens. Our *friends* the Athenians have decided that we will carry owls in our purses to buy our bread, and in our mouths to pay Kiron the ferryman when we die!"

"Perikles has a vision for the future," said Menesarkus.

"A vision that has Athens taking over the known world," scoffed Nauklydes. "I was at the speech on the Akropolis two years ago when Perikles declared, 'War is a *necessity*.' Well, war is coming. And we will suffer for it."

Menesarkus said, "This city has never been taken and—"

"The question comes down to this," Nauklydes interrupted, standing up and slapping his hand on the table, saying, "Do you trust that Athens will defend our city in this coming invasion from Sparta? If the answer is no, then the next question is obvious. Would you rather be an ally and trading partner of Sparta or a victim of their wrath?"

He paused and shook his head. "Athens cannot defeat the Spartan hoplites in a land battle. Even the Athenians admit as much. Perikles's strategy, my old friend, is simple. The Athenians will try to outlast the Spartans and its allies. Blockade their ports. Devastate their economy. All the while hiding behind the vast walls of Athens like a coward who taunts its enemy but hides in his house.

But Sparta has won the backing of King Artaxerxes and his seemingly endless wealth. That has made the Spartans bolder. Soon they will build their own fleet with Persian gold."

"You certainly seem to know a lot about Sparta's intentions," said Menesarkus. "Did the spy caught by the Athenians also tell you of this phantom Spartan fleet?"

"No," replied Nauklydes. "My imagination is better than yours, that's all. Here, I'll paint a picture for you of the coming year. When Sparta eventually invades Attika, the Athenians will abandon the countryside for their walled city. That will leave little landlocked cities like ours exposed to attack, with no relief from the Athenian army. We will be like a badger in a hole. The Spartans will simply dig us out and gut us."

Phakas appeared at the doorway and cleared his throat. Nauklydes waved for him to enter and the steward placed a heavy wine bowl on the desk. Phakas was trying hard not to pant, but the exertion of carrying the heavy thing had taxed him. He breathed laboriously through his nostrils.

"Go away," ordered Nauklydes. "Do not linger while we discuss our business."

Phakas excused himself and scurried out the door.

Nauklydes was starting to feel queasy. He focused his eyes on the ceramic vessel and its design. It had been crafted a hundred years earlier, long before the invasion of the Persians, when artists painted humans as crude black shapes with pointed noses and triangular chins and ludicrously squat bodies, like puppets in a children's shadow theater. But the illustration that ran around the rim was for adults: a comic scene of satyrs balancing wine jars on their massive erect phalluses, engaged in a multitude of sexual positions with flexible boys.

"What did Arkon Apollodoros agree to before he . . . *died*," said Menesarkus, putting a particular emphasis on his final word.

"He had bowed to Perikles's demands, of course," replied Nauklydes, unable to hide the bitterness in his voice. "The old craven fool."

"Is that what you thought of him?"

"Yes," Nauklydes replied, and glared back.

"He was no fool. Nor a coward," said Menesarkus quietly. "But what I cannot sort out is why the Athenians would murder him if he was going along with their demands."

"Listen, Menesarkus," said Nauklydes with a friendly smile, "this business with Nikias and Helladios's son must be weighing on your shoulders. But I assure you, if I am elected arkon, I will make sure that Nikias gets no more than a few years' exile for Lysander's death. He can spend them all happily in Syrakuse, working for me and living with Demetrios."

Nauklydes sat down. And as he did so, Menesarkus got slowly to his feet.

"As I said in the Assembly today, we will have ample warning if the Spartans invade." Menesarkus gestured at the bowl. "I am sorry I will take no wine. Your offer of help for my grandson is impossible to accept. He must have no partial treatment. He is no better or no worse than any citizen of Plataea." He was fingering something in his hand and placed it on the desktop—a shard of pottery. Nauklydes saw it and his eyes opened wide.

"I came to warn you," said Menesarkus. "I will run against you for arkon. And I am fairly certain I will win. I cannot take the chance that you might become the leader of this city. If you do not back down from your pro-Spartan stance I will be forced to call for you to be sharded. And then an assembly of warriors will decide whether or not you are to be banished and your properties confiscated."

Nauklydes stared at the piece of broken pottery in astonishment. He reached for it and turned it over, saw his own name scrawled there. "You would do this to me?" he asked, shaking his head. "Shard me?" His face flushed purple.

"I know two things to be true," said Menesarkus. "Never trust a Spartan and never break an oath. You want us to do both. The Athenians will stand by us. They will send us aid in our time of need. And abandoning our friendship with them would lead to us becoming just another vassal of the Spartan monarchy. The citizens of Plataea respect you. But they will not trust that your intentions are wholly altruistic. You are the wealthiest man in Plataea. You have the most to lose from an invasion. I am willing to give all my land, all my wealth, for the sake of the law. Are you?"

"You would put me on the road?" asked Nauklydes, blinking rapidly. "A vagabond? A pauper? A man without a city?"

"The choice is yours."

"You will not get the votes!" said Nauklydes, and tossed the shard onto the desk with an offhand manner. But his hand shook.

"Will you take that risk?" asked Menesarkus. He went to the door and left without another word.

Nauklydes stood for a time, blinking, shaking his head. His fingers gripped the handles of the wine bowl. He lifted the heavy vessel and flung it against the door, where it exploded in a spray of wine and broken pottery.

Phakas poked his head in the chamber. "What happened?"

"Get in here!"

Phakas made an odd ducking gesture—a signal of obsequiousness—and came into the room and shut the door.

"You will leave the city tonight with a message for our *friend*," said Nauklydes.

Phakas stooped to pick up the pieces of the wine krater. "This was an heirloom of your family," he said quietly.

Nauklydes barred the door, and then went to a lockbox in the corner of the room. Inside were some documents and under these a thick wood dowel. He sat at the desk and stared at the dowel—eyed it as though it were a dangerous snake. He wrapped a ribbon of cloth around the dowel and began writing a message on it.

"Isn't there any other way?" asked Phakas, breaking the silence. "Has it really come to this?"

"Menesarkus threatened to shard me," said Nauklydes. "He has driven me to this decision."

"But will the people listen to you once . . ." Phakas swallowed and it sounded as if he were sending a lump of clay down his throat. ". . . once *it* has happened?"

"They will have no choice," said Nauklydes, "but to see the logic of my decision." He held up his right hand, palm down, with his fingers pointing toward Phakas. "Do you see this ring on my finger?" he asked, wiggling his pinkie with its big ring.

"Your signet, of course—"

"My family crest, a man seizing a bull by the horns."

"Yes, but—"

"The Bull must be brought down," said Nauklydes.

"But he was your teacher. Your mentor."

Nauklydes unwound the ribbon from the dowel. The message he had written while the cloth was on the stick was now a nonsensical collection of random letters. He handed it to Phakas, who slowly coiled the skytale around his finger.

"Menesarkus taught me many things," said Nauklydes. "But the most important lesson he taught me was how to win at all costs. There is only victory."

THIRTEEN

———◆———

Nikias looked around for a weapon. He glanced at Stasius and Leo, who were standing nearby, looking at the armed seer with dazed expressions. He motioned for them to be on guard. But the stranger did not attack them. He stared at the mutilated man with an expression of unmitigated outrage.

"He's a dead man," repeated the seer, tears rolling down his cheeks and into his beard. He glanced at the friends. "The Spartans are gone. The smoke . . . a ruse. They snuck away . . . back to Sparta. Last night, most likely. Your patrols never saw them." He waved Nikias aside. "Now, get out of my way. That is my friend."

Nikias stepped back and the seer went to the mutilated man, put his mouth close to his ear. "Pelias, it's Timarkos," he said softly. "I am here."

The man nodded his head. His body was wracked with sobs, and bloody tears rolled from the pits where his eyes used to be.

"Was it Drako the Skull who did this?" asked Timarkos. Pelias shook his head. "Eurymakus the Theban?"

Pelias nodded vigorously and gagged on his own blood.

"I'll skin him alive," vowed Timarkos. "But now I am going to help you, dear Pelias."

"Is that the same Pelias who plays the harp?" asked Stasius softly. "Beautiful Pelias?"

Timarkos nodded. Stasius sobbed and covered his face with his hands.

How could the wretched young man have ever predicted that such a horrible end would befall him this day? Those old hags the Fates were cruel.

Pelias took in a deep breath. He got on his arm stumps and knees and stretched out his neck. Timarkos held up his sword for the deathblow . . . but stepped back and dropped the weapon. He turned his head away in shame, covering his face with his hands.

"My fault," he said. "I shouldn't have left him on his own. He never would have been caught. I can't do it." He slumped to his haunches.

Pelias grunted angrily. "Do it! Do it!" he seemed to say.

The three Plataeans stared from one to the other. Finally, Nikias picked up the sword and clenched it in his hands, steeling himself.

"Get back," he commanded the others, his voice coming out as a harsh whisper. He placed the sword on Pelias's neck. "Be still, rest now, Pelias," he said with compassion, then brought the blade down with a powerful stroke, severing the head. Blood sprayed from the neck like red vomit.

"Zeus, I've killed a man," thought Nikias. Pelias's neck had been so soft. It had taken no more effort than cutting through a melon. He had known all his life that he would have to kill other men someday. He'd always imagined it happening in battle. A feat of heroism or wrath. But not an act of mercy. Like putting a horse with a broken leg out of its misery. The sword suddenly felt heavy, and there was a dull ache below his sternum.

He wiped his mouth with the back of his hand. The sun went behind a cloud and he instantly felt cold. He glanced at his friends. Stasius had sat down and covered his face with his arm. Leo was staring at him, eyes wide, mouth agape. Nikias tossed aside the sword, held out his hand to Timarkos, and helped him to his feet. Timarkos staggered away without a word and started to gather wood, feeding the fire the Spartans had left burning.

"Who are you?" Nikias asked. "What is going on? Why were you spying on the Assembly today? Why did you try to kill me?"

Timarkos eyed Nikias for a long time. "I am Athenian, and that is all you need to know about me, Menesarkus's heir. I *was* in the rafters of the Assembly Hall, watching the debate. But I was not the only one spying besides you. There was another. The man who . . . the man who butchered my friend. It was that scum Eurymakus."

"How do you know who Nik is?" asked Leo.

"Leo and Stasius," Timarkos said with menace, pointing at each in turn. "Orphan and pimp's heir. I know more than you can imagine." He turned and looked at Nikias. "I have known your grandfather, Nikias, since long before you were born. Ask *him* if you can trust me."

"You work for Perikles, don't you," said Nikias, nodding at the corpse. "You're a whisperer."

Timarkos shrugged and tossed a log on the fire. The black smoke had turned to gray; the fire was coming to life.

"Who is Eurymakus?" asked Nikias. "Why did he torture your companion?"

"Eurymakus is a Theban," said Timarkos. "He did it to send a message to Plataea. To make your people more afraid of the Spartans than they already are. That's his game. Fear. There are spies all over your city. The man you think is a friend—the one who calls himself Chusor—is one of these Spartan spies."

"*Calls* himself Chusor?" asked Leo.

"Chusor is the name of a Phoenician god," replied Timarkos. "In Athens there's a bounty on *this* Chusor's head worth a fortune."

"What did he do?" asked Stasius.

"Murdered a man," replied Timarkos. "Poisoned him."

"Why did the Spartan emissaries leave here?" asked Leo.

Timarkos squinted at them. "Why would any of you trust me to tell you the truth after what you've seen and heard today?" The bonfire was roaring now but he kept feeding the flames. "I could be a Theban trying to trick you. Or a Spartan."

Nikias stared at the headless body of Pelias. "I don't know."

"There is only one man you can trust, Nikias," said Timarkos. "And that's your grandfather."

"What do you know about my family?" asked Nikias.

"There's a scorpion in Plataea," said Timarkos, ignoring his question. "Watch where you step."

Timarkos strode over to the corpse and hoisted the body onto his shoulder. "Get the head, Nikias," he said. When Nikias hesitated he snarled, "Do it!"

Nikias wrapped the head in Stasius's shirt, picked it up, and followed Timarkos to the fire. The Athenian tossed the body onto the flames. "Give me the head." Nikias handed it to him and he threw it on top of the coals. They watched in silence until flames started to consume the body.

"Smells just like an animal on a sacrificial fire," remarked Timarkos with loathing. "Doesn't it?" He let forth a high-pitched whistle and a horse looked up from where it had been grazing behind a stand of trees. The spy walked to the beast, mounted, and rode off without looking back.

"What do we do now?" asked Leo.

Nikias thought of how much trouble he would be in if he didn't go home right now. Everything he knew was crumbling apart. Nothing made sense. He couldn't face his family—his mother, grandmother, and sister. And especially not his grandfather. Nikias felt like fighting. Throwing punches. Smashing anything that got in his way.

He thought of Chusor making the strange weapons with sulfur and beeswax, and his diabolical interest in fatal Skythian poison. The inventor had to be plotting something. He must be the scorpion in Plataea's midst that Timarkos spoke of.

"Nik?" asked Leo again. "What do we do?"

"We can start with the Egyptian," said Stasius, as if reading Nikias's thoughts. "Tonight."

FOURTEEN

———◆———

Menesarkus was able to ride all the way home from Plataea before collapsing in agony because of his sore back. It was all he could manage during the meeting with Nauklydes not to show his pain . . . to reveal his weakness. He slid off his horse and landed on the soft sand of the fighting arena. Saeed called urgently for two burly slaves to carry the master to his bed.

For the first time as an adult, Menesarkus felt as helpless as a suckling babe. In his long life he'd been cut, bashed, speared, and strangled. He'd broken his ribs, an arm, his nose—five or six times at least—and suffered a punctured lung. But he'd never been in as much pain as he was now. It felt as though a knife were digging into his spine. The most disconcerting thing, though, was that his legs had started to go numb—he could hardly feel his feet beneath him when he tried to stand. He lay on his stomach now while Eudoxia applied another poultice of mud and herbs to his lower back. He was miserable. His women were good attendants, this was true. But he hated being at the mercy of his wife and the others.

"Get Nikias," he said.

Eudoxia did not reply for a while. "He never came home," she finally said with worry in her voice.

Menesarkus could not believe his grandson had defied him again. Had the boy lost his mind?

Eudoxia stopped applying the soothing mud and stroked his buttocks. His wife had been mending and sewing up and caring for him for fifty years. He was brutal against his opponents and enemies. But in all their years together he had never raised his hand against her. With her he only *roared* like a monster. He rolled over and she laughed when she looked between his legs.

"Even in your agony you're still ready for battle," she said in amazement.

He touched her cheek and traced his finger down her neck, pulled the dress off her shoulder, caressed her bare skin. He begged her with his eyes. Eudoxia sighed, then removed her dress and undid the knot of her hair. Her long silver mane dropped all the way to her buttocks. Very gently she lay beside him. They had been making love for decades and knew each other well.

After they were both satisfied, Menesarkus lay with his back pressed against his wife's naked chest. "I had a dream last night," he said, craning his neck to look at her with one eye. "In the dream I was chasing my father through the woods. He looked the way he did when I was a child. Before the sickness ate him away. He was fast. I could barely keep up. I called to him but he would not turn back. Finally, I came to a clearing. My father was on his back. He was dead and desiccated. And in front of him stood the old boar—the God of the Mountain—snorting and sharpening his tusks on a stone, as if to guard the corpse. I realized that my father wore a golden amulet that I wanted badly. I would have to kill the boar, however, to get this amulet. But I had no weapon. Only my bare hands."

"And what happened?"

"I picked up a stone and threw it at the boar. This only enraged it and it attacked me, sticking me in the back. The pain woke me up. It was my back hurting me."

Eudoxia kissed his hand. "Would you like something to eat?" she asked.

"Interpret the dream," he commanded. She'd always made sense of his dreams over the years. He could never see the true meaning.

"The amulet is your father's honor. The God of the Mountain is old age. It's simple. I need not consume the vapors of Delphi to see the meaning of this one. You are fighting an enemy against whom we cannot win. You and I are old. We have lost children, and grandchildren. All my hair is silver and your hair is getting thin. Don't let that black beard fool you, Menesarkus. You are an old man. You should, by all rights, be dead." She stood and shook a finger at him. "If you dare move from this bed I will tear off your balls with my bare hands. Now I am going to leave you in peace and quiet and attend to my duties." And with that she got up, put on her dress, tied up her hair, and shut the door behind her.

Menesarkus lay in the dark and shuttered room. He wished that he could wrestle Thanatos, the god of death. He would like to get him in the pankration arena and rip him limb from limb. He would break every rule. Gouge his eyes. Bite his nose.

"But I wouldn't stand a chance right now," he said out loud.

He thought of his meeting with Nauklydes and how strange it was that fate had turned his former Olympic herald into his enemy. The Athenian Timarkos had been the one to put the idea in Menesarkus's head to threaten Nauklydes with sharding. The whisperer, whom Menesarkus had met a dozen times over the last thirty years, had come to the farm early that morning with a message straight from Perikles, sealed in wax with the Athenian arkon's ring stamp. "Keep your oath" was all Perikles had written on the tiny roll of papyrus.

Plataea . . . caught like an olive pit between the grinding stones . . .

He fell into a fitful sleep and dreamt of a tortoise that had been turned on its back . . . an eagle circling above, waiting to come and snatch him in its sharp claws and carry him away.

He awoke with a start calling out for his dead son, Aristo. He crawled out of the bed and made his way slowly down the hall to Nikias's room, using the walls as support. The bed was empty. He saw Aristo's funeral urn sitting by the bed and picked it up, stared at the likeness of his child depicted on it. He didn't notice the crack that had formed along its length.

He thought back to the terrible day when Plataea had been routed on the battlefield by neighboring Thebes, their ancient enemy. The shield wall on the left flank had broken; the sneaky Thebans had used mounted archers to assault that side, surprising the Plataeans with this innovation. Menesarkus's son, Aristo, had become separated from him and Saeed in the panic. After the retreat and the declaration of Theban victory, the two sides came together in peace for the Sorting of the Dead. And that's when Menesarkus had found Aristo.

The young warrior had pushed the dirt around his mouth to smother himself, to stop the agony from the wound to his groin. He'd died with hands cupped around his mouth. To Menesarkus it had looked as though his child were shouting down to Hades. Announcing that his shade was on its way to that dark land of the dead.

Menesarkus had always thought that Nikias would make up for Aristo's untimely death. There was so much promise in that boy. So much strength. But now . . . ?

He squeezed the cold clay urn and it broke apart in his hands like a piece of rotting fruit. He stared in horror at the ashes and bits of bone strewn across his lap.

FIFTEEN

Eurymakus and his favorite wife luxuriated in the radiance of each other's bodies. She leaned against the cool marble of the bedroom wall with him facing the same direction, nestled down between her thighs, arms draped over her legs as she massaged his scalp with fragrant oil. Beneath them was the fur coverlet made from the hides of Theban moles, skins treasured throughout the Oxlands and Attika.

"So good," he said in Persian, his wife's language. He relished the feel of her slender fingertips, the press of her naked breasts against his back. He wound and unwound the silk ribbon around his wrist—the skytale he had just received from Nauklydes. He had washed his hands several times after returning from the Persian Fort, but his hands were still stained in places from the spy Pelias's blood.

"Sell your other wives," said Nihani playfully. "You only need one."

"Will you nurse all my children?" he asked in a gently mocking tone. "Like the statue of Artemis of Ephesus?" Ephesus was the city in Asia Minor where Eurymakus had studied in his youth, before the Athenians took it from the Persians. The statue of the goddess in the temple there had a chest covered with swollen breasts—dozens of them, like bunches of grapes.

Nihani laughed and bit his ear. Eurymakus turned his head, sought her mouth. They kissed passionately, urgently. She reached between his legs. Stroked him a couple of times, toying with him as she nibbled on his earlobe.

"I would sell my others wives for her," thought Eurymakus. "Probably murder them too."

She sang softly as she went back to work, oiling his head. He could hear his slaves moving about in the hall and the voices and cries of his seven children being fed their evening meal. They would not dare disturb his bedchamber, however. They knew to leave him alone when he was with his Nihani.

The events of tonight would go down in the history of Thebes as one of its greatest glories. He'd planned everything so perfectly. So economically. There would be little killing. Hardly any destruction of valuable new slaves or property that would certainly be ruined by a prolonged siege. Nauklydes would deliver his city for nothing more than a promise of friendship with Sparta.

Eurymakus was so certain of his victory he had already sent a messenger with a letter to the court of the Persian king. And he would have given anything to see the looks on the courtiers' faces when it was announced that Plataea had been captured.

For twenty years the court of Artaxerxes had been plotting to turn the tide against the Athenians and their expanding empire—an empire that had gobbled up nearly the entire coastline of Artaxerxes's possessions in Asia Minor as well as fomenting revolt in Egypt and Persia's other Mediterranean tributaries. Eurymakus had been an integral part of these secret plans against Athens, traveling to the seat of the Persian Empire a dozen times. He was a trusted member of the king's inner court. One of his cupbearers. The king praised him once by saying that Eurymakus was his most loyal subject on the Greek mainland.

It was Eurymakus who had suggested to Artaxerxes's viziers to start sending secret payments to Sparta—rich in slaves and land but poor in gold—to help finance their coming war with Athens. The Spartans were the final piece to Eurymakus's scheme to bring down Perikles and his empire. And Plataea was the first move in the coming war—a war that would raise Thebes to its rightful preeminence in the region.

Nihani brushed her husband's hair and tied it into a bun on the top of his head, fastened it with a golden clip. The clip was inset with a green jasper scarab carved with a seated lion. It had been her wedding present to him.

"I said prayers for you last night to Ahura Mazda," she said, naming the Persian god whom they both worshipped. "I saw you riding home from Plataea in a golden chariot."

"A good dream," said Eurymakus.

Nihani had been a gift to him on his last visit to Artaxerxes's court. Before that, she had been a temple prostitute. She had captured his heart at their very first meeting. Her boyish beauty and love skills made his other wives detestable to him. They were good for making children. That was all.

Nihani moved around and knelt in front of him. She pulled back her long black hair, tied it in a knot so it wasn't in her way as she pleased him.

In his mirror of the mind, Eurymakus saw his six hundred handpicked hoplites, the advanced invasion force. Killers to the man. They would assemble in Thebes's stadium at dusk, check over their weapons, pray to Zeus for victory, and then slip across the countryside, dressed all in black.

Nihani hummed as she worked, a low buzz that vibrated on his flesh.

Within five years of Plataea's fall, he mused, the Spartans and Athenians would exhaust themselves in a bloody war. And then a new Persian invasion force would sweep through Attika *and* Sparta and reclaim all of their former Greek territories! Artaxerxes had promised to make Eurymakus his satrap—his local ruler. Eurymakus of Thebes would be, in effect, the king of Greece.

Nihani paused to buckle on the apparatus and Eurymakus got on his hands and knees. She oiled up the black onyx phallus and assumed the man's position.

"Am I your best wife?" she asked huskily.

Eurymakus nodded vigorously, but he was thinking about horses. He only wished Thebes had more horses! His fellow Greeks—even though they had the perfect land for raising fine cavalry—did not understand the value of the mounted archer and spearman. Eurymakus had seen a cavalry ten thousand strong parading at the court of the Persian king—majestic Persian steeds, not the poor, stumpy, ugly horses of Attika. And then he had watched these horsemen in glorious action against the forces of an upstart vassal state, mowing through lines of foot soldiers like Zeus wielding a scythe.

Nihani worked furiously, groaning with lust.

He thought of Nauklydes's masculine face with its incongruously weak mouth. One could tell so much about a man from his mouth. . . .

Nihani reached around and took him in her hand.

A vision of his older brother appeared before Eurymakus's eyes. He saw him naked, standing in the pankration arena, poised to fight.

"Oh, my beautiful brother!" he sputtered.

His cry of pleasure pierced every room in the house. As Nihani satisfied herself Eurymakus planned in detail how he would kill Menesarkus. He'd make the pankrator watch as his women were raped, then hang them all one at a time, saving Menesarkus until the end. The grandson, the fighter Nikias, Eurymakus planned to send to Artaxerxes as a gift. After the youth healed from the castration, of course. He had decided to do this the day he spied on them at Menesarkus's farm. He would personally cut off Nikias's testicles. Make Menesarkus eat them—swallow his own heir's seed!

"Such joy!" he groaned, and thought, "It cannot come soon enough."

Nihani lay down next to him. She was spent and covered with sweat. "I know how to make you happy," she said smugly, and kissed his smiling mouth.

He left her in bed, dressed quickly in black garb, and departed the house. His bodyguard Bogha—a towering Median with braided mustaches reaching down to his pectorals—was waiting in the stables with their mounts. He was dressed in black like his master, a short Persian sword strapped to his back.

"*Magus,*" said Bogha, using the Persian word for wise man, bowing low.

They rode down the cobbled streets of Thebes—streets teeming with activity. Eurymakus saw blacksmiths busily putting a final edge on swords with sparks flying from the grinding wheels. And fletchers stacking high mounds of arrow-filled quivers while shield men packed up armor in leather cases. Warriors marched down the streets in their units, singing songs of war as they headed for their various staging points.

Eurymakus was pleased with how swiftly the citizens had got to work. He'd only given the orders two hours earlier. It didn't surprise him, though. They'd been planning for this day in secret for years.

The invasion of Plataea was about to begin.

SIXTEEN

———— ◆ ————

When Nikias, Leo, and Stasius emerged from the woods near the citadel's entrance, they saw that one of the massive portals was already shut and the gatemen had nearly closed the other.

"What are they doing?" asked Leo, surprised. "It's still an hour before sundown."

The five men put their shoulders to the twenty-foot-tall oak door, straining against its enormous weight and the resistance of the ancient and rusting hinges. They stopped heaving when there was just enough room left for them to pass single file back into the citadel, where they would finish the job: lock the gates from the inside with the crossbars and ground bolts.

"Run!" commanded Nikias, and took off at a sprint.

Stasius was the fastest runner of the three and got there first, waving and shouting at the last of gatemen still on the outside—a sullen thug everyone called "Axe."

Axe turned and glowered as he caught sight of Nikias coming up behind Stasius.

"Pretty Boy and the Runt can enter," said Axe in his jeering tone, referring to Stasius and Leo. "But not you"—pointing a crooked finger at Nikias—"son of Aristo." He blocked the narrow entrance and crossed his arms on his chest.

Nikias knew the Axe had been a friend of Kallisto's brother Lysander. Their gang—mostly city guardsmen—were notorious for their dicing and whoring. A year ago Axe had been tried for the brutal drunken murder of a noncitizen, but General Helladios had used his influence to get his sentence commuted to a mere fine. Nikias could see the look of pure hatred in the man's eyes—the way he was sizing Nikias up like an opponent before a fight. They had, in fact, fought once, but Nikias had soundly beaten the bigger man, humiliating him in public.

"Come on, Axe," said Stasius coyly. "We're having a party at the Thighs. You're invited too."

"Gates are shut," said Axe, smiling crookedly.

"But you shut them too early!" protested Leo.

"Magistrate Nauklydes's orders," said Axe. "Dangerous times, with Spartans about and the arkon dead. And criminal types about," he added, shoving his long chin toward Nikias.

"Go in," said Nikias to his friends in a commanding tone.

"But—"

"Just go." Nikias gave Leo a shove toward the gates. "I'll find a way inside."

Axe stepped aside and Stasius and Leo went through, glancing at Nikias over their shoulders expectantly. Axe turned and followed them in but the door didn't shut all the way. Nikias could hear Axe talking to the other gatemen on the other side of the oak planks. Then Axe strode back into view and the gate closed shut behind him. He was now holding his favorite weapon, a double-headed battle-axe.

"So," said Axe, grinning and running his free hand up and down the length of the haft. "Let's play."

Nikias looked around and realized there was nobody else outside the walls or on the nearby road. He peered up the wall and saw a couple of guards watching them with amused looks on their faces. They turned their heads away and stared up at the sky as if to say, "We don't see anything." Nikias couldn't believe what was happening. A man was threatening to murder him in front of the city gates. Or maybe he just wanted to scare him. . . . Did he expect Menesarkus's heir to tuck tail and run down the road?

Axe raised his thick eyebrows and moved his shoulders from side to side in a taunting way that made Nikias bristle.

"If only I had my whip," thought Nikias. "I'd snap those eyebrows right off your ugly face." He tried to remember where he'd put his Sargatian whip. An image of it flashed in his mind's eye, coiled around his spear in a corner of the barn.

"Hey, Aristo's son," called out a voice from the guard tower on the right-hand side of the gates.

Nikias saw a familiar face in a window—one of his grandfather's old pankration students from the gym.

"Go home, Nik," said the guard in an avuncular tone. "Axe isn't playing around. He and Lysander were shield friends."

"He was like a brother to me!" snarled Axe, shooting daggers at the man in the tower.

"I didn't kill him," said Nikias. "It was an accident. Isokrates was the one—"

Axe spat in Nikias's face. Nikias clenched his teeth, felt his skin flush as the rage boiled up inside him. "Put down your weapon and I'll play," he said slowly, wiping his eye on his sleeve. Big men like Axe were usually cowards without a weapon.

Axe swung the weapon at Nikias's face and Nikias leapt back, surprised at the speed of the attack. The blade had passed within inches of his eyes.

Axe cocked his head to the side. "I'll keep my weapon," he said, and took a step forward. "Now, piss off."

"Do something quickly to get your enemy off his guard," he heard his grandfather's voice say. "Do the opposite of what they think you'll do."

Nikias smiled and said, "Lysander sounded like a piglet when he was speared. I've never heard such a squealing turd—"

Axe bellowed with rage, pulled back his weapon, and swung with all his might at Nikias's head. Nikias had counted on this and ducked aside. Axe's momentum nearly spun him off his feet, with the heavy blade clutched in his hands flying toward the ground. The big man glanced over his shoulder frantically. Nikias's rough fist smashed into his nose. The uppercut that followed a split second after pushed Axe's jaw into his skull with the force of a kicking mule.

Nikias pried the axe from the unconscious man's hands, lifted it over his head, spun around, and slammed it into the portal. The door creaked open a moment later and one of the gatemen poked his head out furtively.

"Let me in *now*," said Nikias, eyes nearly disappearing underneath his angry brows.

SEVENTEEN

———————— ◆ ————————

Kallisto and her fellow huntresses were making their way through a fallow field when they startled a flock of geese. These were the last of the migrating birds heading south for the cold months, resting in the short dry stalks of the scythed wheat. The birds took off with a frantic flapping of wings, fanning out and skimming close to the ground, making it difficult to take aim. Kallisto's companions didn't even try to bring the fowl down, but Kallisto could already taste the fat on her tongue. She let fly with the most perfectly aimed arrow she'd ever loosed from her bow, and one of the geese dropped to the earth like a lead shot.

She ran to it, whooping with triumph all the way. But when she got to her kill she was surprised to find a big male with bristling black crown feathers standing guard over it with outstretched wings. The animal glared at her with what Kallisto could only describe as rage. It honked at her, hissing and showing its pointed tongue, and would not let her or any of the others approach the dead bird.

"The goose's mate," said Nikias's mother, Agathe, who had been hunting by her side. "Its husband."

The animal's humanlike behavior unnerved all of the women. They were reluctant to slaughter the male, yet abhorred the idea of letting its dead mate go to waste. Agathe snatched the dead goose from under its enraged protector and the women ran off, laughing nervously. They made a fire, plucked and roasted the goose on a spit. But the male followed them and stood nearby, honking irately the whole time. The meat caught in Kallisto's throat.

She awoke from the dream, choking. She struggled to move her hands but remembered they were still bound behind her. The pain came back—her cheek where her father had punched her repeatedly. Legs and wrists from the bindings. Scalp where Isokrates had yanked out a clump of hair. Stomach . . . that was the worst. They had starved her for a week in the pottery shed. Bound like an animal. She was so hungry, she'd dreamt of eating the goose. . . .

She'd been wrong about the men of her family. She thought they'd done their worst outside the Cave of Nymphs. But after Lysander died it was as if the madness of the bacchantes had possessed them. If her mother and Akake hadn't thrown themselves on her body, the others surely would have beaten her to death in their wrath.

She wondered what had happened to Nikias. Why hadn't he come for her? Had they already murdered him? Her eyes would no longer make tears. They were as dry as bones. Her heart seemed as though it was shriveling and dying inside her breast. Only a few beats left. . . .

The dream had seemed so real. Not like a dream at all, really. Because it was a memory recalled in perfect clarity. The killing of the goose wife had happened four years ago, right after she'd burned her first bloody rags on the altar of Artemis. Had the entire event been an omen? A terrible prophesy of death?

"Kallisto?"

The voice was spoken so softly she could barely hear it. As though it had been whispered by the clay dust on the floor.

"Kallisto? Sister?"

There was no mistaking it that time. It was Akake's voice. Poor Akake. Always such a gentle creature. A four-year-old trapped inside the body of a man. At first he'd been delighted by all of the excitement—happy to be included in his brothers' game. But she'd seen the look of terror on his face when her father struck her repeatedly in her face. The game was no longer any fun.

"Kallisto," said Akake. "I'm coming to say good-bye."

Kallisto had to swallow four times before she could speak.

"Where are going, Brother?" she asked.

"Not me. *You.* Father is going to sell you to the Makedonian tomorrow."

The Makedonian was a slaver who bought female slaves from around Plataea to sell in Sicily as prostitutes. He was the most odious man Kallisto had ever met. Slovenly. Hairy. Cruel. Her father's rage, it seemed, was limitless. He was going to send his only daughter into a life of constant torment. "A hundred men a day," she'd heard the slaver brag once. "That's how many my best ones service."

"Akake," said Kallisto. "You need to help me."

"I can't," said Akake sadly. "Father will beat me."

"I want you to get a knife," said Kallisto, wriggling toward the door. "I want you to get a knife," she repeated, trying to mask her desperation by making her voice sound lighthearted. "And come back and help me. It won't be difficult, my friend. Just like we do with the rabbits after we shoot them. To put them out of their misery, that's all. Do you hear me, Akake love? Slip the knife in the throat and cut the jugular. I'm like one of those rabbits. I know how you hate to see them kicking their legs with the arrows still in them. Open the door and look at me. My legs are kicking now."

Silence. Several minutes passed in which she wondered if Akake had gone away. Then the shed door opened and Akake's face appeared before her, sniffing like a worried dog.

"I already have a knife," he said proudly, showing her the blade by the light of his lamp. "And sometimes I like to let the nice little rabbits go free. Would you like me to free you, Sister?"

EIGHTEEN

Outside the city walls, a half mile down the road that led from the gate to the east, walked a man in a tattered robe. It was difficult to find one's way on this black night. The walls of Plataea were barely discernible against the black of the horizon behind—the sun had set two hours earlier—and the torches that burned on the battlement's watchtowers seemed to float above the earth.

The man turned and peered at something on the side of the road; a smiling face stared back at him from the darkness. His heart skipped a beat. "Who's there?" asked the vagabond.

The smiling face was rigid, unmoving. The man took a cautious step forward, and then cackled at his own folly. He reached out a hand and touched cool marble. It was a herm road marker. He patted the carved erection for good luck. Thanks to the god of fortune! He could sleep outside the walls of Plataea and then enter the city in the morning and beg some food from old Kallinakos, the kindly priest of the Temple of Zeus.

Behind the herm, in the field of winter wheat, he saw a dark shape move. It was the unmistakable form of a living man rising slowly, stealthily, from where he had been lurking. Then another shadow shape stood up . . . and another. In a matter of seconds half a dozen men had materialized from the field. A black-garbed warrior reached over his left shoulder and gripped the handle of a sword protruding from a scabbard that was strapped to his back. The metal hissed as he pulled it from its sheath.

"Peace—" said the man, raising his hand up high.

The blade whistled. The man's head hit the road with the thud of a dropped melon, followed by his severed hand. Then his body toppled over, his neck's arteries pumping out his blood into the dust.

Eurymakus the Theban wiped the blood from his sword and slid it back into the sheath on his back with a graceful motion. He took off the dead man's robe and wrapped it around his shoulders, then motioned for his men to drag the body off the road. The other warriors crept back into the fields but Eurymakus stayed on the road, shuffling with the gait of an old man, all the way to the walls of Plataea. Once he got there he peered upwards at the Gates of Pausanius. Each of the doors was the span of a man's arms stretched wide—fashioned from the thickest oak and bound with heavy iron straps. Impossible to smash with battering rams. The bastions were staggered at the entrance, creating a curtain wall. On either side of the gates was a tower, perfectly positioned for archers to pick off men foolish enough to try and ram the gates. Rocks could be hurled down from the battlements above to crush the bones of attackers. In Thebes it was accepted as fact that the walls and the gates of Plataea were impassable. Impenetrable to siege warfare. But he, Eurymakus, had made these bastions of stone, these doors of oak and iron, worthless. "There is a weapon stronger than force of arms," he told himself. "I have defeated my enemy with my mind."

He rubbed a silver Theban coin between the thumb and forefinger of his right hand. On one side was stamped an image of the distinctive notched shield of Thebes. On the other the head of Dionysus, "the god who came from the east," his hair wreathed in ivy. Fingers had worn the god's hair smooth over the fifty years or so since the coin had been stamped.

In the right-hand guard tower an oil lamp burned in the window. The silhouette of a man stood there, looking down at him. He could make out the traitor's shape. Eurymakus kissed the coin and tossed it into the window. It clanged on the stone floor. He saw the unmistakable shape of the giant guardsman Zander bend over, pick it up, and then nod.

Eurymakus made a sweeping motion with his arm. One of his men came from his hiding place and let out a croaking sound like that of a frog. Theban warriors rushed from the darkness and formed up behind Eurymakus. They wore no armor. But they did not need bronze for protection. These men had crept across the dark countryside in groups of twos and threes, dressed all in black, sneaking like badgers and foxes, right past the Plataean watchtowers and sentries.

Behind the two massive doors Eurymakus heard a rasping sound as the vertical pins were slid from their sheaths in the ground. And then a crossbar scraped on its tracks as it was removed from the brackets. Slowly, tantalizingly so, the right-hand door opened just wide enough for two men to walk through side by side. The four Plataean gatemen who had betrayed their city appeared hesitantly from behind the door. They waited nervously as Eurymakus strode through the archway, followed by a seemingly endless stream of black-clad warriors.

"They're waiting for you in the Assembly Hall," said one of the Plataean traitors as Eurymakus came to a halt inside the gate. The mass of Thebans hemmed in the four anxious gatemen, forming up ranks around them. The man who had spoken to Eurymakus placed nervous fingers on a purse he held in his other hand—the purse containing their traitor's pay of Persian gold . . . enough to make the four men exceedingly rich.

"And the other twenty gatemen?" asked Eurymakus with his slight Persian accent.

"They drank the drugged wine we gave them," said one of the Plataeans. "They're in there." He pointed at the tower to the right of the gates. "We tied them up and gagged them like we were told. They didn't give us any trouble."

Eurymakus smiled. The powerful drug, laced with the juice of the vision-inducing mushrooms, made men think they were living in a dream . . . made them as helpless as children. He would take pleasure slitting each of their throats.

As quick as a snake he stabbed the gateman nearest him in the heart—the one clutching his bag of gold—while his Theban brethren, taking their cue, hacked off the heads of the other three surprised guards. Eurymakus bent down and snatched the bag of gold from the dead man's hand and tossed it to Bogha, who slipped it inside his tunic. After the last of the four hundred Thebans entered the city, the door was shut and locked with the heavy crossbar. All was quiet. No sound of alarm had been signaled. They had accomplished their first goal. They had breached the enemy's mighty bastions.

A stocky man picked up one of the torches dropped by a dead Plataean gateman. The pitch-fed flame cast the Theban general's rugged features in its yellow-white glow. Tykon was a lean, gray-haired warrior with two deep battle scars on either side of his handsome face. The twenty attack leaders bunched up around him and Eurymakus.

"The rabbits are asleep in their warren," said Eurymakus. "Now terrorize them."

"For the glory of Thebes," said Tykon in his gravelly voice.

A hundred warriors sprinted into the towers on either side of the walls with daggers and short bows in hand. The rest unsheathed their swords and headed out into the citadel. They had trained for this mission for a year and each man knew his way, even in the dark.

Eurymakus kissed his signet ring and followed, tasting the blood of Plataeans on his tongue.

NINETEEN

———————— ◆ ————————

There were a dozen teenagers in the drinking room of the Golden Thighs. All of them were friends from the gymnasium. Every one an athlete. Every one brave. But they'd sat on the cushions in the symposium chamber, listening with abject horror as Stasius and Leo recounted the nightmarish events that had occurred at the Persian Fort that day.

They were all shaken by the story but anxious to avenge young Pelias's mutilation in any way possible. And they were as drunk as satyrs. The wine made them bold and impatient to do something about the Spartan menace, especially after they'd heard that this Timarkos fellow had accused the Egyptian of being a spy for the enemy.

Nikias stood off to the side, arms crossed on his chest, lank hair covering his face. He was desolate. And the wine had only made him more depressed. He felt as though he'd fallen backward down a well. He couldn't stop seeing Pelias's destroyed face and his bloody tears. He couldn't stop thinking of the awful feeling of cutting through the young man's slender neck and the sickening sound it had made. And worst of all, he could still smell Pelias's body burning on the fire. The repulsive odor of singed hair after Timarkos had thrown his severed head onto the flames.

Nikias wanted more than anything to cut off his hair like all his newly shorn friends and burn it on the altar of Zeus. But he'd lost that right. He had to do something to prove that he was worthy of Zeus and his city. He wondered if catching a dangerous spy would count for anything in the eyes of the jury of twelve who would oversee his trial for the death of Lysander. . . .

"But why did the Spartan spy have to be Chusor?" he thought morosely.

Chusor had befriended Nikias years earlier, and the young Plataean had listened countless times with rapt attention to his fantastical stories of journeys in far-off lands. The pyramids of Egypt and talking statues in the sands. The library of Persepolis in Persia—a single building, Chusor had claimed, that was as big as the entire citadel of Plataea. Tales of lizard monsters swimming in the Nile like schools of fish. Molten lava pouring from a volcano in Sicily. Chusor had even been *through* the Gates of Herakles! Not even Odysseus had pulled off that feat. No matter how crazy the stories sounded, he always had the facts—or the scars—to back them up.

And Chusor had taught Nikias things that his grandfather knew nothing about. How some people believed that shades returned to the world in the bodies of newborns. Or the pleasure to be found in studying the natural world—the impossible beauty in something as overlooked as a dragonfly's wing. Or how important it was to ask a woman you loved about what she was thinking . . . about her dreams.

Would they have to torture Chusor tonight to make him admit that he was working for the enemy? What if Timarkos had lied and Chusor was innocent? It all seemed to make sense now, though. Nikias thought of the rumors about Chusor killing a man. He thought of the suspicious map of the citadel he'd seen in the smith's workshop the other night. And the Skythian boy who Chusor had said he'd bought with the single purpose of learning the secret to making a deadly poison. . . .

"Nikiassss?" asked Stasius with a slurred voice. He was holding an old Theban shield and a rusty sword—prizes from the Persian Wars—that he'd taken off the wall, where they'd been displayed for the last fifty years. "We're ready."

"I don't know," said Nikias. "I'm not sure about this."

"Maybe we should wait," suggested Leo. Like Nikias, he wasn't nearly as drunk as the others.

Stasius scowled and shook his head. "Wait for what? The time for waiting is over." He let forth a belch and all the boys in the room laughed except for Nikias and Leo.

They filed out of the bordello and marched quietly down the dark street, armed with cudgels and cooking knives. When they got to Chusor's smithy they stood silently together, lighting torches and passing them around. They peered up at the windows of the second floor, where lamplight flickered.

Nikias glanced at the old shield hanging on a horizontal pole above the entrance to the workshop. Chusor had painted it with the image of the club-footed god Hephaestos—the crippled son of Zeus, loathed by the other gods—in the act of swinging a hammer against an anvil. The figure was artfully portrayed, and the torchlight seemed to make the lifelike image move, especially after a sudden gust caused the sign to swing back and forth a little. The chains holding it to the post squeaked like rats. The wind, Nikias noticed, smelled distinctly of coming rain.

He went to the front door, took a deep breath, and pounded on it. After a while somebody picked up one of the lamps and carried it downstairs. The grate on the door opened.

"Who there?" asked Diokles, staring wide-eyed into the street and the throng of torchbearers.

"It's me," said Nikias. He tried to sound friendly but his voice came out strained. "Open up, Diokles. I need to talk to Chusor."

"Chusor busy," Diokles said, and shut the grate.

Nikias pounded on the door again. The grate opened again.

"What you boys want?" asked Diokles peevishly.

"Open the bloody door!" shouted Stasius, running up and kicking the door with the flat of his foot.

Diokles quickly shut the grate and Nikias heard him running up the stairs.

"Let's break down the Egyptian's door!" shouted Stasius, striking the painted shield above the door with the flat edge of his rusted sword. His ancient blade shattered and one of the chains holding the shield to the pole snapped. Stasius's blade clattered to the street and the shield swung down like a pendulum, nearly braining Nikias.

"Zeus's balls!" cursed Nikias. "Watch it, Stasius!"

Stasius looked at the broken sword in his hand and grinned, then chucked it aside, saying, "Crap Theban sword anyway."

"There are enough of us here," said Hektor. "We can break down the door and pull the Egyptian and his Helot out by their legs."

"Yes! Pound down the door," called out one of the other teens. "Come out, you dirty barbarian!"

"A battering ram is what we need!" declared Stasius. He staggered across the marketplace to a carpenter's workshop on the other side. Sitting on the pavers outside the shop was a massive ten-foot-long oak beam that was meant for the repairs to the Assembly Hall ceiling.

"We can use this as a battering ram," said Stasius, setting down his weapons. "Lay siege to the Egyptian's fortress!"

The teenagers ran across the square to help Stasius, but Nikias stayed near the entrance to Chusor's smithy, brooding. The painted shield dangled precariously, spinning round and round, held by its single chain. Nikias noticed the handle on the back of the shield was broken. His warrior's mind contemplated the fact that a shield with a broken handle would be useless in battle, because you'd have to hold it by the rim with two hands, and that would leave your fingers exposed.

He shook his head with mild disgust as he watched his friends try to lift the heavy beam from the ground. The fact that they were all drunk off their heads made their task difficult. Soon they were laughing and shouting insults at each other, and then one of them let forth an agonized scream as his foot got smashed.

On the second floor of a nearby house, the shutters opened and a woman hissed at them to be quiet. "You'll wake my baby!" she said angrily.

"Sorry!" Stasius hissed back.

Leo ambled back over to Nikias. He was frowning and making a big show of picking a sliver of wood from his hand. He wrapped his arm around an awning pole that held up the shade canopy in front of the smithy and leaned all his weight against it, sighing loudly.

"Maybe this is a stupid idea, Nik," he said under his breath. "These sheep stuffers can't even lift a beam, let alone break down a door. Let's leave the Egyptian alone and go tell your grandfather about Timarkos and poor Pelias—"

Out of the corner of his eye Nikias saw a dark shape rushing from the shadows toward Stasius and the others. It happened so fast, he didn't have time to shout a warning. A black-clad man slashed down with a sword at Stasius's chest, breaking through his clavicle and splitting open his body with a loud cracking of bones.

"Stasius!" screamed Nikias.

Stasius fell to the ground squirming and gasping. And then, like a terrible squall that catches sailors on the sea unawares, a mass of men clad in black descended upon the bewildered teens with a violent fury, chopping and slicing with razor-sharp swords.

TWENTY

———————•———————

Nikias couldn't understand what was happening. It made no sense. His first thought was that Chusor had pulled some terrible trick on them. He saw a friend's head pop from the column of his neck. Another teen held up his arms to ward off a blow and both of his hands went flying.

His friends were being butchered!

Nikias acted without thinking. He leapt up and grabbed the old shield dangling by its single chain from the pole above the workshop entrance. The weight of his body snapped the chain and he clutched the shield on either side by the rim. Leo ripped one of the awning poles free of its canopy and held it like a spearman in a phalanx: left arm rigid out front, right arm bent by his side. They ran to the aid of their friends, yelling fiercely, but they were headed off in the middle of the square by more attackers.

Leo swept the pole from side to side and two of the invaders jumped backward. Nikias raised his shield to protect himself and Leo from a furious sword attack that sent painful shock waves down his arms. His assailant, a broad-shouldered man with a hefty sword, pounded relentlessly on the shield, driving him back toward the wall of the smithy. Nikias was helpless to fight back and lost sight of Leo. He had to keep moving the heavy disk back and forth to prevent the invader from slicing off his vulnerable fingers where they gripped the rim.

"You can't kill a man with defense!" It was his grandfather's voice thundering in his head.

Something caught fire in his brain. Nikias thrust the shield at his attacker with all his might, pushing the surprised invader back half a step. It was all he needed.

Nikias flung the shield downward as hard as he could. The edge of the iron disk landed on one of the invader's feet, breaking his toes. The man screamed and hopped on his good foot, giving Nikias the chance to spin around him and kick out, catching the warrior on the lower back. The man stumbled forward with one knee locked at an awkward angle. Nikias kicked out again and the flat of his foot snapped the man's shinbone. The invader dropped to the ground, shrieking in pain. Nikias leaned over and smashed him in the face with his callused fist, knocking his front teeth down his throat, and the man let go of his sword.

Snatching up the invader's fallen sword, in the same motion Nikias chopped him across the face as though he were cutting through a thick root back on the farm. The blade went clean through the man's head at the eyebrows, sending the top of his skull skittering across the ground.

Nikias whirled around, trying to take in what was happening. Fallen torches lit up the street, showing a tangled mass of dead and writhing bodies in the flickering light. He saw Hektor locked with an opponent, thrashing about violently, screaming indignantly "He's trying to *kill* me!"

Leo was fending off the five remaining attackers with his pole. The invaders poked and prodded at him with their swords, backing the young wrestler against the wall like hunters who'd cornered an animal. All of Nikias's other friends lay still upon the ground.

"Nik! Get over here!" screamed Leo.

Nikias ran at them, swinging his sword at the head of the closest invader with the same mighty stroke he would use to fell a sapling in the woods. Before the man's head hit the ground, Nikias brought the blade against the shoulder of the other and the enemy's arm and sword fell to the street. Leo slammed the pole against the one-armed man's head and the warrior toppled over. The moment he hit the ground, Leo drove the tapered end of the pole through the man's eye and into his brain.

Nikias recklessly charged the other two invaders who'd tried to corner Leo, swinging his sword with a blind fury. The men were overmatched by his sheer strength and his wrath. One of them crumpled to the street, his carotid artery gushing blood. The other, faced with fighting Nikias and Leo by himself, turned and ran down the street and disappeared into the dark.

"Help!" screamed Hektor.

Nikias saw Hektor, twenty paces away, pinned underneath his attacker. The enemy had a long knife grasped in one hand, and with the other was squeezing Hektor's throat. Hektor clutched the enemy's dagger arm with both hands, but the invader was winning the contest of strength.

Nikias reached backward with his sword then flung it forward like a throwing knife. The sword flew through the air, the blade entering one of the invader's ears and protruding from the other with the sound of a melon being pierced. Saeed, who'd taught him that trick, would have been pleased to see it put to such good use.

"Who?" asked the stunned Hektor as he pushed away the still-twitching corpse and got to his feet. "What is going on? Where did they come from?"

"Nikias, where are you?" Stasius called out in a weak voice.

"Stasius!" yelled Nikias. He ran to his friend and dropped to his knees beside him, cradling the back of his head in one hand, lifting Stasius's tunic with the other to reveal the gaping wound to his chest.

"What happened?" Stasius asked, his whole body shuddering, blood gushing from his mouth. "I don't feel well." Air bubbled out from his lungs through the gash that had severed his clavicle, slit open his chest, and separated his ribs. He took in a gasping breath. Leo and Hektor were by his side now, too, shaking their heads in disbelief.

"Don't move," commanded Leo.

"Just stay still," said Hektor. "You'll be fine."

"Nikias," said Stasius. "Why do you look so scared? Why won't my head stop spinning?"

"Invaders!" yelled Nikias at the top of his lungs. The reality of what had happened hit him like a club. "Help! We've been attacked!"

Nikias heard footsteps behind him and turned.

"Hey!" said a dark shape. "It's just me, Myron the sandal maker and Zeno the stonemason."

"What happened?" asked Zeno. "By Zeus, what happened?"

"I don't know," replied Nikias. His jaw trembled spasmodically. "We were standing here . . ." His voice caught in his throat.

"I heard some shouting," said Myron.

"Then I heard screams," added Zeno. "I came right out."

Zeno and Myron moved their torches over the bodies. Out of the twelve young men who'd been in their group, only Nikias, Leo, and Hektor had not been mortally wounded. Five black-clad attackers were also dead.

"It was the Egyptian," said Hektor, his mind in a fog.

"Not the Egyptian," said Zeno. He was bent over one of the dead invaders, fingering something on the man's wrist. "A death tag," he said matter-of-factly, reading the name inscribed there.

Theban warriors, Nikias knew, wore these brass identification bracelets in battle so their bodies could be returned to their families for proper burial rights, even if they were disfigured. "Thebans," he spat with contempt, wiping the blood of the men he'd killed from his face.

"*Dead* Thebans," said Zeno grimly. A handful of other men—residents of the street—had come out of their houses, drawn by the desperate sounds of the fight.

"By Hera!" said Myron, standing up. "The gates must have been breached."

"We've got to warn the city," said Zeno. "We need to get to the garrison, wake up the guards."

"The gates have been breached?" It was Haemon, a butcher. His eyes practically popped out of his head. "We've got to get out!" he cried. "Run to the country-side!" He grabbed one of the torches and took off down the street.

"Wait!" bellowed Zeno.

The sounds of arrows whizzed from the direction Haemon had run. A second later he lurched back into view. An arrow was stuck through his neck and he clawed at it. Another arrow slammed into his back and he crumpled to the street.

From opposite directions, up and down the lane, another twenty Theban warriors came marching into the Old Market. Nikias and the other Plataeans were trapped.

TWENTY-ONE

Two of the residents tried to run back to their homes, but they were soon shot down. Zeno picked up the body of a dead Theban and draped it over his shoulder, using the corpse as a shield.

"Come on!" he roared. "Back to my house!" He ran to his nearby door. The Theban archers shot at him but the arrows stuck in their dead companion, sparing Zeno. The big stonemason held open his door for the others to follow. Myron, crawling on his hands and knees, evaded the deadly projectiles and dove into Zeno's doorway.

"Leo! Hektor! Stand your ground!" he ordered. "Don't panic!"

"Come inside my house, you idiots!" yelled Zeno.

"We're not leaving Stasius!" shouted Nikias. Leo dropped his pole, picked up a sword from the street, and took up a position next to him. Nikias grabbed Hektor by the biceps and yanked him closer.

At the same time Zeno slammed shut his door and locked it.

A man stepped from the throng of Thebans, pointed at Nikias. "Drop your sword," commanded the invader. "Plataea is now under the authority of Thebes."

"You're going to have to cut it from my fingers," said Nikias.

The Theban said, "With pleasure."

A great gust of wind came from the west, as though the god Zephyros had filled his lungs and let forth a mighty exhalation. The wind smelled of rain and the wild herbs of the Kithaeron Mountains, and Nikias thought, "I will never see Kallisto again. . . ."

The door to the smithy opened and something flew over Nikias's head—a sizzling, burning thing that exploded above the attackers. There was a cloud of acrid smoke, followed by agonized screams. Then two armored men—covered in bronze from helm to breast to shin plates—stepped through the doorway, pushed Nikias aside, and strode into the heart of the invaders. One was tall and wielded a massive axe. The other was half his height and clutched heavy iron smithy hammers in either fist. They plowed through the unarmored Thebans, pounding and chopping with the fury of gods.

The explosion had set some of the Thebans on fire—a strange fire that stuck to their skin and would not cease burning. One man tried to tear off his melting clothes, shrieking as his hair caught flame and burned like wool on a sacrificial fire. The Thebans panicked. The men in armor were unstoppable; the Theban swords bounced harmlessly off their stone-hard shells. The Thebans were not used to fighting without armor. They were trained in the phalanx, to stand beside their brothers, with protective carapaces of bronze, shields of thick wood. But they'd left their armor and shields in Thebes, sneaking across the countryside dressed only in thin clothes. And now they were like children with toy swords fighting grown men.

The Thebans broke ranks and scattered back into the maze of streets. After they were gone, Chusor took off his Korinthian helm with its high horsehair plume and held it under one arm.

"Into the smithy," he said.

Nikias dashed over to Stasius. "Help me bring him," he shouted. Chusor gripped Stasius around the legs while Nikias gently cradled his friend's upper body in his arms. Leo helped support his wounded friend's torso. With every step blood poured from Stasius' mouth. They carried him into the workshop and set him down on the floor. Hektor was lying in the corner in the fetal position, shaking and hiding his face. Nikias and Leo knelt by Stasius.

"Stasius," said Leo gently, touching his cold cheek.

"Can you hear us?" asked Nikias, taking his limp hand.

But the beautiful runner did not respond. His eyes had glazed over. He had breathed his life into the dust.

TWENTY-TWO

Nauklydes sat in the arkon's chair in the Assembly Hall, chewing on his fingernails. He had torn the nails off nine of his ten fingers in the last hour. Some of the fingertips bled where he had pulled flesh away. Standing at the back of the hall at attention were two dozen guardsmen—handpicked and loyal followers—who had pledged their lives to support his appropriation of power in exchange for Persian gold.

General Helladios paced back and forth from one side of the speaker's floor to the other, hand clutching the pommel of his sword. He stopped and cocked his head to listen. "Did you hear something?"

"No," said Nauklydes, pressing his fingers to his tunic to stop them from oozing blood. "Axe?" he called out, looking for the big gateman—one of Helladios's personally selected men who'd reported the arrival of the Thebans and then vanished. He looked at the general. "Where has Axe gone?"

"I never liked the idea of giving up the walls to the Thebans," said Helladios, ignoring his question.

"Drako demanded it," replied Nauklydes. "We had no choice. And remember this: we are not giving the city to the Thebans. Everything the Thebans do is in the name of Sparta. Bloodshed will be kept at a minimum. Drako promised me that. The Spartans keep their oaths."

"Some of our men might struggle," said Helladios. "Like the guards on duty on the walls."

Nauklydes shrugged. "The warriors in this hall are the only ones we could trust totally with our plan," he said, and pointed at the silent warriors. "My loyal brethren." He smiled at the men, raised his voice so they could hear. "They know that what we are doing is justified and will benefit the city in the end. Things will be difficult at first. . . ." He nodded his head and bit on a nail. "Yes. Difficult. But once the men in the mountain and border garrisons learn what has happened, that I"—here the briefest of pauses to correct himself—"that *you and I* control the city, they will flock to our side. Especially after the Spartan army arrives in full force and our fellow Plataeans realize there is no choice but to break with Athens once and for all. I know for certain that General Zoticus will unite with us once he finds out what we have done. With him comes the cavalry."

"And those who oppose us?" asked Helladios in a voice meant only for Nauklydes's ears.

"They will be jailed," said Nauklydes in a loud voice, throwing up his arms and rising from his chair. "Come, Helladios. We've had this discussion a dozen times. Now is not the hour to second-guess our actions."

The Assembly Hall door creaked open and Helladios's response died away. A lone figure strode across the gray marble with a dancer's lissome steps. He came to a stop several paces from the magistrate and the general, gave a slight nod, and flicked his eyes at the Plataean warriors at the back of the chamber. Nauklydes was taken aback by how Persian Eurymakus looked at this moment with his dark, almond-shaped eyes, high cheekbones, full lips, and long hair and beard. At his hip was a curved Median sword, the kind used by Persian charioteers. Nauklydes could smell the man's perfume . . . the scent of roses.

"Eurymakus," said Nauklydes. "No Theban has ever set foot in this chamber. Let your entrance be a symbol of a change for the good. You are welcome." He saw Eurymakus fingering something. What was it? A coin?

"I thank you for your gracious welcome," said Eurymakus, looking at the ceiling with an appraising air. The pigeons started cooing above in the rafters.

"Eurymakus, where is Drako?" asked Helladios gruffly. "I expected the king of Sparta's man to be the first to enter the hall, not a Theban whisperer."

"I was given the honor of coming to see you first," said Eurymakus. "Drako will be here soon."

A pigeon flew from its nest and flapped around the dark ceiling. Nauklydes looked up and frowned.

"And where are your men?" asked Helladios, annoyed. "Surely you didn't come alone."

Eurymakus held a hand to his mouth to cover his laugh. "My men are busy. They've taken the guard towers along the walls and now they're clearing the streets. Your citizens are under the impression that an overwhelming force has arrived and they are cowering in their homes, just like I said they would."

"Now we must occupy the rest of the public buildings," said Helladios to Nauklydes. "When dawn comes, the citizens of Plataea must know that we have total control of the hall, the courts, the arkon's offices . . . all of the—"

"That will not be necessary," interrupted Eurymakus. "Whoever controls the Gates of Pausanius and the walls rules Plataea. The rest is meaningless." He gave a dismissive wave of his hand.

A scream in the distance made the Plataeans jump. But Eurymakus remained still and unblinking like a snake.

Helladios drew his sword. "What was that?"

Eurymakus laughed through his nose, covered his mouth with his hand again. "And they thought *Oedipus* was blind," he said in a mocking tone.

Nauklydes noticed the Theban had an odd-looking object attached to his belt—a black onyx box with a dagger handle protruding from it. It looked as though the blade had been driven into solid stone.

Another death shriek erupted outside the building, and several of the Plataean guards unsheathed their weapons. Eurymakus raised his arm over his head in a curious motion and then pointed it at the Plataean warriors standing at the back of the hall. Nauklydes gasped as dozens of arrows sang out from above—from the rafters—and struck the warriors in a hail of deadly missiles. The Plataeans fell to the ground, crying out in their death throes. Helladios took a step toward Eurymakus, but the Theban leapt at him—a small dagger now clutched in his hand—and slashed the Plataean general across the face, dancing away. At the same time dozens of Thebans burst through the doors at the front and back of the hall and descended upon the Plataean warriors who had been struck down, hacking them to pieces with axes and swords.

"Eurymakus! What—" Nauklydes stared at the scene in horror, in disbelief. Helladios had dropped his sword and was staggering around in a circle, clutching at his stomach, sucking in air and gurgling like an animal.

"He'll die soon," explained Eurymakus to Nauklydes, "but it is a painful death. The poison is different from the one we used on your arkon in Athens. As you know, that was meant to mimic a heart attack. This one, however, is concocted to cause the most excruciating agony—an annihilating pain."

Helladios had fallen to the floor. His limbs looked as though invisible hands were twisting them as he thrashed. Something flew out of his mouth, followed by a plume of blood.

"Bit off his tongue," observed Eurymakus. "Now the teeth."

Nauklydes heard a grisly sound emanating from Helladios's mouth: the general was grinding his jaws together with such force the teeth were breaking apart. Blood gushed from Helladios's nostrils and his eyes rolled up into his skull. He stopped moving all at once as though he'd been decapitated.

Eurymakus dipped the dagger into the stone box on his belt, and when he pulled it out again the tip glistened with moisture. He pointed the dagger at Nauklydes. The magistrate turned to flee but was knocked down by four Thebans, who beat him into submission. They tied him up like a calf with his ankles and wrists bound as one.

"I don't understand!" shouted Nauklydes, spitting blood. "Where is Drako? I demand to see Drako!"

"Turn him on his back," said Eurymakus.

Nauklydes struggled wildly as the Thebans rolled him over. "Untie me!"

"Don't move," said Eurymakus softly, holding the poisoned blade an inch from his face. Nauklydes stopped flailing and tried to move his head away from the dagger, but several hands clutched his hair and held his head in place.

"Why?" asked Nauklydes. "Why?"

"Ask *him*," said Eurymakus.

Drako the Spartan appeared behind Eurymakus. Nauklydes never thought he would be so relieved to see the Spartan warrior's mutilated face. "Drako," he spluttered. "Make them stop."

"They do my bidding," said Drako, his constricted, gargled voice escaping from deep in his throat.

"I signed your covenant," said Nauklydes with indignation. "I am arkon now. I did everything you told me to do. I—"

"You're no good to us. We can't have a traitor rule Plataea. Your people would never stand for it."

Eurymakus smiled, showing all his teeth. "You see how it is now?" he said in a wheedling tone. "The traitor Nauklydes. That is how they will remember you."

"Don't kill me," Nauklydes begged of Drako. "Don't let him cut me with that—"

"Take him to his home and keep him there," said Drako. "We will need him later."

Nauklydes cursed and yelled as four Theban warriors started dragging him across the floor. They kicked him in the stomach until he was voiceless, and then shoved a cloth in his mouth. Eurymakus strode over to him and leaned down, grabbed Nauklydes by the back of the head, and whispered in his ear.

"Your son Demetrios—the one you thought was safe in Syrakuse . . ."

Nauklydes stopped breathing at the mention of his son's name, and Eurymakus screwed up his face in mock concern, nodding.

"Yes, Nauklydes. The young man will be in the hands of our agents by now. On his way to Persepolis in the hold of a trireme. Castrated, of course. . . ." Eurymakus paused as Nauklydes started fighting like an angry ox to be free. One of the Thebans put him in a stranglehold to calm him down. "And Demetrios will spend the rest of his days servicing Persian royalty on his hands and knees."

Eurymakus addressed his men. "Nauklydes has a daughter. Let every warrior know he can take his pleasure with her. And let the father watch," he added, as though granting a special favor.

Nauklydes gave a muffled howl. An animal sound—that of a badger caught in a hole, stabbed with a spear.

"Come, Arkon," said one of the Theban warriors with enthusiasm as they hauled him across the marble floor. "Let us take you home. I long to meet this daughter."

Eurymakus went and sat in the black-marble arkon's chair, humming softly to himself. He watched as the Thebans lined up the Plataean corpses and slit the throats of men still breathing. A warrior entered the hall carrying a heavy bag in both hands.

"The heads of Magistrates Periander and Iphikrates," he said. "And General Alexios." He dropped the bag at Eurymakus's feet; it seeped blood on the marble floor.

Eurymakus pulled out Alexios's head and grinned at the face frozen in a silent scream. "How surprised you look." He leaned back in the chair with the head in his lap, stroking the hair as though it were a pet.

"Don't get too used to that seat," said Drako, opening the bag and squinting at the contents. "This city is under Spartan rule now."

"Of course," said Eurymakus, bowing his head obsequiously. "But indulge me, my old friend, for this moment."

"The only men I've ever indulged in my life are my kings. Do not take too much pleasure in this tainted victory."

"Tainted?"

"There is no honor in tricks and poison."

"I have beaten my enemy," said Eurymakus. "You Spartans fight the pankration without rules." He tossed the head of Alexios onto the floor, where it landed facedown with a crunching sound.

"The pankration is a game fought between two men," replied Drako. "War must have rules or else there would be no end to the chaos." He gestured for Eurymakus to stand and glared at the Theban until he obeyed. "I have helped bring about the downfall of a former ally against the Persians. I cannot gloat." He wrapped his red cloak around his shoulders and walked to the doorway with Eurymakus following close behind. When they were on the steps of the Assembly Hall, Drako sniffed the air through the holes where his nose used to be. "Rain is coming soon," he pronounced. "Your reinforcements better set out soon. The Plataeans will hide in their homes for a while, but even rabbits bolt from snakes."

"The messengers have been sent already," said Eurymakus.

Drako regarded Eurymakus with a shrewd look. "I will return from Sparta with the men to occupy the city."

"When?" asked Eurymakus.

Drako cocked his head ever so slightly and raised his eyebrows. It was a look that said, "We will come when we come." "Until that time, Eurymakus, you Thebans are nothing more than caretakers. Kill only the men and their families who are on the list. We don't want to scare any other future city-states in the

Oxlands from joining our alliance. Plataea will be made an example of, but don't turn this into a slaughterhouse."

"I understand," said Eurymakus submissively.

"And keep Nauklydes alive," said Drako. "We'll let the new Plataean government hold a trial and they can execute their traitor themselves."

"How alive must I keep him?" asked Eurymakus.

Drako shrugged and moved nimbly down the steps. Eurymakus watched the Spartan until he had disappeared into the dark of the agora.

Tykon stepped from the shadows where he had been listening, his face set in a scowl. "What will the Spartans do when they come back and find we've killed every man and boy in Plataea and sent all the women to Thebes and Persia as slaves?"

"What *can* they do?" Eurymakus replied, and looking up felt a single raindrop on his cheek. "We are their greatest allies in the war against Athens. I have no fear of the Spartans, Tykon, because I have the ear of King Artaxerxes of Persia. I am the one who gets the Spartans their Persian gold. Without me, they cannot build their precious fleet."

"I just can't see the Spartans taking to water."

"They will have to if they want to destroy the Athenians."

Eurymakus's hulking bodyguard came up the steps with a torch clutched in his giant hand.

"*Magus,* your horses and men are ready," said Bogha in Persian.

"Hold the city until I return," said Eurymakus to Tykon as he followed Bogha down the steps.

There was a flash of lightning over the Kithaeron Mountains, followed almost immediately by a great thunderclap that shook the city. It started to rain hard, soaking everyone to the skin in seconds. The pitch torches sizzled and guttered.

"You'll have to wait for this squall," Tykon shouted over the roar of the driving rain.

Eurymakus covered his head with his cloak and laughed. "Zeus will have to strike me down with a lightning bolt to keep me from Menesarkus," he declared, and thought smugly, "*My* god is far more powerful than the Storm Bringer."

TWENTY-THREE

———————◆———————

The deluge was brief, but more rain fell in that short amount of time than had fallen in the Oxlands for the entire year put together. The streets of Plataea had been turned to swift rivers. The marketplace and agora were ponds three inches deep.

Nikias sat on the floor of the smithy next to Leo and Hektor, arms crossed, hugging his knees to his chest. Leo's head drooped below his shoulders, his face hidden by his arms, but Nikias could tell he was crying because he sniffed every now and then, stifling his sobs. Hektor stared straight ahead with an expression of stupefied gloom, like a painted figure on a funeral jar, as if his spirit had already departed his body for the underworld.

He listened to the drizzling rain outside and the sound of water pouring down the gutters on the roof. Diokles was by the forge sharpening a long knife with a whetstone. He sang a tuneless Helot song in a soft voice, pausing now and then to cock his head toward the door and listen, then shrug and go back to his work. Nikias recognized a few of the strange Helot words—something about Zeus chasing Hera, his wife, angrily across the sky. The thunder was the god's shouts, the rain the tears of the goddess.

Chusor was at the front window, peering through a crack in the shutter. "I count twenty-three men in the market," he said in a distinct whisper.

Nikias wondered how long it would be before the Thebans broke down the door. Or tried to burn them out. He had to find a way to escape from the citadel and warn his grandfather, to raise the men in the countryside and the neighboring towns to come to the aid of Plataea. The longing to flee burned inside him; it felt like a red coal burning below his sternum. What a turn of fate to be trapped *inside* the city. He had spent his entire life thinking of the walls of Plataea as safety—that the farm was the place that was vulnerable to invasion. Perhaps the farm had already been overrun. His grandfather and Saeed murdered. The women and slaves chained and dragged back to Thebes. The thought made him queasy.

A low rumble of thunder in the distance, and then a Theban herald announced for the fifth time in the last hour: "Plataeans! Your city has been taken. If you leave your home you will be killed. Many have already died. Stay calm and you will live to see the dawn."

"The rosy fingers of dawn will be bloody," said Chusor, catching Nikias's gaze.

"You saved my life tonight," said Nikias without emotion. "And theirs," he added, nodding at Leo and Hektor.

"You might wish I had let you all die."

Nikias sucked the blood from a wound on his hand, leaned forward, and spat on the floor. The action made him wince. He'd torn a stomach muscle again fighting the Thebans in the street. His hand went involuntarily to his gut. To the same place where Kallisto's brothers had clubbed him. He thought of her—the way her face had looked the last time they'd made love in the Cave of Nymphs. All of that was so far away now. Maybe she was already dead. He thought of his father's cracked funeral urn . . . that terrible omen. Is this what it had meant?

"Curse the Thebans to Hades," he said through his teeth.

"How did Thebans get into city?" asked Diokles, screwing up his heavy features into a childlike frown.

"Someone betrayed Plataea," said Chusor. "Probably bribed the gatemen."

"Axe," said Nikias, thinking of the man who'd tried to kill him earlier in the evening. Could that thuggish oaf have stooped so low as to betray his own city? "I'll choke the life out of Axe if I catch him. . . ."

Chusor shrugged. "I don't think you are going to get that opportunity, my young friend." He paused and stroked his braided chin beard. "What made you come here tonight with your friends?" There was no anger in his question. Just curiosity.

"The Athenian said you were dangerous," said Nikias. "That you murdered a man. He said you were a spy working for the Spartans."

Chusor squinted at Nikias and cocked his head slightly. "What Athenian?"

"Calls himself Timarkos," said Nikias. "We found one of his own spies tortured nearly to death. I don't care what you did in Athens," he added.

"What did this Athenian look like?" asked Chusor intently.

"Skinny. Blue eyes. Beard like a goat."

"Pointed incisors," said Leo, looking up for the first time and wiping the tears from his face. "Like fangs."

Chusor crossed his big arms on his massive chest, said an oath in a foreign tongue under his breath. "My enemies have found me, it would seem. Timarkos is one of his names. And that Athenian is far more dangerous than I."

"Why do you have a map of the city?" asked Nikias.

"That's my business. I make maps wherever I go. It's none of your concern."

Nikias was not satisfied with this answer, but he did not press him.

"What will the Thebans do to us, Chusor?" asked Leo. "What will they do now?"

"They're going to kill the males," said Chusor. "And they'll send all the women away as slaves. At least, that's what the Syracusans always did when *we* captured an enemy citadel."

"You fought with the Syrakusans?" asked Leo.

Chusor shrugged. "Against my will, I helped them slaughter their neighbors."

"How did you make the fire that stuck to the men?" Nikias asked.

"It's something I've been experimenting with," replied Chusor. "I learned it from old Naxios in Syrakuse."

"Can you make more?"

Chusor glanced up at the ceiling as something scurried across the rooftop.

"Too big for rat," observed Diokles. "Thebans on roof now."

"I don't have the elements on hand," said Chusor to Nikias with a distracted air, his eyes riveted to the ceiling.

"There's got to be something in here we could use," said Leo.

"We can't wait around here forever," said Nikias bitterly. He looked at Chusor. "Give us armor and weapons and let us go out swinging."

"Eye gouges and biting allowed?" asked Chusor with derision. "I'm not ready to throw my life away just yet. I'll take my chances in here."

"You can walk out of here, Chusor," said Leo without rancor. "You and your man Diokles aren't citizens of Plataea. You're useful men. They won't kill you."

"Useful," spat Chusor. "I've been *useful* before. I don't fancy working for the Thebans for the rest of my days."

Nikias looked hard at Chusor. The smith dropped his head and turned away as if contemplating what Leo had said, weighing the possible outcomes of simply walking out the door and into the hands of the enemy.

"Yes," said Chusor in a distant voice. "I have something they would prize very highly indeed."

"Hey! Put that down," said Diokles, springing to his feet. All eyes turned to the stairs where a groggy boy stood, holding a sword in each hand, teeth bared. His wrists and hands were scraped bare and bleeding. His bright red hair was pulled up and tied in a topknot on his head, glowing like bronze in the torchlight.

"Hera's jugs, who's that?" asked Nikias.

"The Skythian boy," said Leo.

"How he get out of chains?" asked Diokles.

"I don't know," said Chusor. "I'd forgotten about him."

"You forgot . . . ?" Nikias shook his head in amazement and stepped back from the wild-looking child. "Who forgets they have a barbarian in their house?"

The Skythian made an uncannily realistic wolf sound, lunging at each man in turn, edging his way toward the front portal.

"He sounds hungry," said Hektor in a detached way, speaking for the first time since the attack.

"Hey, boy, don't go out that door!" said Nikias in a warning tone.

The Skythian spat, pointed at his rear end, and rattled off what sounded like a curse. He fumbled with the bar across the door, his eyes darting back and forth from man to man.

"Don't let him open that door," ordered Nikias.

"Get back!" yelled Chusor.

The instant the Skythian unbarred the door and opened it, three arrows flew into the smithy and clattered against the wall. The Skythian dropped his swords, slammed the door, and barred it in a heartbeat. He turned to the men and gave them what could only be interpreted as a tongue-lashing. When he was done he sat on the floor, crossed his arms on his chest, and started to cry.

At that moment a heap of black dust dropped from the smithy chimney over the forge, followed by two small legs protruding from the flue. A muffled voice screamed for help from inside the duct. Diokles grabbed the legs and pulled out a slender ten-year-old boy covered in soot and soaking wet.

"Mula!" exclaimed Nikias, staring in astonishment at the son of his grand-father's Persian slave.

TWENTY-FOUR

———◆———

"Hello, Young Master," said Mula with a big smile. The black soot made the whites of his eyes and teeth even brighter. "I told Big Master I could find you."

"What are you doing here?" asked Nikias, kneeling in front of Mula and taking him by the shoulders tenderly. For the first time in his life he was happy to see the tag-along pest.

"Big Master can't get out of bed," said Mula. "He ordered me to find you and bring you home. I was in the market when the bad people attacked . . ." He trailed off. The Skythian boy had come over and was looking him up and down with revulsion. The barbarian child pointed at Mula and said something sneering, followed by a harsh laugh. Without warning, Mula attacked him with his fists, cursing him in the same guttural language. Nikias grabbed Mula and pulled him back from the surprised Skythian.

"Mula, what are you doing?" demanded Nikias.

"That boy called me a bad thing," said Mula, kicking out.

"You understand him?" asked Chusor.

"Of course. He speaks Dog Tongue, a stupid kind of Persian that dumb Skythians use. He said I look like a pig's asshole when it's pooping things." Mula wiped the soot from his face.

"I doubt the translation does the insult justice," said Leo, smiling slightly, then moved to the shuttered window and peeked out.

"Mula's sire is my grandfather's Persian slave," explained Nikias to the smith.

"Ask him his name and where he is from," said Chusor.

Shouts outside made everyone turn toward the street.

"More Thebans have arrived," said Leo, one eye to a crack.

Chusor went to one of the wooden mannequins and unstrapped a leather carapace, held it up for Nikias. "Come, Nikias. You must wear armor. Diokles, help Leo and Hektor."

"What's this?" asked Nikias as Chusor slipped the shell over his head. "It's not armor."

"It's something new I invented," said Chusor as he buckled the straps.

Nikias was now encased, front and back, in molded ox hide. "There's no metal plate?" he asked dubiously.

"No," said Chusor. "It's made to be light. For fighting from horseback. Or fighting in the streets," he added, glancing at the door. He reached for a sword and pulled it from its scabbard.

Diokles fit one of the ox-hide carapaces onto Leo and the young wrestler ran his hands over the molded pectorals and rippled stomach muscles.

"These can't possibly do us any good," said Nikias. "Leather's no good against iron—"

Without warning Chusor struck Nikias across the chest with a killing blow from his sword. Nikias staggered from the force of the impact and fell into Leo's arms.

"Hey!" cried Leo. "Nik, are you all right?"

Nikias looked down at his chest in amazement, and saw the slightest indentation in the leather. He smiled at Chusor. "This will work."

Chusor sheathed the sword. "The leather is boiled in a concoction of my invention. It turns an arrowhead nearly as good as bronze. And *this* kind of armor is much cheaper to manufacture. All you need is the hide of an ox."

Mula cleared his throat for attention. He had been speaking quietly with the Skythian boy. "This boy's name is Kolax. He wants me to tell you all that his father is a 'big man' in Athens. His job is to shoot lazy men who refuse to pay their taxes."

"I've never heard of that job," said Chusor with a laugh. "His father must be one of the Skythian archers. Tell him they are the city's police."

"His father left Skythia when Kolax was very small," said Mula. "After his mother was 'laid under the green,' or whatever that means."

Kolax interrupted him with a tirade, pointing at his buttocks.

"He says his father will reward you with gold," continued Mula, "for saving him from the dirty slaver who raped him. And when he catches the slaver he is going to cut off his head, carve the brain from his skull, gild it, and use it to drink wine in his round tent."

"That a *good* revenge," said Diokles, buckling the shoulder straps on Leo's armor.

Chusor handed Nikias, Leo, and Hektor helms. They put them on and eyed each other with satisfaction. Kolax pointed at their armor and spoke.

"Kolax is wondering if those are 'Black Cloaks' out there," said Mula. "And he wants to know if you have some extra 'turtle shells' that will fit him."

"Who are Black Cloaks?" asked Leo.

Mula shrugged. "The enemy of his tribe."

"Tell him," said Nikias, "that we're trapped by *our* tribe's enemy. They will probably try to burn us out. We are going to kill as many of them as we can and make a break for the gates." He glanced at Chusor to see if this impromptu plan met his approval, and the smith nodded back.

"Yes," said Chusor. "That's our only chance."

"Never give up, I say," replied Diokles, clutching heavy war hammers in each hand. "Years ago some Helot people escape Sparta to Mount Ithome. So we can escape too."

"Mount Ithome?" asked Leo with a bitter laugh.

"So he doesn't know?" Nikias asked Chusor.

Chusor frowned and looked away.

"Why they laugh at Mount Ithome," asked Diokles, pointing a hammer at Leo and Nikias.

"That is something I've been meaning to tell you all these years," said Chusor, donning his own leather armor. "Those escaped Helots. Your people. You see . . . the Spartans sent an army to Mount Ithome. The Helots held out for two years. Very brave. But eventually the Spartans won. They killed all the men. Took the women back to Sparta."

"They skinned all the men alive," corrected Leo, causing Chusor to curse and hold up a hand for silence.

"And made their women watch," added Hektor, oblivious to Chusor's protest. "Everybody knows *that* story."

Diokles's chin sank to his chest. The tears came instantly. It looked as though his brain had turned to water and was now pouring from his eyes.

"This a *bad* story," he said quietly. "Very bad story."

"It gets worse," said Nikias.

"What you mean?" asked Diokles.

"The Thebans," said Nikias, his lips pulled back in a fearful grimace. "They are allies of the Spartans. The Spartans are probably on their way here right now. I've met their leader. A noseless warrior named—"

"Master Drako!" uttered Diokles. He blinked several times, squeezing his eyes shut, as though something were digging into the sockets, causing him excruciating pain.

Chusor blocked the front door, thinking Diokles was going to rush into the street. But his servant had no intention of leaving the house. He was in a blind panic, running from corner to corner like a rat trapped in a box with a viper. He picked up two forge hammers and attacked a wall as though he were hammering an entire Spartan phalanx to death.

"Never!" cried Diokles. "Never go back!"

Plaster, dust, and flying chunks of brick filled the air. Within seconds he'd broken a gaping hole through the thin wall that separated Chusor's interior wall from his neighbor's. Chusor grabbed Diokles from behind, wrapped his massive arms around the small man, and held him in a wrestler's embrace. Diokles struggled at first, but Chusor spoke calming words, as though comforting a child throwing a tantrum. Soon Diokles went limp, dropped the hammers.

Nikias, Leo, and Hektor went to the wall and peered through the dust. They could see the stonemason, Zeno, standing in the middle of his main room, holding a lamp in one hand and a short sword in the other, with his two children huddled around his legs, staring back with terror in their little eyes. Myron, still hiding in his friend's house, popped his head into the hole with a comical expression of amazement.

"What are you doing?" roared Zeno. "That's my wall!"

Chusor pulled off a clump of crumbling bricks, held it in his hand, and pondered the implications of what the Helot had done.

"Are all the walls between houses this thin?" asked Leo.

"Every house that's built with their backs to the city walls like ours," replied Zeno.

"There's at least a hundred homes that abut one another," said Chusor, "from here to the barracks and armory."

Nikias, Leo and Hektor exchanged smiles.

"How long can your man keep up the hammering?" asked Nikias.

"All day," said Chusor, a grin breaking on his face. "He was a quarryman in the in mines of Sparta."

"Got any more?" asked Leo.

"Helots?" asked Chusor.

"Hammers," replied Nikias.

As the men went to work destroying the wall in the next room, Nikias took Mula off to the side. "Mula. You know how to swim through the sluice gates, don't you?"

"Of course, Master. Every boy knows how to do it. You sneak through the alley between the theatron and the cavalry stables and you jump into the cistern and—"

"Once we get farther up the street, you'll sneak out the door," said Nikias. "Go to the sluices and get outside the city. You must get back to the farm and warn my grandfather. Tell him what has happened."

Mula nodded. "Will you come with me?" he asked hopefully. "I'm scared."

"I can't fit in the sluice gates," said Nikias. "I'm too big. Only little boys can do it."

"Your slave won't make it alone," said Chusor, who had been listening to the conversation. He glanced over at Kolax. The Skythian had two swords clutched in his hands, twirling them in a figure eight motion in front of his body so fast the blades had become blurs. "Take the Skythian boy with you, Mula. Once you both make it out of Plataea, put him on the road to Athens. Then tell him he's free."

TWENTY-FIVE

Kallisto clung to her brother's back as he ran across the fallow fields that separated their father's farm from Menesarkus's holdings. Every joint in her body ached, but she clung to Akake like a limpet stuck to a stone in the sea. She heard Akake's labored breathing; the big man was tired but he refused to slow down.

"Do they follow?" he asked.

Kallisto craned her neck and wiped her wet hair from her face. "No, Akake love. I see no torches."

Akake giggled. Even though he was scared out of his wits, he was having fun. "I'm the fox," he said. "You're my little rabbit. I stole you from the hunters."

She wrapped her legs around his waist tighter. "Thank you for saving me, Brother."

"Father was bad to hit you," replied Akake sourly. "Very bad." He stopped abruptly.

They had come to a prominent boundary marker, an ancient standing stone carved with words written in the language called Ox Turning. Years ago Nikias had pointed out to her how the script read from right to left, and then left to right, and so on, like an ox turning at the end of a furrow. Nobody knew what the words said anymore; the tongue had been lost to time. But Nikias had brazenly stated that Zeus had carved the words himself, proclaiming that this land had been given to the Nemean tribe for eternity.

"Where we go now, Sister?" asked Akake.

"To Menesarkus's farm."

"Menesarkus a bad man."

"No, he is a nice man."

"Not what Father say."

"Father is wrong."

Akake grunted and forged ahead, straight past the marker. After a while Kallisto could just make out the dark outline of Menesarkus's buildings up ahead. She wondered what Nikias would do when he saw her. She knew her face was swollen and one of her incisors was chipped. Would he think she was ugly now? Undesirable? She thought of how he'd looked at her at the Cave of Nymphs after her brothers had carried off Lysander. Had he been filled with pity then? Or loathing? Or both? Her kin had degraded her, and it seemed like the shame would never go away. If Nikias did spurn her now, where could she go?

They were a hundred paces from the house and she could see a figure standing in the doorway, holding an oil lamp, peering into the farmyard.

"Who's out there?" called a woman's voice. "Nikias, is that you?"

Suddenly Akake dropped her to the ground and lay on top of her. She tried to speak but his big hand covered her mouth.

"I smell horses on the wind," he hissed.

Several dogs started barking violently in an adjacent field, an arrow's shot away. A yelp as one of the animals went abruptly quiet, and then others were silenced. The unmistakable pounding of horse hooves followed these eerie sounds.

"Father has come for us," thought Kallisto. They would kill her this time.

Akake pulled her to her feet and took off running, dragging her along behind him.

"Run!" he screamed. "Run!"

Kallisto couldn't make her feet work. She tripped and fell to the ground. She saw the figure in the doorway of Menesarkus's home toss aside the lamp and slam the door shut. Akake picked her up, put her under one of his massive arms, and started running again. They were twenty paces from the door when a horseman charged up behind. She heard the sound of a blade cutting through the air and the rider charged past. Akake dropped her. A moment later his headless body fell down beside her.

It was as though Kallisto's body had been plunged into fire. She scrambled toward the door as fast as a cat before the rider who had killed Akake could wheel around and come back for her.

She pounded on the door, calling out, "It's Kallisto! Let me in!" But it did not open. She turned and crouched against the archway, trying to make herself small, staring into the dark. More riders were in the farmyard now. Black shapes darting back and forth. Dozens of them. One of them reined up and slid off his mount. He poked at Akake's corpse with his curved blade. Then he turned his gaze toward the house. He saw Kallisto and started forward.

A scraping sound behind her. The door opened. Hands dragged her inside. The door slammed shut and the bar was put back in place.

Kallisto stared at the terrified faces peering down at her in the torchlight: Saeed and Nikias's mother Agathe.

"I'm sorry," said Kallisto through chattering teeth. "My father—"

"Help me," said Saeed, grabbing a heavy chest. Agathe got the other end and they strained to drag it in front of the door.

"Now upstairs."

Saeed and Agathe helped Kallisto to her feet and dashed up the stairs to the master bedchamber. Menesarkus and Eudoxia were sitting up in bed, listening intently, ears cocked toward the window. Phile cowered at their feet. A human's death scream pierced the night. The Persian slave went to the shutters and peered out.

"What is my father doing?" asked Kallisto in shock.

"Those are *raiders* out there," said Saeed. "And they've found the dormitory."

There were twelve adult slaves and their four children living in that dormitory. Saeed moved around the corner room, shutting and locking the wooden shutters on both walls. Outside, a child screamed in terror and was quickly cut off.

"No, no, no!" chanted Eudoxia. "What is happening? Menesarkus? What is happening?"

"Zeus!" gasped Menesarkus. "We've got to help them."

Another strangled squeal came from the yard.

"The front door is bolted," said Saeed coldly. But tears of anguish poured from his eyes. "Can't save them now. We blockade the door with the oak chest. Now we all must go to the roof."

"Helladios's daughter, what are you doing here?" Menesarkus asked upon seeing Kallisto was in the room.

"Where is Nikias?" she asked forlornly, wiping her brother's blood from her face.

"We don't know," said Agathe.

"They're killing them!" said Phile, tearing at her hair. "They're killing them!"

"Who are they?" asked Eudoxia.

Everyone stared toward the shuttered windows with eyes unfocused, listening carefully for any sound. Something crashed into the front door with the force of a giant's fist. Phile shrieked.

"Dogs of Hades!" bellowed Menesarkus. He swung out of the bed, tried to stand, but his legs wouldn't support him and he collapsed. "Get me up!" he said.

A weird rush of energy flooded Kallisto's veins. It felt as though she'd taken the elixir of Artemis, the mushroom brew women drank on the night of the hunt. The mysterious drink that brought visions and a sense that one stood outside one's body, like a shade. She felt that way now. As if her spirit were hovering in the rafters. She bolted from the room. Down the dark hall. Flew down the stairs back to the first floor. Pressed her face against the door. Through the cracks she saw a yellow glow; men were out there holding pitch-resin torches that crackled and hissed as the rain struck the flames. The great door shook on its hinges— another violent blow from a battering ram.

"It won't budge," said a voice on the other side. "Use the axes." The ram made a *thunk ker-thunk* sound as it was tossed aside.

Kallisto's skin crawled with gooseflesh. Those were Thebans out there! She recognized their accents. Her stomach sank. The dreaded enemies were coming to kill them. They'd already butchered the slaves. This was not a dream. She had to do something.

An axe head struck the thick door and squeaked like an animal as it was pulled from the old, dry wood. She turned and started to run back upstairs, bumping into someone blocking her path. Saeed—staring at the door, teeth bared. Agathe, Eudoxia, and Phile stood behind him.

"I've got a spear between my legs that's ready to stab some meat," taunted one of the invaders through the door.

Without warning, Phile started screaming. Saeed clamped his hand over her mouth and hissed at her to be quiet. Outside, the invaders laughed lustily. Another axe joined in the hewing and the two went back to work with a frenzy, now that they knew for certain there was at least *one* woman inside.

"Weapons," said Saeed. "Follow me."

In the undercroft, Saeed handed the women bows and as many quivers as they could carry. He'd prepared these weapons that evening for their practice the next morning. The bows, which were kept in leather bags, had already been strung, the gut coated with beeswax. Each arrow had been checked from flight feathers to head. They hurried back to the main room, set the weapons on the floor.

"I want to cut a gash in one of Menesarkus's whores with my cock!" shouted another voice from beyond the door, just as an axe blade shattered a plank, sending splinters flying. Saeed stepped over to the portal, stood there with his sword drawn as though he would block the marauders' path single-handedly. Phile started weeping uncontrollably and Agathe wrapped her arms around her.

"No time for crying," said Saeed.

But Phile was hysterical. She dropped to her knees and gasped for breath.

"Saeed," said Kallisto. "You go to the roof with Phile and Agathe. Shoot at the raiders from above." When Saeed hesitated, she said, "Eudoxia and I are the fastest shots. We'll kill as many as we can, then join you."

Eudoxia said to the other women, "We do not let them take us. Save an arrow for yourselves. Stick it in your throat." It was the mode of suicide her father had taught her fifty years ago, when the Persians were on the verge of sweeping through their land. She held the point to her larynx. "Here. Right here."

Saeed led Phile and Agathe up the stairs. Another plank split apart. Eudoxia and Kallisto took up the stances they used when shooting at targets in the arena. They slipped arrows in notches, hands hovering over the gut strings like a duo of bards waiting to strum their harps. The top of the door broke apart completely, but the heavy hinges held.

"We're almost there," said one of the axe men.

"I hope you're wet," called out one of the invaders.

"We'll make 'em wet if they aren't," said another.

"I'm getting wet from this rain, so hurry up."

"Shut your bread holes and chop!"

The door was almost completely ruined. The only things holding the splintered pieces together were the heavy iron bands. The Thebans started kicking it, sending large chunks of wood flying into the room. Just then a thundering voice boomed out from the room above, cutting through the din. It was Menesarkus, singing an old war song:

"Stand firm, stand firm!
No shameful flight or fear!
Make your spirit valiant!
Love death and hate your foe!"

The song swelled the women's hearts.

"Aim for their eyes," said Kallisto.

Four men in black appeared through the wreckage of the door, forcing their way into the house, pushing aside the heavy chest that Saeed had used to blockade the door. One marauder held a torch out in front of him, thrusting it into the room to light his way. The last thing he saw in this world was the gleam of an old, gray-haired woman's eye and the flash of a young woman's white teeth as they let go of their bowstrings.

TWENTY-SIX

———◆———

Mula crept through the darkest pathways of Plataea, avoiding the main streets and the enemy. Nikias had told him what to do. He must go back to the farm as quickly as possible and warn the others that the Thebans had taken the city. Menesarkus would know how to save them.

The boy had set out with Kolax, the Skythian, on this exciting adventure. So far they had not seen any Thebans. Mula was certain his master, Menesarkus, and his father would heap praise upon him for bringing them this important message. The lovely Phile would probably cover him with kisses! The notion thrilled him. Maybe the master would give him his own pony. He had no idea how he was going to make it back to the farm quickly, though, as Nikias had ordered.

"I'm thirsty," whispered Kolax as Mula ducked through a tiny space between two buildings. "I wish we had some wine."

"We'll get some when we get to the farm," replied Mula.

"I hear they drink it watered down here," said Kolax. "Like the stuff our mamas give to babies. What is the name of this country again?"

"The Oxlands," replied Mula. "It means land of the oxen."

"Why?"

"Because of all the oxen, I suppose."

"That is a stupid name. My country has many sheep, but we would never call it Sheepland. 'Skythia' means land of the Skythians. A proper name for a place."

"How did you become a slave?" asked Mula.

"I'm not a slave," replied Kolax.

"But the Egyptian bought you," said Mula.

"King Astyanax died," explained Kolax. "His bastard son seized the throne. Twenty other boys whose fathers were enemies of the bastard king were sacrificed, but my uncle helped me escape. He was murdered by Black Cloaks while we fled across the grasslands. I was captured and sold to the slavers. And when my father finds out what happened to me, he is going to go on a killing spree. We will cut off the skulls of our enemies and—"

Mula came to an abrupt stop and Kolax stopped speaking. They saw two men bearing torches—men dressed all in black. They had a Plataean captive with a rope wrapped around his neck.

"By Priapus's towering cock," hissed Kolax. "Those are Black Cloaks."

"Thebans," corrected Mula.

"Black Cloaks eat their prisoners," said Kolax. "You should have told me these were Black Cloaks."

"Thebans," replied Mula. "Not—"

Mula recognized the man with the rope around his neck. He was a famous sprinter named Heraklitus who taught at the gymnasium. If the enemy could catch the fastest man in Plataea, he thought, then how could he and Kolax possibly get away?

Heraklitus saw the alley and decided to make a break for it. He jerked back his upper body, pulling the warrior holding the rope off his feet. The Theban, caught off guard, let go of the rope, allowing Heraklitus to dash in the direction of the narrow passageway. But it was difficult for him to run with his hands bound behind his back. He was too slow.

An arrow whistled from the Theban archer's bow. Heraklitus arched his spine and fell face-first two strides from Mula and Kolax. The Skythian yanked Mula a few steps back and shoved him behind a barrel, covering him with his body.

The Theban who'd shot the arrow dropped his bow, drew a dagger, and leapt on top of the fallen Plataean, grabbing his hair, pulling back his head, and slitting his throat. Dark blood sprayed the rain-slick stones.

The Theban who had lost hold of the rope ran up to the corpse. He peered into the darkness where Mula and Kolax hid, waving the torch in their direction. "Did you hear something in there?" he asked the other. "In that passageway?" He took a step forward, unsheathed his sword.

Mula felt something warm splashing on his thigh. He realized, with humiliation, that he was pissing himself. The Theban poked his sword above the boys' heads. Kolax did a perfect imitation of a frightened cat—a hiss followed by a prolonged meow.

"Just a cat," said the other invader, cleaning off his knife on the corpse's clothes. "Next time, keep a better hold of the rope."

The one with the sword shrugged, sheathed his weapon. Then they went back the way they had come and soon their torches were enveloped by the blackness.

Kolax laughed in a friendly way and ruffled Mula's hair. "Don't be so afraid," he said. "The Black Cloaks kill you *before* they eat you." He squeezed past Mula and into the courtyard.

"Where are you going?" asked Mula frantically.

Kolax was on his hands and knees searching for something in the darkness. After a while he stood up and ran back. He smiled and held out a long, curved, and slender object. "My papa," he said, "would take the skin off my back if I left a bow behind like that sheep raper just did." He held up the bow the Theban had dropped in his haste to knife the escaped prisoner. Then he went to the corpse of Heraklitus and slowly worked the arrow from the wound. He managed to pull it out with the bronze head intact. "And now we have an arrow," he said proudly.

TWENTY-SEVEN

The sound of the water clock draining into its measuring bowl made Tykon the Theban nervous. It echoed in the temple, a steady stream, like a child endlessly urinating into a pot. It seemed to mock him like the rain outside, which had ceased falling torrentially but still drizzled. The streets, in the places where they were unpaved, were thick with mud.

"If the messengers had been able to gallop all the way home along the Kadmean Road in daylight," he pondered aloud to his assistant, "they would have arrived half an hour ago. But at night, picking their way cross-country, slipping on the muddy ground in the pitch-blackness, it would probably take them at least an hour."

"The Kadmean Road must be a foot deep with mud," said his assistant. "The mud on that old road sucks the sandals right off your feet."

"If I were General Straton," said Tykon, naming the man in charge of the reinforcements, "I'd hold off on sending them until daylight. They'll be too vulnerable to attack from the Plataean cavalry stationed at the border towers." Eurymakus's plan had been simple: sneak across the countryside with a small occupation force; take control of the gates and walls, thanks to the treachery of Nauklydes; and then terrorize the citizens until a force of fifteen hundred hoplites could march down the Kadmean Road—under the noses of the watchtowers—and head straight into the citadel. But Eurymakus had not planned on this rain. Or the fact that the moon was hidden by clouds.

Rain and the water clock. The only sounds. He looked around the Temple of Athena, the sacred space he had turned into his command center. There were Theban shields, captured in battles over the years, anchored to the walls as trophies, offerings to the gods. He would make certain these were removed and taken home with honor. One of those shields might belong to his dead grandfather who had been killed by Plataeans fifty years ago at the siege of Thebes, after the Persian invaders had been wiped out and the Greeks had taken revenge on the Thebans, punishing them for allying themselves with the invaders.

He needed fresh air and stepped outside. His two runners and bodyguard fell in behind. It felt good to walk, to be moving and not sitting on his arse. As he approached the gates, one of the doors opened and a rider entered. "The cavalry is already here," he thought for a split second. Then he realized his mind was playing tricks on him. There was no way they could have arrived from Thebes so fast. The rider saw him, rode over, and stayed on his mount. Tykon knew him; it was one of Eurymakus's raiders.

"Eurymakus asks for ten more men," said the man, who was covered in mud from his sandals to the crown of his head.

"Ten?" asked Tykon. "So he hasn't caught the Bull yet?"

"The Bull is in the pen," joked the rider. He looked around. "Things seem quiet here."

"The enemy is afraid, for now," Tykon replied. "I'm worried about the rain, though."

The other laughed. "Our men would plow through six feet of mud to get here, knowing we hold the city."

"Yes," said Tykon without enthusiasm. The rain was making him depressed. The thought of losing even ten men made him feel vulnerable. He put himself in the place of the Plataeans. Imagined what he would be planning right now, locked up inside his home, waiting for death and the destruction of his family. He would make a break for it. He heard laughter from one of the watchtowers and a rattling sound. He realized, with ire, that some of his men were up there rolling knucklebones, the idiots. "Take the men in the tower," he told the rider.

The rider got off his mount and headed inside the building to get his new raiders.

The fact of the matter, Tykon told himself, was that the only important piece of property in the entire city was the gates. Whoever controlled the Gates of Pausanius ruled Plataea. He stared at the hundreds of carts and wagons that had been collected from all over the city. These would be used tomorrow to haul away the spoils of war: women and children, armor, utensils, and silver from the treasury.

"I want these wagons and carts put in a semicircle," said Tykon. "From one gate tower to the other. Add any timbers you can find."

His men got to work immediately. Any Plataeans who tried to get to the gates would have to climb up and over a precarious jumble of wood, exposing themselves to arrows from the walls and towers, with Tykon's spearmen waiting to skewer them if they were lucky enough to make it the fifteen feet across. He reckoned he could hold off several thousand attackers—his own little Thermopylae.

"I'm going to make an inspection," said Tykon, and started walking. Six men fell in behind him. He headed straight for the Old Market. When he got to

Chusor's smithy, he found a dozen archers guarding the building, waiting anxiously for something to happen. Waiting made a soldier feel useless and helpless. Tykon would much rather be fighting. At least then he was in control of his fate.

Darius, one of Tykon's best warriors, approached him. "Why don't we just chop down the door, General? Or burn them out?"

"We want Chusor alive," said Tykon. "He's a valuable asset. Eurymakus marked him as such months ago. The rumor is he knows the secret to liquid fire."

"His attack tonight proved that rumor true," said Darius, and showed his arm where the skin had been severely burned. "At least, in my opinion."

"If that had been liquid fire," said Tykon, "you'd be nothing more than a pile of smoldering bones. That stuff is so powerful it can sink a trireme. Once, in Syrakuse, I saw—"

There was a great flash of lightning and a boom of thunder rocked the world. For a split second Tykon thought Chusor had unleashed some new weapon. Then the rain came pouring down again like a waterfall. "Only Zeus can shake the skies, you fool," he told himself.

Tykon sought protection under the overhang of a building across the street from the smithy. He watched as the street turned once again to a river mud. Water poured off the buildings like cataracts in the spring after the mountain snow melts. The sky lit up from a lightning flash and it was followed closely by another peal of thunder. He shouted at the men to seek shelter with him. It was no good standing in this cloudburst, waiting for Zeus to strike someone down with a bolt.

More waiting.

The torrent was shorter this time. Tykon had a sickening feeling in his gut that traveled all the way up to the bottom of his esophagus. The road to Thebes would be impossible to march on now. The Asopus would surely overflow its banks. They would have to wait even longer for the reinforcements. The hoplites might not arrive until late in the day tomorrow. He glanced down and saw his torch-lit reflection in one of the puddles. His mother had always told him never to look at his own face reflected in a pond. The water nymphs would pull him in and drown him. He didn't believe that anymore, but he still thought it was bad luck. He kicked the puddle, scattering the image.

"You say you've heard nothing all this time?" Tykon asked Darius.

Darius shrugged. "Nothing. There was some hammering about an hour ago. Then it stopped."

"Give me a rock," said Tykon.

"Excuse me?" asked Darius.

"A rock to throw," said Tykon impatiently.

His men searched the ground for a rock. One of them found a stone the size of a coin and handed it to him. Tykon slapped his hand aside, bent down, and prized loose a cobble from the street.

"This will do," he said under his breath. He walked toward the smithy and hurled the cobble at the door. It made a loud crack when it struck the wood.

Nothing happened. "They're gone," said Tykon.

Darius was confused. "I don't understand. How could they—"

"They're not there!" shouted Tykon. He ran to the door, pounded it with his fist, pressed his ear to the door, and listened. Nothing. Not a sound from within. "Bring me an axe!" he ordered.

After destroying one of the shutters with the axe, he crawled through the window and disappeared into the dark smithy. "Give me some light," he demanded.

Darius passed him a torch and Tykon made his way carefully through the dark and cluttered workroom. He saw a warrior's helmeted head; he swung the torch violently and knocked the enemy to the floor. The head flew across the room. Tykon went to it, pushed the thing with his foot. It was made of wood—a dummy used to size the helms. He heard footsteps behind him. He whirled and lunged with the torch.

"It's only me!" said Darius.

Tykon realized his heart was hammering in his chest. He cursed under his breath. He hated when his body reacted in fear. It made him feel weak.

"Drop me down a well," uttered Darius. "Look!"

Tykon's stomach lurched. Darius's outstretched torch illuminated a door-size hole that had been smashed through the wall between the smithy and the house next door. Tykon and Darius stepped through the improvised exit.

Darius ran across the room to the opposite wall. "There's a hole in this wall too!"

They passed into the third house. Another empty room and another hole in the wall and into the next . . .

"They've burrowed through their homes like rats," said Darius. His voice expressed a combination of dread mingled with admiration.

TWENTY-EIGHT

The barracks wall shook as though from an earthquake. Along the middle of the wall the plaster started to crack and flake off to reveal the bricks beneath. These bricks soon flew out like teeth knocked from the mouth of a pankrator. Within minutes the hammers had turned the wall to rubble and it collapsed inward, scattering debris and a plume of dust. Nikias and Chusor were the first to leap into the chamber, swords drawn, torches held out in front of them. Diokles, Leo, Hektor, Zeno, and Myron followed them closely. But there was no enemy in sight.

They had smashed through the walls of nearly fifty homes to get here. Along the way they had collected as many men. Their makeshift army was made up of craftsmen and the aged, slaves and teenage boys. Alone in their houses they had felt like caged animals. Together they were ready to face any foe.

"What's this on the floor?" asked Myron, tripping over something soft.

The men gathered around, holding their torches down by their feet so they could see. The floor was littered with the bodies of men—men whose hands were bound and whose throats had all been slit.

"The city guards," said Zeno, recognizing several faces. "And the archers manning the walls."

"At least sixty bodies here," said Chusor.

Hektor started turning over corpses, looking at their faces. "My father was on the wall tonight," he announced with dread.

"I don't see any torches in the streets," said Nikias, peering out one of the windows. "The Thebans must have abandoned this part of the city."

"Nobody needs to guard the dead," said Myron, nodding at the corpses.

"The Thebans haven't touched the weapons cache," Leo called out from an anteroom. The men who carried nothing more than hammers or butcher knives were given swords. "Where's the enemy? Where are they hiding? Have they left?" he added hopefully.

"They have not left," said Chusor. "They don't need to guard the wineskin when they've got their hand on the stopper."

"What are you talking about?" asked Leo.

"He means they must be guarding the gates to the citadel," said Nikias. "No one can escape over the walls. They're too high. So if you control the gates, you control the way in and the way out of Plataea."

"What do we do now?" asked an old man. His feeble arm was shaking from holding up his torch, and he strained to keep it aloft. All eyes turned to Chusor and Nikias.

"I say we storm the gates," said Nikias.

"Foolish idea," said Chusor. "We'll be slaughtered."

"Well, what else are we supposed to do?" asked Nikias. "We might catch them by surprise."

"Let's think this through," said Chusor. "We need to send out scouts. It will do no good to run about like headless chickens."

"What we need is more men," said Nikias, feeling a sudden anger toward Chusor—an exasperation at his desire to ruminate on the best method for plunging headfirst into a raging river. There was only one thing to do: jump straight in. "I say we start pounding on doors. Raise the city."

"Nikias is right," said Zeno. "What can fifty of us do?"

"My uncle, General Alexios, lives two blocks away," said Nikias, "on Lion Street. I'm going to start with him." If any man knew what to do in a time like this, he thought, it would be Alexios.

Before anyone could argue with him, Nikias opened the door and ran outside with Chusor calling after him, "Watch your back, boy!" The rain was starting to let up but there was about an inch of water underfoot. The streets were eerily deserted. Nikias felt as though he were walking through a gigantic cemetery. He turned a corner onto Lion Street and saw torches in the distance.

"There you are," he said under his breath, hiding his torch behind the wall.

There were four or five Thebans milling about, marching up and down the street, banging on doors. "Do not leave your homes!" they shouted. "You will be killed!"

Nikias waited for a while until the enemy moved down the lane, then dashed across to his uncle's house and knocked softly on the door, speaking in a whisper, "Uncle! It's Nik! Open up." When nobody replied, he pushed on the door. It was unlocked and creaked on its hinges. He felt a sagging sensation in his stomach. He pulled his long dagger from its sheath—much better for fighting at close quarters—and held the torch out. He entered the main room and thrust the flame in first. There was nobody in the room. He turned and moved into the chamber across the hall. Here the furniture was overturned and there was a broken vase on the floor. As he started up the stairs a black shape raced past and he struck out with his torch, only to hear a cat cry out in fright. When he got to the second floor, he pushed open the bedchamber door with the point of his knife and stepped inside.

He swayed . . . felt the air escape from his lips. . . . The room swam as though he were drunk. There was a headless body on the bed—Alexios. He forced himself to enter the next room; he found his uncle's pregnant wife . . . saw her mangled corpse cradling their three-year-old child's dead body.

Somehow Nikias found his way back to the street. He blindly turned a corner and ran straight into someone. For a split second he thought Leo had followed him. "Idiot—" he started to say as they each backed up. He thrust his torch in the other's face and saw a young Theban warrior dressed all in black. The enemy sprang at him, short axe clutched in hand, and chopped at Nikias's chest. The sharp edge of the blade stuck in the boiled leather carapace. Nikias smashed him on the side of the head with the torch and fell on top of him, pummeling his face with his fists.

The Theban was strong and fought to be free. He grabbed Nikias's throat and squeezed. Choking, Nikias clawed at his enemy's face, dug his thumb into the young man's eye—pushed hard until his thumb was in his brain—and scooped the eyeball out, ripping it from the socket. The Theban squirmed free and scrambled away, running like a madman, screaming at the top of his lungs for his companions down the street.

Nikias grabbed his torch and sprinted down a dark alley and out the other side. He came to an archway that led into a private courtyard; it was the entrance to Magistrate Nauklydes's home. He flung his torch away and hid in the shadows just as a gang of Thebans ran past. After their angry voices had faded down the street, Nikias entered the front doorway. The moment he set foot inside, he heard tortured cries emanating from the undercroft. He walked slowly down the stone stairs, heart racing, easing his sword slowly from its scabbard. He'd played down here with Demetrios hundreds of times when they were children. He could have found his way even in the dark.

The large underground chamber was illuminated by the glow of several torches. He could see the headless body of a naked girl sprawled in the corner. Nauklydes lay on his back next to her, hands and ankles tied together, eyes screwed shut but still breathing. On the opposite side of the room two Thebans were raping a woman at the same time. He could not see her face. A third enemy warrior sat on an amphora, holding up a ring to admire it in the torchlight. As Nikias went past Nauklydes, the magistrate opened his eyes. Nikias made a sign for him to be quiet and he nodded vigorously.

Nikias had no plan. He acted on instinct. He stepped forward and swung his sword at the rapist closest to him. He'd meant to take off the enemy's head but his foot slipped on the blood-splattered floor and his sword sliced off the top of the man's cranium. The Theban stood bolt upright and touched his exposed brains, staring at Nikias in surprise.

"Hey!" said the other rapist with an angry scowl. He stupidly kept thrusting into the woman's mouth, giving Nikias time to roll across the floor and cut off all of the man's toes on both feet. The Theban pitched forward on top of the woman with an enraged howl. The third man came at Nikias with a short thrusting sword, hacking across his back, but the enemy's weapon merely bounced off the leather armor. Nikias kicked the Theban's feet out from under him and stuck his sword through his thigh, then leapt up and drove his fist into the man's mouth. He wrenched the sword from the Theban's leg and stabbed him through the heart. The Theban's knees buckled and he sagged backward.

Nikias turned around and saw the man with the missing toes on hands and knees, moving toward a sword. As he reached out for it, Nikias hacked off his hand, then put a foot on the man's back, pinning him in place and lopping off his head.

Nikias moved slowly toward the Theban with the exposed brain. The man was crawling on the floor now, searching for something. He found the top of his own skull and held it up by the hair, staring at it with a bewildered expression. Nikias brought his sword down with a violent chopping motion.

Nikias was breathing as though he had run up the side of the mountain. He wiped the blood from his face. Saw the naked woman cowering in the corner of the room. She was covering her face with her hands, shaking silently.

"Don't cry, don't cry," said Nikias, and held her in his arms. He pulled her hands away from her face. She stared at nothing, her mouth twisted in a weird, constricted smile, as though someone had sliced away her lips. Her face was swollen from the blows of many fists, but he recognized her as one of the magistrate's house slaves. She pushed him away, slapped at his face, and tried to crawl farther into the corner, like a terrified animal.

Nikias staggered over to Nauklydes, cut his bonds, and pulled the rag from his mouth. The magistrate could not speak. His jaw sagged open and he stared at Nikias with a rigid face like a theatrical mask. Nauklydes raised a bloody and mutilated hand, and pointed at the girl's corpse next to him. He crawled to it. The head lay underneath the body, wrapped up in its arms, as if the dead girl had tried to protect it from further degradation. Nauklydes hugged the head against his chest and Nikias saw the once beautiful face of his daughter Penelope frozen in a silent and eternal scream.

"Ahhhh," gasped Nauklydes as sobs were ripped from his chest.

Nikias ran from the chamber—ran blindly up the stairs and into the courtyard that was now filled with torches. He stumbled forward, realized he had left his sword below, and started swinging with his fists.

"Hey!" said Leo.

"Stop!" said Hektor. "It's us."

"What are you doing here?" asked Nikias, wiping the blood from his face.

"Chusor caught a Theban," said Leo. "Brought him back to the barracks. We made him talk."

Nikias grunted. "Where's Chusor now?"

"Still at the barracks, I think," said Leo. "Listen, Nik. It was all a ruse. There were only four hundred Thebans who entered the citadel. And Chusor was right: they're all guarding the gates."

"A trick?" asked Nikias, dumbfounded. "They tricked us?"

"Chusor thinks they were an advance force," said Leo. "They're waiting for reinforcements from Thebes. But the rain must have turned the Kadmean Road to mud and delayed them."

"I found my father in the barracks," said Hektor, seething. "And now I'm going to take some of *their* blood. We've raised the city. We're going to attack the barricade they've put up in front of the gates."

"Come on," said Leo grabbing Nikias by the sleeve, leading him into the street, now teeming with Plataeans.

TWENTY-NINE

———— ◆ ————

Kolax was fearless in the face of many things. He'd broken wild horses, fought bigger boys with his fists, and caught deadly grass vipers to milk the poison from their fangs. But he was deathly afraid of water. Mula had led him through the labyrinth of streets to a massive cistern. Then he'd jumped in and was now treading water, waiting for Kolax to come in. But Kolax couldn't make himself put his legs over the edge and drop the five feet to the water. He held the torch above the dark opening, saw Mula waving his hand impatiently.

"What are you waiting for?" asked Mula. "Hurry, this is the way out."

"Isn't there another way?" asked Kolax.

Mula cursed. "No, this is the only one."

Kolax put the bow on his back, looping the gut strings around his shoulder. He set the torch in a notch in the stone to free his hands. He made to swing his leg over, but it wouldn't move.

Mula splashed the water angrily. "At least I pissed myself for a good reason. Water can't slit your throat."

Kolax gritted his teeth. "Can't do it," he said. "I'll fight my way out of the city."

"Mama's boy," said Mula.

Kolax's upper lip curled back. "You'll pay for that insult, pig's asshole."

Mula made a baby sound and pretended he was sucking on a nipple.

Before Kolax knew what had happened, he was in the water, swimming toward Mula with murder in his heart, his precious arrow clamped in his teeth.

"Finally," shouted Mula, and dove out of sight.

Mula was gone. Kolax froze, started to sink. He took in a big mouthful that made him choke.

Mula popped up beside him. "I found the opening," he said. "Take a deep breath and follow me. You just have to go under the wall here. It's easy."

Kolax stared back, wild-eyed.

"Take a deep breath," Mula repeated, and inhaled deeply, holding his breath, puffing out his cheeks. Kolax obeyed. Mula dove down, pulling Kolax by his hand.

Kolax descended. For a moment his bow tip caught on the stone arch and he thrashed about, screaming in his throat. But Mula yanked on his arm and guided him through the underwater passage. Kolax rose to the surface and gasped for air. He could tell they were in a tiny chamber because of the way their breathing sounded. It echoed off the walls. Mula, still clutching his hand, guided him down a long tunnel. The top of the tunnel was just high enough for the boys to walk at a crouch. The water only came to their knees. Up ahead, Kolax saw the shapes of trees. He felt a wind blowing against his face. They came to a metal grate that Mula pushed aside and squeezed through. They were outside the northern walls. It was still raining hard, but the storm clouds had started to break apart and there was a glow behind the mountains. The moon would rise soon.

"You are a clever, clever boy," said Kolax with admiration.

"Now I need to find a horse," said Mula. He pointed toward the mountains. "The road to Athens is over there."

"Athens?" asked Kolax. "Really?"

"Yes," said Mula. "I'm supposed to set you free now. The Egyptian said so. You can go."

"How many days to walk to Athens?" asked Kolax.

"Four days," said Mula. "Two on a fast horse."

Kolax saw the sad look on the skinny boy's face and said, "I'll go tomorrow. I'm having too much fun now."

They heard the sound of hoofbeats and hid behind a towering plane tree. Kolax gripped his bow and nocked the arrow. Two riders came from the direction of the gates and stopped at the crossroads. They raised their hands in salute, then one took off through a field while the other headed north on the Kadmean Road, straight at them.

"Thebans," said Mula under his breath.

"Black Cloaks," said Kolax.

"You know how to use that?" asked Mula, nodding at the bow.

"You'll see," replied Kolax. "This Black Cloak will chew grass soon."

"Because we've only got one arrow," said Mula.

"Just shut up," said Kolax. "You'll see."

Kolax crept closer to the road, crouched down. He wished he'd had a chance to test the bow, to get a feel for it. Beggars can't pick their portions, though, as his father always said.

As the rider charged past, Kolax leapt from his hiding place, paused for a split second to aim, then let the arrow sing.

But the rider kept going. Mula stomped over to Kolax.

"You missed," he said petulantly.

"I'm going to get my arrow where it fell," said Kolax coldly, and marched down the road. Mula followed. After a few minutes they came upon a crumpled shape. They bent down and touched it. It was a body with an arrow sticking out of its back. Kolax pushed the body over. The arrow had penetrated straight through to the other side, right through the heart.

"You killed him," said Mula in awe.

"He was a good rider," said Kolax, pleased at the reverence in Mula's voice. "He was such a good rider, he stayed on for a while even after I killed him."

The Skythian pushed the arrow through and out the front of the body so the arrowhead would not get pulled off. Then he searched the corpse. He found a leather pouch, which he placed around Mula's neck. There was a sword—he belted this around his own waist—and a dagger, which he handed to Mula. The rider also had a bow but that had broken in his fall. The quiver was full of arrows, however, and in perfect condition. It was just like a Skythian arrow case, with a closable lid. He shook the contents and they made a loud rattle.

"When Skythian warriors want to scare the crap out of the enemy," explained Kolax, "they shake their quivers at the same time. I've heard five thousand men make the 'arrow song,' and it's a noise that would make the bravest warrior want to run home to his sheep." Kolax considered taking the top of the dead man's cranium for a prize, but he reckoned he would save that pleasure for the one who deserved it—the slaver who'd raped him.

"His horse," said Mula, pointing.

The horse, realizing it had lost its rider, had wandered back. It sniffed the body, pushed it with his nose. There was a small fight about who would take the reins and who would ride behind, but Mula won this argument. He knew the way to the farm, which Kolax did not. It was humiliating for Kolax, a horseman born and bred from the plains of Skythia, to ride clutching a Hellene like a tiny child. But he relented. He had a full quiver of arrows and that made him happy. And he'd got his first enemy kill—a Black Cloak. This had been a good night so far, despite the swim.

THIRTY

———◆———

Menesarkus was propped up in a chair in his chamber so he could peer out the small window and try to see what was going on in the farmyard. Eudoxia knelt by his side while Agathe sat on the bed with Phile, who was sobbing inconsolably. He opened the shutter a crack, saw men moving by the shed where the pine pitch was kept—pitch they used to seal the wine jars. They'd been making lots of noise, pulling off doors and moving supplies. Were they stealing from him?

"Maybe they'll leave once they're done looting," he said. He'd never felt so useless and feeble. The sensation was staggering.

An arrow flew from the roof and struck one of the men in the leg.

"Good shot," Menesarkus said. Kallisto and Saeed were still up there, doing their best to keep the raiders at bay.

He was proud of the women. Surprised too. How did they have the courage to stand up to those men, smashing through the door? He'd heard everything. The axes striking the wood. The men taunting the women with their foul talk of rape. He'd known brave men who'd lost their minds waiting for a battle to start. Men who would have run away if they hadn't been so tightly packed together in the phalanx that there was no way out. That is why he'd sung the battle song for them.

And his women had responded by slaughtering at least eight of the invaders. They'd forced the enemy to back away from the door, giving the women enough time to flee upstairs, where they'd barred the heavy door to the second floor.

A sound in the room below made everyone jump. Saeed put his ear to the floorboards and peered through a crack to the ground floor.

"Somebody's down there," he said softly.

"Menesarkus?" asked a man's voice. The stranger's tone was incongruously congenial. "Are you up there?"

Menesarkus looked at Eudoxia and Agathe. "Who is that?" he asked, but they shook their heads.

"What should I call you?" asked the voice. "Hero of the Persian Wars? Winner of the Funeral Games of Lysander? General of Plataea? Or perhaps I should refer to you as Olympic champion. Menesarkus, can you hear me?"

Menesarkus felt goose bumps on his neck and arms. The stranger spoke with a Theban accent. Never had enemy Thebans set foot on his family's land, let alone inside his house. "Who are you?" asked Menesarkus with a harsh croak.

"I want to discuss the terms of your surrender," said the invader. His voice was mellifluous, honeyed.

The old fighter laughed grimly. "Who in Hades are you, skulking around my dining room in the night like a thief?"

"My name is Eurymakus and I am from Thebes. And I bring you news. Your city is taken. You have no hope of rescue."

"Liar," Menesarkus shot back. "Impossible."

"It was treachery," replied Eurymakus. "The guards at the gate were paid off."

"By whom? You?" mocked Menesarkus. "No Plataean would take your Theban coins. They're all clipped round the edges!"

"Menesarkus," said Eurymakus. "I will give safe passage to your family. It is only you that I want."

"Safe passage? Like you gave to my slaves?"

"If you have that much concern for your slaves, then what of your kin?"

"How dare you attack me in this cowardly way! And murder my defenseless slaves. You have no honor! It's against the rules of war. If you have a personal vendetta against me, let us meet on the field of battle or in the pankration arena."

"I am your born enemy," replied the Theban calmly, "as you are mine. But you sowed the seed for my vendetta. First at the Siege of Sardis, where the rules of war were shat upon. And then at Olympia, where another rule was broken. Can't you guess by now who I am? Are you that thickheaded?"

Menesarkus's mouth felt dry. An image flashed before his eyes: the Hippodrome of Olympia . . . a young, handsome Theban lad grabbing the legs of his dead brother, screaming, *You murdered him!*

"Damos the Theban," he finally muttered.

"What was that?" asked Eurymakus. "I could not hear you."

"You're the brother of Damos," replied Menesarkus, louder. "The pankrator I . . ." He paused and shook his head, dropped his chin to his chest. "The pankrator I *defeated* in the Hippodrome."

Silence. At last Eurymakus said, "You and I will settle everything when we are face-to-face. And now I will leave your house. I have tarried too long."

Menesarkus heard a noise in the yard. He opened the shutter and saw some Thebans pushing a farm cart toward the house. The enemy had covered it with skins to protect the contents from the rain. Saeed and Kallisto shot at the men pushing the cart, but the Thebans held the shutters and doors from the outbuildings as shields to protect themselves. They placed the cart at the mouth of the door and left it there before fleeing back to the shadows.

The outer buildings started going up in flames—the barn, the sheds, the storage rooms. They were fed by tree sap and oil that burned despite the rains that had soaked everything. A Theban placed a torch to the ground and a ring of pitch fire erupted around the house. There would be no way for the women to escape now. No cover of darkness.

"The cart is filled with pitch pots and straw," shouted Eurymakus above the roar of the burning buildings. The Theban stood beyond the ring of fire. "We will set it alight unless you come out. We will cook you like meat on a sacrificial fire."

"Zeus watches you!" Menesarkus was shaking with wrath. He wanted to strap on his armor, stride into the throng of enemy, and die fighting like a man. But he could barely move his legs. The muscles in his lower back had gone into uncontrollable spasms. Every breath was a struggle.

"Zeus," replied Eurymakus, "does not exist. I am a believer in the one true God. The seer Zoroaster brought the teachings of Ahura Mazda to this earth. Listen, Menesarkus"—his voice quaked with feeling—"my duty as a disciple of the path of righteousness is to root out demons from the world and slay them. My brother knew that you were a force of evil, but he failed in his pursuit to send your soul into oblivion. I will attain glory in God's eyes, not only by taking vengeance upon you, but also by exterminating your entire city. Give up. You no longer exist. Your line is ended. The bastions of Plataea will crumble by my hand. I am your angel of death."

"He's insane," whispered Agathe.

"A madman," said Eudoxia.

"I will give you a little while to ponder your fate," said Eurymakus.

Menesarkus tried to stand. The pain in his back was mind shattering and he collapsed on the floor. Eudoxia and Agathe were quickly by his side, helping him back to the chair.

"You must try to escape," he said to the women.

"We won't leave you," said Eudoxia.

"But you heard what the Theban said. They're going to burn down the house."

"I will never leave my husband's side."

Eurymakus called out again, "What is your answer, Plataean?"

Menesarkus's eyes filled with tears. His jaw went slack. His vanquished expression scared them more than the Thebans. They saw their deaths written in his eyes.

"Maybe Nikias ran away to Athens," he said softly. "Maybe he's safe."

Agathe turned away.

"Nik will fight them," said Eudoxia. "No matter where he is."

"You must run," said Menesarkus in a strained voice. "To the mountains. To the caves."

Agathe stroked Menesarkus's cheek. "Father," she said. "There are too many of them. They will hunt us. . . ."

Menesarkus said, "You haven't called me 'Father' since Aristo was killed." He looked into her eyes. "I will give myself to this Theban."

Agathe shook her head. "No you will not!"

Eudoxia said, "My beloved, any man who would murder our slaves and their children and threaten to burn our family alive would have no qualms about breaking his word. If Plataea has truly fallen, our fates have already been sealed." She brushed away his tears, kissed her husband on the mouth.

As Menesarkus stared into his wife's eyes, he was filled with her strength. "Go to the roof," he said. "Shoot as many of them as you can, then kill yourselves. Don't let them take you alive."

"*Fear slavery more than death*," said Eudoxia fiercely. It was an ancient Plataean oath that had been on everyone's lips during the first Persian invasion, when their world had been on the very brink of catastrophe.

Menesarkus grunted. Gods, this woman was tough. He loved her more now than ever. "Leave me here," he said, stealing another kiss. "The smoke will get me before the fire."

THIRTY-ONE

———◆———

Mula saw the southernmost boundary marker for the farm and turned the horse onto the path that led through the olive grove. They were less than a quarter of a mile from home. He could hardly wait to get to the house and bring his father and master Menesarkus the important news. The horse had keen night vision and had taken only a few missteps on their two-mile journey from Plataea, but it had refused to do more than a canter, even when urged by the heels of the reckless boys. Despite this they'd made good time. Mula slid off and led the horse through the trees with Kolax still astride.

"These are my master's olives," said Mula. "Do you have olives where you come from?"

"We have sheep," Kolax replied. "Sheep are better than olives. From a sheep you can make milk, cheese, clothing, and a feast."

"You have to crush the olives under a huge stone," said Mula. "To get the oil."

"Where I come from," offered Kolax, "there are lonely men who take a female sheep and—"

"What's that sound," asked Mula. He stopped, cupped a hand to his ear.

Kolax cocked his head. Above the sound of the drizzling rain splattering against the olive leaves, he could hear something . . . men's voices, shouting.

Something moved in the olive trees. A body leapt to the ground. The horse, which had been so reliable up to this point, bolted with Kolax clinging to the mane, and disappeared into the darkness.

Two sets of hands grabbed Mula. They pushed him to the ground, rolled him on his stomach. He felt two knees pressing on his back, holding him down.

"What do we do with him?" asked a voice.

"Slit his throat," replied the other.

"I say we sell his scrawny arse to the slavers."

"Slavery is too good for him. Let's rape his arse, then cut off his head."

"Or rape his *head* and cut off his *arse*."

Mula wailed and tried to get away.

"Quit screaming, you baby," said Theron. He held a rope with a grappling hook on one end, swinging it back and forth like it was a child's toy.

"You little girl," added Orion.

Kallisto's ungainly sixteen-year-old twin brothers lifted Mula up and slapped him playfully.

"We got you," said Theron laughing.

Orion said, "You cry like a girl."

"This one's afraid of a wineskin!"

"Or a dead mouse!"

"Let me go!" cried Mula. "I have to get to the house."

"We've come to find our sister," said Theron. "I'm going to scale the walls of Nikias's house if I have to," he added, swinging the hook and accidentally catching it on Orion's tunic and ripping it.

"Idiot!"

"Sorry, Brother."

Orion glared back at Mula. "We think Kallisto ran away from home and came here," he said.

"And you're going to help us get her back," put in Theron.

"And if you don't, we'll kick your skinny arse."

"Plataea has been taken!" blurted Mula. "The Thebans are in the city."

The twins laughed.

"The boy is quick-witted," said Orion. "I'll give him that."

"We killed one of them and stole his horse," said Mula. "I have to get to the house to tell my father and Master Menesarkus."

Orion made to grab him again, but Mula kicked him in the balls, squeezed between the brothers, and ran toward the house. Theron followed hard on his heels.

"Come back here!" he yelled.

When Mula got to the edge of the farmyard, he froze at the terrifying sight. The house was on fire, surrounded by a ring of flames. The outer buildings were already burned to shells, and the area was crawling with Thebans. Theron came to a sliding halt in the mud behind Mula. Orion was right behind him, clutching his groin as he ran. The brothers stared at the scene, dumbfounded.

"Zeus's balls," said Orion at last.

The pitch flames consuming the house rose ten feet in the air, licking the shutters of the second-story bedroom. They could see people on the roof shooting into the yard below.

"Those are women up there," said Orion.

"Phile," said Mula, pointing.

"Get Isokrates," ordered Theron, and shoved his brother in the direction of their home. Orion ran as though chased by an entire phalanx of Spartans.

Theron put his hands on either side of Mula's head, forced the petrified boy to look him in the face. "Stay here," he insisted. "Don't move. They will kill you if they catch you."

The gawky teen ran around the side of the barn clutching the grappling hook.

THIRTY-TWO

———— ◆ ————

Somehow Menesarkus found himself on the stairs leading up to the roof. He remembered seeing the smoke billowing up through the floorboards. Hearing a voice calling out. Was it Saeed's? His wife's? And he'd thought, "Thanatos has come. Death is in the room." But it was as if his body would not let him die just yet. He felt like one of the automatons in Hephaestos's magic castle—a machine that moved by the will of another man's mind.

He heard himself groaning with every step, but could not actually feel himself making the sound. This had happened to him before, both in the ring and in battle. Men called it "the blood rushing." When a warrior's ikor—his life essence—became enervated and surged through the veins like an opiate, a man no longer felt pain.

The smoke was thick. It blinded him. His hands searched the wall. His feet moved him upward. A memory flashed before his eyes: one of his friends in the Persian Wars who'd got his lower jaw cut clean off in the chaos of a phalanx skirmish and didn't know it had happened until an hour later, when he'd tried to eat his bread and realized that he no longer had any lower teeth. The men had laughed at him. Laughed at the comic horror of it all. Menesarkus would never forget the man's agonized wail or the look of hatred as he had eyed his unscathed companions and their gleaming, laughing teeth. The warrior had marched to an isolated spot, said a prayer to Zeus, stuck his sword handle in the ground, and fallen on it like Ajax on the beach of Ilium.

Menesarkus had reached the top of the stairs. He could feel the wooden door against his hand. He flung it open and staggered out onto the flat rooftop, gasped for air. He rubbed his eyes, slumped against the parapet wall. The driving rain cooled his skin. When his vision cleared he saw all the women lying face-down on the roof, sprawled out as if in their death throes, a single arrow clutched in each of their fists. They did not move.

"My women have killed themselves," he thought.

Eurymakus the Theban had won.

PART II

And there was pandemonium in the streets of Plataea. Thousands of men had been jailed in their homes, waiting for death and the extinction of their city. Now, informed they had been duped by a small force of Theban invaders, they rushed from their doors, frenzied, out for blood, and in various states of readiness: one man wore a bronze corselet but was naked from the waist down; another carried a shield but had no weapon in hand. These battle-hardened men had lost all sense and were no better than insects in a kicked-over hive, running about in disarray. A mob of warriors is useless, you see, without strong men to lead them. . . .
—Papyrus fragment from the "Lost History" of the Peloponnesian War by the "Exiled Scribe"

ONE

———————◆———————

Nikias, Leo, and Hektor got caught up in the rush and were pulled along in a throng of men moving swiftly toward the agora. Someone took up the freedom chant and soon the unearthly sound of thousands of voices crying, "Eleu-eleu-eleu . . ." filled the air. Nikias thought of the pankration championship where his grandfather had killed Damos, with the Hippodrome full of men calling out in unison.

"Nikias!" called out an anxious voice.

Nikias looked over his shoulder and saw Stasius's father, Dorius, running toward them.

"I haven't seen Stasius anywhere," said Dorius. He was twenty years older than Stasius and not nearly as handsome as his son, with a pinched face and big ears. His proudest achievement in life was the respect he'd gotten for producing such a beautiful child. "He was with you last night. Where is he now? I've been so worried—"

"He's dead," said Hektor. "So is my father. And Nikias's uncle Alexios. They're all dead."

Dorius stopped abruptly in the street. A man bumped into him, nearly knocking him over. Nikias put a hand on his shoulder.

"How?" asked Dorius, his lower lip trembling.

"He died bravely," said Hektor.

"The enemy," said Leo. "They surprised us in the street."

"His face?" asked Dorius.

"No," said Nikias. "It was not damaged."

"Where is he now?"

"At Chusor's smithy," said Leo.

"We didn't have time to come and tell you," said Nikias.

Dorius wiped the tears from his eyes, clutched the sword on his hip. He started walking toward the agora. And then he was running. Soon he vanished in the swarm of men.

The three friends fell in with the swelling crowd. Nikias glanced over at Leo and Hektor, saw their eyes shining in the torchlight. Hektor let forth an enraged war whoop.

"Hera's jugs!" exclaimed Leo as they got to the edge of the agora and stopped short. The public square was a slaughterhouse: dead men lay everywhere, stuck full of arrows, clinging to the wooden barricade the Thebans had erected in front of the city gates. Across the open space of the agora, toward the Temple of Athena, a Plataean stepped forward holding up a torch, pointed toward the obstruction, and called out, "Courage! To the barricade again!"

Nikias could make out the shapes of Theban archers crouched and waiting behind the rampart. He scanned the tops of the high citadel walls and saw the enemy there as well. The Plataeans were just out of range of the bows, but if they moved forward toward the barricade they would be exposed to the deadly arrows.

"Stop!" bellowed Chusor from where he stood on the steps of the Assembly Hall. "Form up shields! Form up—"

Nobody heard him. All at once a thousand men spilled out from the various lanes that led to the agora. Nikias felt himself pushed forward. He lost sight of Leo and Hektor as they surged toward the barricade. A Theban arrow, launched from the top of the wall, ripped into the face of the man next to him. Nikias tripped over a corpse and was nearly trampled but managed to scramble to his feet.

"Leo! Hektor!" yelled Nikias.

Nikias and those around him pressed forward until they had reached the wooden wall of carts and wagons. Men heaved and grunted against this impediment and against each other. Nikias was shoved in the back and fell onto the man in front of him, driving him forward a few inches until an iron point erupted from between the man's shoulder blades, then disappeared as it was pulled out. He saw Dorius's dead face for an instant as the brothel owner twisted and fell. Others tried to climb over the bulwark but were shot down or impaled.

"Retreat to the Assembly Hall!" cried a voice. "Retreat to the hall!"

Nikias crawled over a wheel, tried to stand on the upturned wagon, and dodged a spear point that stabbed past his face, thrust through a gap in the jumble of wood. The Theban was completely protected behind the barrier, poking at Nikias with his long spear.

The call of "Retreat!" was taken up by many voices. As Nikias started to get down, an arrow flew from the high wall above the gates and struck him in the chest. He fell backward and landed hard on his side. The arrowhead had pierced the leather but only the very tip had made it through to puncture the skin of his sternum; the leather armor had stopped a shot that should have killed him. A hand grabbed him around the collar of his breastplate, dragged him to his feet.

"Idiot! Do I have to keep saving your hide?" It was Chusor, holding a shield to protect them both. Two arrows hammered it in quick succession. They fell back to the colonnade that surrounded the Assembly Hall and protected them from the enemy archers. Men fled up the steps and into the building, helping the wounded. Chusor, blood smeared and raging, demanded the attention of the Plataeans.

"Listen to me!" he raged as he strode into the hall. "Listen to me! You're acting like animals—rabbits running to and fro, with no sense! Attacking that barricade is suicide, no matter what our numbers. We must think of a stratagem. Use our wits to dig out these vipers!"

Plataeans poured into the vast hall, shouting, "Death to Thebes!" Others took up the chant and soon the chamber resounded with the battle cry. Nikias glanced over and saw Leo leaning against the wall, a hand held to his eyes in an attitude of grief.

"Leo, where is Hektor?" Nikias shouted over the noise.

Leo stepped aside and pointed at the floor—at the corpse of Hektor. His unseeing eyes stared at the ground, toward Hades and his departed shade.

TWO

———————◆———————

Tykon hunkered down behind the barricade, squinting into the rain; the fierce and driving rain that had started up again with the same intensity of the first squall. The Plataeans were out there, across the agora, hidden by the impenetrable darkness of the streets and buildings on the other side of the square. He could hear them—the scrape and clank of their weapons. The occasional shouted order. Every so often an arrow or a lead shot slammed into the barricade.

"They're like children poking a hive of hornets," said Darius, pitching his voice so the other Thebans manning the wooden wall could hear. "We'll give them another sting." He struck the spiked bottom of his spear on a cobblestone.

Tykon was not as confident as his old friend. The assaults on the barricade had proved disastrous for the Plataeans. They'd lost hundreds, while the Thebans had yet to suffer a single casualty. But the enemy must be planning something. They wouldn't have just given up. The Plataeans were too tough for that. They knew attacking the barricade was useless, so they must be discussing another tactic. The fact that the Plataeans hadn't done anything for the last half hour was beginning to unnerve his men and, he admitted, him as well.

Less than two hours had passed since his shocking discovery at the smithy: the Plataeans had dug through their houses like a pack of mountain badgers. He'd sprinted to the barricade, shouting a call of alarm all the way, bursting into the square and startling his men on guard, and had nearly gotten shot for not giving the password. He'd sent his runners to warn the roaming bands of terrorizers—as Eurymakus had named them—to retreat from the citadel back to the gates. A hundred had yet to return. His nephew Perseus was one of the missing.

"We have to assume the ones who haven't come back are all dead," said Darius.

"Yes," replied Tykon.

"We're down to less than three hundred men out of four hundred and fifty."

"I know."

Like any good general, Tykon knew the key to defending a position with archers: holding the higher ground. His best bowmen were positioned behind the stone parapets atop the two highest towers—on either side of the gates—and along the archway that ran between them. The Plataeans had to cross the exposed area of the temple square to get to the barricade—a thousand long paces. His bowmen had decimated their ranks in their disastrous attack. At these close quarters, it was easy work for his archers to find the gaps in breastplates and helms. His spearmen had been there to finish the job.

All Tykon and his men had to do was keep from panicking. He heard some muttering about abandoning the city. They were wondering what was keeping them from just walking out through the gate and fleeing into the night. They could be home in Thebes before sunrise.

"Wineskins all around," Tykon said.

"Thrakian courage?" asked Darius with a smile. "Nothing raises a warrior's spirits like a belly full of wine." He sent a runner off to the towers with the order to pass the skins.

"The messengers have been gone now for half an hour," said Tykon. He'd sent two more riders back to Thebes just before the Plataean attack with an urgent message: "We are waiting for you, our brothers, or death."

"They'll find the army," said Darius with confidence.

Tykon had left his water clock in the temple. It wouldn't do much good in a downpour. The notion of the water clock continually filling with rain and never telling the time struck him as a poetic image for this horrible night that seemed to never end. He glanced up at the Temple of Athena's pediment. One of the statues of life-size nude warriors seemed to move.

"What do you see up there?" Tykon asked Darius. "On the pediment."

"Eh?" asked Darius, squinting up into the rain.

A shout from the direction of the Temple startled Tykon. He saw a small group of black-clad Thebans running toward the bulwark, calling out the password.

"Hold your arrows!" cried Darius. "Our men!"

Plataean archers struck down two of the runners just ten paces from safety. Three made it to the barricade, clambering up and over like rats. They were welcomed behind the wooden wall with slaps on the back and wineskins. Tykon was overjoyed to see that one of the men was Perseus, his twenty-year-old nephew, famous in Thebes for his beauty. Tykon's stomach sank as the youth turned his face into the torchlight. Perseus had lost his left eye. He was smiling with relief, seemingly unaware that he was mutilated. Tykon forced himself to keep his face a mask of stoicism. He could not reveal his true emotions to these men. Neither joy nor pity nor sorrow nor anger. He had to be as solid as a statue.

Kadmus, a grizzled veteran and the oldest of the three men who had just returned, gave a brief report . . . and then Perseus cupped a hand to his missing eye. His mouth went slack and a strange howl erupted from deep in his throat as he realized what he'd lost. Darius wrapped an arm around Perseus, kept the youth from falling over from the shock of his terrible wound.

"This is a botched job," said Tiresius, the third man who had just returned to the barricade. "The reinforcements aren't going to come. Not in this rain. There's thousands of Plataeans out there now. And they're all armored. They're going to attack any minute and rout us. I for one don't want to see how they treat prisoners. Who's with me?"

Before anyone could answer, Tykon let fly with his fist, breaking Tiresius's jaw with a resounding snap, knocking him out cold.

"Opinions I welcome," said Tykon, glowering at his men. "Cowards I will not tolerate." He looked into the eyes of every man standing within the light of the torch as he spoke. "We cannot leave. We have come too far. We are too close to crushing our enemy. Every man from this expedition will go home a hero or go home in a funeral jar. It is that simple. We hold the Gates of Pausanius and that's all that matters." His speech shut up any other dissenters. Some men made to move Tiresius away, but Tykon held up his hand. "Leave this piece of filth where he is," he said. "Kadmus, take Perseus to the gate tower and patch him up." Turning to Darius, he gave the order to douse all the torches. He went to the bulwark again and peered into the darkness.

THREE

———————◆———————

Saeed had gone to the storage room under the house to replenish the arrow sup-
ply for the final stand on the rooftop. He'd been there when the Thebans lit the
burning cart in the house, trapping him below. Now, as he stared at the flames
through the gaps in the floorboards, he smelled the reek of pitch. If he stayed
down there, he would be cooked like a pig in a pit.

He jerked his head rapidly from side to side like a bird, assessing his needs
as Menesarkus had always taught him to do in a crisis. "Never panic," his master had said time and time again over the last fifty years. "And never piss yourself."

Menesarkus had captured Saeed as a war prize almost fifty years earlier at the
rout of the invading Persian king, less than a mile from this farm. Menesarkus,
barely sixteen years old at the time, had slain Saeed's lord, a prince of the king's
own household, in front of the terrified eight-year-old groom's eyes. Rather than
begging for mercy or trying to flee, the resourceful Saeed had set to work strip-
ping the dead prince's plate armor from the corpse so Menesarkus could claim it
as booty. The hundreds of whip scars on the lad's back had told Menesarkus why
he'd be so quick to change masters.

Menesarkus had made Saeed his shield boy after that, and over the years, as
Saeed grew into manhood, they'd fought in dozens of battles together, from
Anatolia to the Greek isles. But the Persian slave had never been trapped inside a
flaming building that was about to come crashing down upon his head. This, he
considered, would be a most dishonorable way to die.

Saeed knelt by a big oak box and flung open the lid. Inside was the plate armor shirt his late Persian lord had worn to battle. He slipped it over his head; it
fit him perfectly, like a tunic made of liquid metal.

A circular object lay against one wall, like a big dish wrapped in leather, balanced on its edge. Saeed grabbed it and ripped off the leather straps, pulling out
the heavy oak and copper-plated shield from inside the sleeve. It was Menesarkus's
own shield, painted with the design of the boxing Minotaur, and it was scarred

with a hundred marks on its burnished surface, souvenirs of the vain attempts by Menesarkus's enemies to kill him over the years.

He slipped his arm through the metal armband in the center of the shield and gripped the wooden handle near the rim. The design of the shield allowed even a thin-armed man like Saeed to support the heavy disk, at least for a time. He snatched one of the short spears from the rack—the kind they used on the farm to skewer badgers trapped in their holes—then reached instinctively for his belt, feeling his Sargatian whip looped there on its breakaway knot, patting it with the knuckles of his spear hand. It was coiled like a snake ready to strike.

He climbed the stairs to the ground floor, holding the shield to protect his face. At the top he was knocked backward by a blast of heat and smoke. The stairway to the second story was completely blocked by fire.

"Master!" he cried, leaping up and slamming the ceiling planks with his shield. Menesarkus's room was directly above. "Master, get out! Go to the roof!"

Saeed retreated to the workshop with the looms at the back of the house, stuck his face in one of the small windows at the top of the wall, gasping for air. The smoke and flames would reach this room soon and he would be dead. He had to figure out a way to get out the front doorway.

He cut a half-finished tapestry from the loom. He knew that oily wool resisted fire, but the flames in the other room were so strong, they would burn through this. He grabbed the water jug in the corner of the room and dumped it onto the woolen covering, soaking it. Then he wrapped himself in the tapestry and ran to the front of the house. The wool sizzled and reeked as it touched the fire. It smelled like a sheep on a sacrificial flame, but the flames did not hurt him. He walked straight through the blaze and leapt out the front door. He tossed aside the singed tapestry, held up his shield.

Five of the enemy stood near the wall at the foot of a tall orchard ladder. They were scaling the walls to the rooftop. A Theban was just about to climb over the parapet. All of the men at the bottom of the ladder faced away from Saeed. They had no idea he was there. They had never expected somebody to emerge from the blazing house alive.

He skewered three of the Thebans with quick, jabbing strokes of his short spear, blocking their swords with his shield, then pulled the ladder from the wall. The man on top clung to the roof ledge, kicking out with his legs for purchase. An arrow shot from the darkness—from the direction of the orchard—and struck him in the back of the skull. The Theban fell to the ground, dead. A loud war cry in the Skythian tongue called out in jubilation.

Saeed turned in the direction of the cry. Eurymakus's giant Median bodyguard ran at him from his blind side and hurled a javelin that pierced straight through his shield, sticking him in the unprotected biceps of his spear arm. Saeed tossed aside the shield and reached for his whip, yanked it loose from his belt, and flung the loop over the head of Bogha, now advancing toward him with short sword raised.

Saeed yanked on the leather thong and it tightened around the Median's neck, choking him. Before Bogha could hack the whip from Saeed's grip, the Persian darted around behind the bigger man and ran in the opposite direction, yanking him off his feet. Saeed threw himself on the ground with his feet on Bogha's shoulders and pulled with all his might. Bogha struggled and kicked, his eyes bulging out of his skull.

Then Saeed heard a child's voice calling out "Father" in Persian.

"*Pidar! Pidar!*" He looked up and couldn't believe what he saw. It was like some horrible nightmare. His boy, his only child—who he thought was safely in the city, looking for Nikias—running toward him across the yard! What evil god had carried Mula here at this moment?

"Go back!" shouted Saeed. "Run away!" His hands went slack on the whip. He jumped to his feet, waving for Mula to stop. But the boy kept coming toward him.

Eurymakus whipped up his bow and shot an arrow that pierced Mula's right breast. The child toppled forward face-first into the dust, three paces from his father. Saeed crawled to his child and, howling in sorrow, covered him with his body to protect him from the enemy. Theban warriors ran from the farmyard and surrounded him, kicking him mercilessly.

"Bind the Persian slave's hands," said Eurymakus to Bogha, who was coughing as he pulled the whip off his neck.

"Yes, *Magus*," replied Bogha, his voice raspy. He used Saeed's own whip to tie his arms, then put Saeed in a headlock and lifted him to his feet.

Eurymakus leaned over the unconscious boy. He noticed something around his neck. It was a dispatch bag. He ripped it from the limp boy's neck and opened it. He twitched when he saw Tykon's writing on the leather scroll. Somehow, one of their messengers had been killed or captured on his way to Thebes. This boy had found the dispatch and had attempted to deliver it to Menesarkus.

He shook the boy, slapped him. "Where did you find this?" he demanded, speaking in Persian. But Mula did not open his eyes.

"Get the ladder back up!" Eurymakus yelled to his men. "Get to the top of the house!"

FOUR

———◆———

Across the square, Tykon saw a figure dash between two buildings. One of his archers unleashed an arrow. It struck stone. A wasted shot. He caught another shadowy glimpse of a man darting through the downpour. Were they planning another one of Chusor's fiery tricks, like the one he'd used at the smithy?

The words of cowardly Tiresius rankled him. He felt in his heart the man was right. It was a botched job. The reinforcements weren't coming. But what had happened? What had gone wrong? The cavalry should have had time to make it to Plataea before the rain came. Unless all the messengers had failed in their mission. He cursed himself for this meandering way of thinking. He needed to stay focused on the task at hand. Stop dwelling on what might have happened.

Would his name and his son's be disgraced back in Thebes? Eurymakus should by rights take the brunt of the blame. It was he who had planned this whole expedition. Where was he now? If they failed tonight and were captured, the Plataeans would show no mercy. Especially in the daylight after they discovered those families who had been slaughtered, cut to pieces in their beds.

His thoughts were interrupted by a deep voice calling across the empty square.

"Thebans! I, Zeno of Plataea, charge you with profaning our city. When our Plataean fathers fought alongside the Spartans and Athenians against the Persian barbarians, your fathers were sucking the Persian king's balls. This city contains many sacred shrines and was named inviolate by the Spartan general Pausanius as a reward for our service to the cause of freedom. You have disgraced yourselves by this skulking attack, unwilling to meet us on the field of battle because you know we would destroy you. Cowards, I call you. And disgraced children of disgraced fathers. You are a cursed people."

Tykon's men grumbled.

"He's got a flair for insults," said Darius with a gruff laugh.

Tykon smiled wryly and grunted. But he'd been struck by some of Zeno's words. He wanted to defend what they'd done. To tell the Plataeans, "You would have attacked us in the same way if you'd been clever enough to make the opportunity." But he couldn't bring himself to speak. He knew his words would sound stupid and weak. So he sat on his haunches, fingering the handle of his short sword.

But a man next to him could not take it. He stood up at full height, exposing his face above the bulwark, and shouted, "We'll rape your sisters, we'll rape your mothers, we'll—" His threat was cut short when something struck him in the forehead with the sound of a thick, dry stick snapped in two. The man's knees buckled and he toppled to the ground, unmoving, unbreathing.

The lead pellet that had killed him bounced off the dead man's head and landed right at Tykon's feet, where it spun crazily on the flat stone. It had all happened so quickly that Tykon didn't even have time to open his mouth to tell the man to sit back down. Now he was minus one more fighter.

"Stay down!" shouted Tykon. "Keep your heads down!"

"Leave the city," commanded Zeno. "Leave us in peace or stay here and die, and let your shades be cursed forever."

Tykon cupped his hands to his mouth and shouted, "You, Plataeans, hear me! Those of you who regretted your fellow citizens breaking with the Oxland League years past, come to us now in peace and we will grant you immunity and welcome you back to our noble confederation of cities. We are a band of friends who stand against the growing tyranny of Athens."

Silence. A shuttered window opened on the second floor of a nearby home. An old crone poked out her head and hurled a chamber pot at the barricade, screaming madly like Medea, "The Oxland League can kiss my hairy arse!" Her curse caused wild laughter from the Plataean side. Shutters opened up and down the street, with insults and objects hurled from dozens of windows. As if on cue, the rain poured down even harder. It was like standing under a waterfall.

Tykon cursed under his breath. If the reinforcements arrived too late . . . to find that Tykon and his men had been overrun . . . gods! Then he would be blamed. His family would be dishonored. His son back in Thebes would be ostracized.

He knew he needed to think more like the wily Odysseus. Or the smith Chusor, for that matter. The one Eurymakus had wanted taken alive. Tykon had to come up with a way of guaranteeing that the reinforcements could enter the city, even if he and all of his men were slaughtered. He strode over to the massive twin portals, ran a hand across the heavy wood. He must figure out a way to destroy the Gates of Pausanius. But it would take hours to chop through the oaken planks that were bound with heavy iron bands.

A shot from a sling slammed into the gate directly above his head. He ducked and crouched low. That one was close. He had thought he was protected here from the enemy's line of sight. He knew the shot couldn't have been random. It had missed his skull by an inch and would have splattered his brains against the gates. He looked up again at the Temple of Athena, and this time he saw one of the statues break free of its marble pediment and scamper over the rooftop!

No. Not a statue. It was a man. He'd been hiding there this whole time, spying on them from above.

"So that's how you got my man," he said under his breath.

He turned back to the gate. Pounded his fist against it. Even the great Akilles was brought down by his heel. The trick was finding the weakness. He realized Perseus was crouched next to him, holding a bandage against the side of his face to staunch the bleeding from his empty eye socket.

"Can we burn the gates down, General?" asked his nephew.

Tykon smiled. Perseus was doing his best to not show his pain. Tykon was proud of his nephew. The young man was thinking like a leader moving on to the task at hand, lost eye be damned.

"No, warrior," he replied. "It's coated with a heavy layer of wax."

"Maybe we can prop the gates open so the Plataeans can't shut them and our reinforcements can march straight in."

"Prop them open with what? Only one of the Titans could put a doorstop down that is big enough."

Perseus stared up at the top of the portal with his one good eye, shielding it from the rain.

"It's no use, nephew," said Tykon.

Perseus said, "When my father and I moved my brother's bed into his new bridal chamber last year, we had to take the portal off the hinges to get it through the doorway. Popped the pins out with a hammer. We'll need a bigger hammer for these hinges," he added.

The solution was too easy, Tykon realized. All this time he'd been trying to figure out how to destroy the gates from the outside—as a besieger. No Plataean would have ever imagined that an enemy would destroy their gates from *within*.

For one of the few times in his entire adult life, Tykon the Theban laughed out loud.

FIVE

———————◆———————

Nikias had been spying on the Thebans from the roof of the Temple of Athena for the last half hour, scouting out the enemy positions, counting their numbers, marking their routines. He'd stripped naked before climbing the fifty feet up the ladder to the top. That way he could maneuver on the slippery marble lintels unencumbered by armor or sodden clothes.

He'd realized that by standing in the pediment at the front of the temple, he blended in amongst the statues of the Plataean heroes and was virtually invisible to the enemy below. When the Theban soldier had exposed himself above the barricade during Zeno's speech, shouting filth about how he was going to rape every woman in Plataea, Nikias had launched a shot from his sling and struck the man down. The satisfaction of hearing the enemy's skull crack like a smashed wine bowl had filled him with a euphoric sense of divine power.

He'd risked killing another one of the invading Thebans—the silhouette he'd picked out and identified as the Theban general. But his lead ball had missed by a hair. The general had spotted him. He was sure of it. It was no matter. He'd seen enough of the enemy positions. It was time to get down and make his report.

He made his way carefully along the eastern side of the roof, out of sight of the Theban bowmen who occupied the gate towers. He paused to stare into the distance, in the direction of his farm. The shape of the Kithaeron range was barely discernible against the black sky and the shadow-filled valley. Across the dark, rolling foothills—to the east, in the direction of Hysiai—a fire burned despite the pouring rain.

At first he thought it was a bonfire, or maybe someone on the road holding a pitch torch. But the instant he shielded his eyes against the rain, there was a flash of lightning in that direction; it lit up the landscape for a split second. The flash was long enough for him to judge the range between where he stood and the fire, and the distance beyond.

He knew, in that moment, that his farm was burning.

A hand grabbed him by the arm and he was so startled he nearly slipped off the pediment, but he was quickly pulled back to safety under the roof by a pair of wiry arms.

"Who's there?" said Nikias, peering into the black.

"Timarkos," hissed a voice from the darkness. "Keep your voice down, idiot boy."

"Do you live in ceilings?" Nikias asked petulantly. He didn't like being caught off guard and was furious with himself for letting the whisperer sneak up on him. "I thought you were on your way back to Athens."

"I've been delayed, it seems," replied Timarkos mirthlessly. "There isn't much time. You've got to get out of the citadel. Raise the countryside. The rain will delay the Theban reinforcements."

"I need to go to my farm!" said Nikias. "I saw it burning."

"Then your grandfather is a dead man," said Timarkos flatly. "But you can still save your city from becoming enslaved."

"How am I supposed to get out?" asked Nikias. "The Thebans control the gates and wall parapets."

"There is a secret passageway," said Timarkos. "An ancient tunnel leading from the Temple of Zeus. Under the altar."

"How do you know this?" asked Nikias.

"No time for explanations," said Timarkos. "You'll need at least a dozen men to push the altar aside."

He started walking toward the rear of the temple ceiling.

"Where are you going?" asked Nikias, exasperated.

"You'll see me again if we both live through this night," said Timarkos over his shoulder. "Now I've got to find the traitor." He stepped swiftly over a rafter and vanished into the darkness, heading toward the far side of the ceiling.

Nikias made his way back to the ladder and descended so fast that halfway down he lost his footing on the rungs. He clutched the two side poles with all his might to slow himself down, but he couldn't get a solid grip on the wet smooth wood. Diokles and Leo, who stood at the bottom of the ladder, grabbed him as he fell. If they had not caught him he would have broken both his legs on the stone pavers.

"Whoa!" shouted Leo. "Not so fast!"

"Theban army come?" asked Diokles anxiously.

Nikias tried to speak but the wind was knocked out of him.

"What did you see?" asked Leo. "Talk, man!"

"Fire." Nikias winced and took off running. He dashed down the lane, across the agora, and up the steps of one of the public buildings, slipping on the marble floor as he ran. "My farm is burning!" he shouted as he burst into a room where

Chusor and a dozen other men were standing over a sand table, looking at a mock-up of the Theban barricade and the city gates.

"How do you know?" asked Chusor.

As Nikias recounted what he'd seen, Diokles and Leo entered the chamber and stood silently in the background. When Nikias described the size of the conflagration, the men exchanged worried looks.

"Were there other fires?" asked Zeno. "In the west? My brother's place, near the crossroads to Kreusis?"

"And my wife's father's house?" asked another. "By the old bridge near the sacred—"

"I didn't see any other fires," interrupted Nikias. "But somebody needs to warn the farms. And then head to the downs and tell the garrisons what has happened. I can raise all the warriors in the countryside and bring back an army to drive out the invaders."

"Nikias," said Chusor, "the Thebans still occupy all of the towers and the tops of the walls. There's no way to get a rope up and climb over the bastions without turning yourself into an easy target."

"We don't want you ending up looking like a stuffed target goose," said Leo.

"There's another way," said Nikias.

Fifteen men put their shoulders against the marble altar and pushed with all their might. The table scraped across the stone slabs of the floor. It was a hateful sound that sent chills up and down the men's spines. When they had moved it three feet or so, Kallinakos, the temple priest, held up his hand for them to stop.

The men stared into a black hole beneath the altar. A sepulchral smell wafted from the opening and into the inner sanctum of the Temple of Zeus where they stood. Brave Greek men feared cavernous holes more than swords, for it made them think of rotting corpses and Hades and the terrible doom to which they would all go someday.

"It was dug long before my grandfather was born," said the priest, an ancient and toothless man with a white beard. "It was one of the Tyrant's secrets. An escape route. How did you know of its existence, lad?" he asked Nikias.

"My grandfather," Nikias lied. "He told me about it when I was a boy."

"I thought the tunnels under Plataea were old wives' tales," said Zeno in awe.

"*My* grandfather used to tell me the Tyrant had many secret tunnels," said Myron. "Filled with treasure."

"I was led to believe the Tyrant's treasures were all found," said Chusor.

"No," said Kallinakos. "Only a tiny portion of his hoard was recovered. The rest lies buried somewhere under the city."

Chusor stroked his chin beard, staring fixedly into the hole.

"We could get our women and children out through here," said a young law clerk.

Nikias lowered himself into the opening. His feet touched bottom with his head just below the level of the floor. He called out for light and Chusor handed him an oil lamp. He looked around in the coffin-size dugout and saw a pile of rocks covering a small opening leading west, in the direction of the city walls. He set the lamp down and pushed aside the biggest rock.

"There's a narrow shaft," said Nikias. "It's partially caved in. There's just enough room for one man to crawl. It doesn't look very stable." He stood up and addressed the law clerk. "You would have to send the women and children in one at a time. They might panic and then . . . they'd be stuck."

"We can't flee the city anyhow," said Zeno. "It doesn't matter if this tunnel were as wide as a road. A man without a city is no better than a slave. And if the Thebans are out in the countryside, our women and children would not make it very far."

The other citizens in the temple voiced their agreement. Zeno was right: death or freedom was the only outcome of tonight's attack.

"Nik," said Leo, "tell everyone what has happened."

"Return to us with an army at your back," said Zeno.

"May Zeus guide your way," said Chusor, and offered Nikias his hand.

Nikias stared at the smith with a lump in his throat. Here was a foreigner, a man whom he'd treated with contempt, happily staying to defend a city that was not his own.

"You can leave," he said to Chusor. "No man here would think less of you and Diokles if you followed me. Especially not after what you've done tonight."

"That's the truth," agreed Myron. "You've fought like a hero today."

"Thanks, but I'll stay and take my chances," said Chusor. "And I have one more pyrotechnic trick left for the enemy. I was explaining it to everyone when you burst into the room, Nik," he added with a smile. "It will make the firestorm in front of the smithy look like a campfire. Besides . . ." He stared into the tunnel and a shadow of terror passed briefly over his manly face. "I don't like tight spaces."

SIX

———— ◆ ————

Menesarkus felt the heat of the burning house through the flat roof. He saw a black shape . . . and then another . . . climb over the parapet wall on the other side. The enemy had scaled the walls with ladders. Soon there were five of them, all in black, creeping toward him like dangerous scorpions.

"We've got him, Eurymakus!" one of the Thebans shouted down to the ground. "He's alive!"

The invaders had cudgels in their hands. One of them carried a coiled piece of rope. He said to the others, "Remember. We take him alive."

"I'll kill you all!" Menesarkus screamed, and swung his fist feebly.

The Thebans laughed.

"How are we going to get the big bastard down?" one of them asked.

They had not noticed the bodies lying on the roof. Menesarkus's women. The Thebans stepped over them. They were anxious to get to the pankrator. Suddenly Agathe, Eudoxia, Phile, and Kallisto rose from the roof nearly in unison, pulled back their bowstrings, and hit their marks with the same steady aim they had displayed shooting rings in the arena. Four Thebans fell dead.

Before any of the women could nock more arrows in their bows, the fifth attacker—the one with the rope—pulled out a knife and lunged at the woman nearest to him, stabbing her in the heart.

"Agathe!" yelled Menesarkus. He lurched forward, crawling across the roof on his knees and palms.

"Mother!" shrieked Phile.

A rattling groan escaped Agathe's lips. She held out her hand toward Phile as she sagged backward and died. The Theban tried to yank his dagger free but her ribs held it fast.

Kallisto, clutching an arrow in her fist, ran at the Theban killer and plunged the arrow straight through his mouth. "Die!" she screamed. "Die!" The arrow sliced through his teeth and tongue and out the back of his neck. He shook his head in surprise, choking on his own blood. He grabbed Kallisto around the throat with one hand and tried to pull the arrow from his mouth with the other.

Menesarkus, moving across the roof on his belly, grabbed the Theban around the ankle and yanked him off his feet. As he fell, Kallisto ripped out the bloody shaft and pounced on the Theban like a cat, driving the weapon through his eye and into his brain, over and over again. He twitched spasmodically, then became still.

Phile ran to her mother, clung to her dead body as sections of the roof started to cave in, flames shooting through the gaps.

"We're going to have to jump," said Kallisto.

She ran to the rear wall of the house. She saw a grappling hook fastened to the wall and a knotted rope attached. The rope moved. Somebody was climbing it! She raised her bow to shoot but a voice called out, "It's me! Theron! Helladios's son."

The awkward young man flung his body over the parapet and took in the scene with his huge protruding eyes. "Sister!" he exclaimed. "What in Zeus—"

"No time to explain," said Kallisto. "The roof is caving in." She went to Phile, dragged her away from her mother's corpse. "Carry Phile and Eudoxia down one at a time," Kallisto said to her brother. "I can manage on my own." She helped Phile onto Theron's back. The sobbing girl wrapped her legs around his waist and locked her arms around his neck, and he lowered himself and Nikias's sister to the ground.

"Help me up!" Menesarkus called to Eudoxia and Kallisto. "Take me to the other side of the roof. I'll distract the enemy while you get down." As they heaved him to the front parapet he said with great emotion, "I thought you were all dead." He looked at his wife. "My beautiful Eudoxia . . . I thought you'd left me."

SEVEN

———◆———

Nikias held the lamp with his arm outstretched. It lit up only a few feet of the tunnel ahead. Beyond the lamplight was an empty and unfathomable darkness. He shuffled his way along the rough floor, using his free hand like the front leg of a tripod, inching forward on his knees and toes. His sternum ached from where the axe tip had punctured his leather armor, making it hard to breathe—that and the suffocating, confining space. At first he could hear the men in the sanctuary above yelling out the battle cry of "Eleu-eleu-elue . . ." to cheer him on. Then their voices became deadened by the rock and earth. And soon the only sound that filled his ears was his own harsh panting.

He reckoned he'd gone twenty paces when he came to a place where he was forced to stop. The tunnel roof had sagged under some tremendous weight. He realized he must be directly under the bastions of Plataea now. The gap between the floor and the ceiling looked too small for him to enter, the tunnel beyond too narrow to crawl any farther. He decided that he would rather take his chances scaling over the city and dodging Theban arrows than squeezing into this rat hole like some kind of worm. He tried to go back and discovered, with a sudden and sickening terror, that the passage wasn't big enough for him to turn around.

His heart pounded in his chest. His stomach sank. He could hear his pulse thumping in his ears. He backed up in a frenzied effort, intending to make his way out rump first, but he struck a low hanging rock and dislodged it from the roof. A pile of dirt and debris fell behind him, sealing off his escape route completely. A dust cloud enveloped him in a choking fog and snuffed out his lamp.

All went black.

Instead of making him hysterical with fear, the utter darkness had a soothing effect on him. He lay very still. It felt as if his body were floating. He remembered sitting at the feet of a traveling bard who had come to Plataea when he was a boy . . . listening to the harpist sing *The Iliad* as he played the harp.

" 'He breathed his life into the dust . . . and a blackness fell over his eyes.' " And now he knew what Homer had meant—the terrible darkness of death. The light of the sun dwindling to black. The end of all sensation. A passage into . . . nothingness.

But then one must awake from this emptiness after some span of time. To live as a shade—a pale, wispy version of oneself, with no more weight than a puff of smoke. His earliest memories were of staring at his dead ancestors' faces on their funeral jars. Looking so morose. And . . . envious. Yes. They envied the living and their warm, heavy flesh.

This was not the way Nikias had imagined he would die. A spear to the groin like his father. A fall from a horse like his cousin. A fist to the temple in the pankration ring like his grandfather's elder brother. All of these he'd imagined. But dying under the ground like some sort of maggot? It was laughable. Pathetic.

He lay for some time, breathing softly. He felt light-headed. Then sleepy.

And then he was walking in a sun-dappled grove—the grove near the Cave of Nymphs where he'd made love with Kallisto . . . less than a week ago? How had he come here now? Had the goddess Artemis magically transported him? Kallisto stood in front of an ancient olive tree and she was naked, both palms resting on her swollen belly. She smiled at him and her voice resonated from the rustling leaves of the trees.

"Your child lives inside me," said her voice, though her lips did not move.

Nikias crouched at her feet, wrapped his arms around her legs, worshipping her as though she were an idol. "Run away with me."

"This is all that matters," said her voice. "I must have a child. And it will be your blood in his veins."

He kissed her foot—

And awoke choking on a mouthful of dirt, in the profound and terrible void of the tunnel. He pounded his fist into the earth, squeezed a handful of stones and dirt. He screamed until his throat was raw. He clawed at the small opening in front of him, pulled himself through the hole, scraping the skin from his shoulders and back. He squirmed on his belly, wriggling like a centipede, afraid that any second he would come to a dead end . . . where he would stay trapped until he starved to death.

Then he felt the slightest hint of a breeze brushing against his face. Air! Cool air smelling of rain! That meant there was an opening. Somewhere up ahead. The wind must have shifted, found its way through the rocks that blocked the entrance to this accursed shaft. The tunnel got wider. He was on hands and knees again, barging ahead recklessly. He tumbled forward. He thought he'd fallen into an abyss. But he only dropped a few feet and landed in a shallow hole that was filled with a few inches of water.

He squatted on his haunches, cupped his hands, and drank the thick muddy water. He could smell rain, hear the wind whistling through the clefts in the rocks. He stood up and put his back against a cold, flat stone and heaved with all his might.

He was inside a small mausoleum in the midst of the sarkophogi, the grave-yard ten paces outside the walls of Plataea. He caught a glimpse of the quarter moon shining through a break in the clouds above the mountaintops. By its light he could see the small footpath that led to a grove of trees below the sarkophogi. Standing there were two Theban soldiers keeping watch on half a dozen horses. They faced the direction of Thebes—northward—with their backs to the grave-yard and captured Plataea.

He stepped out of the crypt like a shade rising from its tomb. He searched the ground, found a sharp rock in the shape of a dragon's tooth, and clenched it in his fist. Then he made his way stealthily down the path toward the unsuspecting invaders. Gripping the rock in both hands, he brained the first guard with a crushing blow to the top of the head. Before the other guard knew what was happening, Nikias kicked him in the groin, grabbed him behind the neck with both hands, and drove his face into an upthrust knee. The man fell when he released him. He picked up the rock again and pounded the man's head to a pulp.

Minutes later, dressed in one of the dead guard's clothes, a Theban sword strapped to his waist, Nikias charged down the eastern road on horseback in the direction of his burning home.

EIGHT

———————◆———————

Eurymakus stood in the farmyard staring up at the roof, waiting for his men to lower Menesarkus. The fire raged. The second floor had started to collapse. Soon the roof would tumble down too. Saeed was on his knees nearby. His hands were bound in front. Mula, the arrow still sticking from his shoulder, lay next to him, unconscious.

"What are you doing?" shouted Eurymakus toward the roof. None of his men had spoken for some time. He'd heard some females screaming and assumed that his men had made short work of them.

There were only two of Eurymakus's raiders and his man Bogha still with him on the ground. He'd lost at least twenty men. They stood with their spears pointed at Saeed and Mula. Bogha had his curved Median blade drawn, waiting for the word to hack them to pieces. As if in response to Eurymakus's question, the head of a Theban appeared at the top of the parapet.

"What's going on up there?" demanded Eurymakus.

The head did not respond. It was a disembodied head stuck to a sword point. Menesarkus was holding the sword. He flung the head at Eurymakus's feet.

"I'll be waiting for you, Eurymakus!" he yelled down, and let forth a mocking laugh, spat at Eurymakus, then tossed another head over the side. Eurymakus had to duck to keep from getting hit by the bloody projectile. "I'll be waiting for you on the banks of the Styx!" Flames roared up behind the old pankrator, as though he stood at the fiery furnace of Hades itself.

"Kill them, Bogha," Eurymakus ordered.

Bogha raised his sword to chop off Mula's head. As he brought down the blade, nimble Saeed dived in front of his child, taking the full force of the sword on his back. His armor had been fashioned by the greatest smith in the Persian Empire, and even though it was fifty years old it deflected the blade as though Bogha had attempted to slice through a rock.

Bogha kicked Saeed aside with his massive foot, raised the sword a second time. As the giant swung down again, an arrow ripped through the back of his sword hand. He let out a wail as his fingers released their grip and the weapon fell from his grasp.

Before the other Thebans could react, Nikias's white mare Photine leapt into the yard. The Skythian Kolax rode her. The child had been trained from before the time he could walk the earth to sit astride a horse and guide it with his knees, thus leaving his hands unencumbered to wield his fearsome bow. He rode in a tight circle around the Thebans. In four heartbeats he shot four arrows—an arrow for each of the enemy. One of the Theban raiders was struck through the eye. The other in the heart. They both died instantly. Bogha got an arrow through the cheek, and the metal head knocked out four of his molars, sliced through the tip of his tongue, and exited the other side of his face. The Median giant staggered away, spitting out chunks of his teeth and tongue.

Eurymakus, however, managed to duck at the last moment, and the arrow intended for his brain sliced off half of his right ear instead. Kolax turned and came back to finish them off. But the agile Theban grabbed a spear and swung, whacking the boy across the chest. Kolax was unhorsed and landed hard on his side, the wind knocked out of him.

Eurymakus leapt on him with his poisoned dagger drawn, hand poised to slit his throat. Kolax snaked aside, bit into the Theban's face, and yanked back his head with all his might. Half of Eurymakus's upper lip came away in the Skythian's mouth. Kolax kicked his way out of the shocked Theban's grasp, spat the lip into the dirt, and scrambled across the yard to where Saeed sat on his haunches by Mula.

Bogha lumbered to Eurymakus and stood by his side. The men stared at each other's ruined faces. Eurymakus was deranged. He could not think straight. All his men but Bogha were dead. A Skythian child had just bitten off his lip. How could that be?

"Demon!" said Eurymakus, pointing his dagger at Kolax.

He glanced up at the roof. Menesarkus had disappeared from sight. The house was consumed in a giant flame that reached for the black sky. This was not the sweet revenge he'd planned—to watch Menesarkus die slowly as he tortured his family before his lidless eyes. Bogha made a brutish sound of alarm. He could not speak with his bloody tongue sliced in two. From around the side of the house, Kallisto and Eudoxia strode toward them, bows at the ready. Hatred was in their eyes. They knelt beside Saeed, Mula, and Kolax, and took up their shooting positions.

A band of horsemen came charging down the road toward the farm. Eurymakus was overcome with relief. It was his reinforcements from Plataea. "Let go! What are you doing?" he yelled in Persian, because Bogha had grabbed him around the waist and was dragging him away from the riders. When Eurymakus glanced back he saw that the riders were not Thebans.

As Isokrates and two dozen of Helladios's slaves entered the farmyard on horseback, Eudoxia and Kallisto shot a final volley at the retreating Thebans. Bogha took an arrow in the shoulder and Eurymakus was hit in the left buttock. But they kept running and disappeared into the dark olive orchard.

Kolax speedily untied Saeed's hands, and the Persian slave, his hands now free, picked up the limp body of Mula and cradled him in his arms, sobbing.

"Isokrates!" shouted Theron, who had just come round the corner from the back of the house with Phile still clinging to his back.

Isokrates dismounted and stared at the inferno of Menesarkus's home, the destroyed and burning buildings, the black-clad Theban corpses scattered across the ground, and the bloodied and wounded members of Menesarkus's household huddled together. His eyes alighted on his sister with surprise and fury. "Kallisto? By Zeus, what are you doing here?"

Kallisto turned away, shaking her head in sorrow. "Leave me be." She dropped to her knees.

"Where is Orion?" asked Theron, looking for his twin.

"We met some enemy on the road," said Isokrates. "We surprised them. Killed them all. Orion was slain."

"My mother is dead too," said Phile.

"And poor Akake," said Kallisto.

"Menesarkus?" asked Isokrates.

Kallisto pointed a finger at the roof, now ablaze, the roaring flames rising twenty feet into the air above the house. The roof beams exploded and crashed to the second floor. Already weakened by the flames, the floor joists sagged, then split and crashed to the ground floor. Smoke, fire, and debris shot from the windows and doors. The house was nothing now but a gutted and burning shell.

NINE

———◆———

The area around the Old Market and Artisans' Lane had been turned into a hive of activity with all the remaining men of Plataea preparing for the assault on the Theban barricade. Swords were sharpened, arrows divided up, bows strung, and armor mended. Word had spread about the gruesome murders at the homes of prestigious citizens. The Thebans were not abiding by any rules of war. The sounds of hammers on metal rang from workshops—the music of impending violence and revenge.

Myron stood outside the hostel for strangers, giving directions to the men who were bringing supplies for the making of Chusor's new weapon: ceramic vessels from Nauklydes's factory; hemp from the rope maker; gypsum—the main ingredient of plaster—gotten from the new bathhouse construction site nearby; beeswax used by temple artists to seal painted marble in a process called enkaustikos; and naptha, a distillation of pine resin that was used as a solvent. The men had to be careful, because the Thebans still manned the walls. Every now and then an arrow flew from one of the towers down to the streets. Sometimes it found its target.

Everyone except Diokles and Leo had been barred access to the smithy. One careless torch, a dropped oil lamp, and the whole place would go up like a volcano. Diokles went about his task of bringing in the materials as they were requested by Chusor, every so often exiting the smithy with a large clay jar—a completed weapon—clutched to his chest with his massive arms. Carrying one of these, he resembled an ant toting a fat larva.

Inside his workshop Chusor put all of the ingredients together. The compounds were extremely volatile and needed to be packed in the clay vessels in the correct proportions. Leo worked as his assistant, measuring out and handing him ingredients. Chusor filled a large empty olive oil jar with dry gypsum that had been mixed with scraps of metal. He covered this with a layer of beeswax. On top of this he poured a measure of liquid naptha. A hemp fuse, soaked in naptha, was placed in the top and sealed with a wax plug. The thing was now ready to be lit and hurled at the enemy. They'd already made six of these "Pandoras," as Chusor called them. They needed at least ten more.

"These are too heavy for one man to throw," commented Leo.

"We will use a sling," said Chusor. "A two-man sling made of rope. Somebody else will light it and let the fuse burn until it reaches the wax stopper. See here?" He gestured at the plug. "When the wax just starts to melt, the Pandora must be hurled at the target or else it will explode, covering your skin with molten fire."

Leo fingered a handful of metal scraps, picked out a broken spear tip. "Why do you mix in these bits of cast-off bronze?"

"The liquid naptha on top burns with tremendous heat," explained Chusor. "In a flash it ignites the dry gypsum—which, compressed inside the jar, bursts forth, sending the fragments flying through the air like tiny arrows, cutting through the flesh of the invaders."

"Oh," said Leo. "Where did you learn to make these fire toys?"

"In Syrakuse. A terrible siege against a rival city in Sicily."

"You were in Syrakuse?" asked Leo, awestruck.

Chusor grunted a yes as he poured the poisonous, vile-smelling naptha into a jar. It brought back a vivid memory: a man burned to the color of charcoal, the flesh sloughing off his body like old clothes, yet still he lived, screaming. . . .

"What is it like? Are the men and women beautiful?"

"No more so than any other place."

"Oh." Leo was disappointed.

"But the city . . . it is beautiful," said Chusor softly. "It's built upon a cliff, and you see the towers from miles away as you approach from the sea. The bay beneath is filled with ships from all over the world, and you hear dozens of different tongues: Phoenician, Persian, Egyptian—"

"Someday I will go to Egypt," interrupted Leo.

"It is a place of wonders," offered Chusor. "The architecture—"

"Did you see a water horse?"

"Watch it," hissed Chusor, for in his excitement Leo had nearly knocked over a container filled with naptha.

"Sorry, Chusor."

They worked in silence for a time, Chusor chewing his lips in concentration, and Leo making a show of being extremely careful. The smith finally said, "I have seen forty thousand of the water horses—the hippopotami—in the shallows of the Nile River." He paused to wipe the sweat from his brow. "One day we went to see that famous talking statue of the Egyptian king Memnon that lies in ruins. The sun was so hot, it burned my scalp through my hat."

"You don't say!"

"The wind blew the sand into our eyes and pelted our uncovered flesh with the pain of needle pricks."

"I have heard of the statue," Leo lied. "Did it speak to *you*?"

"It did speak, though I was the only one of our group to hear it. And it was more like a song than a voice. Like the untuned pluck of a lyre. I had them carve my name on the base of the statue: 'Chusor born of Athens heard Memnon speak twice on a hot day.' It was expensive: they charged by the letter."

"Maybe I will see it someday," said Leo hopefully. "And your graffiti too."

Diokles entered the door. He had an armful of small, empty pots that he placed on the table in front of Chusor.

"Good," said Chusor. "That is the right size. Bring more."

Diokles nodded, picked up the Pandora that Chusor had just finished, and hefted it out the door.

"Honey pots?" asked Leo, nodding at the apple-size vessels.

"These are to be filled with naptha only," explained Chusor, "and plugged with wax. We will hurl them through the windows in the towers, dousing the chambers inside. Then archers shoot in flaming arrows to ignite the volatile liquid. The men inside will be roasted as in a furnace." He waved him away. "Now, stop talking, or else I'm going to plug your mouth with wax."

Chusor went back to work. But his mind would not stay focused. Telling Leo about Egypt had stirred up old memories. Scenes from his past flitted through his head, seemingly disconnected images yet full of hidden portent. His first master, Phidias, old and stooped, feebly carving a marble block and saying, "The figure speaks its way out." His mother, withered like a desiccated mummy, dead on her pallet, a hateful fly sipping at the corner of her mouth. The playwright Euripides raging at his actors during a rehearsal, "Pitiful creatures! Pitiful creatures!" and smashing a theater mask onto the stage. The statue of Memnon in the light of the dying sun, seemingly come to life, its enigmatic smile mocking him. A prostitute he'd bedded in Syrakuse clinging to his feet, begging him not to leave her behind, shouting that she carried his child. And Nikias, the expression on his face before he lowered himself into the tunnel. . . .

How curious it was that Nikias should be the one to lead him to the tunnel. What a strange twist of destiny. The reason he had come to this city in the first place was because of the legend of the Plataean tyrant's buried hoard. He had spent the last three years mapping the citadel, with Diokles the expert digger exploring its sewers and undercrofts in secret by night. But they'd found nothing to make him think the tales of buried wealth—enough gold to buy a small fleet of triremes—were true.

But tonight had changed everything. How ironic that he'd finally found the secret tunnel with the future of the city hanging by a single frayed thread from the spindle of the Fates. If there was one tunnel under Plataea, there were most likely more. The treasure must be down there. The odds of living to find the trove, however, were slim at best.

At least now he knew of an escape route. If the attack on the Theban barricade failed, he would have to force himself to enter that tunnel with Diokles, despite his terror of tight places. He glanced at Leo working silently beside him. The homely lad's brow was fixed in an expression of intense concentration as he measured the volatile ingredients.

"I'm not going to die here with these Plataeans," Chusor thought. "Or be captured by the Thebans. This isn't my city."

But the mere thought of going into that tunnel made his heart start racing. He thought of the prison pits of Syrakuse, where he'd been put into one of the "beehive" cells for a week as a punishment—a space so cramped, he'd barely had room to draw a breath. Where he'd stewed in his own filth in the dark until he nearly lost his mind.

He realized he was sweating profusely and wiped his face on his sleeve. Glancing up, he saw that Leo was staring at him, grinning.

"What are you smiling about?" asked Chusor.

"The Fates."

"What about them?"

"They brought you to us," said Leo. "They were the ones who brought you here. I'll never curse them again."

The young man's words were like daggers to Chusor's conscience. "I'm a coward," he wanted to say. "And the only thing I'm good at is saving my own skin." But he shrugged and said aloud, "The Fates are miserable old hags, Leo. Don't ever let them fool you."

TEN

Nikias galloped into the farmyard and leapt from his horse before it had come to a full stop. The instant his feet hit the ground, he was running toward the house, through the carnage of bodies and smoldering buildings.

"Grandfather!" he yelled. "Mother!"

At the threshold of the main house he recoiled. The front door had completely burned away. The roof and second floor were gone—had collapsed!—and lay in smoking heaps in the center of the house, licked by a myriad of hearth-size blazes, the dying remnants of the great fire that had roared through the building, consuming everything within. There was nothing left but a crumbling, empty stone shell, like a blackened and cracked kiln, the sturdy chimney rising to the height of where the roof used to be.

His family was dead. Burned alive.

He staggered back to the yard. There were corpses sprawled everywhere: black-clad Thebans with arrows sticking through them. His grandfather and the women had put up a good fight—that was plain to see. He hoped none of them had been taken alive. He saw something that made him flinch. Two spears in the ground in the shape of an X, lashed together, with his grandfather's shield hanging at the intersection—the shield with the boxing Minotaur. The old man was dead. Now he knew for certain. And somebody had put up this makeshift memorial to mark the spot. It must have been Saeed.

"Good old Saeed. Loyal to the end," he thought.

He took his grandfather's shield down from the cross of spears and slipped it onto his back with its convex painted surface facing out. He cinched it tight using the leather strap that was built into the shield for just this purpose. Now he could ride without it bouncing around.

Had any of the women survived the attack on the farm? He hoped not. He imagined, with revulsion, his mother and Phile being raped . . . his grandmother humiliated . . . all of them chained . . . beaten . . . dragged back to Thebes to live out the rest of their lives in toil and degradation. How could the Fates weave such a web of misery? How could life change so fast? The day before, he had had a family and a city. But now . . .

He looked around blankly. Somehow he'd found his way to the burned-out husk of the barn without even realizing it. He started searching through the debris, clawing through the charred wreckage. He didn't know why he was doing this or what he was looking for. And then his hand felt a familiar thing made of braided leather. He pulled out his Sargatian whip with a cry of exultation.

He remembered leaving it there, in the corner of the barn, coiled around his spear after the fight with Kallisto's brothers at the Cave of Nymphs. The spear had burned away, but the whip remained. The weapon, intricately braided by Saeed from an entire ox hide soaked in brine, was impervious to fire. He held it to his cheek and felt the heat emanating from it. He thought back to how Kallisto had taken the whip from him that day in the cave . . . wrapped it around his waist . . . pulled him close to her warm body . . .

He would ride to her family's farm now. He would ride there and free her and take her someplace safe. And if any of her brothers tried to stop him, he would strike them down. As he walked back to the smoking ruin of the house, he coiled the whip and tied it to his belt in a breakaway knot using the leather strip that was attached to the whip's handle. It felt good to have the weapon at his hip again, slapping against his leg as he walked.

He got on his Theban horse and kicked the gelding hard, riding fast down the farm's drive and onto the main road.

"Whoa!" he shouted.

He turned his horse and just missed colliding with three horsemen who were galloping up the road from the opposite direction. His mount reared and he had to grab its mane to stay on.

"Nikias!" shouted Saeed. "What are you doing here?"

"Saeed!" yelled Nikias with relief. "You're alive." He glanced at the other two riders. One was Kolax, grinning from ear to ear. The other's face, however, was completely hidden behind a heavy, old-fashioned helm, revealing nothing of the wearer's features through its thin horizontal eye slits and single vertical mouth slot. This stranger wore an old cloak that parted in the middle to reveal a battered breastplate that was too big for the rider's meager frame. At least the resourceful Saeed had found one warrior, albeit a scrawny one, Nikias mused.

"Where is everyone?" he asked. "What in the name of Zeus happened?"

"Thebans came to the farm," said Saeed. "A madman led them."

"So my grandfather is—"

"Yes," said Saeed, dropping his head. "He is dead. But your grandmother and sister are alive."

"Thank the Gods!" declared Nikias. "Where are they?"

"They are at Helladios's farm."

"And my . . . mother?" asked Nikias, his voice catching in his throat.

"She did not make it," said Saeed softly. "They killed her."

The news hit Nikias like a fist to his gut. The world seemed to spin round and tilt at a strange angle. His beautiful mother with the knife-sharp wit. The weaver, the scolder, the healer. The only person he'd ever shed tears in front of without feeling shame. How many times had she comforted him? Tended his wounds? Told him how much she loved him? Her voice echoed in his mind: "Vengeance now, my son. Grieve for me later." He stared into space blankly and asked, "Did Mula make it back to the farm?"

"Yes," said Saeed, wiping his eyes. "But he is dying."

Nikias didn't know what to say. He thought of the little boy, so anxious to be his friend and follow him everywhere. And how he was always spurning Mula, ordering him away like an annoying puppy. When he'd promised to take him hunting the other day, Mula had been so happy.

"I sent him," said Nikias. "It's my fault."

"The boy will live, Nikias!" burst in Kolax, chattering in his strange tongue. "I told your gloomy slave here, but he won't believe me. Mula is strong. And I blessed him with the blood of my ancestors. Put my own blood on his lips. See? I'm painted with the Gryphon of Skythia. My father marked me with needle and ink. And my blood is now a healing potion." He lifted his tunic and turned his back to them revealing a dark blue tattoo of a gryphon—a creature with a lion's body and the wings and head of an eagle—spread across his skin from shoulder to shoulder. He held up a palm to show the slit where he'd drawn his own blood.

Nikias had a vague idea of what Kolax was talking about. The Persian language that Saeed had taught him over the years was similar to the Skythian tongue, but most of Kolax's words sounded like a confusing jumble of nonsense. "Skythian boy," he said in Persian, pointing at Photine. "That's my horse. You take this one."

Kolax understood. He pulled his tunic back down and slid gracefully off the back of the white mare. "I found her in a field by your farm. She's a good animal," he said, and added proudly, "I rode her to battle and killed two men. My tally, though, is three for the night. I'll bet *you* haven't killed more, giant yellow-haired Ox man."

"The Skythian saved us tonight," said Saeed dispassionately. He was too distraught over his son's injury to translate any of Kolax's words. "Saved us from Eurymakus the Theban."

"Eurymakus?" said Nikias, confused. He leapt onto Photine's back and patted her neck. Her muscles rippled at his touch and she let forth a happy whinny.

"He is the brother of Damos," explained Saeed. "The man my master killed in the pankration. He came for revenge."

Nikias thought back to the Olympics, remembering the joy he'd felt when his grandfather had choked the life out of the hated Damos. There'd been a teen-ager in Damos's entourage who'd grabbed the Theban pankrator's legs and tried in vain to pull him from Menesarkus's deadly embrace. The lad had screamed "Murderer!" over and over again and had to be dragged away by the other Theban athletes. There'd nearly been a riot after that, and Menesarkus had to be spirited out of the arena by an armed guard. Nikias had found his way back to their campsite on his own, bristling all the way with the word "Murderer!" echoing in his brain.

Nikias cursed, shaking himself from this memory. He kicked Photine and started riding away. "Tell Kolax he's a brave warrior. Now, all of you, follow me." Saeed and the rider wearing the helm fell in on either side as he headed west in the direction of Plataea.

"The Skythian boy told us what had happened in the city," said Saeed. "We are on our way to warn the farmers. How did you get out of the citadel?"

"I escaped through a tunnel," said Nikias. "The enemy holds the gates. They're waiting for reinforcements to arrive from Thebes. I've got to raise the countryside and get word to the garrisons in the mountains and the watchtowers on the bor-ders." He looked up toward the Kithaerons and then back toward the city. "I don't know which to do first. There's not enough time!"

"Isokrates sent messengers to the mountain garrisons," said the helmeted rider in a voice almost completely muffled from inside the thickly padded face mask. "And he rode to the border towers on the downs to warn General Zoticus."

"Isokrates?" said Nikias distractedly, preoccupied with his thoughts. "He'll just make a mess of everything." He turned off the road and into a field. The other riders followed.

"Where are you going now?" asked Saeed.

"I'm going to Helladios's farm," answered Nikias without looking back.

"Why? Your grandmother and sister are safe," called the helmeted rider.

"What's it to you?" asked Nikias. "I'm going to see if Helladios's daughter is well."

"That's foolish," said the helmeted rider. "There's no time for that."

Nikias kicked Photine and turned sharply around, veered in front of the hel-meted rider's mount, and grabbed the bridle. They both came to an abrupt stop.

"Want to call me a fool again?" asked Nikias. "Because I'll knock your scrawny arse off that horse so fast, you'll—"

The rider took off the helm and a cascade of long brown curls spilled out.

"Kallisto!" Nikias shouted in surprise. "What are you doing on the road? You need to be safe indoors."

"Don't take me back home," she said, glaring at him. "Not to that place. They tried to kill me, Nikias. I'm not going to stay locked in my room, waiting for the enemy or my family to slay me."

"You don't know what kind of danger—"

"Kallisto was at the farm when the attack came," interrupted Saeed. "She is brave. She killed Thebans."

Nikias stared at her in amazement. "What were you doing at our farm?"

"My father was going to sell me to the Makedonian slaver," she said. "He beat me and locked me up. Akake helped me escape. He's dead now. I went to your house to find you. To beg your help. Why didn't you come for me?" she asked with fury. "Why did you leave me with them?"

"I was in jail," said Nikias, exasperated. "Didn't anyone tell you that?"

She dropped her head, confused, searching for words. "They told me nothing." She walked her horse over to Nikias and put her hand on his shoulder. "I couldn't stop the Theban. From killing your mother. I couldn't . . . It happened so fast, Nik. My father is—"

"Your father is dead," interrupted Nikias bluntly. "He was in the citadel. They found his severed head in a sack."

Kallisto chewed on her lip, nodding slowly. "It's what he deserves."

"Let's go back," he said. "I'll take you to some other farm. You can hide there and escape to the mountains if we fail. I've seen what the enemy does to women. They butchered Nauklydes's daughter. War is for men—"

"To Hades with men and their rules!" shouted Kallisto. "To Hades with my dead father's shade! Listen to me now," she said, piercing him with her eyes. "Two weeks ago Magistrate Nauklydes came to our house and I overheard a conversation between him and my father. They were talking about the citizens who opposed their pro-Spartan stance. And how they might have to shard them. They mentioned your grandfather." She wiped away the tears of shame rolling down her cheeks. "Now I know my father was a traitor and I curse his name."

"Why didn't you say something to me about this meeting?" asked Nikias, furious.

"I was going to!" screamed Kallisto, her rage boiling over. "At the cave. And then my brothers found us. Or have you forgotten that day?"

"I haven't forgotten," said Nikias in a low voice. He was thunderstruck. He couldn't believe that Nauklydes had been in league with Helladios. It seemed impossible that the magistrate—his grandfather's old shield man—had done such a heinous thing. Even if what Kallisto said was the truth, who would believe the story? How would he find proof?

"*War is for men*," she said, echoing his words with scorn. "Men made it happen, that's for certain. And the women will suffer, just like always." She put on her helm, dug in her knees, and bolted down the road in the direction of Plataea.

ELEVEN

———◆———

"Don't move, Nephew," said Tykon. "Just lie still."

Perseus could not move even if he had wanted to. His arms and legs were pinned to the floor by four men, each holding a limb. When he tried to speak his tongue would not work; something was shoved into his mouth, it tasted bitter . . . a piece of leather?

"What happened?" asked Tykon. "Who saw it happen?"

"I did," said the man holding his leg. "Perseus was working on one of the gates, hammering away at the hinge pin on top. And all of a sudden he went stiff and fell off the ladder. Landed on the ground twisting and arching his back. We stuck the strap in his mouth so he wouldn't bite off his tongue. I've seen this before. They'll bite off their tongue if you don't give them something to clamp down on."

"He soiled and wet himself," said a man, with a hint of disdain.

"That's normal," said Tykon defensively. "I've seen this happen before to men with head wounds, after a battle."

"And I too," said a second man. "My brother got hit so hard on his helm, it caved in his skull and he had these fits for years."

"And then what?" asked a third.

"Then he choked on his own vomit one night and died."

Perseus stared in confusion at Tykon with his remaining eye. His anxiety seemed amplified, as if having *two* eyes might have diluted his fear. Tykon's greatest worry was that the wound that had destroyed his nephew's eye had also pierced his brain. The young man had not seemed out of his wits a short time earlier, though, when they'd stood together looking at the gates. It had been his ingenious idea to remove the pin hinges from the doors and then rig them with ropes to pull them down from the inside if the Plataeans managed to swarm the barricade. In fact, Perseus had insisted on climbing a ladder and hammering out one of the massive hinge pins himself, exposing his body to enemy arrows.

"Do you know who I am?" Tykon asked Perseus.

Perseus nodded his head slightly.

"Let him go and remove the gag," said Tykon. Once his nephew was free, he asked again, "Who am I?"

Perseus licked lips flecked with foamy vomit. He shook his head and cupped a hand to his ruined eye. "My head hurts here," he said.

"You have been injured," explained Tykon. "In a fight. Do you know where you are?"

"I—" Perseus sat up, stared at Tykon vacuously.

"We're in the gate tower," said Tykon. "In Plataea."

"We're all going to die in here," said Perseus. "Zeus told me."

The men within earshot grumbled. First Tiresius had forewarned of their doom. Now the general's own nephew, after his paroxysm, had divined catastrophe.

If Perseus had been any other man, Tykon would have cut off his head without compunction. He knew his nephew wasn't at fault for his words. He'd seen men's personalities change dramatically after injuries to the brain and especially after seizures. But making this sort of pronouncement could make the men panic and attempt to flee the city. He had to act quickly. He had to be ruthless.

"He has lost his mind," announced Tykon. "He is worthless to us." He waved for Darius. "Take this man outside of the gates and let him find his way home."

The men stopped talking. This was a grave punishment. Perseus might as well go hang himself. Even if he made it back home tonight, he would be treated as a pariah, a coward, scum.

Tykon hissed something in Darius's ear and the man nodded sternly. Then he picked Perseus off the floor and manhandled him out the door of the gate tower. As he went past his uncle, Perseus gave Tykon a ghastly smile, an expression that could have been interpreted as hatred . . . or pity.

Guards opened one of the gates enough to allow Darius and Perseus to squeeze through. Once they were on the other side, Darius led Perseus by the arm away from the city walls.

"I know my way home," said Perseus bitterly. "My memory only left me for a few minutes."

Darius did not speak but clutched Perseus's arm more forcefully.

"You're going to kill me," said Perseus. "Good."

Darius stayed mute. A short walk from the city, they came to the Temple of Androkles. The small shrine was a three-walled pavilion built to worship the ancient savior and hero of Plataea—the Tyrant killer. Darius pushed Perseus inside and stuck his torch in the wall sconce. Perseus squatted on the floor and waited for his death.

"Your uncle knows that it is not your fault," said Darius with tenderness. "He told me to bring you here. He could not have you near the men. Not after what you said."

"He should have killed me himself," said Perseus.

"What did you see in the vision?" asked Darius. "What did Zeus tell you?"

"I'm sorry, Darius," said Perseus. "I spoke . . . without thinking. My mind is altered. The wound. The fit."

"Tell me," Darius insisted, and got down on all fours, peering into his face.

"Zeus was laughing," said Perseus.

"That's all?"

"Yes."

"And you took that to mean—"

"He was *laughing*!" whined Perseus and pawed at his bloody eye. "Don't you see, you fool? Can't you see what I *mean*?"

Darius dropped his head in misery. He got up and went to the entrance to the shrine and paused. "Stay here and rest. When the fighting starts, come back to the city. If you're killed or captured with us, you and your family will not suffer shame." And then he left Perseus alone.

Perseus put his cheek against the cold marble floor and fell into a fitful, fevered sleep. He saw the mocking face of Zeus again. In his dream the god carved a spear from a shaft of wood, then hardened it over a fire as Odysseus had when he made the weapon to blind the Cyclops. Zeus plunged the stake into Perseus's eye. He woke up screaming and clasping his wound. The mocking face of Zeus had showed him Thebes's destiny. Failure. Ignominy. Death.

No shrines in Thebes for Perseus or Tykon.

He could hang himself, he considered . . . or smash his skull against the shrine's altar, but he was dizzy and his head throbbed. He did not have the energy to even stand. When he felt better, he promised himself, he would figure out a way to end his miserable life.

He thought back to the street fight. He had been running a message back to the barricades when he turned a corner and smashed right into an enemy. He struck out at the Plataean with an axe, but it was deflected by his leather armor. Then the enemy got him on his back. He felt a blinding flash of light and searing pain and somehow wriggled free, fled for his life. He hid in the dark, like an animal . . . catching his breath. Finally, he found Tiresius and the others and skulked back to the gates.

The face of the Plataean appeared clearly in his memory—the long blond hair, the fierce eyes . . . Androkles the hero made flesh. What he recalled now—what made him boil with rage—was the manner in which the enemy had mutilated his face: the Plataean had clawed the eyeball out of his skull with his dirty thumb and squeezed it in his hand until it popped.

He lay still on the floor of the temple like a corpse, staring at the strange lights flashing before his eyes. "You're a shade now," echoed a voice in his head as he drifted into another nightmare. "There's nothing to be afraid of, because you're already dead."

TWELVE

———————◆———————

Nikias, Kallisto, and Saeed had not gone half a mile before they came upon a motley assemblage slogging down the road, a man and two teenaged boys astride mules attended by five slaves. The slaves carried armloads of weapons and armor, all of it protected by leather cases and fitted sleeves. They were having trouble hefting the gear through the mire and were barely moving. Nikias knew the riders: General Agape and his two strong sons. Nikias called out a greeting and they turned their heads in surprise.

"Hey, Nik, what are you doing here?" asked Baklydes, the oldest boy. "I thought you'd run away from home after you killed that bastard Lysander."

"No time for talk," said Nikias. "The city is taken. Thebans hold the gates."

"So it's true!" said Agape. "Isokrates's messenger told us as much, but I did not believe it until now. Boys, didn't I say to you earlier, 'I cannot believe that Plataea has fallen into enemy hands, even though Isokrates, the son of a man whom I trust to the highest degree, says it is so?'"

Hesiod, the youngest of Agape's sons and the most quick-witted, ignored his father's digression and said, "The messenger came to us half an hour ago and told us to gather our gear and meet at the Island as fast as we could." The Island was a low hillock just to the north of the city. "But we had to secure the house first and lock the women away," he added almost apologetically, "in case the raiders came and did what they did to you and yours."

"Kronos's chopped balls, you should be there by now!" said Nikias. "If everyone is as slow as you—burdened by armor packed up in traveling cases, and riding mules besides—the Thebans will have planted and harvested wheat and named their bastard children by the time everyone arrives."

"There is an old saying," offered Agape, "about a hare and a tortoise in a race. And the slow—"

"Tonight slow and steady dies," interrupted Nikias. "My mother, my grandfather, my uncle and his family, and two of my friends are rotting! If you want your sons to suck Theban spear poles for the rest of their lives, then by all means, take your sweet time."

"I won't be sucking any Theban's spear pole," shouted Baklydes. "I'll crack their heads open with my bare fists!"

"Where is Isokrates now?" asked Nikias.

"Heading north to the border towers," replied Hesiod. "To warn the cavalry so they can cut off the Theban reinforcements along the Kadmean Road."

"But how does he know the Theban reinforcements are coming from that direction?" asked Nikias.

"He happened upon a dispatch pouch at your house," Agape cut in. "It must have been dropped by one of the Thebans who attacked your grandfather. I did not actually see the pouch, nor the written message, though I assume it was inscribed on papyrus and not—"

"What did it *say*?" interrupted Nikias.

Hesiod spoke before his father could butt in again. "It said that they could not hold the gates for much longer and to come by the quickest path. So Isokrates assumed that meant the Kadmean Road."

"I don't see the wisdom of assembling at the Island," Agape began in his most didactic tone. "I believe we should form up positions based on the old defensive front conceived by the illustrious . . ."

Agape droned on while Nikias and Hesiod exchanged worried looks.

"What should we do, Nik?" whispered Hesiod.

"I don't know," he said. "We could end up chasing after Isokrates and General Zoticus all night. Nobody in Plataea has ever had to fight this kind of battle before."

"The Persians invited everyone to a feast the day before they attacked," said Kallisto. "There were no heralds to announce *this* battle."

"Who's he?" asked Baklydes, pointing at Kallisto.

"My cousin Kallos," said Nikias with a wry smile, using the male version of Kallisto's name. She glanced back at him under her helm and he saw her eyes flash. "This is all going to end up in a hopeless mess," he continued. "Small bands of farmers like you and your family . . . stuck in the mud, burdened by armor and slaves . . ."

"Not exactly an efficient army of liberators," said Hesiod.

Nikias said, "The most important question is this: Are the Theban reinforcements really coming from the northern roads? I think it would be foolhardy of them. Especially with this rain."

He thought back to a day a dozen years earlier when he and his grandfather had ridden to the Lookout. How Menesarkus had told him that no enemy would ever be able to sneak up on Plataea and had scoffed at his childish observation that the enemy could merely sweep around to the west past the border watchtowers and advance over the Oeroe River, the river running from east to west across the Oxlands. His grandfather had laughed at him then. He'd said that the Thebans were not barbarians and played by the rules of war. But the enemy had proven his grandfather wrong on every point. Their entire strategy had relied on treachery and the cover of darkness.

"Slap my stupid arse!" exclaimed Nikias, interrupting Agape, who had moved on from the subject of the allies' positions against the Persians fifty years before to something also close to his heart: the scolding of his slaves. In this case one youngster who had allowed Agape's leather shield case to get into the mud.

"Eh?" asked Agape. "Whose arse are we slapping?"

"What is it, Nik?" said Hesiod.

"The Theban reinforcements," Nikias replied. "Some of them will be coming across country. I'm certain of it. It might take them all night to get here, but they can sweep right around the garrisons and Isokrates and his cavalry. If I were them, I would cross the Asopus near Eutresis, go south, and approach Plataea from the western road. We should look for the enemy there too."

"They'll have to cross at the Victory Bridge at the village of Oeroe," said Kallisto. The bridge in question was at the intersection of the roads to Thespiai and Kreusis. It was less than a mile from the city walls. There stood a tiny village consisting of fifty men.

The clouds parted and a quarter of the moon showed through the rent, illuminating the night with its bright glow.

"We've got to go to the Victory Bridge," said Nikias. "If they're on horseback, they might already be there."

"I'm going with you!" said Hesiod.

"You're not going anywhere, boy!" shouted Agape.

"You'll never keep up with us on that thing," said Kallisto, casting a sideways glance at Hesiod's mule.

"Zeus's blood!" growled Hesiod.

"Ride with the Skythian," said Kallisto.

"The Skythian?" asked Hesiod.

Kallisto pointed at Kolax, who was making his new horse dance around them in a circle, teaching it how to kick out with its hind legs when he prodded its rump with his bow.

THIRTEEN

———— ◆ ————

The river was called the Oeroe, but the Theban cavalry general knew the locals referred to it as "the daughter of the Asopus." It was a smaller river than its namesake but it sprang from the same source—the Kithaeron Mountains—sweeping around the east of Plataea, then turning sharply and running west parallel to the Asopus all the way to the Sea of Korinth. The rains had swelled the banks of the Oeroe River and its tributaries, spilling over the sides and inundating the ground with several inches of water, washing out much of the road that ran from Plataea to Thespiai.

The general's three hundred riders had been forced to get off and walk alongside their mounts for much of the way, but in spite of this they had made good time, going cross-country and skirting the single watchtower in this area on the hill of Pyrgo. They were close now to the stone bridge that spanned the Oeroe, the one the Plataeans called Victory Bridge. Once the general and his men crossed this bridge, they would have only one more mile until they reached Plataea and their brothers holding the city.

He knew there was a small village on the other side of the bridge. The inhabitants of the town relied on the city of Plataea for protection. In times of danger they would retreat, along with the inhabitants of other villages in the valley, to the safety of the city walls, bringing with them their animals and valuables—sometimes even pulling the wooden doors off their homes.

The Theban general's name was Straton, and he had ordered his riders to slay all the men in the village and make quick work of it—no rape. This last part had nothing to do with ethics. They had to work fast to secure this crossing and move on to the city. There would be time enough to enjoy their enemy's wives, daughters, and sons when the city was securely in Theban hands. The last message they had received from Tykon had sounded desperate. He hoped they were not too late.

The fact that they had yet to see a Plataean scout all night boded well. Straton hoped it meant that Tykon and his men had the city sealed up tight and were still waiting for the reinforcements to arrive.

"Probably tasting Plataean wine and women," his second in command, Miltiades, had said merrily a short while ago.

Straton had gone against Eurymakus the spy's original plan of sending all of the reinforcements in a single mass along the Kadmean Road. But his decision to change things had only been because of the extreme rain. At the start of their journey, the horses out in front had so churned up the path with their hooves, they'd made it nearly impossible for the men behind to get a footing. He had decided it was most prudent to split the army up into two mobile attack forces and avoid the roads.

He had sent a small band of three hundred metics and slaves to continue down the Kadmean Road, the old thoroughfare running from Plataea to the north. The men on this road were to act as decoys and draw the Plataeans from their garrisons. General Gennadios, the commander of the hoplites, had swept round to the east in charge of sixteen hundred men—the main force of the army—marching through cultivated fields in the direction of the old Persian Fort along with a hundred mounted archers. At the same time Straton had headed in the opposite direction, leading his three hundred riders over the downs, and then south along a less-traveled road in the direction of Plataea.

He patted his horse on the neck. He was an old stallion who had served Straton well over the years. He would put the beast out to stud if all went well tonight. Maybe even in a field nearby. As one of the victorious generals, Straton would be granted the pick of estates for his reward. He hoped this would please the shade of his grandfather, the only Theban general to win honor in the Battle of Plataea fifty years before. His cavalry unit had routed an enemy group killing six hundred men of Thespiai in a bold headlong charge. If only his grandfather had been in control of the entire army that day . . . They might have won the war against the Greek allies.

Miltiades appeared at his side, a wide grin on his round face.

"There's nobody guarding the bridge," proclaimed Miltiades. "I even rode through the village."

"You didn't see any sign of life?" asked Straton. That could mean the villagers had already been warned and had fled to Plataea. He wouldn't be able to claim this village as a personal war prize and would have to divide up the inhabitants with his fellow commanders. The thought rankled him.

"Don't worry," replied Miltiades, reading his general's face. "I heard a baby crying in one of the houses. They're all in their beds. They have no idea what's coming."

"Riders to me!" said Straton, and his aides galloped off down the line to order the three hundred horsemen to form up on the road.

He could hear the Oeroe long before they got to the bridge—a roar of rushing water. It was a good thing they didn't have to cross through the river, he considered, because their horses wouldn't have been able to ford the rain-swollen waterway. The bridge was narrow; only two riders could pass side by side. He peered into the gloom on the village side as he walked across. He could just make out two rows of buildings on either side of the road, forming a little canyon.

The only sounds were the rain and the roaring river and the faint cry of the baby. Straton thought of his grandchildren safe at home in Thebes. The youngest boy's first teeth had just come in. Two little white stones on the lower jaw.

Straton and about fifty riders had crossed the bridge—nearly filling the entire street from the bridge to the end of the lane—when he gave the signal for men to dismount. He cupped a hand to his mouth and shouted, "Villagers of Oeroe! Open your doors. The city of Plataea is taken. I, Straton of Thebes, am now your master."

The Thebans drew their swords, moved to the doorways, ready to storm the houses. The sound of the crying baby got louder . . . it was moving . . . and now it was outside. Then the rain stopped.

"The rain," said Straton under his breath. "Zeus has decided to dry us off."

"A mother is trying to escape with her baby," commented Miltiades. His voice held the slightest suggestion of pity.

Something caught Straton's eye atop one of the buildings. A little boy stood there holding a torch. It took the Theban a long moment to realize the boy was the one making the crying-baby sound. Next to him was what appeared to be a slender young man in a helm, crouched in an archer's stance. The child's whimpering turned into an eerie laugh that sent a shudder through Straton's body.

"Eh?" asked Straton, perplexed. "What's this?"

The boy hurled the torch toward the Thebans and before it had hit the ground the child had picked up a bow, strung an arrow, and sent the shaft straight through the shoulder of the general. At the same time the archer next to the boy shot Miltiades through the eye.

Shutters flew open. Arrows sang. The horses shrieked and bucked. The Thebans who'd already dismounted ran to and fro, searching for someplace to hide. Doors opened willingly and pulled the invaders into houses, where they were hacked and bludgeoned by many hands—both men's and women's.

On the bridge, ten horses and their riders were slain by a band of javelin throwers who burst from a hiding place in one of the olive mills by the river. Human and animal corpses clogged the narrow passageway. The hundreds of Theban cavalry who had been lucky enough to be on the other side of the river were helpless to come to the aid of their brothers. Some of them tried to cross the river but were swept away. The rest retreated into the night, fleeing from the arrows shot into their midst.

Straton spun his horse round and round in the chaos of the street, searching for a way out of this death trap. A leather whip slipped over his head, tightened around his neck, and yanked him off the back of his mount. Men dragged him into a room, where he was beaten nearly to death. Outside he heard the screaming of his riders. But this only lasted for a few more minutes, and then all was quiet save for an occasional shouted order from the Plataeans or a cry that was quickly silenced.

Then hands lifted him again, pulled him into another room, and threw him on the floor. Straton peered through swollen lids at a face inches from his own—a youth with long blond hair and blood-splattered cheeks who eyed him with the cold stare of an executioner. Next to him was a beautiful young woman wearing battered armor, a helm tucked under one arm, a bow hugged against her chest, and her cheek bleeding from a gash.

The young man unwrapped the leather thong that was still tied around Straton's neck, slowly coiled it around his knuckles menacingly, like a pankrator wrapping his fists for a training bout. Over his shoulder a red-haired barbarian child—the one from the roof—peeked at him, a lunatic smile on his gap-toothed face. He let forth a single babylike cry.

"Stranger," said Nikias to the Theban general, "welcome to my country."

FOURTEEN

———————— ◆ ————————

Tykon and his men were anxious for the Plataeans to attack. The general went up and down the lines of the barricade, giving words of encouragement to his fighters. "Hold your spears high and aim for the eyeholes in the helms, or low at the genitals. And be prepared for an enemy fighter who might try to grab your spear and yank it from your hands. Jab," he told them. "Stick them like boars. Quick jabs. If your spearhead breaks off, don't forget your spike." Tykon knew how one could forget the most basic things in the heat of battle, like the fact that every spear had a spike on the butt end to anchor it to the ground or to serve as a redundant piercing weapon. To the archers on the walls and in the towers he sent this message: "Make your arrows count."

He was just heading back toward the gates, through the endlessly pouring rain, when one of the doors opened a crack and a man—his head covered in a cape—squeezed through. At first Tykon thought it was his nephew, Perseus, come back to redeem himself, and he started to raise a welcoming hand before he realized it was one of his young aides.

"General," he said. "Riders outside the gates."

Tykon allowed himself a sigh of relief. The cavalry had somehow managed to make it from Thebes! He followed the guard outside the walls, anxious to see his brothers. But there were only two riders, drooping on their horses' backs, men and beasts miserable and sodden in the rain.

"Where are the rest of your men?" asked Tykon, thinking they were advance scouts. "Where is the main force?"

One of the horsemen dismounted. He held his cloak over his mouth, walked painfully toward Tykon. When the man got close enough, Tykon could tell by his almond-shaped eyes he was Eurymakus. His hopes vanished. His guts went slack. The cavalry had not come. He recognized the other rider: Bogha, Eurymakus's Median servant. Bogha's jaw hung open, his mouth was a bloody hole.

"What happened?" asked Tykon.

"We were ambushed," replied Eurymakus. His speech sounded strange, garbled. His eyes darted around, focusing on nothing. "We had to walk back from Menesarkus's. We found these horses wandering on the road. So the cavalry has not arrived?"

"No," Tykon said, and glanced upward. "The rain."

Eurymakus spat behind the cloth.

"Where are the rest of your men?" asked Tykon. "I need them now. The Plataeans have broken out of their homes and are going to attack—"

"You let them escape?" asked Eurymakus with disgust.

"I didn't *let* them—"

"They're dead," said Eurymakus, cutting him off. "All my men are dead."

"And Menesarkus?" asked Tykon.

"Burned alive," said Eurymakus.

The rain stopped. It was as though Zeus had slammed shut a giant sluice gate. A few moments later a series of signal flutes blared out across the city.

"The Plataeans are calling their attack!" said Tykon.

Eurymakus pulled the cloth from his mouth. Tykon stared in horror at the man's mangled face. His bloody canine and side teeth were now revealed in a permanent sneer, like that of an angry dog.

Theban voices cried out from the top of the wall, "Fire! Fire! They're burning down the barricade!"

"Get out of my way!"

Tykon whirled to see the coward Tiresius staggering toward them. He'd squeezed through the gate, followed by a billow of thick, white, acrid smoke. He coughed and choked on the poisonous stuff. He held his broken jaw with one hand, glared at Tykon as he pushed by him.

"Get back inside," commanded Tykon.

Tiresius started to draw his sword but Tykon was too fast. The general cut halfway through Tiresius's neck, severing his windpipe. Tiresius clutched his throat, dropped to his knees, and slowly suffocated to death.

A spinning ball of fire sailed past one of the gate towers—hurled from inside the city—and landed near them, cracking open and spewing a stream of fire across the ground.

Eurymakus mounted his horse and dug in his heels. "I go now to find the reinforcements," he said to Tykon, and spat out a mouthful of blood. "You, Tykon, hold this city. Stand until you die."

Tykon watched them go for a moment, then ducked through the gap in the doors. The barricade had turned to a wall of fire. He saw Darius pushing men back toward the flames, barking at them to stand their ground.

"No!" screamed Tykon. "Get them inside the towers!"

The Thebans retreated to the two towers on either side of the gates and slammed shut the portals, blocking out the inferno.

FIFTEEN

Magistrate Nauklydes sat on the floor of his office at the pottery factory. A single lamp glowed in the dark room. "Trapped," he mumbled. "I'm trapped." His hand stroked the lid of the heavy wooden lockbox—the box that held the skytale dowel and his other correspondence with the Thebans and Spartans. "I'll wear a tunic of stones," he said. "A tunic of stones." The door creaked open and Nauklydes curled up in a ball, covered his head with his hands.

"Magistrate?" asked a familiar voice.

"Pha-Phakas? Is that you?"

Nauklydes's assistant crept into the room holding a lamp. When he saw Nauklydes his mouth opened in a silent gasp. "What happened to you?"

"Where have you been?" asked Nauklydes in a child's whiny voice.

"I fled," said Phakas. "I've been hiding on the roof of the factory all night. I always suspected the Thebans of treachery. I tried to warn you."

"You did warn me," said Nauklydes. "Why didn't I listen?" His lower lip curled in a pout. "They did this to me." He held up his right hand. Phakas sucked in his breath, for Nauklydes was now missing his pinkie finger there.

"Theban pigs!" uttered Phakas.

"Daughter!" bawled Nauklydes. "Daughter! Where are you? Come out and stop cowering in the shadows!"

Phakas looked around the room, half expecting Penelope to emerge from the air.

"Where is Penelope?" asked Phakas.

Nauklydes rubbed his hand over the box. "All my secrets are in this box," he said, nodding his head. He leaned forward conspiratorially. "You know all my secrets, Phakas."

"Yes, Magistrate," replied Phakas nervously. "And I will take those secrets to my tomb."

"You weren't coming in here to get the bag of Persian gold out of this box, were you?"

Phakas cleared his throat, shook his head, looked down at the floor. "Gold?" he asked in a thin voice. "I didn't know there was gold," he lied.

"They're going to kill both of us," said Nauklydes.

"Who?"

"Whichever side wins."

"Let's go back to your home for now, Magistrate," said Phakas. "We will think of something later.

"I trusted them," said Nauklydes. "I was mad. But now I feel sane again."

"You have seen horrors—"

"I had a dream just now."

"A dream?"

"I was standing on a plinth outside the walls," Nauklydes said. "My skin was the color of new-forged bronze and gleamed in the sun. In one hand I held a spear, in the other a shield painted with a woman's profile surrounded by four leaping fish. On my head was an ancient helm fashioned from the tusks of boars. I was naked except for sandals on my feet. At the base of the plinth were a gang of satyrs lustily fornicating with both men and women." He became increasingly agitated. "I watched all of this with excitement, yet my own member remained flaccid. In the distance I saw two packs of animals approaching from either direction. From the south came foxes. From the north, slithering snakes. I was the only object that stood in their way. I took off the helmet and balanced it on one of the satyr's phalluses. Then I threw the spear in the direction of the east and started walking with the shield held high. And there stood my son, Demetrios, like a young god, smiling at me and beckoning!" He grabbed Phakas by the collar. "What does it mean? What does it mean?"

"I'm no oracle, Magistrate," said Phakas, licking his lips. "But it seems obvious to me."

"It does?" asked Nauklydes.

"The foxes are Spartans, the snakes are Thebans."

"Of course, idiot!" yelled Nauklydes. "But what about the satyrs? What about the boar-tooth helm? Why do I throw the spear to the east?"

"I—I—" stuttered Phakas. "I think the dream means that you will lead Plataea to victory."

"Victory?"

"You must prepare yourself for battle," Phakas said, and shrugged. "Perhaps?" he added with a mouse-like squeak.

Nauklydes released Phakas and slumped against the wall. He passed a hand over his face. "Menesarkus would laugh at me," he said. "Oh, how he would laugh to see me now." He looked at his destroyed hand and shook his head sadly. "No more hiding," he said. "I won't be captured again. We'll go back to my house. Gather my armor."

"Yes," agreed Phakas. "Let's go back to your house."

Nauklydes held open his left hand. He had been clutching his signet ring. The ring one of the Thebans had cut from his littlest finger to take as a war prize. After Nikias had freed him from his bonds, Nauklydes had found it on the floor of the storeroom. He kissed it now, slipped it on the ring finger of his mutilated hand.

"All my secrets," said Nauklydes wearily. "You know all my secrets." He rapped on the box with a knuckle, then he curled a finger at Phakas. "Come here." Phakas leaned close. "Look in the box," said the magistrate.

He opened it. Phakas peered inside. He could see something there . . . round and covered with blood. He put the lamp closer to it and saw human hair.

A shriek burst from his throat. "Penelope!"

SIXTEEN

The horde of Plataeans was waiting to rush the Theban defenses, staring in awe at the mighty fire created by the Egyptian's destructive genius. Even Chusor was taken aback by the power of his own pyrotechnic invention. The first Pandora jar they'd launched from its makeshift two-man sling had fallen short of its target, but even this errant missile had caused damage, breaking open on the stones of the agora and spreading liquid fire across the ground and under the upturned wagons, igniting the wood in a spectacular explosion. The next ten combustible jars, landing amidst the wooden debris, had started a volcanic blaze that reached the tops of the fifty-foot towers.

Screams of terror and agony rose above the roar of the conflagration. The enemy was trapped between fire and the gates. Chusor wondered if the enemy would flee through the gates and run away or stand to the last man. He reckoned the latter.

At the same time, throughout the city, small bands armed with the naptha-filled pots hurled their bombs through the windows of the towers that interspersed the walls, followed by flaming arrows to set them alight. The confined spaces became instant furnaces, gutted by pitch-fed fires. Men, set alight like human torches, leapt from the walls and turrets to their deaths.

As soon as the flames started to die out along the barricade, fifty Plataeans carrying a massive oak beam lumbered across the agora and rammed into the smoldering wreckage, making a pathway through the charred remains. They were followed close behind by hundreds of armored fighters. Chusor and Zeno led the way. But the area in front of the gates was empty of living men. The smoldering bodies of the enemy lay in crumpled heaps—at least a hundred corpses. The Plataeans shouted victoriously, "Theban pigs!" "It's over!" "We beat them!"

"There aren't enough men here," said Chusor. "Where did they—"

Before he could finish his sentence, the doors to the two gate towers flew open and the remaining two hundred Thebans swarmed from the portals. Tykon ran straight at Chusor and flung his short spear into his chest. The powerful force of the blow knocked Chusor backward and onto the ground. The spear-head pierced the tough leather armor and penetrated an inch into his pectoral muscle. Tykon drew his sword and swung it down at Chusor's head for the kill-ing blow, but the smith grabbed the shaft protruding from his chest and snapped it up against Tykon's blade, deflecting it. Chusor yanked the spear out, flipped it around, and plunged the tip into Tykon's leg. Tykon cursed and hobbled away toward the gates, snaking his way through the confusion of men.

Chusor got up and looked around quickly. Both sides were fighting like wild animals, screaming and kicking, smashing and cutting. Warriors rolled on the ground, gouging out each other's eyes, breaking jaws and teeth. He saw Diokles and Leo, side by side, wading through the brawl, cutting off heads and arms, pounding brains to spongy pulp. The Thebans put up a brave fight, but they were outnumbered twenty to one and losing the battle.

At the gates, Chusor saw Tykon and a dozen Thebans frantically pulling on ropes attached to the two huge portals. The Thebans heaved once, twice, and the doors groaned ominously on their hinges. He realized what was about to happen.

"To me!" cried Chusor. "The Gates of Pausanius! They're pulling down the gates!"

The two doors, no longer held in place by their pins, slipped from their hinges and toppled to the ground, crushing some of the Theban rope pullers as well as Plataeans beneath their massive ironbound oak planks. Tykon jumped back at the last second, just missing death. The way into Plataea was now wide open. Some of the invaders nearest the opening tried to escape and were chased down and slaughtered. But one managed to elude capture and disappeared into the fields.

Chusor strode toward Tykon, sword raised. "It's over!" he said. "Tell your men to throw down their weapons."

Tykon smiled. "You're right," he said. "It's over." He cupped his hands to his mouth and shouted, "Brothers! It is done! Give yourselves to the enemy."

The Thebans within earshot of their general tossed their arms to the side and raised their hands, palms up. Chusor saw one Theban who had called for clem-ency stabbed where he lay on the ground, while others were beaten with fists.

"Stop!" roared Chusor to the Plataeans. "We have defeated them! Stop! By the laws of battle you must not harm the prisoners!" He ran from man to man, pushing Plataean warriors aside, filled with wrath. He grabbed Leo, who was on top of a Theban, punching the man in the face, and grasped his wrist. "It's over, Leo!" he shouted.

Leo stared at him with murder in his eyes, then fell back on his haunches, looking around, nodding his head. "We won?" he asked.

The stunned Plataeans tied up the prisoners and surveyed the damage to the gates. Chusor, Diokles, and Leo stepped through the entrance and stood outside the walls. The sun had just begun to rise and the sky was illuminated by a pink glow. Chusor saw a rider crest the hills to the east and make his way at a canter toward Plataea. The rider stopped just out of arrow range. He seemed perplexed, unsure whether the armored men standing in the ruined gateway were friends or foes. Then the Theban who'd escaped from the melee at the gates leapt from the tall grass where he'd been hiding and ran to the rider, waving and calling out. The rider bolted to him, reached down, grabbed his arm, and swung him up behind him on the horse. They galloped away in the direction the rider had come.

"Theban scout," said Zeno.

Chusor turned to see the stonemason standing next to him. He had a deep gash along his cheek that wept dark blood. He peered in the direction of the rider, lips curled back. "The Theban reinforcements are near"—gesturing to the missing gates—"and we've got a hole in our armor."

SEVENTEEN

———— ◆ ————

A woman of the village of Oeroe sponged clean the cut on Kallisto's face with vinegar and water. They were sitting on the floor in a room filled with wounded villagers. In the next chamber, behind a closed door, Nikias and the other men were interrogating the Theban general. As Kallisto listened to the Theban's agonized screams, she remembered the beatings she had taken from her father and brothers.

"The vinegar stings," said the woman of Oeroe, thinking Kallisto was shivering because of her attentions.

"Yes," said Kallisto. She peered through the open door that led to the street and watched the men moving about on the dirt road, clearing it of the dead, picking weapons from the enemy and making orderly piles.

"Good thing for the Theban they didn't let *me* ask him some questions," said the woman with a crooked smile, nodding toward the closed door. "He would have sung his tale by now."

The Theban general let forth a deranged howl and then started speaking very fast.

"That did the trick," said a wounded man stretched out on the floor next to Kallisto.

Soon the door opened and Nikias strode into the room. His face was drained of blood, his mouth curled in an expression of disgust. Saeed was right behind him, wiping the blood from his dagger onto his legging. Hesiod ran to the door and retched. Kolax bounded out of the room holding something bloody in his hand, then disappeared into the street, imitating the Theban's screams with uncanny accuracy.

"Good work," Nikias said, putting a hand on Saeed's shoulder.

The Persian slave shrugged. "You believe him?"

"I do," said Nikias.

"Is he dead?" asked Kallisto.

"No," said Nikias.

"What did he tell you?" asked Kallisto.

"There's no time to discuss this," said Nikias. "Hesiod!"

Agape's son came back into the room, wiping his mouth on his sleeve. "Yes?"

"Take a man and ride back to the city. You'll have to find a way over the wall. Bring a rope and grappling hook. You've got to tell them what we've learned."

Hesiod nodded. "May the Fates lead you to Zoticus and the others."

"If you see Chusor the smith," said Nikias, "tell him, 'Eye gouges and biting allowed.'"

Hesiod made an attempt at a smile, said good-bye to Kallisto, and departed.

Kallisto kissed the woman who had been tending to her on the cheek. "I'm ready," she said to Nikias, standing up.

Nikias took her by the arm and led her into an empty room.

"What's wrong?" she asked.

"You need to stay here," he said.

"But you know I can fight," she said angrily, though she knew she was on the verge of collapsing from exhaustion. Her body could not take much more.

"You can't come with us!" shouted Nikias. Kallisto reeled from him, backing away from the ferocity in his voice, the anger in his eyes.

"Why?"

"Because it's too dangerous. There's an army of nearly two thousand Thebans marching from the east toward Plataea. We'll be lucky if we can round up a few hundred horsemen to hold them off—"

"But—"

"Kallisto," said Nikias, taking her in his arms. "We ride to our deaths."

She looked into his eyes, saw the agony there. "I'll ride with you, then," she pleaded.

"I can't fight the enemy if I'm afraid of losing you," said Nikias. His eyes welled with tears. "You've got to stay here. And if we lose the city, you and the villagers have got to run to the north."

Kallisto nodded. "I understand," she said, and kissed him on the mouth— kissed him as though it were the last time. "I love you."

"I love you," he replied.

"But for now, love death more," she said fiercely.

She watched Nikias, Saeed, and Kolax gallop out of the village and vanish into the night. She stood at the end of the street for a long time, hugging herself, trying to will away the despair that had seized her soul. As she walked back toward the cluster of houses she saw something fly from the dark on the other side of the river and stick into the chest of a villager. It was an arrow!

"The enemy has returned!" cried a man near the river's edge at the opposite end of the village.

Kallisto pulled off her bow from where it was looped over one shoulder and cupped a hand to her mouth. "Archers to me!" she cried as she ran back toward the little bridge. "Archers to me!"

EIGHTEEN

———— ◆ ————

Tykon and his hundred surviving men sat on the ground in a corner of the agora, their arms bound behind their backs. He watched the Plataeans rushing about, trying to figure out a way to fix the ruined gates. A gang of workers had brought in one of Chusor's inventions, some sort of counterbalanced crane. But even the Egyptian's machine could not lift the massive doors, and the contraption broke from the weight.

Victory in defeat, he thought and said a silent prayer to Zeus. The reinforcements might just arrive in time.

Relatives of the slain Plataeans were hard at work, too, searching for their loved ones, taking the bodies away to homes for private ceremonies. The gloomy sound of the funeral lament could be heard from all over the city. A few of the women had approached the prisoners, shouting angry harangues, but none of the Thebans had been harmed since Chusor's tirade, such was the code of honor that required warriors taken in battle to be treated as inviolable.

A city guardsman flanked by two others approached the prisoners. "Where is the general in charge here? Is he still alive? The one called Tykon."

Tykon got to his feet and looked the Plataean in the eye.

"Me. I am Tykon."

They led him to the Temple of Athena, where Zeno knelt alone in front of the altar with his head drooped in prayer.

"Tykon the Theban," said the guard.

"You violated this sanctuary," said Zeno without looking up. "You stole captured armor and shields."

"At the time this temple was in our control," replied Tykon. "And they were our fathers' and grandfathers' accoutrements, so it is true they were doubly ours."

Zeno turned slowly to face Tykon. His face was rigid.

"There is a bag over there," said Zeno, pointing a finger toward the corner of the temple. "It holds the heads of one of our generals and two of our magistrates. Their family members lie rotting in their beds."

Tykon swallowed. "I followed my orders. That is all. I am a soldier."

"Just as it was the duty of my brethren to *defend* Plataea," spat Zeno.

"You have been allowed to care for your dead," Tykon shot back. "Now let us lay our brothers out in honor."

"Honor? There is no honor in what you did. You are nothing better than pirates . . . or a thief who sneaks into a decent man's house."

"You would have done the same if you'd been clever enough to think of it."

A pause, then Zeno said, "There was a traitor. Tell me his name."

Tykon shrugged. "Let us settle the terms for the corpses of my men. Then I will talk."

One of the corners of Zeno's mouth formed a humorless smile. Tykon chewed on the inside of his lip. Before Zeno could think of a response, an aide appeared at the temple entrance and called urgently for Zeno.

"Keep the honorable Tykon in the temple," said Zeno to his guards. He strode out of the sanctuary. "What is it?" he snapped at the man who had come to get him.

Across the agora he saw Nauklydes standing amongst the prisoners. He was kicking them. Grabbing others by the throat. Shouting in their ears. A huge crowd of Plataeans had gathered around—a thousand or more people. Zeno ran over and muscled his way through the crowd.

"Where is your leader?" cried Nauklydes. "The one called Eurymakus! Where is he? Tell me where he is, you filth!"

Zeno broke through the throng and stared in amazement at Nauklydes. The magistrate's handsome face was deeply altered: eyes sunken in his skull, jaw slack and twisted, lips curled back. His well-knit physique looked misshapen, for he clutched something to his chest with one arm in a way that distorted his posture. He wore nothing but a loincloth and his body was covered with dirt and blood.

"Magistrate!" called out Zeno. "Where have you been?"

Nauklydes stopped thrashing one of the Thebans and glanced at Zeno.

"Recovering," said Nauklydes. "Who are you?"

"Zeno the stonemason," he replied. "The citizens asked me to lead them. All the generals were dead or—"

"They tried to kill me," said Nauklydes. "They poisoned me. Like Arkon Apollodoros. And cut off my finger to get my signet ring." He showed his maimed hand to the crowd. "There is a man I am looking for," he said, clutching his burden to his chest with both hands again, "and his name is Eurymakus. He is the one who did this to me."

"I don't know who you're talking about," said Zeno.

Nauklydes addressed the onlookers. "What should we do with them?" he asked. "They invaded our city like cowards. They murdered our families—the actions of criminals. And yet we *honor* them by sparing their lives?" For a moment he was the old Nauklydes—a rational statesmen, accustomed to holding forth in front of his fellow citizens at the assembly or in the courts of law. Until he savaged one of the prisoners in the face with a brutal kick.

"That's the way," shouted a voice from the crowd.

"We are not barbarians," added somebody else.

"What would you have us do?" asked another.

"I would cut off all their heads," said Nauklydes with a careless wave of his mutilated hand. "It's what they deserve."

"Magistrate, please come with me—" began Zeno, but Nauklydes batted aside his hand.

"Look, Zeno the stonemason," said Nauklydes. "Look what they did to my beloved." His voice quavered and his bloody hand stroked the thing held in the crook of his arm.

Zeno realized, with horror, that Nauklydes touched human hair. A woman in the crowd saw it, too, and started to wail.

Nauklydes held up his daughter's head by the crown, the bloody tendrils of her hair clutched in the fingers of his still functional hand. The crowd groaned at the sight of the desecrated face of Nauklydes's child. The once lovely Penelope had suffered excruciating pain.

"Who will give me their sword?" he asked. "Who will support me in my endeavor?"

"We need these men for negotiations!" yelled Zeno, for several hundred voices were shouting their support for the magistrate. "There is a Theban army on the march, one mile from this city!"

"Then we haven't much time," Nauklydes replied. He grabbed a sword that one of the guards offered to him, took one step toward the nearest Theban, and chopped off his head with a single stroke. "See how easy?"—cutting off another, and still another—"Like scything poppies in a field." Then, in a frenzy of bloodletting, like the crazed and homicidal bacchantes of Dionysus, the crowd fell on the prisoners and tore the rest of the Theban prisoners to shreds.

NINETEEN

——— ◆ ———

Nikias and Saeed galloped along the Kadmean Road, heading north toward Thebes. The Skythian boy, the swiftest rider Nikias had ever seen, was up ahead, acting as scout. Every so often he would ride back to the two, gibber in his barbarian tongue, and give a smile that said, "All clear," then bolt away again. It was like hunting with a manic, tireless dog.

The sun had just come up and the rosy light of morning was a welcome relief to the long, dark night. The smell of wet earth permeated the air. The horses were anxious to feast on grass, and their nostrils flared with anticipation every time they came to a stop to reconnoiter the territory.

Nikias thought about the Theban cavalry general as he rode—saw the man's twisted face as Saeed tortured him; it was emblazoned on his brain. He blamed the Thebans for turning him and his fellow Plataeans into savages. They'd tried to wipe out his family. Destroy his city. They would have turned his sister, grandmother, and Kallisto into whores and slaves. And they butchered his mother. He would have skinned the Theban general's children alive and eaten their beating hearts if that was what it would have taken to make him talk.

The torture had worked. Straton had told them about the ploy to distract the garrisons on the Kadmean Road with a decoy army. Nikias was on his way to find General Zoticus and lead the Plataean cavalry to the real invasion force—the eighteen hundred hoplites, who, General Straton had confessed, were sweeping southeast toward the old Persian Fort across the marshes.

"The Skythian boy found something," Saeed called suddenly.

Nikias pulled on Photine's reins and turned her around.

Kolax had dismounted and was standing over a shape wriggling in the road. The Skythian's arrow was nocked and ready to shoot, but he held back.

"What is it?" asked Nikias.

The normally cheery Kolax wore an expression of trepidation.

Nikias and Saeed dismounted and warily approached the squirming thing. It was a young man in the throes of a violent convulsion, arching his back, twisting from side to side, arms flailing. His mouth was flecked with foam and blood: he'd bitten through part of his tongue. He uttered a hiss in the back of his throat that sounded like "Zeuszeuzeuszeus . . ."

Nikias thought back to the fight in the street after he'd discovered his uncle and his family murdered. He remembered digging out the eye, sticking his thumb into the young man's soft brain behind the socket. He'd felt such pleasure destroying that face, and now here was that very same miserable Theban, in the middle of the road, in the throes of a divine fit, the god's name on his tongue.

The man stopped making noise and snapped open his remaining eyelid. Nikias, Kolax, and Saeed jumped in surprise. He stared upward placidly, his one orb fixed on the sky. He let forth a sigh as one awaking from a nightmare. Then he winced and brought a hand tentatively to his bloody face. He heard Nikias move, glanced over, and locked his eye on him. The Theban's features registered astonished outrage. He tried to move, to reach for Nikias, but he was paralyzed. His body went rigid and he began to shiver as if from cold. His teeth chattered so loudly, they sounded like knucklebone dice rattling in a cup.

Saeed started to draw his sword, but Kolax shook his head.

"You can't kill him," said the Skythian. "He's a shaman. Look how he's shaking. He's seeing the god."

Nikias could understand Kolax's intention if not the words. "Let's get him off the road," he said.

They carried the rigid body over the knee-deep water of the roadside ditch and up onto an embankment on the other side. Nikias left a wineskin next to him, then ran back to his horse, leapt on, and galloped away. Saeed and Kolax mounted and chased after him. The sight of the maimed Theban had unnerved Nikias. He'd wanted to destroy him, put him out of his misery like a dog with a broken leg that could no longer run. But he could not bring himself to do it. The Theban had glared at him with such malevolence . . . the "evil eye" personified.

The incident had upset Kolax too. He no longer bolted ahead but stayed close to the other two riders, looking back over his shoulder now and then as if the one-eyed Theban might somehow be chasing them on foot.

They arrived at the first border garrison—a single tower and ten-foot-high wall enclosing an area about the size of Plataea's gymnasium—to find the gates wide-open and a line of thirty or so Theban prisoners marching through, guarded by a dozen mounted archers.

Kallisto's brother Isokrates was at the head of the riders. "What are *you* doing here?" he asked Nikias, his voice thick with hatred.

"Is the city free?" asked another horseman.

"I broke out," said Nikias. "Where's General Zoticus?"

"He's chasing down the last of this rabble," replied Isokrates with a self-important air.

"Where is Zoticus?" asked Nikias again. "I have important news."

"First tell me if you've seen my father in the citadel," demanded Isokrates. "He was staying with Nauklydes last night and—"

"Your father is dead," said Nikias bluntly. Isokrates blanched. "I am sorry for you. The Thebans killed him. Beheaded him in the Assembly Hall. Our men found his head there in a sack with some others, including my uncle Alexios's. Many have died tonight. My grandfather, my mother—"

"Just tell *me*," said Isokrates, cutting him off, "this news you were to deliver to Zoticus. I'm on my way back to report to him now."

"These men you've captured," said Nikias, gesturing at the prisoners. "They were a decoy. The real force is coming from the east. Eighteen hundred hoplites strong."

The garrison men erupted in a cacophony of alarmed questions: How had he heard about the army coming from the east? What proof did he have? Where *exactly* were they coming from? What *had* happened in the city tonight?

"Listen to me," said Nikias, his voice rising with impatience. "The Thebans butchered us in the streets tonight. At least five hundred of us were killed. Maybe more. They created a barricade around the gates and we attacked it—thousands of us, and not a man got to them. They are waiting for a force of men to come and join them. And then they will take their time dividing up our women and children like animals at a summer fair. We captured a Theban general at Oeroe and tortured him. Saeed cut off his balls and started on his fingers before the Theban told me that the main force went to the southeast and is coming by way of the Persian Fort. For all I know, they might already be at the Gates of Pausanius. So let's quit this useless talk and take some action."

The men shifted uncomfortably. Their rout of the Thebans on the Kadmean Road *had* been too easy. Nikias's description of what had happened in the city made everything more real. The stakes were beyond anything they could ever have imagined before tonight.

"How do you know this Theban didn't lie to you?" Isokrates scoffed.

"It's intuition," replied Nikias. "Now, whoever is with me, follow hard. We've got to find Zoticus and his cavalry."

Nikias, Kolax, and Saeed set out at full gallop, followed by a dozen riders—all the horsemen who'd remained at the garrison. Isokrates raced up beside Nikias and sneered, "You'd better be right about this."

Nikias ignored him and kicked Photine hard, pulling away from the mass of riders, leading them onward into a landscape lit by the rising sun.

TWENTY

Chusor watched the slaughter of the Theban prisoners from high above.

He was standing on the walkway that spanned the city gates, working to rig a series of pulleys and ropes to hoist the giant portals back into place, when it happened.

As soon as Chusor had caught sight of Nauklydes raging at the prisoners, he knew there was going to be trouble. He felt like a patron at a play—in the back row of the Theater of Dionysus—watching a tragedy unfold. The acoustics of the agora carried every word the magistrate said the fifty yards to Chusor's ear. The bloodbath happened so quickly, there was nothing he or the other men fixing the gates could do to stop it. And so they all watched in mute shock as the blood of the hostages was spilled, desecrating the stones of the agora. Within minutes the place was littered with body parts—heads and limbs the people of Plataea now tossed into carts like some hideous harvest.

Chusor could see Phakas scurrying around, whispering in the ears of different citizens. Soon Nauklydes's assistant had gathered a small crowd who went to the magistrate and surrounded him. Nauklydes stood with arms crossed, watching the sorting of the Theban dead. He was no longer holding his daughter's head. It sat at his feet. Phakas whipped off his cloak, stooped quickly, and wrapped it up. The fat steward spirited the object away.

Krates, the master of the walls, said to Nauklydes, "The arkon and all the magistrates are dead except for you. You must assume the temporary position of arkon until an election can be held."

Nauklydes covered his mouth with his bloody hand and nodded his head. "I am the obvious choice," he said. "But the city needs a general now more than an arkon." He turned and shouted, "Phakas! Phakas! Bring me my armor."

Nauklydes's armor—an exquisite corselet, helm, and greaves fashioned by Chusor in his workshop—was hurriedly brought to him, and he dressed for battle in full view of the public, with Phakas kneeling before him, lashing the bronze guards to his master's shins.

"Like watching the birth of a tyrant," said Chusor under his breath. He looked down, directly beneath the walkway on which he was standing, and saw Diokles working hard to rig the gates with pulleys and ropes. Chusor realized that he and the Helot could flee now. He had silver at his smithy. Enough for the two of them to buy passage on a boat at the port of Kreusis. All they had to do was walk through the gates, head over the Oeroe Bridge, and hike the eight miles to the port. They'd be long gone before the battle even started.

He looked up and saw Nauklydes striding about the city like an avenging god, towering over men in his horsetail-plumed helm, barking out a flurry of orders. The agora was an anthill of activity now: slaves carting away the dead, archers scavenging for arrows, peltasts loading up with missiles, and men arranging themselves into phalanx units. He saw Leo, still wearing the leather cuirass, donning a helm and falling into a row.

"The new arkon comes our way," said one of the men working with Chusor.

Nauklydes, with Phakas in attendance, stepped on top of one of the downed gates.

"You men!" Nauklydes called, pointing at the workers on the wall above. "Cease this activity."

"Magistrate—" Chusor began.

"Arkon," Phakas interrupted. "He is arkon now."

"Arkon," said Chusor, "I think we can get the gates back up before—"

"No more hiding behind walls," declared Nauklydes. "We meet the Thebans in the field. That is my command. These gates did not protect us last night. They will not protect us now. Chusor the smith, you and your men dress yourself in your armor and join up with Zeno's phalanx."

"He's cracked," muttered one of Chusor's work crew. "A cracked stone."

Just then a scout rode up to the entrance from outside the walls and leapt from his horse. "A force of Theban hoplites have arrived at the old Persian Fort," he announced breathlessly.

"You see?" shouted Nauklydes almost gleefully. "Gates no longer protect us." He turned to the scout and asked how many fighters he'd seen on the road.

"Perhaps two thousand," replied the scout.

Chusor and the men reluctantly stopped their work and left the wall, entering one of the gate towers and descending the stairs to the agora. A welcome sight awaited them there: around a hundred men from the countryside, along with their armor-bearing slaves, were marching through the entrance to the citadel.

"Hey! Agape!" shouted a city dweller, for he'd caught sight of his old shield companion General Agape and his strapping sons, Baklydes and Hesiod. "Where did you come from?"

"From the Island" was Agape's fullmouthed reply. "I gathered up everyone who had assembled there and marched back to the city on the instructions of Menesarkus's heir, the young and hasty—or should I say hotheaded—Nikias, who—"

"You saw Nikias?" asked Chusor.

"He's headed north," Hesiod answered. "To find Zoticus. We captured a Theban cavalry general at the river Oeroe. The Theban told us about the relief force coming from the east." He paused and eyed Chusor. "You're Chusor the smith, aren't you? Nik had a message for you. 'Eye gouges and biting allowed.'"

Chusor's lips curved into a ruthless smile. Eye gouges and biting: those two attacks weren't allowed in the Olympic pankration event. Nikias was telling him, "I'm not playing by the rules anymore." He was glad the young pankrator had made it through the tunnel. He was also impressed that he had been able to thwart a Theban cavalry crossing at the Oeroe.

Phakas ran up to Agape and pulled on his sleeve. "General Agape, Arkon Nauklydes wishes to convene with you immediately."

"Arkon?" asked Agape. "When I left the city last he was still a . . ."

Chusor went off to find his armor; he'd left it in the Temple of Athena for safekeeping while he worked on the gates. As he made his way through the throngs in the agora, followed by his shadow, Diokles, he thought about Nikias's message. The meaning was simple: Nikias was going to fight to his last tooth and fingernail. What would the young pankrator think if he returned to Plataea and Chusor had scurried away like a frightened rabbit? Did he really care so much about the young man's opinion that he was willing to risk his freedom and his life? Or was it a matter of honor to remain?

"Sentimental fool," he cursed under his breath.

"Eh?" asked Diokles.

"We can leave the city, you know," said Chusor.

"Run?" asked Diokles. "We have run from too many places."

"Yes, we have. And we're still alive *because* we've run."

Diokles scratched his head thoughtfully. "Legs tired. Sick of running."

"But what about the Spartans?"

"If Mount Ithome and the Helots all dead there," said Diokles as they walked up the steps to the Temple of Athena, "I don't have anyplace to go. The Masters not take me alive, though."

The moment they stepped inside the sanctuary, a firm hand grasped Chusor around the biceps. "Hey—Zeno!" Chusor said.

"Don't speak," ordered the stonemason. "Just come with me."

He led Chusor and Diokles to the inner sanctum, where Tykon sat on the floor, gagged and bound at the ankles and wrists. The Theban stared at the two with half-closed lids.

"He's the last Theban," explained Zeno. "Their leader. Name's Tykon. I was interrogating him when Nauklydes appeared in the agora. I cannot trust the new arkon with him. He will kill him. We must know who the traitor is."

"What are you going to do with him?" asked Chusor.

"We have to keep him safe until after the battle. Then I can deal with him if I'm still alive."

Tykon grunted. Zeno undid the gag. The Theban licked his cracked lips, cleared his throat.

"Where are you holding my men?" asked Tykon.

"Your men are dead," replied Zeno. "Nauklydes ordered their execution."

Tykon ground his teeth so loudly, it sounded like two rough stones rubbing together. "Nauklydes was the traitor," he said at last.

Zeno and Chusor exchanged surprised glances.

"Why?" asked Zeno. "For what reason could he possibly—"

"Spartans," cut in Tykon. "Nauklydes is afraid of the Spartans."

Diokles twitched and let out a worried grunt at the name of his former masters.

"Nauklydes has made some arrangement with Sparta?" asked Zeno in disbelief.

Tykon shrugged and said, "Believe me or don't. It does not matter now. Your city is dead no matter if we succeed today or not. The Spartans will come eventually. . . . Nauklydes feared them even more than us. That was his undoing. And your doom."

Drums pounded in the agora along with battle pipes.

"Warriors, assemble!" shouted the heralds.

Zeno turned to Chusor and said, "Take the Theban someplace he will not be found."

Back in his workshop, Chusor fastened shackles to Tykon's ankles and wrists. These fetters—which the city's jail had commissioned from the smith—attached to each other by iron rods, making it impossible for the Theban prisoner to walk or move his arms. Diokles finished the job by hammering home the locking pins with quick, violent strokes. If he had missed, he would have crippled Tykon for life, but the Helot's aim was true.

The Theban had not spoken since Chusor had carried him out of the Temple of Zeus, slung over his shoulder like a corpse. He stared morosely at the wall now, sucking air through his teeth. The faint sound of Theban war flutes playing in the distance, however, made Tykon sit up and cock his head.

"Theban warriors are coming," said Chusor to Diokles. "We must go now."

Chusor locked Tykon in the storage room, a windowless chamber with only one entrance. He went back to the main room and scavenged the place, looking for any remaining pyrotechnic weapons. He was worried about the fact that the crazed Nauklydes had all but abandoned the defense of the gates. If the Theban general had half a brain, he would lead a cavalry assault through the Plataean lines and ride straight into the city. He wished they had not used up all the naptha; all he could find in the smithy was a cracked and empty container that once held the flammable liquid.

He sighed, motioned to Diokles that he was ready to leave, and then exclaimed, "Forgetful Chusor!" slapping himself on the forehead with his palm. He rummaged under a table near the anvil, grabbed a heavy leather bag; its contents clattered with a metallic sound as the bag shifted in his grip.

Diokles insisted on toting the heavy bag and took it from Chusor's hands. The Helot pointed at Chusor's head and then at his own bulging biceps. "You're the brains, I'm the brawn" was his unspoken meaning.

TWENTY-ONE

———◆———

"God will lead us to victory," said Eurymakus. He was walking with a limp and gingerly touching his wounded lip with his index finger. His left buttock ached fiercely where one of Menesarkus's women had shot him, and his right ear burned where it had been sliced in half by the Skythian boy's arrow. Bogha slogged along next to him, barely coherent.

After leaving Tykon at the gates, they'd ridden down the Kadmean Road, searching for the army of Theban hoplites that was supposed to be on the march to Plataea. But they'd galloped straight into a Plataean cavalry patrol and had narrowly escaped capture. Bogha's mount had taken several arrows from the pursuing Plataeans and died soon after they'd eluded the enemy riders. They'd both ridden on Eurymakus's mount for a while until his horse went three-legged lame. Eurymakus had stabbed it with his poisoned dagger in a fit of pique, watching with cold fury as the big animal trembled violently and died within seconds.

Now they were trudging across a muddy field in the direction of the old Persian Fort. Eurymakus glanced at Bogha. The Median's bloody stump of a severed tongue lolled from his mouth. He still had the stub of a broken arrow shaft protruding from his shoulder.

"God will show us the way to victory," repeated Eurymakus.

"Yesh, *Magush*," replied Bogha despondently. He could no longer make an *s* sound with his ruined mouth.

"God told me what to do," said Eurymakus, thinking out loud. "I cannot be blamed for the failing of Tykon and the others. There is some demon at work here other than Menesarkus and his witches. And once we find that demon and cleanse him from the earth, Plataea will fall."

"Yesh, *Magush*."

God had told Eurymakus how to destroy Menesarkus and his city five years earlier at the Temple of Zarathustra in Sardis. Eurymakus had picked the sacred mushrooms in a glade on Mount Timolus with the magi, drank the *parahaoma* tea made from the boiled fungi, and then stared at the sacred flames of the seer's eternal fire until the vision came: an army of men in black, marching at night, slipping through an open gate and into a dark city. Manipulating Nauklydes had taken years but it had been easy. The spy had used all of the techniques taught to him by the Persian king's whisperer to turn Nauklydes's own fear and greed against him.

But something had upset God's stratagem tonight. It had all started with the rain—the most rain Eurymakus had ever seen fall in one night in the Oxlands! There was only one explanation. There was an evil at work. God's enemy—the Demon King—had called forth the tempest, and then the ruler of the under-world had emboldened the Plataeans trapped in the city . . . told them to escape.

In a pouch around his neck were some of the dried mushrooms from the Holy Mountain. He wished that he could make some of the tea right now and ask God what to do. Perhaps he should set off for Persia immediately and report to King Artaxerxes's whisperer? There was no going back to Thebes. Generals there had been hanged for losing skirmishes, let alone losing the lives of four hundred warriors.

The one great consolation was that he had rid the earth of Menesarkus. The sight of the old pankrator standing on the rooftop, waiting to be consumed by the flames, was a joy to behold—the perfect ending for an unbeliever. He would have gladly given an arm to see that, let alone a few meager pieces of flesh. He imagined his brother Damos sitting on a shining lotus at the foot of God, smiling at him. Revenge was sweeter than figs soaked in honey. Justice fed the soul. His only wish was that he could have toyed with his brother's murderer for a while, like he'd done with the Athenian spy he'd killed and left in the Persian Fort.

"*Magush!*" cried Bogha.

Barely a spear's throw away, a hundred Theban slaves were plodding through a muddy field. Six warriors were barking at them to hurry up, but the slaves—overburdened by their heavy packs—were making little progress.

"You," called Eurymakus to their leader. "Where is the army?"

The warrior whirled and grabbed for his sword, but when he caught sight of Eurymakus and Bogha he relaxed.

"Eurymakus," said the warrior, bowing. "They're up ahead. Follow that stream to the old Persian Fort and—"

Eurymakus turned abruptly from him and started walking toward the fort with Bogha lumbering after him like a big dog.

"I told you," said Eurymakus. "Did I not tell you God would lead us to them?"

"Yesh, *Magush*," replied Bogha, managing a ghastly smile.

They walked another mile before they came across the stragglers—weary foot soldiers, their legs caked in mud to their groins. Up ahead, through a line of trees, Eurymakus could see a gathering of officers and the army of hoplites in a field behind them, forming ranks. He limped into their midst.

"General Gennadios!" shouted Eurymakus haughtily. "Where is General Straton?"

"Eurymakus, what are you doing here?" General Gennadios was a white-haired fifty-year-old with the tanned, wrinkled face of an old man and the muscular body of an athlete half his age. "Have you come from the city? What news do you bring?"

"Tell me why you are dawdling here," asked Eurymakus in a domineering tone. "Tykon and his men were making a last stand at the Gates of Pausanius when I left the city. There is no time to be lost."

"We had a hard time of it in the rain," shot back Gennadios. "We quick marched through this muck for the last five hours. We've been waiting for General Straton—"

"And is he lost too?" scoffed Eurymakus.

"Straton took the cavalry to the west, toward the Oeroe bridge—"

"That was not the plan!"

"You are not in command of this expedition," sputtered Gennadios. "You are merely an advisor, Eurymakus. Remember your place."

Eurymakus put a hand to his wounded lip and spat out some blood. Just then, one of Gennadios's scouts entered the camp on horseback. Sitting behind him was Darius, Tykon's second in command, bloodied from the fighting at the gates. He leapt from the horse, shot a surprised look at Eurymakus, and went straight to Gennadios.

"General," said Darius, "the four hundred have fallen defending the Gates of Pausanius. I was the only one to escape."

Warriors within earshot groaned and cursed.

"Then we have failed," said Gennadios, giving Eurymakus a dark look.

"No!" said Darius. "We pulled down the gates. The way to Plataea is wide open. Nothing stands between the army and victory."

"The gates are down?" asked Gennadios with wonder.

"Like a gaping hole in a breastplate over the heart," said Darius.

"Any sign of Plataean cavalry?" asked Gennadios.

"None, General," replied the scout who had rescued Darius from the citadel. "And the Plataeans are milling about like ants whose nest has been kicked open."

"To the Four Hundred!" the men cheered. "The Four Hundred!"

"How did the Plataeans escape from their homes and attack the gates in the first place?" Gennadios asked Eurymakus over the din of the excited men.

"I do not know," replied Eurymakus. "I . . . I was not there."

Gennadios looked at him in surprise. "What do you mean? Were you *lost*?" he asked with a sneer.

Eurymakus felt a trembling in the earth and sensed what was coming moments before he heard the shout of "Riders!" He saw a troop of at least two hundred horsemen charging across the plains, directly at them. Were they Plataean? His stomach sank and he recited a prayer to the One God. But the approaching riders called out the password. They were Theban!

"General Gennadios!" shouted the lead rider as he came to a stop, smiling happily. "We found you."

"Where is General Straton?" asked Gennadios. "Where are the other riders?"

"Taken," the young man said, and dropped his head. "At the bridge of Oeroe. The enemy was waiting for us. They killed fifty of our men. An ambush. We tried to cross the bridge again but were thwarted a second time. So we went farther west and forded the river where it was shallower. More riders were lost in the raging waters. We skirted along the mountains and came directly here. I kept to the plan and hoped to find you on the march. But we were afraid you might have been bogged down."

"You are to be commended for your efforts," said Gennadios. "I will lead the cavalry now."

"The glory will all be yours now," said Eurymakus, seeing the excitement in Gennadios's eyes. "With both Straton and Tykon dead or captured."

Gennadios glanced at him. Forced himself to look stoic. "Yes," he said. "But the glory goes to Thebes, not me."

"No, the glory goes to Ahura Mazda," thought Eurymakus.

"You and your shield man may take two of the riderless horses, Eurymakus," Gennadios added in a loud voice. "You seem to have *lost* yours."

"Get the horses," Eurymakus hissed to Bogha.

"Form up ranks," Gennadios commanded his lieutenants. And turning to the men nearby he shouted, "There is only one mile between us and victory! To victory, brothers! March and ride to victory!"

The closest warriors took up a joyful shout. The eighteen hundred men formed ranks and walked fast across the sodden grass with the two hundred riders trotting out front. Word spread of the heroism of the four hundred invaders—how they had held the Gates of Pausanius against overwhelming forces and pulled down the massive doors to the city in the midst of their defeat.

Soon the lead riders crested the low hills and caught their first glimpse of the walls in the early morning sunlight. Eurymakus, out front with General Gennadios, smiled despite the pain it caused his ruined lip. The missing gates in the bastions made Eurymakus think of a pankrator with two missing incisors. He could see the Plataeans outside the walls in phalanx formation, twenty or so shields deep, around two thousand strong. Only about half seemed to be wearing armor.

"They've formed up in the field in front of the walls," observed Gennadios eagerly.

"A tactical blunder," said Eurymakus. "They have nowhere to run but back into the city. And there is not a single enemy horse in sight!"

A spontaneous cheer erupted from the Thebans. There were treasures and pleasures held inside those walls. The men were filled with lust to seize them.

Eurymakus slowed his horse and rode beside Bogha. "Stay close to me," he said in an undertone.

"Yesh, *Magush*," replied Bogha.

"If things go bad," said Eurymakus, "we head south for Sparta."

"The One God blesh ush," said Bogha, and fished a fragment of tooth from his jaw.

TWENTY-TWO

Like every Plataean male, Leo had been taught since earliest childhood to dance "the Warrior's Dance," a simulation of the phalanx maneuver. It was performed at festivals, funerals, and celebrations by various age groups, from toddlers to teens. But the choreography had in no way prepared him for the reality of actually standing in a phalanx, waiting for a real battle to begin, weighed down by sixty pounds of armor, and pressed in on all sides by similarly outfitted, metal-clad, shield-bearing warriors. The claustrophobia was intense. Leo could see nothing of the battlefield, only the bronze backs and horsetail-plumed helms of the men in front and on either side. The smell of urine and feces was overwhelming. A youth in front of him squatted for the third time and let forth a stream of fear-induced diarrhea that splattered on Leo's foot. He did not even have the wherewithal to complain.

". . . and that's called 'battlefield discharge,'" Agape was saying with a hearty laugh. The old farmer was walking the lines, giving encouragement. As the last surviving general, Nauklydes had put him in charge of the right wing. Behind Leo were Agape's sons, Hesiod and Baklydes.

"Better than an enema," responded an amused voice several rows away.

Somebody let forth a massive fart and the men burst into laughter. The joviality served as a potent counterattack to the fear. In a chain reaction, old and young alike squatted to take relief, farting, pissing, and defecating. Some even bent over to puke.

"How is a dead coward twice disgraced?" asked Agape in a cheerful tone as he passed by his boys.

"How?" asked Baklydes, even though he knew the joke.

"First a defeated coward, then a coward's *corpse*!"

Howls of laughter—more than the jest deserved. But their nerves were frayed. Leo had always thought Agape was an old windbag, but he now felt a powerful respect for him. A knuckle rapped on his helm. He turned to see the old man himself smiling at him.

"Keep your pot on the back of your forehead until the fighting starts," said Agape in a softer voice. Leo noticed that Agape, as well as his two sons, wore their helms in the at-rest position, revealing their faces. "Help prevent your brain from getting too hot."

Leo smiled sheepishly. He'd been so anxious to be ready for the battle that he'd been wearing his helm all the way down over his face since they'd marched out of the city.

"Thanks, General Agape," said Leo, sliding the helm back.

"Alkidas's shade will be on your right," said Agape, naming Leo's dead father.

The mention of his father's name swelled Leo's heart. He bit his lip, concentrated on what he had to do. He knew that the right side of a hoplite—his spear arm—was the most exposed. His instructors at the gymnasium had told him that most of the disasters that occurred in phalanx battles were because men panicked and edged together toward their shield companions to their right, seeking out the cover of their shields. If too many men did this, then the entire phalanx turned and drifted apart rather than walking straight ahead and plowing through the enemy with shields and weapons held high.

Nauklydes rode by the front of the line on a black charger. Because Leo was so far back in the phalanx, he could see only the top part of the new arkon's torso and the horse's rump. It looked as though Nauklydes were a giant centaur towering above the men.

"Brothers!" the arkon shouted. "The enemy has arranged themselves into their formations and are poised to attack. Their cavalry will hit us first. Hold your shaft tightly and stab the butt spike into the ground to anchor the spear. Keep your shield up, your spear tip high. Tense the muscles of your legs and stomach. When the enemy first hits us, it will feel like you've been punched by Zeus's own fist. But don't panic. Stay strong. Stand firm. May the son of Kronos make you strong, Ares guide your hand, and Athena protect you!" To Leo, Nauklydes seemed like a different man from the crazed killer who'd cut down the Theban prisoners in the agora. He was totally confident, excited for the battle to begin. "Remember," roared Nauklydes. "Zeus loves a Plataean!"

The men cheered with gusto at the mention of the old adage. Hoplites as well as archers on the wall took up the call of "Zeus loves a Plataean!" Nauklydes rode away to the next section and Leo could hear him begin his speech all over again. "Brothers! The enemy . . ."

"Where is that goat stuffer Nikias?" asked Baklydes. "We need Zoticus and the cavalry. We can't hold out against two thousand hoplites *and* mounted archers as well."

"Shut it, boy," said Agape from three rows up, where he stood at the front of the phalanx. "Cavalry is no match for hoplites with long spears. When my own father and grandfather were charged near the Shrine of Androkles, they—"

"Sorry, Father," called out Baklydes, "but—"

"Nikias will be here, Baky," Hesiod interrupted. "Listen to Father and stop flapping your jaw."

"Shut your arse, Hes," said Baklydes, "or I'll sort you out, Brother."

Leo turned around and said, "Not exactly the best time to be fighting, you two."

"Shut up, Leo!" replied the brothers at the same time.

The sound of battle flutes blared from the direction of the enemy and the cry of "Thebes! Thebes! Thebes!" roared from nearly two thousand voices. The violence of the enemy's cries carried across the air, an audible tremor that struck fear into the hearts of the Plataeans. As the Theban cavalry got closer and closer, the ground beneath the feet of the defenders rumbled like the foreshock of an earthquake. When the enemy riders finally hit the front of the line, the crash of spears on shields split the air with the noise of lightning.

Leo realized he had nothing left in his bowels or bladder.

TWENTY-THREE

———◆———

From Gennadios's position—just out of bow-shot range—the battle seemed to be going exactly as he'd planned, and his heart raced with excitement. His cavalry had slammed into the Plataean lines, causing much damage, and then retreated just as they'd been ordered. His archers and peltasts had been harassing the two wing sections of the Plataean formations, attacking and retreating, drawing the enemy ranks forward and away from the middle block, spreading them thinner and thinner.

He would grind the Plataeans down until they were exhausted, then send the cavalry back for a final decimating charge. It was almost time. The middle Plataean phalanx was a jumble of confusion now, and the wing formations were leaking down the slope in front of the citadel, the enemy hoplites moving farther and farther apart from their shield companions as they were pulled toward the archers and their badgering attacks.

Gennadios had a lump in his throat the size of a boiled egg. He had to force himself to swallow. His remaining men, split into two formations of one thousand men each, as well as the bulk of the cavalry, were waiting for him to call the signal to attack. He forced himself to swallow and roared, "Now!"

The Theban soldiers, unencumbered by armor, sprinted swiftly up the gentle slopes with such speed, the surprised Plataeans were caught off guard. The men in the front ranks panicked and turned, causing a jumble and confusion. The Theban phalanxes slowly converged on the center, driving the Plataeans back on themselves and into the center phalanx, like deer herded into a killing trap.

"Riders!" Gennadios called out. His remaining two hundred horsemen charged straight ahead at the middle phalanx, plowing into the surprised men with their long spears, grinding toward their destination—the entrance to Plataea.

Gennadios, with his bodyguard of a dozen riders, charged up the hill. Eurymakus and Bogha followed close behind.

———

Leo stood in the center of chaos; he heard the clamor of clashing weapons, the screams of anger, agony and death, and saw spear points seeking out his face and groin.

There was a hoplite in front of him who'd been speared through the head and yet remained standing, as lifeless as a doll, held up by the crush of men around him. Leo held a broken spear shaft and stabbed wildly at the enemy faces that appeared all around.

"Fall back in line!"

It was old Agape, trying to bring order back to the broken phalanx. A blade chopped off the tip of Leo's spear and he stumbled backward, tossing aside the useless weapon, holding his fists up like a pankrator.

"Your sword, fool!"

It was Hesiod, standing at his side, raising up his shield, protecting them both from an enemy spear. Leo fumbled for the handle of his weapon, drew the blade. Something hit him on the back of the head and he stumbled forward in the mud. He looked up to see a Theban with a raised spear, ready to plunge it into his face. Leo swept out with his sword, a furious stroke that cut off the man's leg at the knee. Leo scrambled to his feet, turned to see Hesiod staring at the ground in shock: his arm had been cut off at the elbow. He reached down to pick up his severed arm, but Leo grabbed him by the rim of his bronze corselet and pulled him back to the walls, where Agape was reassembling a phalanx for a last stand.

Chusor and Diokles entered the agora just as twenty mounted Theban archers breached the lines and charged into the city. The Thebans whirled about, picking off the surprised archers from the unprotected walkways along the walls, spearing wounded warriors where they lay. One of the enemy riders caught sight of Chusor and Diokles and shot an arrow in their direction. The shaft buzzed across the agora and struck the rucksack gripped in Diokles's hands. The Helot emitted a pained gasp and pitched forward.

"They're coming for us," said Chusor as six of the horsemen broke off from the troop and headed their way. There was nowhere to run. He helped Diokles to his feet. The Helot's arms were limp at his sides, yet somehow the heavy bag remained attached to his chest. Diokles stared at it curiously. The bag of metal spikes had thwarted the arrowhead that had struck him, but the force of the shaft had driven one of the points deep between his ribs, pinning the bag to his body like a big tack.

"Shit!" was all Diokles managed to say.

The six Theban riders galloped straight at Chusor and Diokles with long spears held low to impale them. Chusor wrenched the leather bag from the

Helot's body, pulled open the flap, and hurled the contents across the stone pavers. The metal plane tree pods—the ones he'd shown to Nikias in his workshop a week earlier—bounced crazily on their spiked points.

The lead horse, barely two spear lengths away, stepped onto one of the barbs, stopped dead in its tracks with a high-pitched scream, and sent its rider flying over its head. The other horses reared, staring at the metal things, snorting warily.

Chusor grabbed the spear from the downed rider and gutted him with a sweeping stroke. Then he rushed the other horses, nimbly stepping over the artichokes, spearing two of the surprised riders—one in the face, the other in the throat.

A horse bucked its rider off and he landed face-first on the ground. The Theban stood up, clawing at his face and the spike that was stuck through his forehead and into his brain. Diokles ran over to the man, snatched the dagger from the Theban's belt, and disemboweled him with his own blade.

"This way!" yelled Chusor.

They ran the fifty paces to the gate tower on the right, avoiding the arrows of the other Theban riders that sailed across the agora. Chusor kicked open the door, and the two dashed up the stairs to the platform at the top where three Plataean archers stood helplessly watching the rout taking place beneath their city walls.

Chusor and Diokles went to the edge and peered over. The Thebans had encircled the Plataeans—completely enveloped them and pushed them back to the walls. They could see Nauklydes, still astride his white charger, hacking violently at the enemy with his sword—an enemy that was slowly but inevitably pressing toward him.

"Why aren't you shooting?" Chusor yelled at the archers. He grabbed one of the immobile archer's bows, wrenched it from his grasp. "Give me some arrows," he demanded.

"We're out," the archer replied, and gestured at the empty quivers littering the stones.

For a fleeting moment Chusor thought of escaping the citadel through the secret tunnel below the Temple of Zeus. There was still time for him and Diokles to make their way to safety in the confusion of the battle—before the Thebans stormed the gates and captured the city once and for all. They could wait in the tunnel until nightfall, then emerge from the exit under cover of darkness.

But a voice in his head said, "Gods damn you, Chusor, you pitiful creature. You coward!" He felt a sort of relief wash over him. He was sick of running. He looked over the edge of the tower. He could easily leap over the side before the Thebans captured him. Death would be certain and sudden.

And then he saw a thing that made him cry out in exultation: a mass of horsemen coming north from the direction of the Kadmean Road, storming up the hill toward the backs of the Thebans. The enemy had no idea what was about to hit them.

"The border cavalry!" shouted one of the archers in joy.

"Nikias!" shouted Chusor. He could see the lad's white horse out in front, and Nikias's long blond hair flying behind his head like the mane of a lion.

"Look!" said Diokles in alarm, pulling on Chusor's arm.

"I see them, Diokles," Chusor replied. "They're Plataean horsemen. From the border garrisons."

"No," said Diokles. "Over there."

Chusor turned in the direction of the Helot's outstretched finger, which pointed east to the tops of the Kithaeron Mountains. Through a break in the trees, Chusor saw a thin line snaking down the mountains about five miles away from Plataea, like a line of ants. But these were marching men. And they were dressed in the unmistakable crimson cloaks of Spartans.

"The Masters have come for me," said Diokles in despair.

TWENTY-FOUR

Nikias pulled away from the other Plataean riders as the cavalry climbed the slope to the citadel. He held a short javelin poised above his head. On his back was strapped his grandfather's shield. Behind him were over two hundred horsemen—all of those who'd been stationed on the northern borders. They screamed a single word as they charged toward the enemy: "*Thanatos!*"

Nikias felt as though he were connected to Photine. He was no longer merely riding the horse—he'd melded with her and become a mighty centaur. The sounds of the thunderous hoof beats and the screaming of the Plataean cavalry behind him seemed to propel him forward, as though he were held in the hand of a swiftly moving god.

The line of enemy Thebans was fast approaching. Nikias could see their faces clearly now—see the expressions of surprise and fear. Their archers had begun shooting at him. An arrow flew past his head and he laughed. Nothing could stop him. Zeus was his shield. He picked his target: the tallest Theban standing at the back of the enemy phalanx. His javelin flew from his hand like a lightning bolt and smote the enemy through the face.

And then, with a prodigious sound—a gut-rattling crash like nothing he'd ever heard before—he and the other riders slammed into the Theban line, mowing down the enemy, trampling them underfoot, pushing them into their comrades, driving them toward the gates of the citadel and the Plataean hoplites. Screams of men. Screams of horses. The clash of metal and wood and the liquid squelch of severed flesh.

The crush and chaos of battle.

Nikias pulled his sword from its scabbard and chopped downward, back and forth. Heads and arms and hands dropped to the mud. The air reeked of blood and vomit, sweat and shit.

"Drive them forward!" he heard Zoticus cry above the pandemonium. "Into the arms of our brothers!"

As Nikias turned toward Zoticus's voice, a Theban ran at him from his blind side and clouted him across the chest with his pole, knocking him off Photine. Nikias landed hard on his back and lay there, stunned for a moment, gaping up at the battle. There was a ringing in his ears that distorted all of the sounds. He was no longer a centaur. No longer in the hand of a god. He was momentarily helpless, with the shield on his back stuck in the mud, belly exposed like a flipped-over beetle.

He heaved himself to a sitting position. Photine was right next to him, bucking insanely, turning round and round as though she'd lost her mind. Nikias had to duck to avoid getting brained by her hooves.

A Theban armed with a long spear noticed Nikias and stepped toward him. The man's face was twisted with wrath. He was hunting a human. And the golden-haired Plataean he'd just knocked off his mount was his prey. Nikias realized, with a sickening lurch in his stomach, that his sword hand was empty. He was helpless to deflect the warrior's coming attack.

The Theban thrashed Photine in the nose with his spear pole to get her out of the way—to give himself a clean thrust at Nikias. It was a crucial mistake. Photine jerked her head indignantly as her nostrils spurted blood. Her ears went flat, her eyes bulged from her head, and she wheeled round, intentionally kicking backward at the Theban's head, smashing the man's face to pulp with the force of a sledgehammer.

"Photine! Wait!" shouted Nikias as his vengeful mare gave one last kick at the air and galloped away, barreling through the mass of warriors, neighing with terror.

Nikias stood shakily. Everything was happening so fast, yet he saw it all with an eerie clarity, as though the world had become a series of painted pictures on a wall.

He caught a glimpse of Kolax shooting three Thebans dead in as many heartbeats, and then disappearing into a mass of enemy horsemen, whooping maniacally in his Skythian tongue. He saw Leo not twenty paces away, his face covered with blood, screaming like a lunatic and cutting a Theban warrior's head straight down the middle. He saw Zoticus's horse rear and dance with a beautiful grace, and heard the horse master calling out "*Thanatos!*" in elation. And out of the corner of his eye, high above the citadel, Nikias caught sight of the black flash of a crow's wings against the pinkish-gray morning sky—a crow with a single white tail feather. The rain had stopped completely. The sun would shine today.

He'd never felt so alive, nor so close to death. Suddenly an axe swung in front of his face and he jerked back. A giant Median with long braided mustaches towered over him. The grim-faced warrior, who had the shaft of an arrow protruding from his shoulder, brought his battle-axe down again to cut off Nikias's head, but the young pankrator feinted quickly to one side. The Median's axe drove itself into the earth where Nikias had just been and carried the man forward, unbalancing him. Nikias snatched at the arrow sticking out of the Median's shoulder and twisted it viciously. The Median howled in pain and flung back his head, giving Nikias the opening to deliver a punishing uppercut to the Median's throat.

The Median reached for his own neck, gagging. Nikias grabbed the warrior's two long mustaches and pulled down as hard as he could, wrenching the man's jaw out of its socket. The Median screamed and backed away, sputtering like an angry ox.

But three more Thebans came running over and surrounded Nikias, cutting him off from his brethren. Nikias deflected a spear thrust by turning his shielded back to an attacker. Another Theban stabbed at his chest from the opposite side, but Chusor's leather armor turned the spear point and it snapped off. Nikias realized, with sudden despair, that he couldn't keep fending off the enemy attacks without any weapon at hand.

He slipped off the heavy shield and held it by one of the straps, spinning around in a tight circle with the big disk whistling through the air so fast that it became a blur. The Thebans stepped back to keep from getting hammered by this makeshift weapon. Nikias let the momentum of the shield carry him toward the nearest Theban and the rim of the shield crashed into the invader's head, crushing his skull inside his helm like an egg smashed inside a cup.

But the shield pulled Nikias off balance and he stumbled, falling flat on his face. The Median had recovered his senses and rushed up behind him, weapon raised. There was nowhere for Nikias to run now. As the giant brought his axe down for the deathblow, something thin and brown whipped around the Median's neck—the brown leather plaits of a Sargatian whip—and pulled the Median sideways, causing the axe blow to glance off the edge of Nikias's leather armor.

"Saeed!" shouted Nikias joyfully.

The Persian heaved on the whip with one hand and tossed Nikias a short spear with the other. Nikias jumped up, caught the spear, and in the same motion thrust the iron tip into the throat of the Theban behind him, then rammed it in the opposite direction, sending the butt spike through the mouth of another enemy warrior who was coming at him with his sword raised. Nikias pulled the spear out of the dead man's face in a spray of blood and teeth.

He glanced at Saeed, who was dangling with his feet off the ground, clinging like a child's doll to the Median's neck as the enraged giant tried to shake the skinny Persian off his back.

Nikias let the spear slide through his blood-soaked hands so that he was holding it by the end like a club. He swung it with all his might at the Median's knees, breaking them both with a loud crack. The giant's legs buckled and he fell backward. As he hit the ground, Saeed squirmed out from under him, put both of his feet on the Median's shoulders, pushed off as hard as he could, and constricted the whip, trapping the enemy's desperate screams in his throat. Saeed wasn't going to let the Median escape from him a second time.

"For my son," Saeed hissed in Persian. As fast as a scorpion's tail, he let go of the whip, pulled a dagger from his hip sheath, and buried the blade into the Median's brain. The giant's legs shot out at the same time, as rigid as poles, then went flaccid.

Nikias locked eyes with Saeed for an instant.

"Fight!" ordered Saeed, springing to his feet and heading back into the fray.

TWENTY-FIVE

◆

Nikias snapped his head from side to side, searching for the enemy. He saw a riderless horse nearby and jumped onto its back, spinning the animal around to survey the battle from a higher position. But all he saw was confusion: men fighting for their lives, weapons flashing in the morning sun, a seething mass of men and metal. He could barely tell who was Theban and who was Plataean anymore, as the warriors still standing were covered with so much mud and blood. He spotted Kolax mounted on a horse twenty feet away, pointing his bow at Nikias and screaming for him to get out of the way.

Nikias turned his horse and swung the spear without looking. His pole caught a Theban's downward-plunging sword, breaking the enemy's right arm near the shoulder and sending his weapon to the dirt.

"That is Eurymakus!" yelled Saeed as he staved off a Theban warrior with one whip-wielding hand, pointing at Nikias's attacker with the other. "Kill him!"

Nikias drove his mount into Eurymakus's horse and swiped at the Theban's eyes with his spear tip, but Eurymakus ducked, pulled out a dagger with his unhurt hand, and stabbed Nikias's mount in the flank. The animal screeched as though it had been skewered with a hot poker. It reared and fell backward as all four of its legs gave out at the same time. The horse crashed to the ground, pinning Nikias's torso and both of his arms underneath it. Nikias's leather carapace, as strong as bronze, kept him from being crushed by the weight of the horse. But he was trapped.

"Poison!" shouted Kolax in Skythian as two Theban spearmen came at him, prodding at his body with their long poles and preventing him from using his bow. Kolax swung his bow back and forth like a club, knocking the deadly spear points from side to side.

"Saeed!" gasped Nikias. "Kolax!" He craned his neck but could not see either one of his companions. The horse's body and legs shuddered with spasms as the poison entered the animal's heart.

Eurymakus slid off his mount and ran to Nikias. The Theban sprawled over the belly of the dying horse and peered down at Nikias, who was struggling to free himself. Eurymakus held his poisoned blade inches from Nikias's nose. The Theban's mutilated lip curled back and he said, "I know you. Spawn of Menesarkus." He uttered something in Persian that sounded like a prayer.

"Murderer!" yelled Nikias, desperately trying to free his arms.

An arrow whistled past Eurymakus's ear. The Theban spy flinched and looked up. Kolax had turned his horse around and was making it kick out with its hind legs, forcing the spearmen near him to give ground. Kolax swiveled round so he sat backward astride his horse, facing Eurymakus, and notched another arrow to the strings. Eurymakus cursed under his breath and ducked behind the horse's stomach. Kolax let fly again and his dart slammed into the horse's ribs. Then a Theban rider came at Kolax with a battle-axe and the Skythian ducked, fell off his horse, and vanished into the melee.

Eurymakus crept over the dead horse again, eyes searching fearfully for Kolax, dagger held out in front, broken right arm dangling by his side. Nikias had never felt such terror. There was no escape now. Death was coming.

Nikias sucked in a deep breath and with one last effort arched his back, straining every muscle in his body. Something unexpected happened. It was as though the stuff in his veins had changed to ikor—the blood of the gods. He no longer felt pain, or fear. Only an intense power surging through him.

As he arched his spine, pushing into the ground with the back of his head, digging into the earth with his heels, the horse carcass rose a few inches. It gave him just enough room to move his left arm. He grabbed the handle of his Sargatian whip, pulling it away from his belt and snapping the breakaway knot. In one motion he slid the whip out from under the dead horse, raised his arm behind his head, and cracked it hard at Eurymakus, who was now directly over him, leaning forward to stab with the poisoned blade.

The whip coiled itself around the surprised Theban's broken arm. Nikias pulled sideways on the whip and Eurymakus's arm jerked upward against his will, barely brushing against the poisoned dagger in his other hand.

Eurymakus jumped back and gasped in disbelief, staring at his right palm. There was a tiny scratch there. Just enough to draw blood. In a flash Eurymakus picked up a fallen sword from the ground and chopped off his own right arm at the elbow. He stared at the stump of his arm, which was now spitting blood, and waited . . . waited to see if he had acted fast enough to stop the poison. A few seconds later he took a step back toward Nikias, sword raised.

"Look what you did!" he screeched, spittle flying from his lips. "I'll pluck out your eyes! I'll feed you your own balls to—"

"Retreat! Retreat!" called a Theban-accented voice.

A throng of men, some fleeing for their lives, some giving chase, ran into Eurymakus, knocking him off balance. And then the spy was swept up into the maelstrom of warriors, and Nikias lost sight of his enemy.

"Someone help me out of here!" he shouted with frustration.

He felt hands under each armpit pulling him out from under the horse, dragging him in the opposite direction of the retreating enemy.

"Nice of you to join us, Nik," said Leo on one side of him.

"You cut it close, didn't you?" asked Baklydes on the other.

Nikias broke free from their grasps, stumbled to his feet, and ran to the place where he'd last seen Eurymakus, ignoring his friends' shouts for him to come back. He was lost to the world, focused only on one thing: finding the man who'd killed his mother and grandfather. Who'd burned his farm. Who'd tried to destroy his city. But the Theban was gone. He'd vanished with the mass of retreating warriors.

"You lose something?" asked Leo, holding up Eurymakus's severed arm, still wrapped tightly in the Sargatian whip. Before Nikias could answer, Leo chucked the arm at his feet and collapsed in exhaustion on the ground next to Baklydes, who was squatting on his haunches and wiping Theban brains from his cheek.

Nikias scanned the battlefield. It was strewn with over a thousand dead and maimed men. Exhausted hoplites made an effort to chase the retreating Thebans down the hill, but most could only stagger a few yards before falling to the ground, trying to catch their breath. He looked toward the gaping entrance to the city. The few Theban riders who'd breached the Plataean line and made it inside the citadel were now attempting to escape, but they were cut off by a mass of Plataean spearmen. Nikias could plainly see the towering figure of Chusor leading this charge, trapping the enemy cavalry inside the walls.

"To me!" cried Zoticus. Nikias looked back at the battlefield. The horse master was still astride his horse and completely unscathed. He waved for the other riders to follow him. "Hunt them down!"

Nearly seventy of the Theban cavalry had survived the melee. They'd fallen back and formed a moving screen between themselves and the thousand or so Thebans retreating on foot. Nikias watched as Zoticus speared the Theban general Gennadios in the back from thirty feet away, then chased down the impaled rider—who had somehow managed to stay atop his mount—and cut off the Theban's head. Gennadios's horse kept running with the headless rider spewing a fountain of blood high into the air. Zoticus leaned over and stuck the head onto the point of his sword and held it aloft for the enemy to see.

"There!" shouted Nikias. He'd caught sight of Eurymakus, a hundred paces away, and felt the blood rush again—a thrill of excited fury that made his flesh tingle. The Theban leapt up from where he'd been hiding behind a pile of dead men and horses. He'd tied off the stump of his severed arm with a ragged Plataean pennant he'd ripped from a phalanx commander's spear pole. He grabbed the headless body of Gennadios and yanked it off the horse. Eurymakus clutched the animal's mane with his remaining hand, pulled himself onto its back, and charged down the hill, away from the citadel and in the opposite direction of Thebes and the retreating army.

Nikias cupped his hands to his mouth and screamed in the direction of Zoticus in an effort to get his attention. But the Plataean horse master was chasing after the throng of enemy riders, followed hard by Kolax. The Skythian boy was barking like an insane hound, shooting Theban stragglers at will.

Nikias glanced to his right. A wounded horse stood there, trembling and snorting. Blood was oozing from a huge gash in its flank. The beast was too far gone to ride.

He glanced down. A dead Theban archer lay sprawled in the mud at his feet, bow clutched in his dead fingers, arrow still nocked. Swiftly he took the bow and arrow in hand and knelt, fitting the arrow to the gut, sighting down the glinting bronze arrowhead, pulling back and taking aim at Eurymakus.

The Theban was riding fast, leaning so far forward on his horse that his face was pressed against the animal's pumping neck. Soon he would be out of range. Nikias let himself feel the distance. Adjusted for the wind and the pull of the earth goddess Gaia. He thought, "Artemis, guide my hand," and let fly. He knew the instant he'd released the arrow his aim was true.

But either by bad luck or the invisible hand of some Theban-loving god, Eurymakus's horse stumbled, dropping its head. The arrow passed so close to the Theban's skull that the hair on the top of his head puffed out from the breeze made by the flying shaft. Eurymakus's horse recovered its footing, and the Theban glanced back with a sneer in Nikias's direction, the pennant strapped to his amputated arm flapping wildly.

Nikias looked around frantically for another arrow. Precious seconds passed, and Eurymakus soon became a tiny figure in the distance. Nikias threw aside the bow and ran to the wounded horse. He gripped the reins and swung himself onto its back. But the startled animal—traumatized by the battle and its injury—bucked him off and he landed hard, whipping back his head against a shield that lay on the muddy ground. His vision went black.

TWENTY-SIX

———◆———

By the time the sun was at its zenith, Spartan scavenging parties were hard at work, roaming the countryside in search of provisions. These warriors had been camped on the southern side of the Kithaeron Mountains for the last two weeks, waiting for General Drako to return from his mission in the Oxlands, and they had nearly exhausted the provisions of their vassals the Megarians in whose territory they had lingered.

After Drako had arrived the night before with news of the successful Theban sneak attack, the army had marched over the mountains and waited on the summit to the southeast of Plataea. Their march had taken them, ever so briefly, through Athenian territory, an act of war in and of itself.

Drako had intended on marching his men straight through the open gates of Plataea just after dawn and occupying the citadel as guests and allies of the Theban conquerors. But when they'd arrived in the Oxland valley, soon after the aftermath of the miraculous Plataean victory, Drako was baffled about what to do. He didn't have enough men to storm the citadel—even one with missing gates. His Spartans were trained to fight phalanx to phalanx on a flat field of engagement, not to storm the walls of a citadel against enemy archers who held the higher ground.

Furthermore, Sparta hadn't declared war on Plataea, and Drako was not about to break the rules of war. Faced with this strange turn of events (and the obvious bungling of that Theban Eurymakus), he'd brought his two thousand men to the old Persian Fort to reassess the situation.

The Spartans did not steal anything from their Plataean "hosts," as they called the locals; they paid for all they took with Persian gold. They did not threaten any of the men or women in the countryside who were fleeing to the citadel with their precious belongings. Rather, they acted with a politeness that unnerved the Plataeans who met them. Even though the two were not officially at war, there were enough red-clad warriors and their Helot slaves on the roads to make it seem like Plataea had already been defeated and colonized.

Two Spartan horsemen entered a deserted and burnt farmyard. Unlike common Spartan foot soldiers, who dressed in nothing more than sandals and dirty red cloaks, these riders were outfitted as scouts with leggings, high buckskin boots, and light plate-armor cuirasses. Their robes were spun from the finest crimson cloth and they wore signet rings—signets that identified them as members of the royal houses.

The younger of the two cavalry officers got down off his horse and held the reins for his superior so he could dismount. This was done as a show of deference rather than out of necessity. The commander was perfectly capable of getting off a horse by himself.

"Don't do that anymore," said Arkilokus as his feet touched the ground. "Don't hold my reins." They spoke in Dorik, the Greek dialect of their homeland.

"Yes, Prince Arkilokus," replied Hippius, bowing slightly and, looking about the place, observed, "This farm is destroyed."

"Yes, Hippius," replied Arkilokus with a dismissive tone. "It would appear so." Arkilokus was big for a Spartan. Practically a giant compared to Hippius, who, like most of his race, was short and sinewy. While Hippius had dark hair, Arkilokus's was sandy-colored. The commander could have easily put on Oxlander clothing and not gotten a second glance. He stared at the ruined farm with a curious look. "What happened here?" he asked under his breath, scratching his thin blond beard.

A gang of Helot slaves soon entered the yard. They were yoked to carts like beasts, six men to a cart. The wagons were filled with bags of wheat, caged chickens, and tied-up pigs. A dozen Spartan warriors with spears brought up the rear.

Hippius ordered the Helots to start searching the grounds, while Arkilokus went off by himself. Almost all of the buildings—main house and sheds—were uninhabitable, irreparable. The only animals that could be seen were some smoke-blackened ducks waddling about, picking through the dirt for fallen seed. He looked in the doorway of the ruined slave quarters, saw the mangled bodies of the men, women, and children who had been butchered there. The flies were so loud, they sounded like bees in an orchard. He did not flinch or cover his nose from the stench. He'd seen worse. He'd *done* worse.

He saw a beautiful white mare grazing in a field nearby and shouted at Hippius to go and capture it for him. He made his way across the farmyard and saw the marks of many feet and horses' hooves. Here and there the ground was stained with black blood.

He went into the ruins of the house, ducked under charred beams, and climbed over heaps of bricks. The hearth and the entire chimney still stood in the center of the room but they were surrounded by debris. He sifted through the rubble until he found the broken remains of a funeral jar. He picked up the shard that bore the face of a dignified, thoughtful-looking man with only the first three letters of the name still legible—"Ari . . ." He spat on the shard and rubbed it on his cloak to clean it. He held it up to the light, studied it, and then tossed it aside.

A faint groaning sound made him turn. It was coming from the chimney! He went to it, put his ear to the stones. He cursed and looked around for a tool. He wrenched a large flagstone from the floor, then set to work slamming it into the chimney. He pulled the loose bricks apart and a hand reached out, desperately pulling at the blocks.

"Get me out of here!" bellowed a Plataean-accented voice.

Arkilokus pulled out more bricks until he could see a bearded face that was coated in black soot—a face that looked as though it had been carved from a chunk of charcoal. The owner of the face was curled up inside the chimney in the fetal position, stuck like a stopper in a bathtub.

"What is this, then?" asked Arkilokus with a profoundly un-Spartan look of surprise, speaking in perfectly accented Attik Greek.

"You cursed goat pleaser!" replied the stuck man. "Get me out of here immediately."

"Who are you, old man?" asked Arkilokus.

"Who do you think I am?" came the reply. "Now, stop gawking and help me out of this forsaken chimney."

"Are you injured, ancient one?"

"What do you think, dung for brains? And you can call me 'General.'"

"Well, General, how did you—"

"I crawled in here from the rooftop to escape the fire, rat brain. By Zephyros, you're a question-asking fool!"

The Spartan's mouth formed a wry, lopsided smile. "Put your arm around my shoulder, Grandsire the General. Let me help you."

The Plataean reached out and wrapped his arms around Arkilokus's shoulders. The Spartan heaved him forth and set him down on the ground.

"Gods!" yelled the freed man. "Arggghhh!"

"Back injury?" asked Arkilokus.

"I hurt my spine the other day," replied the Plataean. "Fighting," he added, as though to regain some of his dignity.

"Ahh, I've heard injuries to the spine are vexing," said Arkilokus, and clicked his tongue.

Two of the Spartan prince's force, drawn by the commotion, ran up with a flash of red cloaks. The soot-covered man looked all three up and down and the expression on his thunderstruck face showed that he'd realized that the men standing in front of him, including his rescuer, were Spartans.

"Hera's jugs," cursed Menesarkus, the Bull of the Oxlands.

PART III

There was a sect of Thebans whose religious beliefs were strange, even to their fellow citizens, for many folks of that city shunned the Greek gods and ascribed to the mystical teachings of the Persians, whom they desired to imitate in all things. The devoted disciples of the god Ahura Mazda saw themselves as warriors in that deity's earthly army. Their mission in life was to root out and destroy the unbelievers. . . .

—**Papyrus fragment from the "Lost History" of the Peloponnesian War by the "Exiled Scribe"**

ONE

———◆———

Eurymakus stood at the edge of the Great Abyss that separated earth from the heavenly realm. He was clothed all in white silk. His face was unmarred by blood or wounds of any kind. Raising the palm of his right hand to his forehead he gave a salute to the one God—Ahura Mazda the Giver of All Life. He called to Daena, his guardian angel, to show him the invisible bridge across the Chasm of Damnation. He waited expectantly for her to appear. If he had lived a good life, Eurymakus knew, Daena would be beautiful—a reflection of his inner beauty. He called again, but his voice was drowned out by the furious winds that whipped through the canyon. The winds tore the white clothes from his body to reveal the putrid signs of a decaying corpse.

A wrinkled hand attached to a wizened arm reached out from the pit, feeling its way along the precipice, its fingertips like a fleshy spider. Eurymakus tried to move but he was rooted in place. He could not flee. The hideous hand touched his foot and pounced, grabbing him around the ankle and yanking him off his feet. As Eurymakus tried desperately to stay on the edge of the cliff, the dark shape of an old hag rose up, engulfed him in her skeletal arms, and pulled him over into the oblivion with a triumphant cackle of glee. . . .

Eurymakus opened his eyes and let forth a stifled scream. He could not remember where he was. He looked around, saw he was in a field tent. It was day. He heard the sounds of men moving outside. He rolled over and saw a candle burning on the ground. Next to it was a cup of mushroom tea—the sacred tea that had shown him the terrible vision. He tried to put his right hand to his face to touch his throbbing lip, and saw a bloody stump where his arm used to be. It was tied off at the end with a tourniquet.

He was in the Spartan camp, he remembered all at once. At the Persian Fort. The Thebans had been defeated and he had fled the field of battle. He had run straight into the Spartan forces.

He lay back and covered his eyes with his good arm. He imagined he was back in Persepolis, the great capital of the Persian empire, where he and his brother Damos had gone to live after escaping the siege of Sardis in Anatolia. He saw himself sitting in one of the palace's quieter gardens, by a tiled fountain, listening to the caged bulbuls—the nightingales.

In Persepolis, Damos's great beauty and physical prowess had caught the eye of the king's entourage, and he had become a lover of the aged Xerxes himself. Eurymakus, who had showed wit and wile, had been singled out by the king's court whisperer and trained in the arts of subterfuge and spy-work. Over the years he had traveled to the farthest corners of the empire with various whisperers—along the well-laid royal roads that enabled messengers to ride nearly fifty miles a day—learning staggering truths. The empire was not held together by threat of war, or even the might of the king's armies, but rather through deception, fear, well-timed assassinations, and—most important—bribery.

After Damos had been killed in the Olympics, Eurymakus had retreated back to the court of Artaxerxes, the son of Xerxes, who'd devised his own senile father's murder with poison. It was during the long journey to Persepolis that Eurymakus had first dreamt up his plan to bring down Plataea . . . and eventually all of Greece. Five years later he'd returned to Thebes with a few sacks full of gold darics and put his scheme into motion. The gold had kept coming and the plan had kept working flawlessly. Until he'd attacked Menesarkus's farmhouse, of course. And then everything had crumbled and turned to shit, like a temple built on a dung heap.

The tent flap opened and Drako entered. "Done with your prayers?" he asked, his rough voice scraping in Eurymakus's ears like a rasp on a horse's hoof.

Eurymakus glared at the Spartan. "Don't understand . . ." he said groggily.

"Don't understand what?" asked Drako.

"The battle—demons—"

"There were none of your demons on the fields of Plataea," said Drako. "Only men fighting for their lives. And you and your Thebans let glory slip through your fingers." He shook his head with contempt.

"Tykon—" began Eurymakus.

"What about him?" asked Drako. "He's either dead or a prisoner."

"He failed," said Eurymakus. "Not I."

"That's not how a Theban court will see it," said Drako.

"I can't go back there."

"Get used to the idea."

"Your army was waiting on the other side of the mountain," said Eurymakus, touching his lip and wincing. "You lied to me. You said you were on your way back to Sparta with the news and—"

"Do you think I would trust a snake like you with Plataea?" asked Drako. "My mistake was that I had confidence you could at least hold the city until dawn."

The men stared at each other, neither turning away. Finally, Eurymakus rolled over on his side and covered his eyes with his arm. The image of the hell hag appeared before his eyes. He wondered why God would send him such a cruel vision. He wished Bogha were there. He had loved the big Median—loved him like a favorite horse or a dog. He'd watched helplessly from across the battlefield as Menesarkus's Persian slave killed him.

"Leave me," ordered Eurymakus. "I need to rest. And let's stop this foolish talk of me going back to Thebes. I'm staying here with you. I am your liaison with Artaxerxes. You won't hand me over to my people. I'm worth my weight in gold."

"A little less weight now, it would seem," said Drako eyeing Eurymakus's missing arm.

"Get out, noseless skull!" said Eurymakus with venom.

"Someday, Theban," said Drako, "you will no longer have the protection of the Persian king. And then I'll give you a lesson in Spartan civility."

After the Spartan had gone, Eurymakus turned to look at his signet ring—the gold and carnelian ring given to him by Artaxerxes himself. The ring that was his passport to move freely along the vast network of roads of the Persian kingdom. The ring containing an invaluable secret that was far more precious to him than mere flesh and blood and bone.

But his arm and signet ring were gone. Lost in the muddy battlefield of accursed Plataea.

TWO

———————◆———————

An ominous sign, yet difficult to interpret. Zeus's disembodied head—as big as the city of Plataea—racing across the blue sky, jaw agape, chasing down a tiny, bee-sized ox fleeing from his hungry mouth. It could mean so many things. . . .

Menesarkus lay flat on his back in a wagon as it rumbled down the road. The enormous white thundercloud resembling the face of the god towered directly overhead. Zeus had nearly caught up to the smaller scud of mist—the miniature ox. With a shift in the wind the god's "mouth" appeared to open wider and wider. Soon it would devour its vaporous prey.

"There is no way to escape the will of the Storm Bringer."

The voice in Menesarkus's mind was his grandfather's. The brain was a wonderful organ, he thought, to remember the exact tone, cadence, and timbre of the long-dead man's manner of speech. It was his grandfather who had taught him to read not only letters but portents in the clouds as well.

Was the ox symbolic of Thebes about to be destroyed by Plataea? Or was it the other way around?

He wondered if men in the city, a short ride from here, were watching the sky now—if they, too, were seeing this omen. He thought of Nikias. Had his grandson earned glory on the battlefield? Or was his corpse already rotting in the morning sun, morphing into a hideous mockery of his youthful beauty?

The wagon jolted. Menesarkus's injured spine sent a shiver of pain through his body. He stifled a gasp, pushed himself up on his elbows to a sitting position. He took a look around at the landscape, recognized instantly where they were heading—to the Persian Fort. This was good news. It meant that the city was still in Plataean hands. Otherwise the Spartans would not be digging into position with their backs to friendly Thebes, as the Persians had done those fifty years ago. Instead they would be camped directly outside the city walls. He eyed the three Spartan warriors walking a few paces behind the wagon. Their lean faces showed the stereotypical blank expression of their race. He wondered what had happened to the young commander who'd got him out of the chimney. The last time he'd seen the blond-haired Spartan, he was riding away on Nikias's mare, Photine.

"This is the road held by your ancestors in the second position," remarked Menesarkus, more to himself than the nearby Spartans. "I and my phalanx were just there"—pointing to a hillock—"and we joined your kin in the final push against the enemy position. The crazed Spartan Aristo broke from the pack and slew a dozen Persians before as many arrows brought him down. I later heard you buried him without honor, a punishment for breaking ranks. Foolish notion. He should have had a temple built in his honor. Why, I named my own son after him."

There was no response from the warriors. Not even the slightest hint of interest. But then one of them made a quick motion and Menesarkus saw the other two respond with barely perceptible nods. Menesarkus knew the Spartans could speak to each other with their hands. He'd even learned a little of their "battle sign," as they called it. The Spartan warrior had signed "Hallowed ground" to his companions.

Menesarkus thought back to his journey to Sparta. It was a year after the victory against the Persians. He had been chosen to go along with a contingent of Plataean warriors, invited as honored guests of one of the royal families to participate in funeral games for Lysander, leader of the "Three Hundred" who had held off the passes of Thermopylae for a week. Stalling Xerxes and his army of a million men and giving the allies time to organize their defense of Greece.

Menesarkus recalled seeing the Eurotas valley surrounding the city of Sparta as though it were yesterday. It had been like entering an upside down world. The lush valley, fed by two rivers, contained hundreds of buildings, both public and private, as well as a myriad of gardens and orchards—a city five times the size and vastly more populated than Plataea. And, astonishingly, there was not a single wall or fortification in sight.

"Our shields make our walls."

It was the ancient Spartan motto. And they had proved this saying for centuries by meeting and defeating any army that attempted to invade their lands. But it was still disconcerting to see so many people seemingly living a life free of care. He suddenly felt ashamed of his own walled city. It seemed confined and claustrophobic compared to this astonishing, rambling Elysium. As though he and his fellow Plataeans—living behind cramped walls—were some kind of rude insects. Bees in a compact hive or ants in a mound of dirt.

He became friends with several full-blooded Spartan warriors during that summer, and he won great honor during the funeral games. He took the pankration event in a no-rules bout in which he'd reduced their champion—the nastiest and deadliest fighter that the young Menesarkus had yet faced—to a comatose heap of ruined flesh. Rather than being shunned after this victory, he gained the admiration of his hosts and spent the rest of his stay in Sparta training members of the royal family in his boxing techniques.

"Zeus's balls!"

The curse escaped Menesarkus's lips as the wagon bounced over a stone aggravating his injury. He craned his neck and saw a small stone bridge that led over a stream. They would be at the Persian Fort in a few minutes. He glanced back at the clouds. They'd changed dramatically in the short time he'd been daydreaming about his trip to Sparta. The ox entering Zeus's mouth now resembled a penis penetrating a disembodied vagina. That could be interpreted in many different ways. . . .

Plataeans, he knew, could never accept the Spartans as overlords. They found them too strange. Hardly even Greek. They looked and sounded different from the men of Attika and the Oxlands, the true scions of Zeus. Physically the Spartans were darker and shorter. They spoke with those outlandish Dorik accents. They bowed to not one but *two* kings and lived in packs of men. They were so unused to women that they shaved the heads of their new wives to make the marriage bed tolerable. Besides that, they let their women wrestle naked in public. This he'd witnessed with his own eyes, and the sight of those muscular Spartan beauties grappling in the sand had given him a massive erection—actually pulled the knot of his dog tie loose!—much to the disdain of the Spartan males standing nearby.

He'd ended up bedding one of those girl wrestlers. The handsome Helena. So muscular and dusky compared to his pale Plataean wife back home. Helena had sought him out at a palace party after his victory at the games. She'd worn one of those delightful short chiton dresses, one of the few decent Spartan innovations, in Menesarkus's opinion, that flashed the insides of her thighs and the hair of her bush with each step. She'd told him that her father had given her permission to bed Menesarkus. Came right out and said that to his face. Her father wanted her to have the great pankrator's seed. Menesarkus had heard rumors about Spartan "wise sex"—breeding by design. And here was proof. It was only after they'd made love, off and on for the next week, that Menesarkus discovered who her father was: the king regent Pleistoanax.

One of the three warriors escorting the wagon broke off and loped on ahead—most likely, Menesarkus thought, to inform the Spartan general of his arrival. The pankrator wondered how he would be treated. Would they bind him in chains and take him back to Sparta as a prisoner to rot in some prison pit? Or would he be accorded the rights of a general captured on the field of battle?

He saw that the Spartans had moved into the Persian Fort like swallows returning to ancient nests. There were guards manning the gate and archers striding along the tops of the grass-covered walls as confidently as if they were in Sparta and not on enemy territory.

There were hundreds of slaves hard at work, gathering wood for fires, bringing water from the river, and slaughtering animals outside the berms. Others brought stone from the fields to rebuild the guard towers that had crumbled over the decades. The Helots looked exactly the same as they had when Menesarkus had first seen them fifty years earlier—with squat bodies and glossy black bristle of close-cropped hair, wearing their dung-colored knee-length smocks.

For that matter their Spartan masters had not change an iota, either. He could see hundreds of them in the distance, squatting on the ground in small groups, or unpacking weapons and armor, hair as long as a woman's and their beards trimmed to a sharp point at the chin. That consistency over the decades, in everything from architecture to dress, was the trademark of the Spartan people. While fashions and hairstyles—even laws—changed in Attika and the Oxlands, Sparta remained immutable.

The cart rolled over the wooden bridge that spanned the dike and entered the camp. The Spartan who had gone off to report Menesarkus's arrival returned at the same wolf-like lope, whispered something to his companions, and motioned for the driver of the wagon. They unharnessed the Helots, pulled the wagon into a stand of bushes and trees, and then, without even glancing at him, all headed off to the center of the camp.

The old fighter's face turned as red as a Spartan's cloak. They'd left him alone with disdain. Like some sort of vagabond cripple!

The young commander who'd dug him out of the chimney galloped into camp astride Photine. Without thinking, Menesarkus barked at him in Dorik. "Hey, you! Get off that stolen horse and help me out of this damned cart!"

Arkilokus reined up, leapt from Photine's back, and strode quickly to Menesarkus. "You certainly have balls," he said, "to address me like that."

"I am a general of Plataea, sparse beard," replied Menesarkus. "I've got balls bigger than you and your sire put together. Now help me off this forsaken wagon."

Arkilokus's mouth twisted into a lopsided smile. "Put your arm around my shoulder, grandsire. Good, now give me all your weight," he added with a gently mocking tone. "I can hold your old bones up."

For the first time Menesarkus realized how big the Spartan was. Nearly his own height and build with broad shoulders—incredibly brawny for a Spartan.

"Thank you," said Menesarkus with an effort at civility. He was able to walk fairly well with the Spartan supporting most of the weight of his upper body.

"Where am I to take you, then?" asked the young commander. "A little stroll about our camp? Are you a spy?" He stifled a laugh.

"Take me to whoever is leading this invasion force," replied Menesarkus.

They made their way in silence through the scattered groups of Spartan warriors, who stared at them with perplexed and sometimes hostile looks.

"That horse you took is my grandson's," said Menesarkus.

"I'll pay you gold for her," said Arkilokus. "You'll come out all right."

"I don't want money," said Menesarkus. "I want the horse."

"Too bad," said Arkilokus.

A sentry spotted them and ran to the center of the compound where a group of officers conversed over a map spread out on a small field table. Menesarkus spotted Drako instantly.

"What is this?" shouted Drako with ire. "What are you doing, Commander?" With his lips curled back in a sneer, his noseless face looked even more porcine than usual.

"General Drako," replied Arkilokus, "I bring an honored guest. A Plataean general. I found him alone. He is injured—"

"I am fully aware of his presence in the camp," spat Drako. He stood with his hands on his hips, glaring fiercely at his subordinate, avoiding Menesarkus's eyes. Menesarkus had seen Spartans break the noses of their subordinates for lesser crimes than bringing an enemy into the heart of camp. He waited expectantly for a blow to fall on the young commander's face. He glanced over and saw that his helper was not cowering. Rather, he was glaring back at his superior.

"Then you will not mind," began Arkilokus, "that I have—"

"You have overstepped your place, Prince," cut in Drako.

Prince Arkilokus! Menesarkus remembered where he'd seen him before. He was a champion four-horse charioteer. He'd watched him beat an Athenian nobleman to take the crown at the Olympics the year before. Only the very wealthy could afford to compete in that expensive sport. Only a Spartan royal. His lineage was the only way he could get away with such insolent behavior toward his general. The tension between the two Spartans was palpable. He noticed that the other warriors regarded Drako and Arkilokus anxiously. Obviously there was bad blood between these two. Menesarkus felt guilty for putting the young royal in such a tight spot. The only thing for it was to play the Bull. He turned to Drako and spoke for all to hear.

"I am Menesarkus. Hero of the Persian Wars. Victor of the Funeral Games of Lysander. Olympic champion. General of Plataea. I, who stormed this very site fifty years ago with members of the Spartan royal family—as well as you, Drako!—at my side . . . am I to be treated like a vermin-ridden beggar at the door of a rich man's house? I am overcome by your rude behavior. I could weep, I am so insulted. Is this what things have come to? We have sunk low. Very low indeed." The moment Menesarkus had announced his name, Arkilokus's strong arms had gripped him tighter, as if, Menesarkus thought, to offer support for his outrage.

Drako chewed his teeth and looked Menesarkus up and down. His expression changed from rage to resignation.

And then Menesarkus saw a man who made his heart skip a beat—a one-armed Theban, his bloody stump tied with a tourniquet at the elbow, limping into the center of the camp in heated conversation with another Spartan. He stood out amongst the red-cloaked warriors because of his Persian hair and beard and the fact he was clothed all in black. Even though Menesarkus had only seen the enemy by torchlight, he recognized him immediately: Eurymakus.

"You!" yelled Menesarkus. "Coward! Murderer!"

Eurymakus pulled up short, his face twisted in open-mouthed surprise and indignation. Rage surged through Menesarkus's body, making him fierce, making him strong. He broke free of Arkilokus and threw a punch that caught Eurymakus off his guard, striking him on the side of the head, sending him to the dirt.

THREE

———◆———

Nikias awoke from a dreamless stupor to the cawing of excited crows mingled with the morbid sounds of keening women:

"Today the sky is black as night, today the day is as dark as a tomb . . ."

Baklydes and Leo stared down at him. They had stripped off their armor and were as naked as pankrators. Their faces, arms and legs were splattered with blood and mud, but the areas that had been protected by armor were strikingly clean. They looked like tortoises without their shells.

"Nik appears to be awake," observed Baklydes.

"How many fingers?" asked Leo, showing his middle finger.

"Goat fondler," said Nikias groggily.

"He'll live," said Leo.

Baklydes helped Nikias sit up and he looked around him with bleary eyes. The hillside swarmed with men carting off wounded Plataeans. Binding captured Thebans in chains. Putting lame horses and dying enemy warriors out of their respective miseries.

"Did Saeed survive?" Nikias asked, watching a pair of crows stabbing at the face of a Theban corpse and fighting over a piece of flesh.

"Saeed's the one who dragged you over here with your shield," said Leo. "Then he found a horse and rode for Helladios's farm. Said he was going to see his son before he died."

Nikias sat up, turned around, and glanced down at the shield his head had been propped up on. He saw the familiar boxing Minotaur and laughed even though he felt nauseated and his neck ached fiercely. He'd been beaten blind several times before in fights and falls from horses, and knew his brain had been "rattled," as his grandfather used to say.

"Tell me what happened," demanded Nikias.

"You fell off a horse," said Leo. "And the Minotaur on your own shield knocked you out."

"And then?"

"Zoticus chased the Theban hoplites as far as the northern crossroads; they killed a hundred more of them. Then their horses started to give out and they had to come back."

"How many dead on our side?" asked Nikias.

"Get your bearings first, Nik," said Baklydes. "You've had a rough time."

"We're still counting the dead," said Leo. "And it's not over."

"What do you mean?"

"There's another army."

Nikias shut his eyes, shook his head from side to side. The world spun.

"Spartans," said Baklydes.

Nikias rolled over and puked.

"That was *my* reaction," said Leo.

"I don't understand," said Nikias, wiping his mouth.

"We'll find out soon enough," said Leo. "The Spartans are setting up base at the old Persian Fort. We thought they were going to march straight for the citadel, but for some reason they went to the fort. We've seen a few mounted Spartan scouts riding around, but they haven't done anything aggressive. They've even been leaving the refugees alone. All the farm families have been pouring in from the countryside."

"How many Spartans?" asked Nikias.

"Two thousand, maybe. Plus a couple thousand more of those Helot slaves."

Nikias cursed. Everything tonight and this morning had been for nothing. "Why are the Fates against us?" he growled.

"We've stayed alive so far," said Leo. "The Spartans have never laid siege to a city the size of Plataea. It's not their method. At least, that's what Zoticus says. They haven't attacked yet because they have no cavalry. We can put three hundred riders in the field now, what with the captured horses. We trapped almost fifty Theban riders in the city."

"And the Egyptian will have the gates up soon enough," added Baklydes.

Nikias tried to turn his head to look over his shoulder, but his neck was so stiff he could barely move it. So he shifted his whole body around to peer at the entrance to the city. One of the gates was nearly up, hovering inches above the ground, suspended by a dozen ropes pulled by hundreds of men. Even with his blurred vision, Nikias could make out the distinct figure of Chusor directing the workers. "His name's Chusor," he said softly.

"Eh?" asked Baklydes.

"Nik's right. Call him Chusor," said Leo.

"Who, Nikias?" asked Baklydes stupidly.

"No, arse brains, the *smith*," said Leo. "*His* name is Chusor."

"What happened after I escaped through the tunnel?" Nikias asked Leo.

Leo told him about the destruction of the barricade and the appearance of Nauklydes, his demented speech, and the subsequent slaughter of the bound prisoners.

"I can't condemn what they did," said Nikias. "Not after what I've seen. What I've lost."

"The Thebans are no better than thieves or pirates," said Baklydes.

"But how will this affect peace negotiations?" asked Leo.

"To Hades with peace," said Nikias. Turning to Baklydes, he asked, "Did your father and brother live?"

"They did," said Baklydes. "My old man would talk Thanatos himself to death. But Hesiod lost his arm."

"Too bad for Hesiod," said Nikias. He felt lucky to have made it through the night and dawn with nothing more than a few cuts and a cracked head.

"He'll be all right," said Baklydes, unconcerned. "He's lucky he didn't lose both."

"Speaking of arms," said Leo, and he kicked at something lying on the ground. Nikias saw Eurymakus's severed arm, still wrapped in his Sargatian whip. The spy's appendage, drained of blood, had turned pale and was snaked with livid blue veins.

"I reckoned you'd want your whip back," said Leo, reaching for it.

"Don't touch it!" warned Nikias. "It's got poison in it."

He bent down and inspected the hand. There was a signet on the ring finger. He pulled it off and put it in a small pouch strapped to his belt for safekeeping. Then he tore the tunic off a dead Theban and wrapped the whip's handle with it, carefully unwinding the whip from the arm and cleaning off Eurymakus's blood. He realized that the whip had saved the Theban spy's life, cutting off the flow of blood in his arm and giving Eurymakus enough time to hack off his own arm.

"Thebans don't really have the dragon's blood, you know?" said Baklydes.

"I told you," said Nikias. "It's got *poison*—"

"Look," interrupted Leo, pointing to the path that wended its way along the bottom of the walls of Plataea. A line of prisoners was being led up the road from the direction of the village of Oeroe.

"Those are the Theban cavalry we captured," said Nikias.

"Looks to be thirty more prisoners," said Baklydes.

Nikias saw the castrated Theban general Straton walking out in front of his men, wincing with every step.

Two men rounded the corner of the walls bearing a body on a stretcher. Even from this distance Nikias could see they carried a woman, for her long hair dragged in the mud behind her.

And then it hit him—like a spear through his heart. He sprinted across the field, leaping over corpses. When he got to Kallisto, he saw her eyes were closed and her chest and head were wrapped with linen bandages. Blood had soaked through both wounds. He shouted her name several times but she did not open her eyes or react to his voice. The stretcher bearers set her down and Nikias knelt by her, took one of her hands, and held it. Leo, Baklydes, and Saeed ran up and stood at his side.

"How?" Nikias asked the stretcher bearers. "What happened to her?"

"The Thebans came back to the bridge a second time," one of them replied. "They tried to clear the bridge so they could pass. But Kallisto led a charge of archers across the bridge—crawling over the dead Theban horses—and shot a dozen of the enemy before they took her down. She cracked her skull on the stone bridge as she fell. My own wife took the arrow out clean. But both wounds are bad."

"What was Kallisto doing at Oeroe?" asked Baklydes.

"She begged to come with me," said Nikias. "I don't know where to take her," he said numbly. He felt like grabbing fistfuls of dirt and covering himself and Kallisto until they disappeared, absorbed into the earth. No more pain. No more longing. Nothing. Just the cool earth and silence. "My uncle's house is defiled with corpses . . ." he said in a distant voice. "They were butchered last night."

"Our farm is too far away," said Baklydes.

"So is ours," said Homer.

Leo said, "I know where to take her."

FOUR

A blinding pain shot up Menesarkus's spine after punching Eurymakus in the head and he lost control of his legs, dropping to his knees. Arkilokus picked him up and dragged him away from the stunned Theban, who had fallen flat on his back, nearly knocked senseless from the blow.

"This man tried to murder my family!" said Menesarkus with fury. "He is responsible for the deaths of my daughter-in-law and my slaves."

Eurymakus shook his head. He reached for the poisoned dagger at his hip. But he'd left both his sword arm and tainted blade on the fields of Plataea. He got slowly to his feet, swayed, looked about unsteadily, then fell on his rump. "Menesarkus, old friend," he said with a contemptuous smile, made even more ghastly because of the chunk of flesh missing from his upper lip. "So good to see you here. It appears I get to have the pleasure of killing you again." He tried to get up again but Drako held up his hand.

"Stay where you are, Eurymakus," said Drako.

"I demand the right to fight him," said Menesarkus. "I name this a blood feud and by Spartan law you must accept."

"Oh, I accept," said Eurymakus, getting up on one knee.

"Some fight that would be," observed Drako. "A one-armed man and a cripple? Is that what qualifies as sport in the Oxlands?" His joke brought smiles to the faces of his men, but not laughter.

"You make a good point, General Drako," said Arkilokus. "We are not on Spartan soil. We don't have to honor a blood feud even if—"

"This has nothing to do with you, Arkilokus," burst out Eurymakus harshly. And then he bowed slightly to the royal. "You must forgive me, my prince. The loss of my arm in battle . . . the crushing defeat have made me—"

"Shut up, all of you," croaked Drako with his constricted voice. "Help our honored guest to my tent," he said, and motioned for two burly Helots to take over for Arkilokus and lead Menesarkus to a field tent nearby.

"Make your report to the officers," Drako commanded Arkilokus. He turned to the fuming Eurymakus and said in a low voice, "Control your emotions, Theban. He is my prisoner now. You had your chance." He marched away from them with his short, quick steps and entered the tent.

"It's the badger's tail for your supper," said Arkilokus to the Theban spy with a smirk. "Though you seem to have already eaten part of your lip. Perhaps you're full?"

Eurymakus slit the Spartan prince's throat with his eyes.

FIVE

Menesarkus sat in a folding field chair with Drako cross-legged on the floor in front of him. "That was quite a performance," said the Spartan.

"Nothing that I said was untrue," replied Menesarkus.

Drako cocked his head, took in a deep breath . . . and sighed. Menesarkus could not remember ever having heard a Spartan sigh before. It was disconcerting, especially coming from this grizzled veteran with the eyes of a murderer and the face of a boar.

"There is no reason to conceal anything from you," said Drako with a shrug. "Thebes has failed in their attempt to take your city."

"Because you arrived too late to help," spat Menesarkus.

"We are in alliance with Thebes," said Drako. "That is no secret. We knew what the Thebans were going to do. That I will admit. But we came to prevent them from slaughtering your brothers and sisters. We came here to protect you from Thebes."

Menesarkus snorted. What the Spartan was saying was preposterous. "Why?" he asked.

"Because a strong Plataea as an ally is worth more to us than a stronger Thebes," replied Drako without artifice. He scratched his beard like a dog going after a flea. "When I came to your home the other week, I spoke the truth. If you had only joined our league, none of this would have happened. We would have made Thebes subject to your citadel. But you rebuffed us—"

"Because you are Athens's enemy!" blurted Menesarkus. "How could we go against our protector?"

"Because they will leave you out to dry like a gutted fish on a rack," replied Drako with scorn. "Our war with Athens is unstoppable. It is already set in motion. Your city has escaped doom today. But if you continue to cling to Perikles like a screaming toddler clutching his mother's leg, well, he will eventually cast you aside."

Fish on a rack. Toddler at his mother's leg. This was a poetic sort of Spartan. Menesarkus felt an overwhelming sense of despair. Everything Drako had said was true. He felt as though he were caught at the edge of a shore, pounded down by the endlessly crashing waves. . . .

"You have a choice," said Drako. "We are simple men. We honor old alliances and friendships. Plataea stood side by side with us against the Persians, while the Thebans offered both Darius and Xerxes water and earth like simpering slaves. We have not forgotten that in Sparta. A strong Plataea could help us defeat the tyranny of Athens. And you can save your families from death and degradation. You can see that we do not have enough manpower to attack Plataea . . . at least, not today. I will not toy with your military mind. You have seen our camp. This is an occupation force, not an army to besiege a walled citadel. But we will not abandon the Persian Fort. We will hold this ground until more men come from Sparta along with Persian siege masters. And then we *will* lay siege to Plataea and bring its walls to the ground if it takes fifty years. But I would much rather have one crippled Menesarkus as an ally than even a hundred of the strongest Theban warriors."

A wave of pain wracked Menesarkus's body. He slipped from the chair and landed on his side. Drako called out and guards entered the tent with drawn swords, thinking their general was under attack.

"Lay him out on the bedding," Drako said. "And bring him some wine mixed with poppy."

Several hours passed in a blissful stupor. The opium made the pain go away and filled Menesarkus with a wonderful feeling of peace. He realized that he was alone in the tent. He heard the sounds of the camp. At one point he thought he recognized a Plataean accent nearby.

There came a passage of time. He had no idea how long. Was it hours or days? Finally, the flap opened and a man entered. He stood for a while silently watching Menesarkus.

"Is that you, Theban goat groper?" asked Menesarkus with a laugh. The drug made even the prospect of death a whimsical notion. He half expected the Spartans to allow Eurymakus to slit his throat. "Have you come to kill me?"

"Why would I kill you?" asked Arkilokus. He knelt by Menesarkus's side, uncovered a small oil lamp. "Although you did call me 'goat pleaser' when we first met. I *have* beaten men senseless for less than that." The flickering light showed his ironic smile.

"You would kill me because I have seen too much," said Menesarkus.

"You've seen nothing, Plataean," said Arkilokus in a gently teasing tone. "Except what we want you to see."

"I heard a Plataean voice outside a while back. Was that in my dream?"

"Not your dream. An emissary from your city. He came on his own, defying your arkon Nauklydes. Said his name was Isokrates—"

"Nauklydes is not arkon," cut in Menesarkus with a chuckle. His eyes unfocused and he drifted off for a moment. "He's my Olympic herald."

Arkilokus took his hand, slapped him gently on the cheek. "Wake up, old man."

"What is it?" asked Menesarkus, grabbing the Spartan's hand. The knuckles were overlarge and severely callused. Several of the fingers had been broken and healed slightly crooked. "You're a pankrator," he said with surprise.

"All my life," replied Arkilokus. "It runs in the family."

"A wealthy Spartan like you could never fight in public," said Menesarkus. "It would be beneath contempt for you to enter with commoners like me." He laughed as if to say, "Poor coddled royal."

"Too true," replied Arkilokus. "I watched you beat Damos the Theban. I cheered for you even though it infuriated Drako, who wanted you to lose."

"You and I would have been a good match," said Menesarkus. "With me in my prime."

"The gods have a sense of humor, do they not?" asked Arkilokus. His voice had lost its tone of sarcasm. "Eh, Menesarkus the great pankrator?"

The Spartan's rough hand trembled as though in fear, thought Menesarkus. Or was it excitement?

"You think my predicament humorous?" asked Menesarkus.

"Rather the coincidence of our meeting," replied Arkilokus.

Menesarkus squinted. "You remind me of someone. . . . I can't figure it out. . . ."

"Shall I get you a mirror?"

"Eh?"

"You were acquainted with somebody *I* once knew," stated Arkilokus. "Somebody very dear to me."

"Where?"

"In Sparta, of course. The drug has made you stupid. Think."

"Really? What was his name?"

"*Her* name," said Arkilokus. "Some called her 'king's daughter.' You see, I have known about *you* my entire life."

The skin of Menesarkus's forearms broke out in gooseflesh. He imagined he could see her strutting toward him in her thigh-flashing dress. He could taste her lips on his mouth as though he'd kissed her only yesterday. He said, "Helena . . . king's daughter . . ."

"I simply called her 'Grandmother,'" said Arkilokus, and felt Menesarkus's hand clutch his shoulder in a death grip. "Now do you see why I said, 'The gods have a sense of humor'? Eh, Plataean?" He leaned forward so his mouth was nearly kissing Menesarkus's cheek. His words came out as the faintest whisper: "Eh, *Grandfather*?"

SIX

It was an hour after midnight by the time Chusor completed work on the Gates of Pausanius. When the massive doors were finally hung into place by torchlight and the hinge pins hammered down, a great cheer went up from the gathering of onlookers—over ten thousand men and women, including residents of Plataea and refugees from the countryside, who had stayed up until long after dusk to see their beloved gates restored.

Arkon Nauklydes went and stood before the crowd. His face was haggard. There was a bandage around his upper body where he had taken a spear to the pectoral, and his wounded hand was wrapped in linen. He cleared his throat. Licked his lips. His eyes blinked rapidly and he rubbed them with the back of one hand.

"Speak, Nauklydes!" called out a man from the audience, and soon the entire crowd was chanting his name.

"Nauklydes saved us!" cried out a voice.

"What can we do about the Spartans?" asked another.

"The arkon will lead us!"

Nauklydes held up a hand for silence. When the crowd calmed down, he declared in a resonant voice that was at odds with his exhausted demeanor, "Zeus led us this day! Not Nauklydes. Nauklydes is nothing more than an instrument of that god. I am honored that you have chosen me as your interim arkon. Other men are better than I to hold this illustrious office. But they are dead. My wise old mentor, Menesarkus . . ." He dropped his chin to his chest, fought back tears. ". . . he would have told you all to defy the Spartans. He would have told you that these walls—which have never been breached save by treachery—can protect us from the Red Cloaks. . . ." He gazed at the thousands of eyes staring back with anticipation. "Nauklydes agrees," he said, nodding his head. "Nauklydes agrees!" he repeated, raising his voice to a shout. "The Spartans are treacherous foxes. They came to the Oxlands hard on the heels of the Theban snakes like carrion after a kill. They must have been in league with the

Thebans. There is no other explanation. Many of you saw the Spartan heralds come to the walls this evening, asking to meet with me in council. I sent them back to the Persian Fort with these words in their ears: 'Plataea will never be the servants of the Spartan dual kings. Plataea will never give up these walls. Plataea will never cower to the demands of men who conspire with our enemies to bring us down by subterfuge and deceit.'

The Plataeans raised their voices in support of Nauklydes. The arkon blinked rapidly, jutting forth his chin. "We met the Thebans on the fields of Plataea as warriors. And we beat them. Nauklydes used no sly trick with his sword today. Nauklydes saw the enemy, and the enemy saw Nauklydes, and Nauklydes slew him!"

The crowd roared and clapped. Nauklydes held up his hand again, and when the people had quieted down he said, "Now let us make a sacrifice to Zeus and ask the god to watch over us in the coming days. Let the smoke from the burning entrails of the hundred oxen float upward and please Zeus's nose. May we please him with our devotion."

Six strong warriors led a huge bull ox weighing over fourteen hundred pounds through the crowd. They quickly tied its legs together. The animal, hogtied and on its back—a most unnatural position for an ox—was terrified and cried out plaintively. Kallinakos, the head priest of the Temple of Zeus, walked up and handed a long knife to Nauklydes. The arkon slit a small puncture in the animal's throat. Thick blood poured from the slit onto the stones in front of the Gates of Pausanius, staining the gray slabs with blood. Kallinakos let the blood pump out for about a minute, then signaled that there was enough and clamped shut the wound with his aged hand.

The audience had become somber, their eyes riveted on the ox. The six warriors untied its legs and stood it back up on its four hooves. Then it was bound with a thick rope around its neck and another attached to its tail. Three of the warriors pulled on the neck rope while the others stretched the tail. The dazed and bled ox stood rooted, pulling back with its neck and digging in with its hindquarters, lowing deep in its throat. There were another ninety-nine oxen tied up in Plataea's abattoir, which stood a stone's throw over the city's eastern walls. These oxen were all to be slaughtered for the hecatomb—the feast of one hundred oxen—after the ritual had been completed. As if in response to their brother ox, the herd of doomed animals started lowing with terror, a sound that sent shivers up Chusor's spine where he stood atop the wall, looking down on the scene.

General Zoticus stepped forward carrying a massive cleaver. He positioned himself in front of the ox, lifted the blade, and brought it down with a brutal blow that broke through the spine with the sound of a snapping branch, nearly slicing the beast's entire head from its neck. The audience let forth a collective breath as the ox dropped to its knees and toppled while its lifeblood spurted across the stones.

The ox was slaughtered and its guts burned in a large fire pit. The meat of the animal was taken off to be cooked for the famished crowds—many of whom had not eaten since the night before. Phakas announced, in a forced offhand manner, that Arkon Nauklydes had paid for the hecatomb out of his own coffers.

Chusor had seen enough. Even though his stomach growled with hunger pangs, he had no appetite for this meat. His friend Zeno the stonemason had taken a spear to the guts in the battle, and the thought of gorging himself on ox meat while that good man was unable even to sip water made him sick. He grabbed a torch and left the wall, walking down the stairs of a guard tower to the streets below. He made his way along Artisans' Lane to the marketplace. Lamps glowed in his smithy. He knew Diokles was there, standing guard on Tykon the Theban. Next door, the portal to Zeno's house was open. He entered and saw Zeno laid out on a bed in the front room. His wife squatted by his side; their children had fallen asleep at his feet. Blankets had been hung over the holes in the walls to give Zeno some privacy in his last hours. The room reeked of death.

Chusor sat by Zeno and took his hand. "Zeno?" he asked softly. The stonemason's eyes were closed but he was still breathing . . . just barely.

"Not much longer now," Zeno's wife, Xanthippus, said quietly, wiping her tear-swollen eyes with her palms. "And then I'll claw my face with these daggers." She held up her fingers and showed long nails she had clipped to sharp points.

Chusor had lain in bed many nights listening through the thin wall to the arguments between Zeno and Xanthippus. More often than not, though, the stonemason and his woman would make up and then make love like crazed cats, crying out their expressions of undying love . . . words that were such a comical contrast to their precoital viciousness.

Zeno stirred and opened his eyes a little. He looked at Xanthippus and smiled. Then he noticed Chusor and said, "Ah. Did you finish hanging the gates?"

"They're shut and locked, neighbor," said Chusor. "No more worries tonight."

Zeno took in a deep breath, sighed, and shut his eyes. "Keep watch on my family, will you, Chusor?" he asked in a fading voice. "You're my friend and . . ." His voice trailed off and his whole body convulsed . . . once . . . twice . . . and then he was gone.

Xanthippus placed her fingers at the top of her forehead and dragged the nails down her cheeks and neck to her clavicles. Red welts formed and then the blood wept from the lines like red sap. Chusor left her there, keening and rocking back and forth.

When he opened the door to his smithy, he saw a woman lying in the alcove at the back of the room, with Nikias sitting on the floor nearby, head drooped on his chest in sleep. Leo sat at the table chewing miserably on a hunk of stale bread, his face turned toward the wailing coming from Zeno's home.

"Who's that?" Chusor asked, pointing at Kallisto.

"Nik's Kallisto," said Leo. "She was wounded at Oeroe—"

Nikias opened his eyes, saw Chusor, and got to his feet. "Chusor, I hope you don't mind—"

Chusor went to Nikias and embraced him.

"I saw you charge the Thebans today," said Chusor. "I was on the tower. You were brave, Nikias."

"The woman I told you about," said Nikias, pulling away from Chusor and gesturing at Kallisto.

"She is welcome in my home," said Chusor.

"We didn't have any other place to go," said Nikias. He turned in the direction of Zeno's house and the sobs emanating from that room.

Chusor leaned over Kallisto. Nikias had combed her long hair and braided it in an old-fashioned 'warrior's knot.' And he had cleaned all of the dirt and blood from her face. Chusor pulled back the blanket and lifted the bandage over her chest.

"It's from an arrow," said Nikias. "The head was pulled out clean."

"I am no physician," said Chusor, "but this does not look mortal." He touched her head, felt the heat emanating from a livid welt that ran all the way across her forehead. "One can never tell with a head wound, though. It could be bleeding under the cranium."

"She seems lost in a nightmare," said Nikias. "She mumbles in her sleep. Nonsense words."

"She is very pale," said Chusor. "She has obviously lost a lot of blood. Keep changing the linens. And see what morning brings. I have some poppy here. We can give her that to ease her dreams. The arrow wound needs a poultice to draw out any infection."

Chusor opened his spice cabinet and brought back some dried poppy resin. He put Leo to work crushing it in a mortar, then went off to the back of the house to look for Diokles. The Helot was wide-awake, sitting cross-legged on the floor in front of the room in which Tykon was kept. He had a large axe clutched in one hand.

"He still there," said Diokles, nodding at the door.

Chusor smiled at Diokles and opened the portal. Tykon was sitting on his haunches. Like Diokles, he was on guard, glaring back at Chusor with the eyes of a captured wolf. They stared at each other for a few moments without speaking before Chusor shut the door and locked it.

"Keep up your watch," Chusor said to Diokles.

Diokles grunted and shifted the axe to his other hand.

Back in the eating area, Chusor found that Leo had fallen asleep with his face on the table and was snoring loudly, the crust of bread still lodged in his mouth. Chusor finished grinding the opium powder and mixed it with some wine in a cup. Then he made a compound of herbs and some clay in a bowl. After he was done, he handed the cup of liquid poppy to Nikias and said, "Spoon it into her mouth, just a tiny sip at a time, until this is all gone."

Nikias nodded and took the bowl, went and knelt by Kallisto, started giving her the elixir. Chusor undid the linens over her chest wound, cleaned it with vinegar, and applied the mixture of clay and herbs.

"I need to talk to you, Nikias," Chusor said as he tended to Kallisto.

Nikias was concentrating so hard on giving Kallisto the poppy-laced wine that he did not hear him.

"Nikias?"

"What is it?" asked Nikias, eyes wide. "Is she all right?"

"Just listen to me," said Chusor. "Nauklydes is the traitor. I have proof. A captured Theban general who is under lock and key in my home. But it will be difficult to prove any of these accusations. Nauklydes has firmly established himself as the new arkon. The people have flocked to him. He has changed his song completely and calls for defiance of the Spartans. Helladios was one of his co-conspirators."

Nikias shook his head. "I knew he hated my grandfather, but betray Plataea? That's insane."

After Nikias had administered all of the opium, Chusor said, "Leave her for a while. There is nothing more you can do now. Follow me."

He led Nikias to the storeroom at the back of the house. They entered the makeshift cell, shut the door behind them. The bound and helpless Tykon eyed the two with contempt.

"I'm not afraid of torture," said Tykon. "I'm dead anyway."

"We're not going to torture you," said Chusor.

"Unless you lie to us," said Nikias. "If you help us convict the traitor, you'll eventually be traded back to Thebes."

Tykon's eyes narrowed. "As I said, I'm already dead. My wife would slit her wrists and kill our children if I walked through our door now. And then I'd be tried and hanged by a Theban court for managing to be the only survivor of a failed expedition in which over four hundred men perished. I was dead hours ago. You're talking to a ghost. You think you're doing me a favor? If we had taken this city, you'd both be my slaves now. Get out of my sight." He spit on the floor at Chusor's feet.

"Why do you hate Plataea so much?" asked Nikias. "Why did you want to exterminate us? Like a hive of wasps?"

Tykon smiled at Nikias. "I know who you are, Nikias. And I've got a story for you. Perhaps one your grandfather the hero never told."

"Go on," said Nikias, squatting on his heels.

"Twenty years ago," said Tykon, "a combined force of Plataeans and Athenians attacked our colony of Sardis in Anatolia. They besieged the city for three months. The men and women ran out of water and turned to drinking the blood of animals. And when the animals were all dead, the people quenched their thirst with their own piss. When the city finally gave itself up, they rounded up every man whom they suspected of being a Persian collaborator. Do you know how preposterous that was? Sardis is in Persia, after all. We paid our taxes to the satrap of Lydia! We were not vassals of the Athenians. These six hundred men were executed and their corpses dishonored . . . defiled."

"How?" asked Nikias. "How were they defiled?"

"Had their heads cut off and stuck on spears to rot in the sun." Tykon's lips curled back in disgust. "And then . . . and then the Plataeans defiled the wives of those men . . . in public . . . raped *our mothers* in front of the dead eyes of their husbands." Tykon looked Nikias in the eyes. "Three of us escaped that siege. We were teenagers at the time. I and my two best friends—Damos and his little brother, Eurymakus."

"Damos?" asked Nikias. "Damos the pankrator?"

"General Menesarkus was also at the siege of Sardis," Tykon said. "Both him and his brother, Alexios. They were the ones in charge of the Plataean forces. Those are the sorts of men you sprang from, young Nikias."

"Eurymakus has had his revenge," said Nikias bitterly. "He killed my grand-father and my mother."

"I only wish I could have been there to see the old Bull slaughtered," said Tykon. "And your mother, too, for that matter."

Nikias stood up and kicked Tykon in the face as hard as he could. The Theban's jaw snapped shut with a loud clack of teeth smashing together. He was about to kick him again when Chusor grabbed him and pushed him up against the wall.

"Leave him, Nik," he said. "He can't fight back."

Nikias breathed hard through his nose. Unclenched his fists. "Let me go, I won't touch him."

Chusor released his grip and Nikias went to Tykon, squatted down in front of him. "Why did Nauklydes betray us?" Nikias asked the Theban.

Tykon let the blood dribble out of his mouth and ran his tongue over the place where his tooth had cut his lip from the kick. "I'm through talking," he said. "But you can try and beat it out of me if you want."

He sat back and grinned mirthlessly at Nikias.

SEVEN

———— ◆ ————

Chusor told Nikias to go for a walk to cool off. He promised to sit by Kallisto and watch her while he was gone. The dark streets teemed with people—refugees from the countryside, city dwellers scavenging for food and water, armed guards on night watch making their rounds. Lamentations had ceased in most neighborhoods. Everyone was exhausted beyond memory. The cries for the dead would begin anew in the morning.

"Nikias!" The deep stern voice stopped Nikias in his paces. It was General Zoticus and his entourage, walking across the agora from the cavalry stables. The general held a rope. Tied to it was an angry redheaded boy.

"Kolax," said Nikias. The last time he had seen the Skythian, he'd been galloping across the fields toward Thebes, shooting down the enemy, screaming with joy.

"You brought this one to the battle, yes?" asked Zoticus, and handed him the end of the rope before Nikias could reply.

"What did he do?" asked Nikias.

"He refused to come back when I called off the attack," said Zoticus. "I had to chase him halfway to Thebes." He smacked Kolax on the side of the head. "You . . . come . . . back . . . when . . . I . . . call," he said slowly, using sign language for the barbarian child's benefit.

"I could have killed ten more of them," whined Kolax in Skythian.

"I think he's complaining that I kept him from his fun," said Zoticus, and tweaked Kolax's nose.

Kolax grimaced and tried to kick Zoticus in the shin, but Zoticus moved his leg aside and laughed. Nikias had never before seen anyone try to kick the fearsome general, and was shocked that Zoticus did not punch the boy in the face—a punishment he'd meted out to a youthful Nikias for the slightest transgression in the riding arena at the gym where Zoticus taught boys how to throw the javelin from horseback.

"As dumb as a cat," said Zoticus with an expression of fondness. He ruffled Kolax's head. "Best rider I've ever seen, though. Shoots like an Athenian guardsman too. Tell Chusor that if he ever wants to sell him to me, name his price. I'm off to bed. And you should be too," he added in a warning tone.

Zoticus strode down the street with his men. Kolax watched him go, cursing in Skythian under his breath.

"Prick," said Kolax in Greek.

"So you have learned some of my language," said Nikias.

Kolax shrugged and said, "Mula."

Nikias untied Kolax's ropes. "You stay by my side or I'll tie you up again. Understand?"

Kolax rubbed his rope-burned wrists and nodded.

There were torches burning in the outdoor colonnades near the Assembly Hall. Nikias could see some men eating a late meal engaged in a heated discussion. Guards were posted at the main entrance to the building, preventing anyone from going inside. Nearby was a crowd of warriors standing in front of a bonfire, waiting to go on guard duty, drinking and talking, winding down from the day. One of them saw Nikias and raised his cup.

"Aristo's son!" he shouted. "You made your father's shade proud today."

The other men raised their cups and gave an "Eleleu" cheer. Nikias felt proud.

"And the little barbarian," called out another. "He made Zoticus look like he rode a mule!"

"To the new Hero Androkles and the little Skythian archer!"

"I wish my grandfather were alive to hear this," said Nikias under his breath.

"The village seer always said praise would be heaped upon my head, like an endless pile of prime sheep dung," said Kolax in a self-satisfied way, grinning. He was obviously enjoying the attention. "Where are we going?" he added.

Nikias knew by the tone of his voice what he was asking. "Don't know," he replied.

He led Kolax back toward the direction of the Temple of Athena. Here the streets were dark and nearly deserted. Up ahead he saw ten men bearing torches heading straight at them. Nikias's hackles went up and Kolax sensed the danger as well.

"Go to Saeed," said Nikias. "To the farm where you took Mula last night!"

Kolax nodded with understanding, then bolted like a rabbit and disappeared into the shadows. When the men got close, Nikias recognized them: warriors who had been loyal to General Helladios, all armed, and Axe—the guardsman who had tried to stop him from entering the city last night. Nikias turned to run but was met by another half dozen men, all with bows strung and ready to shoot.

"We've been looking for you," said Axe with a crooked smile, rubbing the still-sore jaw that Nikias had punched in their brawl outside the gates. "Isokrates wants to talk to you."

"I don't particularly want to talk to him," said Nikias.

Several men grabbed Nikias by his arms.

"Come with us," said Axe.

"What are you doing?" asked Nikias.

"Just shut up."

Nikias's instincts told him to make a break for it, but it seemed so undignified to try to flee and be shot down in the back like an animal. "Isokrates is a coward," he said, "if he won't fight me alone, in the open. . . ."

They walked in silence for two blocks, then turned down an even darker street. Nikias's heart raced. Perhaps this had nothing to do with Kallisto. Maybe Isokrates had known all along that his father, Helladios, was a traitor. And now he was carrying out his plan—to wipe out Menesarkus's family and end all opposition to Nauklydes.

They led him to a dark building; Nikias recognized it as the home of one of Helladios's relatives. Axe took up position at the entrance and the warriors shoved Nikias through the door. Inside the main room Nikias saw Isokrates poring over a map with three other men. The floor was covered with sleeping bodies—Isokrates's male cousins—many of them snoring loudly.

Nikias expected Isokrates to sneer and hurl some insult at him. But instead he gave him a civil nod of the head and pointed to a door.

"In here," he said.

Nikias entered a dark room with no other exit or windows. Isokrates told him to take a seat at a small table and shut the door behind them for privacy, then sat and stared at Nikias across the table without speaking, tapping his finger on the boards.

"What is this about?" asked Nikias.

"You and I are now the heads of our families," said Isokrates. "Both of us are now in danger of losing our farms as well. And most important . . . our city."

Nikias had not thought about the fact that with his grandfather dead he was now responsible for his entire family. "We need to get our women into the city," said Nikias. "They're all at your farm—"

"I saw them today," said Isokrates. "After the battle. My mother, your grandmother and youngest sister. However, my sister—the willful girl—has run away someplace."

Nikias held back telling Isokrates about Kallisto. If he'd thought the man cared at all for his sister, he would have said something about her injuries . . . and her heroism. But he knew that Isokrates felt nothing for Kallisto but murderous contempt.

"They are safe for the time being," said Isokrates. "The Spartans will not harm them."

"How do you know that?"

"I rode to the Persian Fort to meet the Red Cloaks."

"You did what?" asked Nikias.

"I rode to their camp," repeated Isokrates. "After the new arkon turned away the Spartan messengers from the walls. I acted on my own volition."

"And what happened?"

"I met with their general. A noseless creature named Drako."

"What did he say?"

"They wish to discuss terms," replied Isokrates. He stroked his long thin nose. "This city cannot hold out against a prolonged siege, Aristo's son. Those Spartans at the Persian Fort are just an advance guard. But with us holed up like badgers inside these walls, they can destroy every farm in the plains. We have only enough grain in the city's storage sheds for one year. They can starve us out. My father warned that this might happen."

Nikias could see the logic of Isokrates's argument. His grandfather had also warned him of this possibility. What Nikias could not understand, however, was why Isokrates—a man who had hated his guts his entire life—was taking him into his confidence. He did not trust him enough to tell him what his own sister had revealed: that their father, Helladios, had plotted to betray the city along with Nauklydes.

"I have never liked you, Nikias," Isokrates said bluntly, breaking the silence. "You've been a sharp stick up my arse for more years than I care to remember. And after you . . . after you were part of Lysander's *accidental* death, I freely admit I wanted to kill you with my own hands. But you have shown yourself to be a leader today. And brave. If you had not stopped the Theban cavalry at Oeroe, we all might be dead now. Some are calling you a new Hero Androkles. I think it is all nonsense and so should you," he added with a snort.

"Of course. Nonsense," said Nikias, trying best not to smile. "I did my duty, that is all."

Isokrates nodded his head, stared at the flickering lamp on the table. "In that respect we are of the same mind. We know our duty." A pause, then: "The Spartans are going to offer Plataea a treaty."

Nikias said, "We should accept it."

"But Nauklydes is going to turn them away," replied Isokrates. "Tomorrow there will be an assembly. Nauklydes will do his best to tell us all we are perfectly safe behind these walls. But I know it will be a disaster for Plataea if we take this course. As did my father. Up until today I have been a supporter of Nauklydes. I thought he was a wise man. But he has changed since the invasion. Perhaps it is the murder of his daughter. She was to be my betrothed. . . ." He closed his eyes for a moment, then opened them wide. "Or maybe he is terrified of Spartan treachery. Whatever the case, I cannot back a leader who acts in such an imprudent manner. And the slaughter of the Theban prisoners is a stain on our city that will last forever. It weakens any ability we have to come to terms with the Thebans. Those prisoners were worth so much to us alive." Then in a nonchalant way he added, "I need all the support I can muster. With your grandfather dead, you are the head of an old and honorable tribe. And an excellent match for my sister."

"You're offering me Kallisto's hand?" Nikias asked in amazement.

"If you can find her," Isokrates replied in a vexed tone. "The obstinate creature . . ."

"But I'm not a citizen yet," said Nikias cautiously. "How can I help you sway anyone? I have no vote."

"The young people will follow your lead," replied Isokrates. "We might need some fists to back us up if there's trouble."

"Now, that's a depressing thought," said Nikias.

Isokrates let forth a sigh that metamorphosed into a gigantic yawn. "I've got to get some sleep now," he said. "We'll talk more in the morning."

"I have your promise," said Nikias warily. "Your sister's hand in marriage? And you forgive the accident with your brother Lysander?"

"Do I have your support?" asked Isokrates.

"As though I were your own brother," said Nikias, and held out his hand.

"All is forgiven."

Down the street from this house, hidden in the shadows, a band of thirty men armed with cudgels lurked in the dark. Phakas, the servant of Nauklydes, stood licking his lips incessantly, glancing nervously at general Zoticus, who stood by his side.

"If Isokrates and his kin resist, they must be killed," hissed Phakas, taking an urgent yet utterly theatrical step toward the house where Isokrates and Nikias were cementing their alliance. He had no intention of joining Zoticus and his men in this violent endeavor. He merely wanted *them* to spring to action now.

"We'll handle this," replied Zoticus calmly, pushing Phakas firmly against the wall with one of his powerful hands. "Go back to your master and tell him I have everything firmly in my grasp."

Phakas obeyed, skulking away into the black alley.

Axe, still standing guard outside the house, glanced in the direction of Zoticus, took off his helm, and set it on the threshold. It was the sign to Zoticus that all the men in the house had gone to sleep.

Zoticus pursed his lips and whistled—the same call he used for his riders to charge. The gang rushed down the street toward the house.

EIGHT

At dawn a warm wind blew down from the heights of the Kithaeron Mountains and into the streets of Plataea, carrying with it the heady scent of pines. Chusor, sitting alone at the kitchen table in his workshop and picking discontentedly at a plate of food, breathed in the aroma of the breeze as if it were a physic—a remedy for the hollow feeling in his gut. The fragrance spoke to him.

You can still leave this doomed place . . .

The crazed slaughter of the Theban prisoners had been weighing heavily on his conscience. Nauklydes was insane and would lead the Plataeans to their destruction. That much was obvious. Last night, after Chusor had ordered Nikias to go for a walk to cool his head, he had brooded for a long time, alone in the dark. And then, without thinking, he had lit several oil lamps and started gathering up his belongings.

Chusor had planned on telling Nikias that he would be leaving at dawn. But the lad had never returned. And now the smith was worried.

He glanced over at his traveling pack sitting by the door. It contained the small amount of silver he had saved over the last two years, a few clothes, a notebook filled with designs for his inventions, and his cherished copy of Herodotus—two thick scrolls, tightly rolled. He'd packed only a few of his best tools, for he needed to travel light. Everything else would have to stay behind. All that he'd built here in Plataea.

But was he truly willing to leave Diokles behind as well?

He sighed and stared down the hallway to the storeroom door at the other end of the house. The Helot was in there, guarding the Theban prisoner. No matter how much Chusor had pleaded with Diokles the night before, he would not consent to flee the citadel with him. The stubborn mule seemed resigned to die here. He could hear him faintly now, humming to himself—a dispiriting and tuneless song in his own tongue that must be driving the bound Tykon mad.

The wind shifted and brought with it the dry reek of woodsmoke wafting through the open window, coming from the other homes in Artisans' Lane. The men and women of Plataea were awaking to another day. They had survived the Theban sneak attack and the terrible battle at the gates. But would they outlast the single-minded and ruthless Spartans?

He leaned back and closed his eyes, trying to recall the exotic aromas of far-away places he'd been to. Spicy cedar oil from Tyre. The wholesome pulp of Nile papyrus. The warm spray of seawater crashing against the oak bow of a ship as it passed the Gates of Herakles. The one fragrance he could not recall, however, was the natural perfume of his mother's skin . . . and this made him chew his lip in consternation. He had loved her with all his heart. And she had died a slave, never knowing that her child had been granted his freedom.

But what had he made of his life as a free man? Would she be proud of him? Was merely practicing the art of survival a good enough reason to be alive on this earth?

He had come to Plataea in search of a legendary treasure. But he had ended up forging an honest life for himself *and* Diokles, far from the men who wanted both of them dead. He liked this new Chusor whom people respected and trusted. He didn't want to go back to being the man that he'd become before he'd discovered this place—a man bent by desperation. A mercenary and a pirate.

And a killer . . .

Respect and friendship were worth far more than gold, he mused sadly. But you couldn't have either one of those things if you were a shade.

He opened his eyes and pushed the ceramic plate away from him so hard that it skidded across the table, flying off the other side and falling to the floor where it shattered. He got up and strode down the hall to the storeroom door, grabbing the iron ring and flinging open the portal. Tykon lay on his side, arms tied behind his back, ankles bound, staring into space with a numb expression. Diokles was squatting in the corner, hugging his favorite forge hammers to his chest.

Chusor said crossly, "Come on, Diokles. Sun is up. Time to eat. Time to go."

"Not hungry," replied Diokles glumly. "Not going with you. The Helots of Mount Ithome. The ones who run from Sparta—they all dead now."

"Yes, but—"

"*You* told me that story, Chusor!" shouted Diokles, slamming one of his hammers against the stone floor like a sullen child. "Nowhere for me to go now! This city as safe as any, I reckon. Masters can't get me in here. Plataea walls—they nice and high. Masters can't climb walls. Why?" he asked with a disparaging smile. "Because no walls built around cities in Sparta. So Masters can't practice climbing walls. See? Diokles not so dumb after all. Chusor not only smart one here. This Helot sick of leaving places whenever Chusor say go!" He started humming louder, as if to drown out any reply Chusor might offer, and stared sullenly at the ceiling.

Tykon glanced at Chusor and said, "Kill me now," in a bored voice.

Chusor shut the door and stood in the hallway for a moment, tugging on his long braided beard with an exasperated gesture. How could he argue with Diokles's idiotic logic? The Helot knew nothing of siege towers or starvation—the tools of an enemy blockade. He sighed. Arguing with him would serve no purpose. And Diokles was just too strong to drag out of the storeroom by force.

"Maybe I could drug him into oblivion?" he thought. By the time Diokles woke up—safely in the hold of some merchant ship with Chusor—they'd be all the way across the Bay of Korinth, on their way to the colonies . . .

He wandered around the house, brooding in a black mood, until he found himself climbing the stairs to the second floor. He had carried Kallisto up here last night, putting her in his own bed to provide her with a more comfortable resting place. He stood in the doorway to his bedchamber, gazing at Kallisto's motionless body on the bed, watching her shallow breathing. A sudden snoring sound made him glance over to the foot of the bed where Leo was fast asleep on the floor. He had helped Chusor keep watch on Kallisto throughout the night, but had finally succumbed to Morpheus's song a few hours before dawn.

Chusor went over and knelt by Kallisto's side, scrutinizing her face. Her skin was deathly pale—almost translucent. She looked beautiful, though, like a goddess carved from ivory. But it was a frail kind of beauty, like a flower about to shed its leaves and die. He put a hand on her forehead. She had a slight fever, but she was no longer talking in her sleep. He didn't know if this was a good or bad sign. He said her name aloud, but she made no reply. When he pulled back one of her eyelids to look at her pupil, he saw that it was extremely dilated—he could barely see the ring of her iris. And she didn't move a muscle at his touch.

He wished his friend Ezekiel the Babylonian was here. Ezekiel was a doctor working in Athens whom he had known in his youth. A physician who'd been trained in Persia—at the court of Persepolis—where doctors knew far more about caring for the human body than the Greeks did. Ezekiel would know how to best help the girl recover her senses. Chusor, however, was at a loss. He'd seen something in one of Ezekiel's books, about an operation performed to relieve pressure on the brain . . .

A crow landed on the window ledge and cawed loudly, startling Chusor from his reverie, and waking Leo who sat upright, exclaiming, "Are we under attack again?"

"I don't believe the avians have allied themselves with the Spartans," replied Chusor lightly, then added under his breath, "yet." He squinted at the crow and made a gesture with his hand to ward off evil. He did not consider himself to be a superstitious man, but *this* was definitely not a good omen. When the crow started defecating on the windowsill, he flung a pillow at it, hissing angrily, "Be gone!"

The black bird turned with a flap of wings, showing a single white tail feather as it soared to the rooftop of the house across the lane.

"I had the strangest dream," said Leo, staring sadly at Kallisto.

"You'll have to tell me later," said Chusor. "I'm going to look for Nikias. And you must change the poultice on Kallisto's wound, and give her more juice of the poppy."

Leo looked distraught. "Nik hasn't returned?" he asked, standing up and rubbing his eyes vigorously as if to banish his fatigue. "Something must have happened to him. He would have never left Kallisto all night otherwise."

"That's what I was thinking as well," replied Chusor. "I'll be back in no more than an hour."

He left the bedchamber and hurried down the stairs to the main room of his workshop. He glanced at a leaf-bladed sword hanging over the hearth. He wondered if he should bring the weapon with him in his search for Nikias. He'd seen how the Plataeans had butchered the Theban prisoners. They were filled with bloodlust. Perhaps they'd already started turning on each other. Maybe Nikias had been murdered in the streets. He was just about to reach for the sword when the front door swung open, and Myron the sandal maker poked in his head.

"Chusor, I need to talk to you," said Myron with a chastened look on his round face.

"What is it, Myron?" asked Chusor irritably.

"Please," he replied, stroking his brow nervously where it was stained with a permanent dark brown streak, caused by decades of wiping away the sweat with fingers covered in tanners' oil. "It's about the Theban prisoner."

"Gods!" Chusor cursed. "I told you not to tell anybody about him."

"I know, I know," replied Myron guiltily. "Just come with me to the Guild Hall."

Leo bounded down the stairs and stopped short when he caught sight of Chusor and Myron. He glanced back and forth at the two of them with a worried expression.

"What is it?" asked Leo. "What's wrong? Is something happening?"

"It's not your concern, lad," Myron told him. "The men of the guild need to speak to Chusor. Alone."

Chusor looked briefly at the sword hanging over the fireplace, and then stared at Myron who was smiling back at him in a friendly way. Chusor realized he would look foolish grabbing the weapon and carrying it through the streets, so he left it there and followed Myron out the door, saying over his shoulder to Leo, "Tend to the girl. I'll be back soon."

Myron and Chusor headed down the street toward the Guild Hall—a tall building made of black marble. They passed five city guardsmen who were standing at ease, speaking quietly to each other near a marketplace stall. Chusor saw one of them glance surreptitiously at him as he and Myron went past, and every instinct screamed at him to run.

But he kept on walking.

Myron led him up the steps to the Guild Hall and paused in front of the shut doors. The oak portals were twice as tall as a man and beautifully carved with various scenes showing craftsmen at their work: potters, woodworkers, smiths, shield-makers, stone-carvers, weavers, and even sandal makers.

Myron put one hand on the door and placed the other on Chusor's arm. "Don't be afraid," he whispered hastily. "'The sandals have been cut,' as the old saying goes, 'and now we must wear them.'"

"What on earth are you talking—"

"Don't do anything foolish," Myron interrupted with a sudden urgency. "You have to trust me now, my friend."

Chusor heard noises from behind: heavy footsteps and the clank of armor. He whipped around and saw that the five guardsmen they had passed in the street were now jogging purposefully toward the steps of the Guild Hall, fanning out in a semicircle with their weapons drawn, barring any attempt he might make at an escape.

NINE

Myron opened the door and nudged Chusor into the hall. It was a spacious room, two stories high, with benches on three walls forming a miniature assembly floor in the center of the chamber. Lamps burned in sconces on the walls, illuminating the faces of two dozen stern-faced men. Chusor quickly glanced from face to face. He knew every man there. Myron sat down amongst them, caught the smith's eye, and turned away sheepishly. Chusor heard a sound of metal behind him—armed city guards barring the door.

"What's going on?" asked Chusor, pulse racing.

Krates, the leader of the guild, stood up and faced Chusor. He was the master of the walls, the man responsible for maintaining the city's bastions. He was in his early fifties with beard and hair of gray and a lean, sinewy body. Krates had lost some teeth during a fight in his youth and had a habit of talking out of the side of his mouth. He was one of the few men of Artisans' Lane who openly disliked Chusor and let him know it, and he was a great friend and supporter of Nauklydes.

"Chusor the metic," said Krates, "you have entered this Guild Hall to stand trial."

Chusor laughed so hard that Krates jerked back as though he'd been punched in the nose.

"On what charges?" asked Chusor.

"You are indicted on grounds of"—the slightest pause—"illegal behavior."

"Where are we, Athens?" mocked Chusor.

"To be more specific," Krates continued, "for aiding the Theban—General Tykon."

Chusor stopped laughing and shot a frustrated glance at Myron, who squirmed uneasily.

"I was not *aiding* the Theban," said Chusor. "I was *protecting* him until the iron cooled down."

"Then you admit that you have been keeping him in your care?"

"I do not deny that he is in my house, bound with ropes and guarded. He is an important witness."

Krates offered a thin smile and then said, "Since you are not a citizen of this city-state, you fall under the guild's jurisdiction. And we hand out swift justice to metics who commit crimes against this city."

Chusor clenched his teeth, cursed under his breath. Soon after he'd moved to Plataea, there was a metic bread maker who'd been accused of cutting the flour in his loaves with sawdust. He'd confessed to his crime under torture. He'd been whipped, stripped naked, and left for dead on the outskirts of town. This "truth by pain" law existed everywhere in the Greek world. In Athens, only slaves or spies could be tortured under criminal proceedings. But here in Plataea things were different. Any noncitizen was at risk. Chusor had always believed this method of interrogation illogical. A vicious liar could convict an innocent man if he was stalwart enough to undergo the agony. And an honest man could be coerced into retracting his accusation merely to put a stop to the pain. Would these men—these friends he'd helped save tonight!—persecute him in such a vile and unscientific way?

As if on cue, Myron stepped forward and proclaimed, "I nominate Chusor the smith to our guild."

Krates whirled on Myron. "That is a stupid suggestion! There's never been a metic in our guild. Under what rules do you make this proposition?"

"Based on the extraordinary service rendered to Plataea this day by the defendant."

"You cannot do this," said Krates with a wave of his hand.

"I need only a second and third nomination to proceed to a vote," said Myron.

"I second," said Simon the blacksmith, standing up.

"I third," called another.

"A general call in favor," declared Myron.

A roar of approval erupted from a vast majority of the seated men. Chusor felt a surge of pride. These men *were* his friends.

"A call in opposition," stated Myron.

There came a response that was clearly below the decibel level of the first, with the supporters of Chusor scowling and hissing at these supporters of Krates.

Myron announced, "Chusor the smith is now a member of our guild and accorded all rights as a member. He cannot be coerced into giving testimony."

Krates pointed a long finger at Myron. "You, Myron, are a fool. The arkon Nauklydes will hear of this."

Myron shrugged and gestured for Chusor to take a seat on one of the benches. The moment he sat down next to the smiling sandal maker, there was a pounding on the door and the guards quickly lifted the bar. Armed men entered and dragged Tykon to the center of the room, tossing him to the floor.

Chusor bristled with indignation. Tykon had been under his protection. Under his roof! But the guardsmen had entered his home, uninvited, and taken the Theban by force. He hoped they hadn't hurt Diokles to get Tykon. But he reckoned the Helot was smart enough not to fight a gang of armed Plataeans over an enemy warrior. He shot daggers at Myron who stared at his hands with a hangdog expression, refusing to meet Chusor's eyes.

Slowly, Tykon managed to move to a kneeling position, despite the fact that his ankles and wrists were still bound. No one made any attempt to help him. The men in the hall were glaring at the Theban with utter hatred. On his knees, in the middle of the floor and trussed like an animal, Tykon reminded Chusor of an ox waiting to be sacrificed.

Tykon slowly scanned the faces in the room, one after the other, until his eyes locked onto Chusor's sad, pitying gaze. Tykon squinted ever so slightly, and then gave Chusor an inscrutable smile. "So, this is how it goes," he seemed to say.

"Am I accorded no rights as a prisoner of war?" Tykon asked of no one in particular. His bland tone said that he didn't give a grain of wheat one way or the other.

Krates walked in a circle around the Theban. On his face was a look of disgust and hatred. "City, tribe, and name," he demanded.

"Thebes. Tribe Kadmaeus. Tykon, son of Symmakos."

"Rank?"

"General."

"How did you come to be with that man sitting over there—namely, Chusor the smith?"

"He carried me to his house."

"*Carried* you?" asked Krates with mock surprise. "Were you drunk? Tired from your efforts? You don't seem to be injured."

"Neither. I was bound."

"Bound by whom? Were you captured?"

"Yes. Captured by one called Zeno."

"Zeno is dead," called out one of the guild members.

Myron said, "The prisoner has named a witness who is deceased."

Krates turned to Chusor. "And why did Zeno entrust this Theban to you and not a fellow Plataean?"

"Perhaps *because* I am not a Plataean," said Chusor. "The slaughter of the prisoners had just occurred. Zeno was afraid that Tykon would also be murdered."

"Why 'afraid'?" asked Krates with a laugh. "Afraid of a single Theban?"

"Of his knowledge," said Chusor.

"What knowledge?" demanded Krates.

"He knows the name of the traitor," said Chusor.

The guildsmen erupted into excited talk.

"This is valuable information, to be sure," exclaimed a man.

"Who betrayed us to the enemy?" demanded another.

"Tell us you, stinking Theban scum!" shouted a third.

Krates smiled sarcastically and addressed Tykon. "Ah! Yes, of course. Important information in that wily Theban brain. Please, Tykon the general, tell us the name of the traitor and save your hide for another hour or two. Let me guess. It was a person of high standing in our city. Someone whom we would never suspect, eh?"

Tykon crossed his arms on his chest, dropped his head. His torso and shoulders started moving up and down. At first Chusor thought the general was crying, then Tykon looked up and Chusor could see the Theban was laughing.

Tykon looked straight at Chusor, and said, "That's the traitor right there. Chusor the Egyptian."

TEN

———————◆———————

"Let me out of here, Zoticus! Damn you!"

Nikias pounded furiously on the heavy door of a jail cell, as though it were an enemy that he might beat into submission. He'd been locked in the pitch-black chamber for at least six hours—ever since he'd been dragged from the home where Isokrates and his followers had been massacred.

His voice was hoarse from shouting and his fists ached from pummeling the heavy wooden portal. After Kallisto's brother Lysander had died, Nikias had been imprisoned in this same cell, accused of his murder. And now he was trapped here again, like a rat in a box.

He kicked at the door with the flat of his foot, cursing violently as a burst of pain shot from his heel to his spine. He slid to the floor and sat with his back against the cold stones of the wall, breathing hard, staring into the darkness, seething with frustration.

Scenes from last night's attack played incessantly before his eyes. He saw Zoticus and his gang of cutthroats bursting into the house where he and Isokrates had been meeting, catching the men completely by surprise and killing them with a cold-blooded efficiency. He saw Isokrates, stabbed through the heart, eyes bulging with astonishment as he died. He saw the warrior Axe, chopping men to pieces, a savage grin fixed on his ghastly face as the walls were splattered with blood.

Nikias had grabbed a chair, swinging it from side to side like a cudgel, smashing heads until the chair had broken apart in his hands. But it had been impossible for him to maneuver in such a tight space, and he was quickly overwhelmed, brought down by five of Zoticus's men. Axe had been about to kill him, raising his weapon for the deathblow, when the cavalry general had stepped in, wrenching the battle-ax from the huge warrior's grasp.

"Not this one!" Zoticus had shouted. "Nauklydes wants him alive. Take him to the jail."

Nauklydes . . . Nauklydes . . .

The name of the new arkon echoed in Nikias's tired brain, mocking him. Last night, he hadn't believed Tykon's claim that Nauklydes was the traitor. Or perhaps he hadn't *wanted* to believe him. But now, after seeing what Nauklydes had ordered done to his own brethren, Nikias felt in his heart that everything Tykon had said was the truth. Even the terrible story about how Nikias's grandfather had allowed the Plataean warriors to rape Theban women at the siege of Sardis carried weight. And if *that* hideous tale was accurate, then Tykon's reason for attacking Plataea was easy enough to understand: he had wanted revenge.

Nikias thought of Kallisto and instantly felt a pain in his chest—a sensation like a needle stabbing at his heart. He was overcome by a wave of doom and desolation. He pictured Kallisto's body, rigid and lifeless. Her eyes extinguished of their spark. He felt sick to his stomach and wrapped his arms around his belly, curling into ball and falling into a fitful sleep. He dreamt that he and Kallisto were in the Cave of Nymphs, languishing in each other's arms. She said to him, "There's no poem compared to this," but when he looked into her eyes they were brown and shriveled like raisins. He heard a noise coming from her throat, like a mouse scrabbling in the walls of a house, and he tried to scream—

"No!" he blurted out as he awoke to the raspy sound of a key scraping in the cell door's lock. He sprang to his feet, fists clenched. The portal creaked open on its rusted hinges and the small room was lit by the glow of a torch, followed by the rangy bowlegged figure of a man, peering at Nikias from dour, deep-set eyes.

"Let's go," said Zoticus.

Nikias stood rooted to the spot. "Where?" he asked suspiciously.

"The arkon is setting you free," Zoticus said with a benevolent air. "He has no grudge with you. Nor do I. You were in the wrong place at the wrong time. I spoke up for you, just so you know. We've already lost enough men without sacrificing someone as brave as you. You'll be one of my cavalry captains soon enough," he added with a paternal tone. "You're a better rider and fighter than any of my men. We need you to kill Spartans." He gestured with the flaming torch toward the hallway outside the cell. "Now come on. I need to fill this hole with someone who *should* be here."

Nikias wondered if Zoticus knew that Nauklydes had betrayed his city. If not, would the cavalry general believe Nikias if he was to tell him what Tykon had claimed? "Zoticus . . ." he began hesitantly, "are you certain you're following the right man?"

"I'm not certain of anything, lad," he replied. "All I know is that we're in for the fight of our lives. It's the Persian invasions all over again. And we need a strong man who can lead the charge. I'm sorry that your grandfather is dead. He could have led us. But Nauklydes proved himself on the battlefield against the Thebans. That's all that matters to me."

He led Nikias out of the underground prison to the street above where Axe and a dozen other armed men were loitering in the bright morning light, eating breakfast where they stood. Axe leered at Nikias, smiling dangerously. Nikias suppressed the overwhelming urge to drive his fist into the man's face as he passed by.

"Stay out of trouble," Zoticus said when they were out of earshot of the other men. "And stay away from Axe," he added under his breath. "He doesn't like you." He pushed Nikias in the back, sending him on his way

Every man Nikias saw in the street was a potential enemy . . . just like General Zoticus and Axe and the others who had killed Isokrates and his kin. Plataea was turning into a city of barbarians, Nikias mused morosely. And the thought brought him low. The real enemies were Thebes and Sparta, not fellow citizens. Men who had banded together to defeat the invaders—who'd sacrificed their bodies for their brothers—now looked at each other with suspicion.

The tension was palpable. He saw two men shouting violent threats at each other over who had the rights to purchase a bag of barley flour. Armed guards bearing shields with hastily painted insignias—a huge *N* for Nauklydes—strode up to a man who was painting a pro-Spartan message on the side of his house and yelled at him to stop, threatening to throw him in the jail. Nikias wanted to shout what he knew—that Nauklydes was the traitor! But how could he prove it?

He started running in the direction of Artisans' Lane. He was dreading what he might find at Chusor's smithy—a house of death and Kallisto's cold body. When he got to the crowded marketplace he was brought to a halt by an unexpected sight: Leo was sitting on the steps in front of the Guild Hall, his body wracked with sobs, his face buried in his hands.

"Leo!" said Nikias, running over to him. "What's going on? What's happened to Kallisto?"

Leo peered up at Nikias with a face full of indignation. "Where have you been, Nik?"

"I was jailed," he replied sharply. "Is Kallisto alive?"

"I was trying to find Chusor," said Leo in a dazed tone.

Nikias grabbed Leo and shook him hard, repeating, "Is Kallisto alive?"

"Yes!" shouted Leo, shoving Nikias away and hiding his face in the crook of one arm. "She's just the same. She still hasn't spoken or opened her eyes."

Nikias let forth a relieved exhalation. "Thank Zeus," he said softly, but added crossly, "So who's watching over her?"

"Diokles," said Leo. "I was afraid somebody might try to hurt her. He's barricaded the door to the smithy. Everyone has gone crazy, haven't they?" He spoke these last words in a high-pitched tearful voice, like a little boy. "I had to find Chusor. He went away and never came back."

"Where did he go?"

Leo looked up at him and wiped away his tears. "Myron came to the smithy a couple of hours ago. He told Chusor he needed him to come with him here to the Guild Hall. A few minutes later some city guardsmen came looking for Tykon and dragged him away." His face was twisted into a tormented grimace and tears poured from his eyes again.

"Where is Chusor?" Nikias asked, forcing his own voice to sound calm.

"He's dead," said Leo softly.

Nikias felt like the air had been sucked from his lungs. "What happened?"

Without another word Leo stood and led him through the Guild Hall doors and into the main chamber. The place was empty of men. Nikias saw that ropes were hanging from the rafters. The ends of the ropes were red. On the floor, under the ropes, were fingernails that had been ripped out whole. And chunks of flesh and innards.

Nikias reeled.

A man had been hung by his arms here and tortured. Gutted like an animal.

"No," said Nikias. "Not Chusor. I *know* who the traitor is."

He staggered blindly from the building. He'd seen blood before. He'd killed men with his bare hands. He'd even witnessed the torture of the Theban cavalry general. But no act of violence had ever seemed this despicable. This pointless. They'd gotten the wrong man. He breathed slowly through his nose to steady himself, then strode down the street. He wanted to find somebody to punch. He wanted to wrestle an enemy to the ground and strangle the life out of them. But who *was* the enemy? Who was he *supposed* to fight?

"Where are you going?" asked Leo, running to catch up with him.

"I don't know," said Nikias. Everything he saw was a blur. Chusor was dead. They'd killed him. And what had they done with Tykon? He was a valuable prisoner. Surely they wouldn't have been stupid enough to kill him too? They had most likely taken him to Nauklydes. But the arkon would put the Theban to death for certain, just to cover his own tracks.

"Why have you stopped in front of Nauklydes's pottery factory?" Leo asked.

Nikias looked up and saw where his feet had brought him. "I need to find proof that Nauklydes is the traitor," he said.

There was nobody working in the big building today. It was completely empty. They walked through the long colonnade, past the slabs of clay, the painters' stalls and the storage areas with the packed up vases. The long rows of potters' wheels were at rest and the clay ovens were cold. All was eerily quiet.

At the end of the hallway was a locked door.

"That's the door to Nauklydes's private office," said Nikias.

ELEVEN

———————— ◆ ————————

Nikias found a hammer lying next to a packing crate and started pounding on the lock.

"What are you doing?" asked Leo, putting his hand on Nikias's wrist to stop him.

"Trying to get in," he replied. "What does it look like?"

Leo stood on his tiptoes and reached along the sill at the top of the door. His fingers grasped something: a key. He fit it in the lock.

"How did you know?" asked Nikias.

"All the shopkeepers do it," said Leo. "Why not a pottery factory owner?"

They went into the dark room.

"Box," said Nikias, pointing to the heavy oak container.

"Now you can use the hammer," said Leo.

Nikias smashed the lock until it broke away, and then lifted the lid.

"Too dark," said Nikias.

They dragged the box into the light of the main workroom and dumped the contents on the floor. Papyrus scrolls spilled out. Leo picked up the wooden skytale dowel.

"What's this?" he asked. Nikias shook his head, so Leo tossed it aside.

Nikias picked up a small scroll and started reading it. Leo saw a leather coin purse still in the box, bulging with coins. He grabbed it and stuck it in his shirt without Nikias seeing.

"I found something," said Nikias, nodding at the scroll in his hands.

Leo peered over his shoulder, scanning the page. "A list of citizens' names? What's that for?"

A man stepped from behind one of the columns and Nikias and Leo sprang to their feet. The Athenian spy Timarkos walked over to them and held out his hand for the scroll. "Let me see that," he demanded. Nikias handed it to him and he scrutinized it for a while before saying, "It's Nauklydes's death list."

The last time Nikias had seen the scrawny spy had been on the night of the sneak attack, when they'd spoken on the roof of the Temple of Athena. What had Timarkos been doing since that night? Sneaking around the city, most likely, lurking in the shadows while other men had fought and died. Nikias doubted that he would get a straight answer out of Timarkos about his activities, even if he were to ask him the question bluntly. He was a whisperer. It was his job to bluff and deceive.

He stared into the older man's bright blue eyes, and Timarkos stared right back without blinking, his hollow-cheeked face completely unreadable. Should Nikias trust him? At the Persian Fort Timarkos had told him that Chusor was the traitor, and now Nikias knew *that* tale to be a falsehood. But the spy had also revealed to him the whereabouts of the hidden tunnel, enabling him to escape from the citadel and raise the cavalry. That secret knowledge had no doubt saved Plataea from falling to the Theban reinforcements.

He looked at the death list in Timarkos's hands, then glanced at Leo who was staring expectantly at him, waiting for him to say something. Nikias swept his hand through his hair with agitation. What should he do with this death list? How could he use it to expose Nauklydes without getting killed? The two men he had trusted most in the world, Chusor and his grandfather, were dead. He had no one else to go to for counsel.

"So what do we do now?" Nikias asked Timarkos. "We know who the traitor is but we can't touch him."

"Nauklydes must be killed," said Timarkos, "and a true Athenian loyalist installed to power. Someone like Menesarkus—"

"He's dead," said Nikias. "My grandfather is dead."

"And you know this for certain?" asked Timarkos.

"Yes," replied Nikias. "He was burned alive at our house."

Timarkos pursed his lips. "I had hoped he might have escaped and was in hiding."

"The Bull of the Oxlands wouldn't hide from anyone," said Leo with a laugh.

"So now what?" asked Nikias. "Do you Athenians support Nauklydes until you can think of someone better to put in his place?"

"You think Athens wants a madman and a traitor in control of this city?" replied Timarkos with an admonishing tone. He turned away and stared into space, wiped his mouth with an angry gesture. "It was Nauklydes who handed over Pelias to the Thebans."

"Your companion?" asked Leo. "The one Nikias . . ." His voice trailed off and he looked away. "The one he helped to the afterlife."

Nikias saw the mutilated spy's face before his eyes—saw him as he'd looked in the Persian Fort, crawling on the stumps of his hands and feet, crying out in agony. He remembered the sickening sound of his sword crunching through the young man's neck. How many days had it been since he and his three friends had gone on a lark to catch a glimpse of the Spartans? Five? Six? It seemed like a year.

"Pelias was Nauklydes's lover," explained Timarkos. "Working to get information out of him. We've been keeping an eye on Nauklydes, you see, for some time. Eurymakus the Theban must have suspected Pelias. The whisperer was waiting for him at Nauklydes's home."

"So what do we do?" asked Leo.

"I've been watching the citizens of Plataea all morning," said Timarkos. "Listening to their debates in the streets. They are of two minds. They either blindly support Nauklydes and will follow him to Hades. Or they think he's a tyrant in the making and won't let themselves be cowed by him. Your people could end up slaughtering each other in the streets of Plataea before this is over."

"Civil war," said Nikias, dismayed. "It hasn't happened since the days of the Last Tyrant."

They heard the sound of a horse galloping down the street. "All citizens to the Assembly Hall!" shouted the crier as he rode past. "All citizens to the Assembly Hall! All citizens . . ."

"What's going on?" asked Nikias.

"A chance for Nauklydes to present himself to the citizens of Plataea," said Timarkos. "And set forth his vision for the future." He took something from the folds of his cloak. It was a strange device that neither of the two young Plataeans had seen before: a thin tube attached to leather straps.

"What's that?" asked Leo.

"A pig sticker," explained Timarkos. "Hold out your arm, Nikias," he commanded.

With a far-off look in his eyes, Nikias obeyed and the whisperer fit it onto his muscular forearm. "Chusor told me about these," said Nikias.

"That's a weapon used by thieves and pirates," said Leo.

Nikias tested it with a flick of his wrist. A skewer shot out of the tube with a metallic hiss and locked into place.

Nikias said, "It's what Eurymakus used to cut me in the rafters of the Assembly Hall, isn't it?"

"Yes. And it's an efficient tool," replied Timarkos. "With you sleeve pulled down, it's completely hidden."

Leo was aghast. "You want Nik to kill Magistrate Nauklydes?"

"Arkon," corrected Timarkos. "He is Arkon Nauklydes now." After a pause he said, "It's not whether or not I want him to do it. He knows it has to be done."

"This is crazy," said Leo. "Take that thing off, Nikias."

"You would be a hero in many a man's eyes," said Timarkos. "And Athens would hold you in the highest esteem. Besides"—he tugged on his goat's beard, gave his slanted smile—"Nauklydes will kill you and everyone who's left of your family if you don't. And then he'll murder the late Helladios's daughter, Kallisto. You know I speak the truth."

Nikias rubbed the scar across his chin. He glanced at Timarkos, who was nodding his head, and then at Leo, who was rubbing his temples and gritting his teeth as though he was suffering from an agonizing headache.

"Nik, you can't just walk up to Nauklydes—" began Leo.

"Go to Kallisto and stay with her, Leo," said Nikias. "Promise me you'll find a way to keep her safe."

"I promise," said Leo, "but—"

Nikias waved for Leo to be silent and got up to leave. His face was set in an expressionless mask. "Are you coming with me?" he asked Timarkos.

"No," replied Timarkos. "I can't be seen with you. But you'll know where I'll be." The spy pointed upward.

"The roof?" asked Leo, perplexed.

"The rafters," said Nikias. He pushed the pig sticker blade back into the tube, and rolled down his sleeve, hiding the deadly contraption.

TWELVE

—————◆—————

Arkilokus rode his new horse out past the double sets of sentries and into Plataean territory. This prince was no "trembler," the name the Spartans gave for warriors who lacked courage in battle. It was true that members of the royal family were not sent off to join a herd of boys at the age of seven to be whipped and beaten and taught to steal for food, and made to endure all weather in nothing more than a single garment. The upbringing for members of Spartan royalty was quite different from that of lesser men. But it was still full of physical hardships and suffering. Every single day of his life, as soon as he could walk, he had trained from sunup until sundown in the arts of war. His father had brought to the palace men from around the known world to instruct him. Skythian archers, Rhodian peltasts, Aethiopian horsemen, Kretan wrestlers. Blood blisters, torn muscles, broken bones, concussions . . . he'd had them all by the age of ten.

At the age of fourteen, with rapport between Sparta and its former enemy Persia at an all-time high, he went east to learn charioteering at the court of Xerxes in Persepolis. He lived amongst the Persians for four years, training in their splendid hippodromes. He learned how to judge racing horses and inspect his wicker chariots and wooden spokes. Rig the complicated reins and yokes and straps. Sometimes he and the other charioteers raced on the vast, flat desert plains—where four horses pulled a man on wheels faster than a diving hawk—hunting buck and lion with spear or bow. Once he had survived a head-on crash with another charioteer, who had died instantly from his wounds.

He had met the spy Eurymakus in Persepolis as well—learned of the Theban's undying hatred for Menesarkus, and the man's devotion to the strange religion and his worship of the foreign god, Ahura Mazda. Eurymakus had sought out his friendship—they were nearly the same age—but Arkilokus had never liked the Theban who was training under the tutelage of Artaxerxes's nefarious whisperer. Eurymakus reminded him of one of the pet snakes the king kept in a cage in his bedroom.

By the end of his stay in Persia, Arkilokus had taken more lovers than he could count, and fought four men to the death in blood duels, most all on account of those same lovers. Arkilokus knew he could outride, outshoot, and outfight any man in Sparta. And Drako knew it too. But still he treated him like a coddled fool. He had not wanted him on this expedition. Arkilokus had been forced to beg his father to allow him to come.

He found himself back at Menesarkus's farm. Perhaps he'd gone there on purpose, or maybe the horse—wanting to go home—had led him there. He tied the mare up and went into the ruins. He found the pottery shard with the man's face he had tossed aside the day before. Now he knew the man depicted on the shard was his uncle, Menesarkus's only child, Aristo. He put the shard in a pouch he wore around his neck and tucked it under his shirt.

"The man whose seed made my daughter was a living Herakles," his grandmother Helena used to tell him. He'd loved his grandmother more than any of his relatives. His mother had died giving birth to Arkilokus, and thus earned a tombstone with her name on it for her efforts. His grandmother had taken over the maternal role. She was ravishingly beautiful, even in her old age. He wondered what it would have been like to grow up in a household with Menesarkus and Helena together?

Without a doubt Menesarkus had a kingly air about him. He was the sort of man whom men would follow to their deaths. That made him dangerous. They were lucky to have him safely in the camp where they could keep an eye on him. Bend him to their way of thinking. In Arkilokus's opinion they should have sought him out in the first place rather than trusting the slippery Theban Eurymakus and his pathetic army of invaders. The Overseers—the five elected citizens who advised the Spartan dual kings—had committed a colossal blunder by trusting the Theban snake.

Drako had sent Eurymakus back to Thebes, escorted by an armed guard, to report his disastrous failure to his own people, thus preventing him from sneaking off to Persia. Arkilokus hoped the Thebans would execute him. But he reckoned the spy was too powerful to get what he deserved.

Arkilokus made an inspection of the vineyards and orchards. He was impressed with the careful rows, the expert pruning. It would be a bountiful harvest this summer because of the recent rain. But this farm was nothing when compared to his father's vast estate in Lakonia, where five thousand of his personal Helots worked the earth. It was a shock to know that a part of his ancestry had come from this meager little place.

He mounted up and headed back to the main road, where he came across some mountain refugees—a family carrying everything they owned in baskets and sacks—heading toward the citadel. They shepherded a flock of goats that bleated dolefully as he trotted past.

"Has the city fallen?" asked the patriarch of the family. He had assumed that Arkilokus was Plataean like himself.

"Not yet," said Arkilokus over his shoulder. "But soon."

The young commander decided to ride all the way to Plataea and inspect the fortifications again as he'd done the day before. He was formulating a siege plan based on what he'd learned in Persia from Xerxes's engineers. Persians used siege warfare on their enemies all the time, unlike his own people, who knew nothing about this kind of fighting. He hoped that they would not have to lay siege to the city. He was convinced that the Plataeans could still be coerced into joining the Spartan League, even after this debacle. *Thebes is the enemy, not Sparta.* That was the approach he'd used with Menesarkus the night before. But the old man had stuck firmly to the fact that Plataea had signed an oath with Athens.

"It's written in stone in our agora," Menesarkus had said. "I'll show it to you whenever you like."

As soon as Sparta was in control of Plataea, Arkilokus would ask his father to make him the governor. "I will allow Menesarkus to keep his farm," he said aloud, and patted his new horse on the neck. The old man could retire there and live out his days in peace. And his grandson—Nikias the pankrator, Arkilokus's cousin—would be allowed to serve in some capacity under the governor's rule. Benevolence was the mark of the Herakladean kings. One of his ancestors used to sit by the river once a week and listen to the complaints of every Spartan citizen, no matter how lowly. At least, that's what his grandmother Helena used to tell him.

It felt good to gallop across the open country with the fresh smells of morning wafting up from the earth. He had a sensation of invincibility. As though he were a god. Indestructible. This was good chariot country. He would set up a racetrack and welcome all gentlemen challengers from throughout the Oxlands. He kicked his horse and it picked up speed, snorting playfully.

The city walls and towers came into view a mile in the distance. The bastions resembled a Persian fortress in the red light of dawn, and for a moment he imagined he was back in the East.

From out of nowhere a figure sprang from the tall grass, arms flailing and screaming. The white horse balked—stopped dead as though it had run into a stone wall. Arkilokus was pitched headlong over the neck of his mount, and the city was suddenly upside down. He landed on his back and his head struck against the hard ground. He tried to cry out but could not move his mouth. The white mare trampled on his chest as it ran away in fright, but he felt nothing. His entire body was paralyzed.

The face of a young man appeared before him. The stranger had a bloody hole where his right eye had been torn out. The blood had dried to a thick crust on his cheek in a stream that ran all the way down to the bottom of his chin, like red tears. His breath reeked of bile.

"I thought you were my enemy," said the Cyclops. "One Plataean looks like another." And then he was gone, striding through the grass toward the Kithaeron Mountains, flapping his arms as though he were a flightless bird.

A short while later a scavenging patrol, on its way back from outlying farms, found the motionless rider.

"Hey, that's Photine," one of them said, pointing at the horse now running across the fields. "Nikias's filly."

"Who's that on the ground?"

"I don't recognize him."

"Zeus's balls! He's a Spartan!"

They carried the stunned Spartan prisoner into the city.

THIRTEEN

———◆———

After morning inspections Drako made a decision he felt would either cost him his seat on the Council of Elders or win it for him outright. He met with Menesarkus alone in his campaign tent and said to the pankrator, "General Menesarkus, you are free to leave this camp."

The juice of the poppy had relaxed Menesarkus's back muscles over the night, so the spasms had nearly stopped. He was able to stand up straight and face the Spartan with decorum. But his face could not hide his astonished reaction at this pronouncement—this remarkable turn of events. He'd reckoned he'd be sent off to Sparta to spend the rest of his pathetic days as a prisoner.

Drako continued, "Your arkon Nauklydes sent us a message at dawn refusing to meet with me for a second time. I have ordered riders to Sparta asking for another seven thousand reinforcements. You have seen our numbers in this camp. Now you know how many will be here to lay siege to your city. I hope you see how fruitless it would be for you Plataeans to continue in this stubborn support of Athens—a city that will, no doubt, turn its back on you."

"I thank you for your candor, General Drako," replied Menesarkus. "You know that if we were to accept this treaty, we would first need permission from Athens. An envoy must be sent."

"Then I would send your envoy immediately," replied Drako. "But first you will have to bring down the arkon Nauklydes. He is the greatest impediment to your survival. I can tell you now that Nauklydes conspired with the Theban Eurymakus to overthrow your city."

"Preposterous—"

Drako held up a hand to stop Menesarkus. He pointed to a leather dispatch bag that lay on the folding map table.

"Here is evidence," he said.

"What is it?" asked Menesarkus.

"Proof that will convict Nauklydes of treason against Plataea. You must take it back to your city and face your Assembly and convince them not only to depose Nauklydes but to make an alliance with Sparta."

"I can't believe that a magistrate of—"

"You do not have much time," interrupted Drako. "Nauklydes, it seems, already has a great following for his anti-Spartan course. It will be difficult to persuade your fellow citizens, I fear. But if anyone can plead our case, it is you. However, if your accusations against Nauklydes fail, you will, I'm certain, be put to death. Nauklydes will wipe out your entire family as well. He was completely aware of Eurymakus's plans to murder you and exterminate your household. In fact, he helped make the plan." And one final knife in his ribs to urge him on: "Your heir, Nikias, was to be castrated and sent to Persia as a gift."

"Where is he now?" Menesarkus asked with a growl. "This Theban Eurymakus."

"Don't concern yourself with him," Drako replied. Then: "If you succeed today you and I will soon have a conversation of a different sort. For you will certainly be the next arkon. All the men who might oppose you are dead."

FOURTEEN

"All citizens to the Assembly Hall! All citizens to the Assembly Hall!"

The town criers ran from house to building to temple to public latrine, shouting their news. The men of Plataea poured into the streets and filed into the Assembly Hall. There were only two thousand three hundred and twenty-seven full-fledged citizens out of the twenty thousand inhabitants of Plataea at the last census and now this number had been reduced by at least seven hundred dead since the Theban invasion, and another two hundred or so too severely wounded to leave their homes. Still, it was a testament to the intimacy of Plataean society that the half dozen Assembly Hall gatekeepers—whose duty was to keep out minors and noncitizens—knew all of their fellow citizens who were still alive by sight.

Nikias wasn't about to let the gatekeepers thwart him from the Assembly Hall. He disguised his face with a bloody cloth and said in a garbled voice, "I'm Proteus." It was the name of a young citizen he knew who'd been speared through the cheek during the "Battle of the Gates," as it was now being called. The Assembly Hall gatekeepers nodded and let him pass through and into the Courtyard of Laws. Here it was packed with men inching their way to the hall doors at the other end of the quadrangle.

Nikias saw two massive urns filled with small round ballot stones—white for no, black for yes. As the men passed into the courtyard, they grabbed a stone of each color, and Nikias did the same. The marble stones felt cold and dry in his sweaty palm and he clutched them tightly.

Nikias inched his way into one of the covered porticos on either side of the quadrangle and waited in the shadows as the citizens slowly filed into the Assembly Hall through the two doors set on either end of the building. It seemed as if they were taking forever to enter, and Nikias's heart beat faster with every passing minute.

He thought back to that morning two days ago when his grandfather had got him out of jail and brought him here to try and talk some sense into him. He wished the Bull were here now. It seemed impossible that the Bull of the Ox-lands was nothing more palpable now than a wisp of smoke.

Would his grandfather be pleased with what he was about to do?

From inside the building he heard the rumble and groan of the wood bleach-ers as the thousands of citizens stepped up the venerable old planks, finding their seats. The hall was filled with the excited buzz of voices.

Nikias glanced down and opened his fist, stared at the two ballot stones. Nauklydes was going to ask them to vote to break with Athens. To go to war with Sparta. "But there will be no voting today," he thought grimly.

Swift punishment and then chaos. . . .

He clutched the pig sticker strapped to his wrist. He would strike down the arkon at the start of his speech—before he could pollute the citizens' ears with his lies. Nikias would be executed for such a heinous crime. The "City's Man"— the public executioner—always stood at the back of the hall with his sharp axe. His position there was symbolic. Executions always took place in the agora and never with an axe. But Nikias was about to do something that had never before taken place in this hallowed chamber. He knew there would be swift punish-ment for his act.

The alternative, however, was to let the man who'd betrayed Plataea to the Thebans live. A man seemingly bent on destroying his own city and people . . . and Nikias's family. No. He could not let that happen. He would sacrifice his own life for the good of the city like Androkles the Hero—the Tyrant Killer. Maybe someday they would remember him and his tribe's name with the same reverence as the Hero.

Through the open doors he heard the Assembly clerk call the meeting to order. The men in the hall quieted down. There followed a few seconds of si-lence before the clerk said, "Nauklydes, son of Speusippos of the tribe Dionysios, arkon of Plataea."

"Fellow citizens," called Nauklydes. "I welcome you to this Assembly Hall, built eighty-three years ago as a symbol of our city's break with the Oxlands League and our alliance with our good friend Athens. We Plataeans have met here for over eight decades to vote on important matters—to steer the ship of our great city toward prosperity. Now we face a peril that threatens our very existence, much in the same way our grandfathers and fathers did with the Persian invasions."

Nikias forced himself to move. He ran to the nearest Assembly Hall door, flattened himself against the black marble wall, and peeked around the corner of the doorway. Now he could see the area in front of the bleachers called the speaker's floor. He saw Nauklydes standing there. The new arkon looked stately and imposing—as if he'd grown to match the lofty station he'd only recently assumed.

Nikias started to tremble uncontrollably. Could he really run out onto that floor and cut the arkon down in front of every citizen in Plataea? Stab him with the pig sticker—the weapon of a murderer? Nauklydes was only a few paces away. Nikias could run to him in a matter of seconds and stab him in the back and straight into his heart. The arkon would die immediately. He had the sensation of being in a nightmare. How had he gone from a hero to an assassin in one day?

Nauklydes continued: "All men think that the age they live in is the most important to their civilization. Well, I will argue, friends, that this age is the most important for Plataea and our way of life. The Theban grass vipers have had their heads cut off"—cheers from the crowd—"but now the Spartan foxes are at the door. Listen to me, brothers. The Spartans are a greater menace than either King Darius or his son Xerxes. For the Persian kings had hoped to bring us under their empire as vassal states. The Spartans, however, would make us, like the lowly Helots, their beasts . . . their slaves."

The room erupted into angry shouts: "Death to Sparta!" "Better dead than a slave!" They stomped the wooden planks beneath their feet, and the din was thunderous.

Nikias flicked the blade from the sheath hidden under his sleeve. "A downward stroke to the chest, through the ribs, and into the heart. Death is instantaneous." It was the Bull's voice in his head. But Nikias could not make himself move. *No shameful flight or fear!* His grandfather had taught him the battle poem—taught it to him as a child to turn his heart and guts into iron.

"This city cannot be taken by the Spartans!" cried Nauklydes. "We are too mighty! Too courageous! Our walls are too high for their low minds. Only by treachery can we be defeated. And that is why traitors—or men with betrayal in their hearts—must be rooted from our midst."

Nikias tried to slow his breathing. Tried to make his shoulders loose. Tried to will away the sensation that his feet and legs were carved from marble blocks.

Make your spirit valiant! Love death and hate your foe!

He was so focused on steeling himself for murder he didn't notice the figure of a man shuffling across the Courtyard of Laws from the direction of the front gates. A bull of a man, striding forward with a heavy-footed grace.

Nikias tensed the muscles in his legs to run. But a powerful hand grabbed his wrist—the wrist with the pig sticker.

"That won't work now," whispered a familiar voice in his ear. "We've got to kill his *idea* first and *then* cut down the man."

"Grandfather!" Nikias grabbed Menesarkus, embraced him so hard that the old man winced in pain. He looked into his grandfather's eyes through a blur of tears. "Grandfather," he said again. "I thought you were dead. I thought—"

"There's no time to talk, Nik," said Menesarkus. "Put away that blade. Sit on the floor by the bleachers and don't speak until I call you."

"But Nauklydes is the one who betrayed the city," said Nikias in a rush.

"I know," said Menesarkus. "I know everything."

Nikias thrust the scroll into his grandfather's hands. "I found this in Nauklydes's office—a list of all the men to be executed after the invasion."

Menesarkus opened the scroll, looked at it quickly. "You have done well. Now give me the reins . . . give me the reins, my son."

Nikias obeyed. He watched Menesarkus limp slowly, painfully into the hall—directly onto the speaker's floor—holding a long staff for support. Nikias thought he looked like Tiresius the seer in Sophokles's play. He stopped ten paces from the arkon and waited for the cheers for Nauklydes to die down.

"It's Menesarkus!" a voice called out.

"The general is alive!" yelled another.

"The Bull lives!"

Nikias slipped through the doorway into the hall and sat on the floor next to the lowest level of bleachers.

Enthusiastic applause filled the hall. Nauklydes noticed Menesarkus with a start and held up his hand for the crowd to be silent. "General Menesarkus," he said. "You have made a curious entrance to this Assembly. But I am pleased to see you. So many good men have died over the last two days. It is good to know you have survived, somehow, unscathed." The implication was: "Where were you during the defense of Plataea?" He held up his bandaged right hand to display his wound.

"My brave brothers," boomed Menesarkus, ignoring Nauklydes and addressing the crowd in his stentorian voice, "you lionhearted sons of Zeus. I have heard the news of the victory of the gates, and I have just returned from the Spartan camp where I met with their general Drako. The important information I bring could not wait any longer. And so I apologize to our arkon for interrupting the arkon's *discourse*." His repetition of the word "arkon" made the title seem somehow unseemly.

"Is your news so important that it cannot wait for another forum?" asked Nauklydes. "Or have you convinced the Spartans to decamp and go back home?"

This provoked scattered laughter from the crowd.

"No, Nauklydes," said Menesarkus with a half smile. "My skills as a diplomat are not *that* good."

"Then maybe your news should wait," said Nauklydes with growing annoyance. "It is polite to let a speaker finish before tipping over his water clock."

"I reckoned," said Menesarkus, scratching his beard, "in these days of tumult that maybe we should forget about etiquette and go back to a day when men voiced their concerns without such formality. Hundreds of years ago our ancestors stood on this very spot and shouted each other down in a wooden hall with a dirt floor."

"Men of Homer's age used to debate with their fists too," said Nauklydes. "I would not presume to fight you, General, for I'm certain you would win a battle of brawn."

"My wits are not completely gone," replied Menesarkus. "I'm confident I could beat you both ways."

Nervous laughter erupted from the crowd. Everyone there had seen these two men debate for years and years. Before, there had always been a good-natured rivalry. But now there was something menacing in their voices. A threat of violence underneath the surface.

"I think you had better leave the floor," said Nauklydes.

"I think not," replied Menesarkus.

Nauklydes turned and walked away petulantly, as if he were going to leave the Assembly. He stopped and whirled on Menesarkus and yelled, "Get out!" To his guards he barked, "Take this man out!" And to the General Assembly: "I order him out of the hall!"

Some guards made a move toward the floor but men leapt from the benches and stopped them. The hall erupted into pandemonium. Men got in each other's faces, pushing and shoving. There were two factions, those in support of the arkon and those against. And there was no clear majority.

A man seated on the benches near Nikias caught sight of him and said, "What are you doing here, Aristo's son? You're not of age yet. Get out."

Nikias held a fist under his nose and replied, "Next thing you say, old duffer, tell it to my fist."

The man took a look at Nikias's huge fist—gnarled with scars and scabs—and sank down.

"Plataea!"

A piercing bellow blared from the floor. A voice so loud it reverberated off the walls like a thunderclap.

"Plataea!" yelled Menesarkus again. It was the voice he used on the battlefield. The call for the phalanx to charge the enemy's shield wall. "Plataea!" The men in the hall quieted down. It was instinct to follow their general's call.

"Speak, General!" cried a voice from the top of the bleachers. Many others echoed his request.

"Listen to me!" said Menesarkus. "The Spartans have offered us a peace treaty which Nauklydes, in his *wisdom*, has refused outright. The Spartan general told me today that seven thousand more warriors are on their way from Sparta"—gasps from the crowd—"and they will lay siege to this city and eventually they will wear us down, starve us out."

"And you would sign a pact with these two-kinged men?" asked Nauklydes. "And break our old alliance with Athens?"

"I would first send envoys to Athens and beg them to release us from this allegiance. Because the Athenians can no longer protect us."

"*Beg* them?" laughed Nauklydes.

"Beg on my knees if I had to," replied Menesarkus. "Because we cannot break the alliance. It is our codes and laws and respect for alliances that set us apart from the barbarians. Athens holds our fate in its hands and I tremble at what might happen if they reject our plea."

"I never thought I'd see the brave Menesarkus turn fawnhearted," mocked Nauklydes.

"And I never thought I'd see an honorable man like you hand over his city to the enemy!" shot back Menesarkus.

There was a grumble from the crowd.

"This is a dangerous accusation," threatened Nauklydes. "And beyond outrageous."

Menesarkus took a step toward Nauklydes and pointed the tip of his staff at him. "Nauklydes spoke earlier of men with 'betrayal in their hearts.' The arkon said, 'We need to root these men out of our midst.' Well, I agree with him wholeheartedly." His next utterance came out as a fierce roar: "Men of Plataea, you see before you the traitor who opened our gates to the enemy! I accuse Nauklydes of betrayal against the State!" He threw his staff in Nauklydes's direction. It clattered across the floor and Nauklydes had to hop over it to keep from having the stick hit him in the ankles.

Menesarkus's accusation hit the men in the Assembly like a shock wave. Never had such an indictment been made in this hall! Thousands of men groused and murmured. Menesarkus, they knew, was among the most honorable. Even the supporters of Nauklydes believed he was brave and honest beyond censure. If a man of his stature made this claim . . .

Myron the sandal maker stood up in the front row and pitched his voice above the noise. "What proof do you have, Menesarkus, of this accusation?"

"I have physical proof," said Menesarkus, and held aloft the Spartan dispatch bag he carried. "And every man in this room will see it. And when you see it, you will weep as I did to know that this man, for his own advancement, made a pact to sacrifice every man in this room and every one of your families."

Nauklydes's face turned the color of the gray marble floor. He shook his head slowly. He knew all eyes were on him but for once he was speechless. Finally he blurted, "Is this a trial or a public debate?"

"It began as you giving a speech," said Menesarkus. "And then it turned into an argument between us two. And now I propose we move on to your trial."

"You can't do that!" said Phakas running onto the floor. "General Menesarkus has lost his mind."

"This man is not a citizen of Plataea," said Menesarkus coldly. "Guards, seize him."

The guards loyal to Nauklydes stood rooted, unsure of what to do. But there were guards who had served with Menesarkus on many campaigns, and they rushed the floor and dragged off Phakas, kicking and yelling.

"Keep him near at hand," said Menesarkus. "I'll need to interrogate him shortly."

"You can't do this," said Nauklydes weakly. "I am arkon."

"You might have forgotten, Nauklydes," replied Menesarkus, "that I am the seniormost general alive in Plataea. And by the laws inscribed on these walls, I can bring charges against any man in Plataea, even the arkon. I can also call for an immediate trial during a time of war. It is an ancient law created to mete out indiscretions on the battlefield."

"You mean you propose to have a trial *now*?" asked the stunned Nauklydes.

"Yes," said Menesarkus.

"And I suppose you will pick the jury of twelve," said Nauklydes with scorn.

Menesarkus smiled and swept his hand in the direction of the thousands of men sitting on the benches watching intently. "On the contrary. I propose that every man in this room serves as the jury. They will hear the evidence against you, and they will convict you, and then I will pronounce your sentence."

Nauklydes waved for his entourage led by Zoticus. "This has gone too far. General Zoticus, take Menesarkus to the jail."

Zoticus hesitated, then walked to the bleachers and took a seat with the other citizens—sat with arms folded across his chest, glaring at Nauklydes.

Krates stepped forward and cleared his throat. Nikias tensed. This was the man who was responsible for killing Chusor. There would be a reckoning with this man, he promised himself.

"The Artisans' Guild will present evidence supporting General Menesarkus's accusation," announced Krates. He went and stood next to Menesarkus. "And since the general cannot legally act as prosecution, I volunteer my services."

This pronouncement sent another shock wave through the crowd. "Nauklydes's own man has joined Menesarkus!" "To prosecute the arkon!"

Nauklydes stepped back and fumbled for his chair, then sat with eyes unfocused, his jaw muscles working as he clenched and unclenched his teeth.

"What is this evidence?" asked Menesarkus.

Krates leaned in and cupped his hand to Menesarkus's ear, spoke swiftly. The old pankrator's eyes narrowed.

"Were you going to sit on this evidence of yours?" asked Menesarkus crossly.

"We did not know how to corroborate our testimony," explained Krates. "It is the testimony of an enemy combatant and therefore suspect. But since you claim that you have physical evidence . . ." He twisted his misshapen mouth uneasily, glanced at the bag clutched in Menesarkus's hand. "There should be a formal accusation," he added, ever the stickler for procedure." Looking around the hall, he announced, "We need clerks to keep records." Two law clerks volunteered and hurriedly got writing material and styluses from the Assembly Hall office.

Krates noticed Nikias and said, "Your grandson cannot stay, General Menesarkus. He's underage."

"I'm going to ask him to tell everyone what he saw," replied Menesarkus.

After the clerks had arranged themselves at their tables, Krates called on Menesarkus to make his formal accusation.

"I accuse Nauklydes of treason."

"Is this the only accusation?" asked Krates.

"I could accuse him of many things," said Menesarkus. "Multiple homicide, cowardly behavior, misleading the state, and corruption. But treason is more than enough to sentence him to the death he deserves."

"And what are the specifics of this charge?"

"That Nauklydes of his own decision collaborated with Eurymakus of Thebes and Drako, general of Sparta, to murder the gatehouse guards and allow an expeditionary force to enter Plataea with the intention of executing our magistrates, opposing generals, and other leading citizens. He would then become arkon, place the state under the control of Sparta, and break our alliance with Athens."

There were murmurs of disbelief. Then a voice shouted from the seats, "Tyrant!" Several others repeated the call until Krates shouted them down and they were silent.

"And how does Nauklydes respond to these assertions?" asked Krates.

"My very actions would seem to contradict the accusation," said Nauklydes, his eyes open wide in an expression of astonished distress. "My entire household was murdered upon the invasion. My own daughter butchered. I was tortured by the Thebans and only by great fortune escaped with my life. I led the army against the Theban reinforcements and brought us to an overwhelming victory. And my speech today was a plea for Plataea to continue our relationship with Athens and defy the Spartan menace."

"Let him go!" shouted a man in the stands.

"He's innocent!" roared another.

"Silence!" shouted Krates. "Silence!" Turning to Nauklydes, he said, "You did not say whether you were guilty or innocent."

"Innocent," said Nauklydes. "Of all your ludicrous accusations."

"And how do you contradict his claim?" Krates said to Menesarkus.

"His actions clearly contradict the truth," said Menesarkus. "And that is why he has been so deceptive. The answer is simple, however. Eurymakus and the Spartans deceived Nauklydes and tried to murder him as well. And now the arkon knows that the only way to secure his life is for the brave citizens of Plataea to protect him inside these walls. His ruthless instigation of the murder of the Theban prisoners"—addressing the entire Assembly now—"is a shame on our city that will live for thousands of years . . . until the end of civilization."

Krates nodded his head. Waited for someone to shout. But a pall had fallen over the thousands of citizen jurists. "You may respond to Menesarkus's accusation," he said to Nauklydes.

The arkon shook his head. "It's all supposition. He's trying to manipulate you. Fill your heads with lies. Next he'll claim that I'm a Spartan in disguise! That I cut off my own finger!" He unwrapped the linen bandage on his right hand to show his missing finger.

Menesarkus stared at Nauklydes's hand for a long moment, and then nodded his head. He motioned at Krates.

"Bring Chusor the Egyptian," called out Krates.

FIFTEEN

Nikias's heart leapt. Chusor was alive! Behind him the hall doors opened and he saw two guards enter with the smith.

"Chusor," whispered Nikias as Chusor walked past, but the smith didn't hear him and strode onto the speaker's floor. Nikias could not see a single mark of torture on the man's body. But his face was fixed in a sullen mask.

Krates said, "I present Chusor, a metic of Athenian birth, to present testimony against Nauklydes."

"Metics are not allowed to testify in trials of betrayal against the state," said Nauklydes. "Who is your father, Chusor the smith?" he prodded. "Eh? The rumor is you were born a slave!"

"I am no man's heir, that is the truth," said Chusor, defiant and dignified. "I am a bastard born. My mother was a slave but I was given my freedom in my youth."

"Chusor's lineage makes no difference in this trial," said Krates. "He is here simply to relate what transpired between himself and Zeno, who *was* a citizen."

"Zeno is dead," said Nauklydes. "This is a rumor."

The memorist—one of the clerks responsible for knowing the written laws—stood up and stated, "A dead citizen's actions may be told and not count as a rumor."

Nauklydes crossed his arms on his chest. "Well, let the foreigner speak," he said, waving impatiently. "Come, now, Chusor the Egyptian, let us hear what you have to say. And remember that slander will beget swift punishment."

"Please don't badger Chusor," said Krates. "And do not threaten him, Arkon. He is now a member of our guild." Then, turning to Chusor, he requested him to relate what had happened last night between himself and Zeno.

"I was going to get my armor," said Chusor, with a glower at Krates. "I'd left it in the Temple of Athena for safekeeping. Zeno asked me to follow him into the sanctuary. He'd captured a Theban who had taken refuge there. This Theban claimed to know the name of the traitor who had let the Theban force into the city."

"And why would he offer that information?" asked Nauklydes. "To spare his life, no doubt."

"He said that he did not care one way or the other if he lived or died," said Chusor. "He seemed to tell the information out of spite."

"Well, where is this witness?" asked Nauklydes. "This Theban?"

"He was tortured to draw out the truth," said Krates. "He did not survive the torture."

"What you did to him was barbaric," said Chusor to Krates.

"Yes, yes," answered Krates peevishly. "You've already made your feelings known on that matter." To the guards: "Take the witness Chusor away."

Nikias caught Chusor's gaze as the smith was led down the hall and out of the building. Chusor squinted at Nikias and shook his head in disgust. "Barbarians," he said under his breath as he passed.

After he was gone, Nauklydes raised his arms in exasperation. "This is your witness?" he asked. "A metic smith?" He gave an exasperated laugh.

"The Theban prisoner gave a list of facts under torture," said Krates. "And these facts were witnessed by every living member of the Artisans' Guild. I ask them to please stand and show themselves." Twenty-four men—all of them sitting in the same section of the benches—stood up. Krates brought forth a piece of parchment and read, "Tykon of the tribe Kadmae of Thebes did swear, under torture, to the following facts. He on several occasions witnessed Phakas, steward of Nauklydes, entering the city of Thebes and meeting with Drako the Spartan *and* Eurymakus the Theban. That he, Tykon, did participate in councils of war in Thebes at which Nauklydes's name was mentioned as the traitor; that Eurymakus betrayed and captured Nauklydes in this Assembly Hall where General Helladios—a coconspirator—was executed." He stopped reading. "Would the members of the Artisans' Guild verify that I have read these charges correctly?" The artisans called out "Yes!" nearly in unison, then sat. Krates walked over and handed the sheet to the clerk.

Nauklydes looked back and forth from one end of the benches to the other on both sides of the room. "You heard the metic Chusor state that the Theban said these things out of spite. What he says about my manager Phakas and Helladios, well, I cannot speak for them. Perhaps Phakas is a traitor who worked in league with Helladios." Phakas cried out in surprise from the back of the room but was quickly silenced. "I tell you, brothers," continued Nauklydes, "that everything this Theban said about me is a lie. There is no truth in them. I ask you, my friends, how *you* would feel if you were in my place now? If *you* had survived through that terrible night of invasion and fire and battle and death only to be accused of monstrous crimes by the enemy! If you had wounds to show from that enemy"—holding up his maimed hand—"and beloved ones dead and not yet buried! *Murdered* by that enemy!" His voice broke with emotion. Tears rolled down his cheeks. "You would feel as I do now. You would feel betrayed by your brothers. You would feel like stabbing a knife into your own heart to stop the pain. I have been maligned." He searched the faces on the benches. Pleaded to them with his eyes.

There was a silence that lasted for ten seconds before someone shouted, "Nauklydes has been slandered by the enemy!"

"Maligned by a Theban murderer!" cried another.

"This trial is absurd," bellowed a third.

An explosion of quarreling voices filled the hall.

"Next person to take the floor and speak their truth," called out Krates. But nobody listened to him. The Assembly guards had to be called and they pushed men back into their seats. It took ten minutes to regain order. All during this time Nauklydes stood stock-still with his head downcast, a hurt and noble expression on his fine-looking face.

Nikias noticed that his grandfather was kneading the base of his back with his fist. His face was fixed in a grimace of pain. Or was it fear? Menesarkus glanced over at him and Nikias saw dread in his grandfather's eyes. He knew he was losing.

"My grandson Nikias," said Menesarkus at last. He motioned for Nikias, who stepped onto the floor and took a position next to his grandfather. "My grandson is no enemy. Speak to the Assembly, Nik."

Nikias could feel every eye in the room boring into him. He'd never felt so timid in his life. "Helladios's daughter Kallisto," he said hesitantly, "overheard Nauklydes speaking to her father. And they were talking about those who opposed them and their pro-Spartan stance. Men who would have to be dealt with. My grandfather was one of these men."

Nauklydes shook his head in frustration. "Ridiculous!"

"When was this?" Krates asked Nikias.

"Two weeks—ago," said Nikias haltingly. His throat was so dry, his words had started catching in his throat. "And this morning I broke into Nauklydes's office at his pottery factory—and found a scroll in a lockbox. On the scroll was written out a list of names . . . a death list."

Men stood up and shook their fists at Nauklydes while others shouted them down in defense of the arkon. Nauklydes walked over to Nikias and stared at him. Nikias expected him to yell at him and belittle him in front of everyone. But the arkon did just the opposite. He put his hand on Nikias's shoulder.

"Young Nikias's bravery is a fact," Nauklydes said calmly, "and he should be honored for it. I heard about his daring escape to the countryside to raise the warriors there. And I saw him riding out in front of the cavalry in the Battle of the Gates. Besides all of that, he saved me from the three men who murdered my daughter and tortured me. Cut down three Theban warriors by himself!"

Menesarkus looked at Nikias and asked, "Is this true?"

"Yes," said Nikias.

"Slew them in my house," Nauklydes continued. "The house I had not left all evening. The house where the Thebans had pulled my daughter and myself out of our beds. The story that I was in the Assembly Hall during the invasion is absurd. I ask young Nikias to tell everyone that I was found in my home, bound and gagged."

"Noted," said the clerk.

"I did indeed go to see Helladios several weeks ago at his farm," Nauklydes explained. "At his urgent request. He told me that Menesarkus stood in the way of peace, and that he needed to be sharded from our city. I told him that this was a dangerous course; that Menesarkus did not deserve to have such a vicious thing happen to him—a thing that would jeopardize his entire family if it were carried through." He pointed an accusing finger at Menesarkus. "Even though this man, my former mentor, came to me in secret not a week later and threatened *me* with the very same act!"

The assembly turned their eyes on Menesarkus.

"Is this true?" asked Krates.

"Yes," said Menesarkus, shoulders slumping. "I threatened to have Nauklydes sharded."

This new twist in the story emboldened the Nauklydes supporters, who started yelling for the trial to be ended.

"As you all can see," said Nauklydes, waving his hands for silence, "Helladios's daughter lied when she spoke to Nikias about what had transpired in my meeting with her father. I ask you, who here hasn't been accused of something outlandish by a woman? Next she'll be telling us she's been raped by the west wind!"

"She's not a liar, Nauklydes," Nikias shouted over the scattered laughter that had erupted after the arkon's crude joke. He took a step forward angrily and was restrained by his grandfather's hand. "If you call her one, then you give that same insult to me." Rage had loosened his tongue and made him forget his nerves. "Explain why you are still alive while my uncle Alexios, General Helladios, and the others are all dead. And why was the death list in the box in your office."

"As I told everyone already," said Nauklydes. "I would be dead if not for you, young Nikias. And as for the second question, well, evidence can be planted. The traitor Helladios's daughter duped you. *That* is obvious. She knew her father had betrayed the city and was afraid of what would happen to her as the child of such a person. She, like the rest of her family, would be cast out from our society."

"You're not walking out of this Assembly Hall without telling the truth," said Nikias dangerously.

Nauklydes's eyes twitched. The congenial smile faded from his lips. "You had better watch yourself," he warned under his breath. "You're like the little satyr who put his prick where it didn't belong." Turning to the crowd, he smiled with mock sympathy. "Young Nikias was in love with Kallisto. Many here know that he has been meeting with her and defiling her in secret for months. And remember, Nikias is still accused of murdering Helladios's son Lysander. If any trial should be held now, it is *his*. Not mine."

The crowd booed Nikias and called out jeers. "Sit down, lawbreaker!" "Lysander's killer!" "Liar!"

Menesarkus's head slowly sank. Nikias felt his guts churn.

"Another enemy," said Nauklydes, shaking his head sadly. "And someone for whom I had such great hopes."

"It seems everyone in Plataea is conspiring to fabricate fantastical tales about your behavior," said Menesarkus at last. His voice was barely audible above the noise.

"You have not shown any proof!" said Nauklydes almost jovially. "And *that* is the truth, Menesarkus."

Menesarkus glanced at Nikias, who smiled back and made a subtle gesture— the pankration sign . . . a hand punching into an open palm. The old pankrator responded with a nod and an almost imperceptible smile on his bearded lips. He turned to Nauklydes. "Yes, you're right, Arkon." He pulled forth, from the dispatch bag, the evidence given to him by Drako. He held a scroll to Nauklydes's face. "Is this not the stamp made by your signet ring?"

Nauklydes's eyes grew wide. "The Spartans cut off my finger to get my signet," he muttered, for he saw his doom in what Menesarkus held: the copy of the treaty he'd signed with the Spartans. "They stole it to forge my signet seal—"

"And yet, your signet ring is on your *other* finger there," said Menesarkus with a predatory smile.

Nauklydes instinctively covered his ring with his left hand. Most of the men in the hall saw this action. Some of them gasped.

"What is this document in your possession?" asked Krates.

"It is an agreement," said Menesarkus, "signed in secret, making Plataea a Spartan protectorate under Nauklydes's rule. It was signed by Nauklydes and stamped with his family signet—the child pulling down the rampaging ox. The ring is an heirloom of his house. There exists none other like it. I noticed it right off when he undid his bandages to show us all his wounds."

The hall was absolutely quiet. Nikias could hear a single fly buzzing in the rafters. His thoughts raced back to the night of the sneak attack. He saw Nauklydes, bound and gagged, on the floor of the undercroft. And the slave girl brutally raped. All at once he remembered something—when he'd come down the stairs he'd seen one of the enemy warriors holding up a ring and admiring it. Nikias realized that the Theban must have hacked it from Nauklydes's hand moments before he, Nikias, had arrived on the scene. The Theban had taken the signet as a trophy, to bring back home to show his family. The Spartans hadn't cut Nauklydes's ring from his finger to forge his seal on a treaty. No. Nauklydes had signed it *willingly*. And then he'd stamped his family's ancient emblem in the wax, thus sealing Plataea's doom.

But the cunning Spartans had betrayed him. And the citizens of Plataea had refused to be conquered.

Nikias locked eyes with his grandfather. The old pankrator looked exhausted but relieved. He nodded slightly to his grandson, as if to say, "This fight is finished."

"And here," said Menesarkus, holding a small scroll aloft and addressing the assembly, "is the aforementioned list of thirty names of prominent citizens to be executed by Nauklydes, and others to be jailed. Nearly half of the names of this list, I have been told, are now dead." He took the two documents to the clerk and laid them on the table. The clerk recoiled as if Menesarkus had just put down a putrid limb from a corpse. "Neither Nauklydes's name nor Helladios's appears on the list."

"Lies," raged Nauklydes. "Lies!"

A half dozen of Nauklydes's most loyal followers charged the floor and were struck down and hauled away by the guards. Fistfights broke out in the benches.

"If you believe me, brothers, fight for me!" shouted Nauklydes. "Stand by me now!"

"This man would have us tear out each other's throats before admitting his guilt," proclaimed Menesarkus. "Guards! Bring the prisoner Phakas back here."

The guards dragged a terrified Phakas back and held him down at Menesarkus's feet. The crowd settled down and watched expectantly.

"We've seen too many friends and family die, Phakas," said Menesarkus. "Nauklydes was willing to throw you to the dogs already. We'll skin you alive if you don't tell the truth now."

Phakas heaved up his guts on the floor, but he was already confessing before the last retch shook his body. He told everything. Details of when his master first started talking to Eurymakus, dates, amounts of money that were spent bribing guards, secret routes he took to Thebes, the murder of Isokrates, and more of his master's dark secrets.

"Enough!" shouted Menesarkus at last. "We've heard enough."

The guards dragged Phakas out of the chamber and then rushed back and cleaned up his bile and blood from the sacred floor of the Assembly.

During Phakas's confession Nauklydes had turned to stone. He'd sat in the arkon's chair, unmoving and unblinking. Then he slowly dragged his fingernails down his face. The self-inflicted wounds turned to livid marks on his white skin.

"I have nothing more to say," said Menesarkus. "I have wept myself dry already. There's been no tragedy written to compare to this. Let the jury cast their ballots. If you believe Nauklydes is guilty, put a black stone in the jar."

The clerks put empty ballot containers on the floor and waited for the men to line up and drop in their stones. But not a citizen moved from the rows of seats. Nauklydes's eyes darted across the faces in the crowd, and for an instant his countenance registered hope.

And then a black stone sailed from the top row of the benches, landed on the marble, and skidded up to Nauklydes's foot. Another flew from the opposite side of the hall and hit the arkon in the head, dropped with a clatter to the floor. Within moments, like a sudden squall of black hail, two thousand and more of the small dark stones rained down on the miserable arkon.

Nikias looked at his palm. There was still an impression dug into his skin from where he'd clasped the ballot stones throughout the trial. He didn't remember throwing the black stone, but his hand now held only the white one.

Menesarkus walked over to the arkon's chair and dropped the black stone he'd been holding onto Nauklydes's lap. He stared at Nauklydes's dumbfounded face and said, "I pronounce death, Nauklydes. A tunic of stones. The execution will take place tomorrow morning in the agora." He turned to the assemblage of men and declared, "Nauklydes's possessions will be handed over to the city and his body will not be buried within the borders of Plataea."

SIXTEEN

Nikias wandered back through the city in a daze. The sun was shining brightly, but the citadel seemed full of shadows. Full of ghosts. He smelled food cooking in homes and shops, but he felt no pangs of hunger. The black and gray marble of Plataea's buildings glowed eerily in the light, as though they were made of something brittle that could shatter and crumble at any moment. And the dirt-colored walls surrounding the buildings appeared fragile, too, as though they were made of nothing more substantial than eggshells.

He remembered how, when he and Nauklydes's son, Demetrios, were little boys, the two had spent hours lovingly re-creating the walls and buildings of Plataea with rocks and sticks. Now he wished he were as big as a Titan so he could scoop his hand under the entire valley, stride across the sea, and set it down someplace far away and safe. He had discovered Plataea's dreadful secret: it was vulnerable, just like a man, and it could die. All of Plataea could have been swept away, obliterated, merely by the traitorous actions of one man.

He heard the city criers riding through the streets, announcing the news of Nauklydes's death sentence. Women stood in doorways, covering their mouths with their hands, expressions of astonishment and wonder.

What a terrible gut blow his old friend Demetrios was in for if he ever returned to Plataea. His sister butchered. His father executed and his bones scattered far from the family tomb. All of his family's possessions confiscated by the city-state. And the appalling shame of being the son of a traitor.

He thought of Kallisto lying unconscious and felt a sudden stab in his stomach. What did anything matter if she were to die? Why did he leave her at the bridge of Oeroe? He felt like slamming his fist into a wall. He wanted to punish himself.

He heard his name and whipped his head toward an alleyway. Timarkos stood there, beckoning him. Nikias hesitated and then followed the whisperer into the shadows.

"Your grandfather just won the bout of his life," said Timarkos. "And I saw him fight Damos the Theban at the Eighty-fourth. He made Nauklydes look like a fool."

"Nauklydes is insane," said Nikias flatly. "There's no other explanation for his betrayal." He realized, with chagrin, that he was still wearing the assassin's weapon on his forearm.

Timarkos laughed through his nose. "You've a lot to learn, Nikias, about the minds of men."

Nikias smiled without humor. "Tell me, then, whisperer: Why did Nauklydes betray his city? His friends?" He started unbuckling the straps on the pig sticker.

"Because he was afraid," said Timarkos.

"Afraid of the Thebans?" scoffed Nikias. "Afraid of the Spartans? These walls have never been besieged. None of this would have happened if not for his treachery." Freeing himself from the spy's cunning tool, he tossed it at Timarkos's fact.

"Nauklydes was afraid of his own vulnerability," replied Timarkos. "Most men's ruthless actions are committed to achieve power, and once men gain that power, they'll do anything they can to keep it firmly in their grasp."

"I don't need your lessons in philosophy," Nikias said, and started to walk away.

"Wait," said Timarkos. "I'm curious about something."

Nikias stopped and glared at him.

"Would you have killed Nauklydes today," asked Timarkos, "if your grandfather had not arrived?" He stooped and snatched the pig sticker from the muck of the alley.

"Of course," replied Nikias. "I trusted you. And as it turned out, you told me the truth about him. But you lied to me about Chusor. He's no Spartan spy. And now I suspect you've got some personal grudge against him."

Timarkos met Nikias's gaze and raised his eyebrows slightly.

"Yes," said Timarkos, "I think you *would* have killed Nauklydes. You are a courageous young man, Nikias. The heir of the Hero Androkles. And yet, if the entire city of Plataea were filled with warriors like you, Plataea would still fall. Your grandfather plays a dangerous game. I can't tell if he really wants to break with Athens or if he's just trying to buy time with the Spartans. Either way, he makes one or the other the enemy of Plataea. The Spartans won't back down. And Athens won't let Plataea go. Perhaps your grandfather sees something I don't."

"Why don't you ask him?" asked Nikias.

"I haven't got time," said Timarkos with a sigh of resignation. "I must return to Athens with news about what has taken place here. Other men will decide what happens now." He quickly strapped the pig sticker to his forearm.

"What do you mean?" asked Nikias. "What other men?"

"Humans think the gods rule the world," said Timarkos. "But it's really just a handful of mortals."

"Kings and arkons?" spat Nikias.

Timarkos spoke sadly. "Oh, no, young Nikias. Ugly men like me who creep in rafters and skulk in alleyways. We're the ones who make the puppets dance."

Nikias suddenly felt a burning hatred for the Athenian. He wanted to strike him down and kick him to a bloody pulp. He thought of Pelias, the young harpist who Eurymakus the Theban had tortured. The man Nikias had put out of his misery at the old Persian Fort because Timarkos had become so overwrought with emotion, he couldn't lift the sword. "Was Pelias a puppet?" he asked. "Because he wept and bled like a man."

Timarkos's eyes narrowed. Then he smiled and bowed. "That blow was better than a fist, Nikias. You're learning. Your grandfather should send *you* begging to Perikles. You might be able to sway the arkon's heart of stone." He turned and walked down the alley. "And be careful of Chusor," he said without looking back. "He'll betray you in the end. He betrays everyone." The spy rounded a corner and disappeared from view.

Nikias made his way to Chusor's smithy. He moved into the busy marketplace, now crowded with more refugees. The people had dazed expressions, as if they were walking in a waking nightmare. Many of the women went unveiled, too exhausted from the recent tumult to bother with mere propriety.

He wondered if his grandmother and Phile were still at Helladios's farm. He hoped Saeed had made it there. He hoped he'd seen Mula before the boy died. As soon as Nikias had checked on Kallisto, he decided, he would get a horse and cart and ride out to fetch his women back to the city. He realized that they would have had no word that Menesarkus was alive.

When he got to Chusor's smithy, he noticed the painted shield bearing the image of the god Hephaestos leaning against the wall by the door. Somebody must have found it in the street where Nikias had dropped it after the Thebans' sneak attack. The paint was chipped off from the blows of enemy swords, nearly obliterating the image of the smith. It would have to be redone.

"The gods don't loathe Hephaestos because he's misshapen," Chusor had told him once. "They hate him because he's cleverer than they."

Leo appeared in the doorway of the smithy, chewing on a hunk of bread. When he saw Nikias standing there, he beamed and declared, "Chusor is alive!"

"I know," said Nikias.

"He was just here," continued Leo excitedly. "He told me what happened in the Assembly Hall. Then he went to get a drink."

"Where's Diokles?" asked Nikias.

"Still in the storeroom," said Leo. "He keeps saying, 'The Masters can't climb walls,' the poor scared Helot."

"He'll come out when he's hungry enough," said Nikias.

"I'm glad you didn't have to kill Nauklydes," said Leo brightly. "Aren't you?"

"Of course," said Nikias. "Don't be an idiot." His head was swimming. It seemed like every single muscle in his body had started aching all at once.

"Chusor said he was going to get drunk," said Leo, frowning. "Said he wanted to be alone." And then, looking curiously at Nikias, he added, "You don't seem too happy he's alive."

"I'm happy," said Nikias peevishly. "What do you want me to do? Go running to him and kiss his balls?"

Leo looked hurt but he didn't say anything.

"I'm sorry," said Nikias. "I'm just so tired."

"So it's to be a tunic of stones," said Leo with awe in his voice. "That's—"

"Did you hear something?" Nikias asked, cutting him off. He peered in the direction of the stairs leading up to the second floor—to the bedroom where Kallisto lay unconscious.

"I didn't hear—"

Nikias sprang to his feet and sprinted up the stairs, bursting into Kallisto's chamber. She lay on her back with her eyes wide open, staring at the ceiling. At first he thought she was dead, but then her eyes rolled toward him and her lips parted. Her voice was raw and weak, but she said his name. He went to her bed, sank to his knees by her side, reached for her hand, and took it gently, covering it with kisses.

"Where am I?" Kallisto asked fearfully.

"With me," Nikias replied in a soothing tone, his heart swelling with love and relief. "Nothing to be afraid of. You were injured. You've been asleep for two days."

She stared into space for a while, squinting with a perplexed expression, as if trying to recall some distant memory. "I thought you were dead," she said at last, and a faint smile appeared on her mouth. "But it was just a dream, wasn't it?"

"Just a dream," he repeated softly.

After a time she said with a feeble laugh, "I've never seen *that* before."

"Never seen what?"

"I've never seen you cry."

"Nikias! Are you in there?" It was a familiar voice calling from the street outside.

"It's Saeed," said Kallisto, closing her eyes. "Dear old Saeed."

Nikias let go of her hand and tenderly laid it by her side. He went to the shuttered window and pushed it open, stared down into the street. Saeed stood there smiling and holding a dark-haired shape curled up in his arms.

"Mula!" shouted Nikias joyfully. "Mula's alive!" he said to Kallisto, grinning from ear to ear. "I'll be right back." He bounded down the stairs, flying out the front door and up to the Persian slave and his child.

"I made it to the farm that night, Master," said Mula in a tiny voice. "I did as you asked."

"I know," said Nikias. He carefully took the wounded boy from Saeed's arms and held him in his arms. Mula's face was ashen, but there was a light in his eyes. His shoulder was wrapped in clean linens where the arrow had pierced him.

"You're not mad at me?" Mula asked in a trembling tone.

"Never!" declared Nikias. "You did a hero's work that night. And I'm going to buy you one of Chusor's beautiful daggers as a reward. And take you hunting with me as soon as the Spartans are gone."

"I'm so glad you're not mad at me," said Mula, and then he closed his eyes and sighed deeply.

"The Skythian boy saved him," said Saeed. "His gryphon's blood brought my child back to life."

"Where is that little barbarian?" asked Nikias fondly. Saeed pointed across the market to where Kolax was walking between Nikias's grandmother and sister, holding each woman by the hand and shepherding them through the crowded square, cursing at people to get out of their way. Eudoxia and Phile wore the same stupefied expressions as the other refugees. Walking behind them was Kallisto's brother Theron, struggling under the weight of Phile's and Eudoxia's belongings, which were stuffed into leather bags and lashed to his back.

Nikias handed Mula back to Saeed with care. "Take him up to Kallisto's room," he said, then loped across the crowded square. When Phile caught sight of her brother, she brought a hand to her mouth, collapsed to her knees, and let forth a strange cry of hysterical relief. "My brother! Oh, my brother!" Eudoxia saw him and raised her face heavenward and uttered a full-throated prayer to the goddess.

Nikias kissed his grandmother on the cheek, then knelt by Phile and wrapped his arms around her sobbing body. Eudoxia leaned over and covered her two grandchildren with her trembling arms. None of them could speak.

Kolax stood next to Theron and grimaced, apparently disturbed by the sounds of Nikias's sobs. "Skythian men only cry at the funerals of their favorite horses," he remarked to Theron. "Poor Nikias. His beautiful white mare must have died."

"Grandfather is alive," said Nikias at last, his voice choked with emotion. "Grandfather is alive. Did you hear me, Phile?" And looking up at Eudoxia he said, "Grandmother? Do you understand? Your husband is alive!"

SEVENTEEN

———◆———

Death by a "tunic of stones" was reserved for the most heinous of all crimes: betrayal of one's city. If the Thebans had succeeded in capturing Plataea due to Nauklydes's deceit, every male citizen would have been executed, their wives and daughters raped and sold into slavery, and their male children murdered, thus snuffing out their lines forever.

The agora, therefore, was filled to overflowing with the men and women and children of the city who had come to see the most wretched Plataean in the history of their people smashed like a venomous snake. In the center of the square was a plinth on which stood the statue of the Hero Androkles. Beneath the plinth, pavers had been pried up and a shallow pit dug. The crowd watched quietly as Nauklydes was buried up to his waist and shackled into place. Nobody jeered. The people were bereaved that one of their own—a man who had lived among them their entire lives, done business with them, and led his brothers in arms to victory on the field of battle—had deceived them . . . had nearly destroyed their way of life.

Each of the twenty executioners received one stone, the size of a loaf of barley bread, weighing about as much as a human head. They were made to stand fifteen paces from the condemned man. If the stone throwers had been allowed to stand any closer the first rock might have caused the deathblow. That would have been too merciful. The purpose of the dreaded "tunic" was to inflict massive pain, dishonor, and a lingering death.

Menesarkus stepped from the crowd, went and stood in front of Nauklydes. The deposed arkon pressed his chin to his chest, his eyes clamped shut. Even though Menesarkus knew the man's heart was corrupt, Nauklydes's face still appeared noble and intelligent.

"Like Prometheus chained to the rock," he thought.

Menesarkus said in a somber voice, "Nauklydes, your sentence was pronounced, your judgment read, and now your execution must take place. Do you have anything to say?"

"Old friend," replied Nauklydes, looking up at him beseechingly, speaking in a whisper so only Menesarkus could hear, "I think I am insane. I have had visions . . . waking visions. And pains in my skull. Voices telling me what to do. How else could I have betrayed Plataea? It wasn't just for selfish reasons. Zeus possessed me. A madness took me . . . like the madness of Herakles. I did not want to do any of it. But I just kept getting pulled along, as though I were caught in a swift river. I did it all for my son, Demetrios. To save my heir from the Spartan menace."

"But what of *my* heir?" asked Menesarkus. "What of *other men's* sons and grandsons?"

Nauklydes shook his head forlornly.

"Who poisoned Arkon Apollodoros?" asked Menesarkus. "In Athens."

"It was one of Eurymakus's agents," replied Nauklydes. "I knew of the deed but I was not the one to lace his food with the poison. The Thebans have many tentacles, even in Athens."

Menesarkus made to go, and Nauklydes reached out to grab his hem. But the chains stopped him short with a clatter. "Wait! Menesarkus!"

"Be quick, this is unseemly," replied Menesarkus curtly.

"What gave you the idea to threaten me that day?" he asked. "When you said you would have me sharded."

Menesarkus bit his lip. "It was an Athenian whisperer. One of Perikles's men. He came to my house and told me it was Perikles's order."

"Timarkos?" asked Nauklydes. "The one with blue eyes?" When he saw Menesarkus's surprised look, he said, "Don't trust him. Timarkos has his own agenda. And don't trust the Spartans. They are treacherous."

"The traitor speaks of treachery," said Menesarkus.

"I left you a letter with the warden at the jail," said Nauklydes. "I wrote up a plan last night—a plan that you *must* follow if Athens refuses to release us from the alliance. Please do me the honor of reading it."

"I will," said Menesarkus.

Nauklydes nodded slowly. "I have only one request. That you commission a funeral jar for my daughter and use some of my confiscated funds for the upkeep of my family's tomb."

"I will grant you that," said Menesarkus, and walked back to the crowd.

"I thank you," called out Nauklydes. "Your punishment is just."

The first executioner was so nervous, his stone landed two feet from Nauklydes's face. The second man threw too hard and his rock landed all the way on the other side. The crowd groaned. The executioners were turning tragedy into comedy. The third man to heft his rock was a skilled discus champion named Boulos, an old drinking friend of Nauklydes. The condemned man saw him and smiled bravely.

"Give me your best, Boulos!" he said.

Boulos stepped to the line and heaved his stone, turned the instant it left his hands, for he knew it would hit its mark and did not wish to see. The rock struck Nauklydes squarely in the mouth. And in the blink of an eye the handsome man's face was destroyed. Nauklydes let forth a howl that sent half the crowd fleeing for their homes. By the time the last stone was hurled at the traitor's body, both of Nauklydes's arms were broken, his nose crushed, his collarbone smashed, his skull shattered, and one eye turned to pulp. The stones surrounded him, encased him in a rocky tunic.

And yet Nauklydes lived.

The ones who had stayed to the end could hear his ragged breath whistling through one nostril—a defective flute with split reed. Every so often his head lolled from side to side, like a poppy pod on a broken stem.

Menesarkus ordered four guards to stand over the prisoner until he was dead. The crowd slowly dispersed but Menesarkus stayed where he was, staring at his former Olympic herald. The old pankrator had one arm across his stomach with the other elbow resting on it, the fingers of that hand pensively kneading his lower lip.

Nikias, who had watched the execution from beginning to end, walked over and stood by his grandfather's side. "What did he say to you?" he asked. "Before you gave the order." When Menesarkus did not respond, Nikias decided to leave him alone. "Good-bye, Grandfather," he said.

Menesarkus stirred from his reverie and said, "I'll never forget seeing your face at the end of my fight with Damos. Pushed up against the wooden gate. Surrounded by Spartans. How a ten-year-old boy made it all the way from our lodgings on the outskirts of Olympia and sneaked into the Hippodrome, I still can't comprehend."

"I wanted to see the fight," said Nikias. "I was angry that little boys weren't allowed. And I was eight years old, not ten."

"And you found out why I forbade you from the fight, didn't you?"

"I was stronger than you thought," said Nikias.

"I was about to give up," said Menesarkus. "Before I heard you shouting, I almost yielded."

"I would have rather seen you die that day than submit to Damos," said Nikias.

Menesarkus grunted. He turned and looked into his grandson's eyes with a profound sadness. "If I had to sacrifice you to save this city, I would," said Arkon Menesarkus abruptly. His eyes seemed to ask for forgiveness, and then they became as hard as voting stones.

Nikias nodded with understanding. "And I would do the same."

"Without this city, we as a people are nothing. The city stands above the individual. You must always fear slavery more than death. Understand? If you learn anything from me, let it be that."

"I understand," said Nikias.

"You will never have Kallisto as your wife," said Menesarkus, turning to stare at Nauklydes again.

Nikias's mouth opened in shock. "But Isokrates promised me Kallisto before he died. I haven't had a chance to tell you—"

"You will not join yourself to the daughter of a traitor."

Nikias, devastated by this new blow, left his grandfather standing watch over Nauklydes. The old pankrator stayed for several hours, arms crossed on chest, as still as a statue. He was thinking of the siege of Sardis—of row after row of Theban heads stuck to spear points . . . and the terrible crying of the women as they'd been raped. He was thinking of the aftermath of the Battle of the Koronea, when he'd found his son's corpse. And then Menesarkus recalled, with gnawing guilt, the terrible joy he'd felt in the Hippodrome when he'd squeezed the throat of Damos the Theban and had felt his body jerking—as though in the throes of coitus—as the spark of life was snuffed out. . . .

He was overcome by a black and abysmal despair. He could not fight it. The feeling pounded him over and over again, like a ceaseless wave. With a prayer to Zeus on his lips he left Nauklydes alone and limped out of the agora.

The Traitor Nauklydes, as he would forever more be called, died alone. A rumor went around the city that when men came to fetch his corpse in the morning they found a crow sitting on Nauklydes's ruined head, cawing raucously—a crow with a single white tail feather.

EIGHTEEN

———◆———

After Nauklydes's body was carted off in a wagon and dumped in an open field past the farthest boundary marker, the citizens of Plataea gathered for another Assembly. They chose five new magistrates and elected them, and then those men nominated Menesarkus as arkon. There was a vote. This time in the proper way—by secret ballot. The citizens reached into a funnel and placed their voting rock in one of two urns. The no urn proved unnecessary, however: when it was emptied, it did not contain a single ballot.

The new arkon's first official business was to meet with the Spartan envoy. General Drako and ten of his men marched through the gates to the sound of flute music. Thousands of Plataeans ran to the agora to see the enemy Spartans, and the sight of the hideously mutilated warrior caused much excitement. Drako was welcomed by the new arkon at his public offices. The meeting was brief and courteous. It lasted just long enough for the Spartans to once again make their official declaration of friendship to Plataea in exchange for Plataea's promise to break formal diplomatic ties with Athens.

Menesarkus said to Drako, "The envoys will be sent to Athens today. We trust that your army will not interfere with them as they will be passing close by the Persian Fort on their way to the pass of Megaris and the long road to Athens." Drako assured him they would be unmolested.

Before leaving Menesarkus's company, Drako told the arkon (in a hushed aside) that he hoped Menesarkus would notify him if any Spartans were ever captured and held in Plataea. To which the arkon nodded vigorously saying, "Of course, of course." Then Menesarkus added with a perplexed air, "But surely you aren't missing any men?" Drako did not reply to this question.

When the sun was at its zenith, Krates, the leader of the expedition to Athens; his second in command, Agape; their dozen clerks and assistants; and a guard of twenty cavalry left the city gates and took the eastern road. They stopped at the Temple of the Hero Androkles and sacrificed a black ram on the altar. The intestines were twisted, which Krates interpreted as "confusion" and Agape took to mean "coalescence."

Menesarkus had a long day of work at the arkon's office. There were many things to arrange: the planning of foraging parties to bring in supplies. Work crews to fix damage done by the invasion and battle. The shifting of men and resources from the watchtowers along the borders. The housing, feeding, and guarding of the two hundred Theban prisoners captured in the battle outside the gates and at Oeroe. And the counting of all the money in the treasury. Fortunately he had a staff of competent yet exhausted public officials and workers.

Near the end of the day, when he found a moment alone, he broke the seal on the letter Nauklydes had written him and read it several times. The missive had been penned, surprisingly, in straightforward prose. No mention of "voices" or "prophesies." It was a battle plan and a list of potential agents. After he had digested the contents, Menesarkus folded the letter, along with Nauklydes's signet ring, and locked it in his office's heavy oak and iron strongbox for safekeeping. Then he went to the prison and signed the death warrant for Phakas. He was to be taken into the mountains, beheaded, and thrown into a chasm.

Kiton, also known as Axe—a city gateman whom Phakas had also implicated in treachery—had been issued a death warrant. But he was nowhere to be found in the city. One witness had last seen him leaving the Gates of Pausanius, heading down the road toward Athens.

General Zoticus was given a severe reprimand for his part in the attack on Isokrates and his kin. But the cavalry general was not charged with any crimes. Plataea had already lost too many good men to throw another on the altar of revenge. Menesarkus was convinced that Zoticus knew nothing of the invasion plot but had been duped into trusting the charismatic Nauklydes after the invasion. Zoticus was given the assignment of finding another three hundred horses to build up their stock and headed north to Makedon to fulfill this task.

In the back of the prison was a locked chamber—a room used for political prisoners or citizens of high standing awaiting trial. It had windows, so the air was not mephitic, and was furnished with a desk and a comfortable bed. Outside the door stood a physician and his attendant, who were speaking in low voices.

"How is he?" asked Menesarkus as he approached them, leaning on his staff.

"He seems better today, Arkon," replied the physician. "He says there is a tingling in his toes. This is a good sign. It may mean the paralysis is only temporary."

Menesarkus entered alone, shut the door behind him. He sat down on a chair near the bed and stared at the young man lying motionless there. Years ago,

Menesarkus remembered, during the Messenian Wars—the conflict Sparta had waged with its close neighbor—a Spartan warrior had been captured and taken prisoner by their enemy. The Spartans had paid five times his weight in silver to have him released—such was the value they placed on a single full-blooded warrior.

Menesarkus thought, "If one Spartan is worth his weight in silver, then what is the value of a future Spartan *king*?"

Arkilokus opened his eyes and gave his grandfather a questioning look.

"The gods have a sense of humor," said Menesarkus bitterly. "Eh, *Grandson*?"

NINETEEN

Chusor had been very drunk for two days running.

He'd spent most of the time since Nauklydes's trial at a little wineshop at the end of a twisting alley near Sex Factory Lane.

There had been a festive atmosphere in the city ever since Nauklydes was given the tunic of stones. There'd been a lottery to decide who would be the twenty lucky men who got the honor to throw the execution stones. Chusor had heard one particularly wealthy merchant brag that he'd paid a thousand drachmas to take another man's place on the death squad—enough coin to buy a house.

"Barbarians," said Chusor under his breath. "You think you're civilized? Well, you're not. You're a pack of blood-hungry wild dogs." He'd never been an unruly drunk. He didn't want to have these feelings of rage.

But he couldn't get Tykon the Theban's screams out of his head. At first the Theban had refused to recant his accusation against Chusor. So the men of the guild had strung him up like an animal for slaughter and, eventually, they'd persuaded the tough Theban to tell the truth. Chusor had never before seen artisans' tools put to such ghastly use.

He knew the men of the guild had had every right to torture Tykon. The Theban invader would have ordered the execution of every one of them, raped their daughters, and smashed their infant boys' heads against the walls with his own hands. But it was all just such a waste. And torture made men worse than animals.

Chusor lifted his cup and purposefully spilled a little of his wine on the stone floor as an offering. "Tykon," he said looking down at the ground, in the direction of Hades and the current abode of Tykon's shade. "Honor means nothing. Revenge even less. You had your life and you pissed it away."

Now Tykon's part in the story was over, mused Chusor, but the deeds he'd committed would perpetuate more violence and suffering.

"Agony begets agony begets agony," he droned. "Until the end of time."

"What's that?" asked the wineshop owner from the back of the room. "You want some more wine?"

"Indeed!" called out Chusor, staring blearily at the table.

Somebody sat down across from him.

"Find another table," growled Chusor without looking up. "I'm drinking alone."

"Hello, Chusor," said Nikias.

Chusor lifted his head, focused his eyes. A smile curled on one side of his mouth. "Bring a whole jug for me and my friend," he called out to the owner. "The young Nemean lion!"

The shopkeeper brought one jug filled with wine and another brimming with water along with a clean drinking cup. Nikias waved away the water and poured the wine directly into his vessel. "I'm having it straight," he said. "Skythian-style."

"Good idea," said Chusor. "I've been drinking uncut all day."

Nikias took a long swig and sat back in the chair. "I came here to thank you. Without you we might all be dead."

"You still might die," said Chusor. "The Spartans aren't going anywhere." He peered into Nikias's eyes. There was something different there. What was it? Dejection? Dread?

"My grandfather is sending an envoy to Athens," said Nikias, brushing his long hair from his eyes with a quick swipe of his fingers. "To ask the Athenians to release Plataea from our alliance with them."

"They won't agree to that," said Chusor. "I know Perikles. I *know* him, Nikias," he added with particular emphasis. "He'll dig in his heels. If they let Plataea go, then who's next? One of the islands—Naxos, say—will try to break away. And Athens will see its empire start to crumble. They'd rather have Plataea pulled apart to the last stone than see you join with Sparta. At least that way you'd serve as a symbol of undying obedience."

"That's what my grandfather thinks as well," said Nikias.

"Then why is he sending the envoy?"

"Principle."

"To Hades with principle!" shouted Chusor. "Enough of this constant killing and destruction."

They sat in silence for a time, drinking their wine, listening to the voices coming from the food stalls and taverns.

"Kallisto woke up," said Nikias, smiling.

Chusor smiled back. There was nothing cynical about the look on his face now. He raised his cup. "Thank the Gods," he said.

"You helped save her too," said Nikias.

Two men walked by the wineshop talking about the execution.

". . . a joy to see Nauklydes's jaw smashed clean off," said one.

"My stone took out one of his traitor's eyes," replied the other.

Chusor mumbled something under his breath.

"What did you say?" asked Nikias.

"I said, 'Pitiful creatures,'" replied Chusor. "It's what the playwright Euripides always says about mankind. Not 'pit*iless*' or 'vicious' or 'stupid,' like I would say. Just a sneering 'Pitiful creatures,' as if we are nothing more than a superior sort of dog."

"I've only seen one of his plays," said Nikias. "My grandfather loves those two shriveled old foreskins Sophokles and Aeskylus."

"Did you know," said Chusor, "that the Athenians invented a word for you Plataeans and Thebans and the rest of you dirt-farming Oxlanders? 'The anesthetized.' That's what they call you. Because you're all so numb and dumb."

Chusor instantly regretted his tirade. He didn't know why he'd said such a hateful thing to Nikias just now. But instead of appearing insulted, Nikias leaned forward and whispered in a conspiratorial tone, "What else?"

"Eh?" asked Chusor.

"What else do they think in Athens," asked Nikias. "What should a hick like me be on the lookout for? How do I fit in? Who do I go to if I'm in trouble and need help?"

Chusor sighed. "You sound like you're going to do something imprudent."

"My grandfather can't leave Plataea," said Nikias. "So he's got to send somebody else as an envoy to Athens. It's going to be skinny Krates and General Agape the windbag."

"Your grandfather knows what he's doing," said Chusor. "Old and tired men showing up at Perikles's court on bended knee. His cynic's heart might just be moved by their ingenuous . . . pitifulness. Athens is a dangerous place, Nik."

Nikias gave a hearty belly laugh. "And Plataea isn't?"

"What do you hope to achieve in Athens?" asked Chusor.

Without hesitating Nikias replied, "Speak to Perikles myself."

Chusor tried to hide his smile. "You'll have better luck bringing back the Minotaur's horns."

"I know," said Nikias. "But I've got to try. My grandfather wants me to stay here and help scavenge for *supplies*! And if I can do something extraordinary, he'll have to let me marry Kallisto."

Chusor took a long drink, then stared into the bottom of his empty cup. There was a painted image there of two satyrs engaged in obscene pleasure. "Drinking and sex," he observed. "If only men would stick to those two activities, there would be very little killing in the world." After a pause he said, "Listen, Nik. The envoys *will* fail. I have no doubt about that."

"Then we will have to fight the Spartans," replied Nikias. "My grandfather will not allow us to break our oath."

"You will have to dig in for a long siege," said Chusor. "There is a chance that you can outlast the Spartans. They can't keep ten thousand men here for very long. Especially if they are planning to wage a prolonged assault on the cities of Attika. And they know nothing of siege craft."

"That's why we need you," said Nikias. "You will be assigned the job of master of the walls tomorrow in place of Krates. I convinced my grandfather you are the man for the job, now that Krates is leaving for Athens. And everyone on his council agrees. Devise some new way of fending off attacks. Trick them. Trap them. Send them home with their tails between their legs."

Chusor grinned. "You think I'm capable of holding off an army of Spartans?"

"If anybody can figure out a way, it's you," Nikias replied. "Hephaestos is cleverer than the other gods, remember?"

"Ah, flattery," said Chusor. "Even I am not immune."

It was late and the shopkeeper started to close his wineshop. Chusor paid up and he and Nikias walked back to the smithy. They entered the house quietly, keeping their voices down because Nikias's grandmother and sister were asleep upstairs in one of the rooms alongside Kallisto. Mula, Kolax, Saeed, and Leo were bedded down in the other chamber. Diokles was still in the storeroom, and they could hear him snoring loudly.

Chusor and Nikias went to the kitchen to talk and eat. It was the first time either one of them had felt hungry in days. They stuffed themselves with bread and cheese and dried figs. And they consumed an entire smoked ham between them, conversing long into the night.

Chusor told Nikias all about Athenian society. How the city was a snake pit of spies, whisperers, and secret societies all vying for power. He also told Nikias of his misadventure with a hetaera—the regal courtesans of Athens—and her lover General Kleon, a dangerous man who'd been vying for power with Perikles for decades.

"The Athenian spy said your real name isn't Chusor," said Nikias. "Was that a lie?"

Chusor didn't reply. He got up and went to a small desk in the corner of the kitchen, lit an oil lamp, and sat down. He took out a sheet of papyrus from a slot in the desk, along with a little writing box containing a quill and bottle of ink. He sat in silence for a while, then started to write.

"I hope I didn't insult you," said Nikias. "I don't need to know about your name."

The smith stopped his quill for a moment and said, without rancor, "My old name was a slave's name. Chusor is the pet name my mother called me. As a child, I was always making things to amuse her, you see. And Chusor is the name of the Phoenician god of invention." He started writing again, and did not pause until he was done a few minutes later. Holding up the sheet, he blew on it to dry the ink. Then he rolled up the papyrus and held it forth.

"What is this?" asked Nikias.

"It's a letter of introduction of sorts—to the hetaera I knew in Athens," explained Chusor. "She is well connected and will help you if you get into trouble. Something you're good at," he added sardonically. "And I've put down some directions for how to find the home of an old friend of mine: a doctor named Ezekiel. Go to him if you get injured. Something else you're good at, I might add."

Nikias smiled and took the tiny scroll, tucking it into his tunic for safe-keeping.

"Are you going to Athens alone?" Chusor asked.

"Yes."

Chusor grunted. He reckoned Nikias's chances were better that way. "Don't come back alone," he said.

"What do you mean?" asked Nikias.

"Find men," explained Chusor. "Men looking for adventure. Men who hate the Spartans. Preferably archers or peltasts. You'll need many of those. A good archer can hold off ten men during a siege assault. And you Plataeans are terrible bowmen. At least, the men amongst you."

He handed Nikias a heavy leather pouch.

"What's this?"

"Persian gold," said Chusor.

"Where did you get this?" Nikias asked, peering into the bag. There was enough gold in the bag to buy ten farms.

"I found it at Nauklydes's place," said Leo's voice. He had been watching them for some time, sitting on the landing that led to the second floor. He stepped down the dark stairs and into the lamplight of the kitchen.

"You stole it?" asked Nikias.

Leo shrugged. "But I felt guilty keeping it. What am I going to do with all that gold? So I gave it to Chusor." He looked into Nikias's eyes sadly. "You're go-ing, aren't you?"

"Yes," said Nikias. "At dawn. And I have to go alone."

"I reckoned you would. Why can't I come with you?"

"Because, brother," said Nikias, "Plataea needs every warrior it has left."

Nikias went over to Leo and wrapped his arms around him in a powerful hug. "Help my grandmother and sister watch over Kallisto for me."

"I will," Leo promised.

"Give these mercenaries one coin up front," Chusor instructed Nikias. "Promise them a rate of one gold piece per month once they get here. Tell them about Sex Factory Lane and all the beautiful whores. Tell them the city is stocked with food and wine. Or that there's a vast treasure buried beneath the streets. Make it seem like a lark," he said, handing him another bag, this one filled with lead shot for slings. "And you might need these too. They're my own design: far more aerodynamic than those dog-shit-shaped lumps you Plataeans fling about."

Nikias took the proffered items, clutched them against his chest with one arm, and then held out his free right hand. Chusor grasped it.

"Thanks, Chusor."

Chusor said, "I figure if the Spartans do send reinforcements, they'll be here in a month."

"I'll be back long before then," said Nikias confidently. "And then we'll have a proper drinking party." He went into the main room of the house and Chusor and Leo followed him.

Nikias put his hand on the front door latch and was about to open it when something caught his eye: a full travel pack lying on the floor. Nikias had seen Chusor wearing this pack before, whenever the smith had set out on one of his long journeys—trading for supplies in neighboring city-states, or searching in the mountains for minerals and plants to use in his experiments. The pack was of Chusor's own design, with a rigid frame and padded leather straps.

Nikias looked at Leo and his friend nodded, turned away with tears in his eyes. The expression on his face showed he already knew Chusor was planning on leaving Plataea for good.

"This was never my city," said Chusor.

Nikias smiled. "May Hermes guide you, Chusor," he replied softly. Then he looked at Leo and said, "If you remember anything I say, Leo, remember this: the city means nothing without the ones we love whose walls it protects."

He opened the heavy door and departed.

EPILOGUE

———◆———

"I weep for all these dead and say my last farewells. And raise my hand to all the divinities of the air, to serve as witnesses of these things. . . ."
—**Euripides of Athens**

The Well of Gargaphia was a sacred shrine devoted to Kore, the unfortunate goddess captured by Hades and taken down to his underworld kingdom. The crumbling temple, which lay one and a half miles from the citadel at the foot of the Kithaeron Mountains, had been built long before Plataea was founded. Its four walls were rough-hewn stone from the adjacent slopes, and its ancient roof beams—cut from the glade nearby—were rotted out at the ends where they had been exposed to centuries of sun and rain.

Every year the farmers who lived in the vicinity and cherished the shrine put a new roof on it made of reeds gathered from swamps by the Asopus River. They were the same reeds used to make the famous aulos pipes of the Oxlands, and sometimes, when the wind hit the roof, it sang a mournful tune. Inside the small structure was an opening for the well. Sacred water was brought to the surface using a copper cup attached to a rope.

Nikias sat inside the temple listening to the wind singing in the reeds. He had been there for an hour or so, waiting for the sun to rise. Outside the door he could see Photine's white head grazing happily on the lush grass that grew from the moist ground around the well.

He took something out of his belt pouch and studied it with an expression of distaste. It was the signet ring he'd taken off the severed hand of Eurymakus after the Battle of the Gates. It was made of yellow gold and set with some sort of red gemstone and carved with the impression of a crowned Persian king holding a bow and a spear. Nikias didn't know why he'd taken it off the amputated hand. Maybe he'd wanted a piece of his enemy, to remind him of the menace who'd tried to wipe out his family and city.

He thought of tossing the ring into the well, but he put it back into his pouch instead. Then he stood up and reached for a leather wineskin that he'd filled with water from the well, one cup at a time. It would have been easier to fill it from the creek nearby, but he wanted to drink this blessed water on his journey to Athens, a charm to ward off bad luck.

He went outside and untied Photine, mounted, and headed up a goat path. He carried few belongings besides the wineskin. Tied to his back was a pack containing the gold, the lead shot, and the letter of introduction to the courtesan given to him by Chusor, as well as a change of clothes, a loaf of bread, and some olives. His only weapons were a short sword that he wore on his hip in an old leather scabbard, a long dagger strapped to his lower back, and his trusty Sargatian whip. The sword was one of Menesarkus's old weapons with his seal set in gold on the pommel: the boxing Minotaur. His grandfather had given it to him in honor of his recent feats in battle.

When he got to the Cave of Nymphs he gazed down on the plains of Plataea, illuminated by the morning sun. He thought of all the people he loved whom those walls protected. His brave grandmother and pretty Phile. His Zeus-like grandfather. Loyal Saeed and skinny Mula. Lighthearted Leo. The wily Chusor.

And the woman he vowed to marry—the goddess on earth Kallisto. His grandmother and sister had promised to look out for her. To nurse Kallisto back to full health while he was away. They'd also promised to speak to the arkon Menesarkus on her behalf. They hoped to convince his grandfather that Kallisto shouldn't have to suffer because of her father's treachery.

He thought back to the day they'd made love in the cave. Before everything had started to crumble. How her hair had smelled like sun-warmed wild herbs and the sweat of her horse where she'd pressed her head against the animal's neck in their frantic race up the mountainside. And how her eyes had transfixed him. How she'd whispered, "I will have you." He wanted her so badly now, it made his stomach ache, like a pang of hunger to a starving man.

He squeezed Photine with his legs and turned her away from the vista. His grandfather would be furious when he found out he'd left. But Menesarkus had always told him, "Enter the pankration arena to win." If that meant he had to speak to the Athenian arkon Perikles himself, as Timarkos the whisperer had suggested, then so be it. The Hero Androkles wouldn't have spent these perilous days collecting grain and cheese. Or rounding up sheep. No! He would have done what Nikias was doing now. The arena had shifted to Athens. At least for now. So Athens was where he had to go.

A voice echoed from inside the cave, startling him.

"Never to see whole, never to love, never to gain honor again!"

"Who's in there?" shouted Nikias.

A figure, ragged, crazed, his single eye blazing with hatred, stumbled out.

Nikias recognized the Theban whose eye he'd plucked out. The same one he'd found days ago on the Kadmean Road in the throes of a fit.

"You!" exclaimed Perseus. "Eye grabber! Honor taker!" He lunged at Nikias but the pankrator knocked down the deranged Theban with a kick.

"What are *you* doing here?" asked Nikias in surprise. "Go back to Thebes!"

Perseus jumped up, grabbed a handful of rocks, and threw them at Nikias's face, spitting and cursing insanely. Nikias kicked Photine hard and charged up the hill.

"Nothing but death and sorrow for you, Plataean!" the Theban shouted after him. "Nothing but pain and . . ." His voice trailed off, blown away on the wind that had whipped up from the plains with the setting of the sun.

Nikias rode fast, not looking back. By the time he got to the top of the mountain, both horse and rider were exhausted and had to rest. He let Photine wander off to find some grass to eat. He sat on the ground, cradling his head in his hands. This second encounter with the young Theban had shaken him. It was a bad sign.

"Nothing but death and sorrow for you, Plataean."

Nikias should have killed him then and there for uttering such a curse. Cut him down with his sword. But something had stayed his hand . . . again.

"Death and sorrow . . ."

A rider charged up the hill. Even in the dim light of dawn, with one glance Nikias knew who it was.

"Hey Nik," shouted Kolax in Skythian. "I saw you leaving and I followed. Are you going hunting? I heard there are giant pigs up in these mountains. I would like to make a fancy necklace from the tusks. Maybe I'll give it to your sister Phile. She's got excellent hips for breeding, though she cries too much."

Nikias waved Kolax away. "Curse your barbarian talk," he said. "I can barely understand a word you're saying. But you can't come with me. I'm going to Athens."

"Athens?" proclaimed Kolax. "You know the way to Athens? I've got to come with you." And then he switched to broken Greek, speaking to Nikias in his own language. "My father. Archer. In Athens!" He pantomimed the pulling of a bowstring, watching the arrow strike home, and thumped his chest triumphantly.

"What did you say?" asked Nikias, startled by the revelation.

"My father," repeated Kolax, still speaking in broken Greek. "He city archer. Shoot arrows." He switched back to Skythian and said, "I've got to bring him back here to kill these Red Cloaks. He doesn't know I was stolen from Skythia. That our tribe was betrayed by the bastard son of King Astyanax and—"

"Gods, shut up for once!" cried Nikias.

Kolax stopped talking and scowled, grinding his teeth.

Nikias climbed onto Photine's muscular back. Stroked her neck. He might as well take the boy with him, he thought. Kolax was sort of like having a boisterous dog—a dog that could shoot a bow and arrow with the skill of a master archer. He'd proved himself many times over, from the defense of Oeroe to the battle at the Gates of Pausanius. He said, "You can go to Athens with me—"

Kolax made his captured Theban horse dance in circles, and let forth a Skythian war whoop. "Yes, yes! To Athens! We'll find my father and—"

"—but you *must* come back when I call," demanded Nikias. He put his fingers to his lips and gave a piercing whistle. "That means you come to me." He made a beckoning gesture.

"Yes, I understand," replied Kolax. "The whistle means you're in trouble *again* and you need my help. Let's go!"

As nimble Photine picked her way over the rocky peaks, Nikias thought of the letter Chusor had written for him—the introduction to the courtesan in Athens. He'd read it by lamplight, over and over again, while a newborn baby—a child who'd been made fatherless by the Theban invasion—screamed in the women's quarters of the house next door . . . inconsolable cries that lasted for hours despite the constant lullabies sung to him by the child's exhausted mother and the other women of the house. . . .

> *My Sophia,*
>
> *Not a single day has gone by since we parted that I have not thought of you. I have traveled the known world trying to forget you, and yet you still shine in my memory as brightly as the sun. My offer to you is the same as when I first made it. If you accept it, send word back to me through the owner of this letter and I will come for you on my winged horse. Forgive me for asking again—an exile feeds on hope.*
>
> *If you receive this message, you will know that the bearer is in need of help. His name is Nikias, grandson of Menesarkus, the great Olympian of Plataea. And though he is not yet of full age, he is in fact the bravest man I have ever known. Treat him as though he were my brother. He is a Plataean born and bred. The men of Athens scorn his people and call them coarse farmers, but I know the truth: they are bighearted, gallant, and fearless beyond measure.*
> *Blessings,*
> *The son of no man*

ACKNOWLEDGMENTS

I am indebted to James Howard Kunstler, who did something most authors are unwilling to ever do for another writer: he introduced me to his literary agent. Adam Chromy, for his part, never gave up trying to get The Warrior Trilogy published.

I am grateful to my friend David Wheeler, who read this manuscript many times and offered valuable suggestions; Elyse Cheney for her much needed encouragement; my cousin Mariko for her wordsmithery; and my editor, Peter Joseph at Thomas Dunne Books, who took the chance on *Sons of Zeus* and helped shape it into a better story.

Finally, I couldn't have written this tale if I hadn't first gone on a remarkable journey of the imagination to ancient Greece with Gregory C. Carr.